THE CAPRICORN PEOPLE

Aaron Fletcher

LEISURE BOOKS  NEW YORK CITY

A LEISURE BOOK

Published by

Dorchester Publishing Co., Inc.
41 E. 60 St.
New York City

Printed in the United States of America

PART ONE

Chapter 1

A HAND SHOOK GARRITY'S SHOULDER, and he woke with a start. A lantern shone in his eyes, and his surroundings were strange. He was on a ship, with heavy beams overhead and the tangy scent of seawater blending with the smells of tar, hemp, and damp wood. Then he looked at the smiling face of the man holding the lantern, and memory returned. The man was Thomas Mabry, a seaman and a friend from the time they had attended grammar school together as boys.

"Wake up, Earl," Mabry chuckled. "You can't sog about all day in a bunk, you know."

Garrity sat up on the edge of the bunk, and he winced and held his head. "Bloody hell," he groaned. "My head's nigh to bursting, Tom."

"Aye, I'm a bit worse for a tot too much myself," Mabry replied ruefully. "But tea's heating in the galley, and I'll see if I can find something to put in it that'll set us right. You can have a wash at the water butt on the deck, if you wish."

Garrity yawned and nodded. Pulling on his boots,

he picked up his hat and followed Mabry to the door. Mabry's appearance belied his words. His tanned, youthful face was bright and alert in the light of the lantern, and he was neat and clean in his long frock coat, tricorn, and white cravat. He opened the cabin door, and Garrity followed him along a low, narrow passageway that opened out onto the main deck by the steps leading up to the quarterdeck.

The stars were dimming in the east as a blush of light spread across the horizon, and the ship bobbed gently in the low swell rolling across the bay. The masts and spars of other ships anchored nearby were silhouetted against the sky, and anchor lights dotted the harbor. The town of Sydney lay on the slope overlooking the harbor. Lighted windows in the town gleamed faintly, and lanterns moved along the waterfront and the streets.

Sailors were dark shadows in the dim light as they moved about on the ship, their bare feet soundless on the deck. The water cask was at the base of the mainmast. Mabry filled a wooden bucket for Garrity and walked back across the deck. Garrity took off his coat and shirt and washed. Then he dressed, and took the bucket to the rail to empty it.

A dawn breeze whispered through the rigging, and the thin, gray first light of dawn spread across the harbor as Garrity walked back across the deck. Mabry was at the foot of the steps leading up to the quarterdeck, holding two steaming pannikins and talking to another man. He turned as Garrity approached.

"Did that take away some of the cobwebs, Earl?" He laughed. "Here, this will put an end to any that might be left. Captain Spencer, this is my friend Earl Garrity."

Spencer was a short, stout man, wearing a tricorn and a frock coat with wide pockets and brass buttons. He touched his tricorn and nodded amiably. "Mr. Mabry has often spoken of you. I'm pleased to meet you. Your family owns a large sheep station in the outback. Is that right?"

"I'm pleased to meet you, Captain," Garrity replied, taking a sip from the pannikin. The tea was strong, liberally laced with rum, and he took a deep drink as he glanced around at the ship. "Aye, my family owns Wayamba Station, but I'd gladly trade my share of it for this."

"Would you now?" Spencer chuckled. "Well, I'll assure you that nothing could be easier. Port Jackson is overrun with forecastle hands, but there's a scarcity of men for the quarterdeck. An educated man can quickly qualify as an officer. Like Mr. Mabry here."

"Earl knows how to deal with men," Mabry said. "We were discussing the subject last night, and I told him that was the main thing a ship's officer has to know."

"That's quite true," Spencer agreed. "I can teach a man navigation and the handling of a ship, but how to deal with the crew is another thing again. And if you can do that, you've already learned much of what you need to know. What do you say, Mr. Garrity? Are you ready to sign the ship's articles?"

Garrity smiled, shaking his head and taking a drink from his pannikin. "No, they're looking for me to get back to Wayamba Station with some goods I was sent to fetch. Tom tells me that you're sailing today for New Zealand."

"Aye, our hatches are battened down on a good load of trade goods, and we'll be going back there to load lumber and spars. There's always a good demand for those, and they bring a tidy profit."

"Do you ever have any trouble with the cannibals there?"

"No, but I don't venture to make landfall anywhere but the white settlement on North Island. Some have tried to make a better profit dealing direct with the natives at other places along the coast. Some of them have ended up in a pot." He turned to Mabry. "Did you tell him about what I have in the box in my cabin?"

"No, sir," Mabry laughed. "I'll fetch it, and he can have a look. And perhaps I'd best fetch him another pannikin of tea."

Garrity drained his pannikin and shook his head as he handed it to Mabry. "No, I'm much obliged, but that's enough for me. That's the strongest tea I've had in a while, and I'll need my wits about me."

Spencer and Mabry laughed. Mabry took the pannikin and went into the passageway to the cabins. Spencer glanced up at the rigging, then he looked back at Garrity. "Do you come to Sydney very often, Mr. Garrity?"

"Not nearly as often as I'd like, Captain Spencer. I'm here now because some things we ordered from England came in, and we need them before the shearing."

"You haven't come for supplies for the station, then?"

"No, we use tons of supplies, and we don't have the wagons to haul that much. A carter brings our supplies out when the shearing has been done, and he hauls the wool back. Our factor here is Cummings, and they see to that for us."

"Aye, Cummings Brothers is a good firm. The owners of my ship deal with them. They provide a good quality of trade goods." He turned as Mabry came out of the passageway with a wooden box. "Ah, here we are. Let's see what Mr. Garrity thinks of this."

Full dawn had broken, and the sun was coming up over the horizon. Spencer looked at Garrity with a smile of anticipation, then slowly removed the lid from the box. It contained a preserved human head. The preservation process had given the dark skin a texture of shriveled leather. The black, coarse hair was tied up in a sheaf, and the lips and eyelids had been sewn with thick twine. The features were covered with a deeply-etched pattern of tattoos, and the face was fiercely savage.

"Bloody hell," Garrity murmured, shaking his head. "Do they all look like that?"

Spencer nodded, smiling at Garrity's reaction. "Aye, and worse. I've seen some with those tattoos all over their shoulders, arms, and chest, as well as their face. It gives you a turn when you see a canoe full of them come alongside, doesn't it, Mr. Mabry?"

"It does and all," Mabry agreed. "They're a blood-thirsty lot. From what I was told at the white settlement, they always save the head and eat the rest when

11

they kill someone."

"I got this from one of the chiefs who live around the white settlement," Spencer said. "There used to be a thriving trade in heads, but the Governor here stopped it. Just as well. Bartering human heads is a heathenish way of making a profit."

"How do the people at the white settlement keep peace with them?" Garrity asked. "It appears they have a perilous life."

"Aye, they do," Spencer replied, closing the box. "But the Maoris aren't fools, even though they're savages. Those around the settlement know they can get trade goods from the traders, so they mostly leave them be. A few missionaries are also there, and whalers put in there to sell their cargoes and victual their ships. Still, people disappear now and then, and everyone knows what's happened to them. Sure you don't want a sip of tea?"

Garrity smiled, shaking his head. "No, I'll forego it. And I'd best leave before I end up going with you, whether I want to or no. It's been a pleasure meeting you, Captain Spencer."

"It's been a pleasure for me as well, Mr. Garrity, and I'll look forward to seeing you again. Mr. Mabry, we have ample time if you'd like to see Mr. Garrity ashore."

"Aye, I would like to, sir," Mabry replied. "I'll be back directly."

Garrity and Mabry crossed the deck to the rail. Crewmen were dipping up water with buckets on long ropes and washing down the deck. Two of them put their buckets down and trotted across the deck when

Mabry called them. The two sailors scrambled down the ladder and readied the oars in the boat. Garrity and Mabry went after them.

The sun was inching higher into the sky, and the dawn breeze was dying away. It was January, late in the Australian summer, and the intensity of the early morning sun warned of the torrid heat that would settle during the afternoon. The sailors plied the oars, guiding the boat through a line of ships at anchor, rowing toward the piers reaching out from the waterfront. The ships bustled with activity, bare feet slapping back and forth on the decks as officers barked orders.

Garrity and Mabry talked as the boat crossed the harbor. There were ships everywhere, their weathered hulls crusted with salt. On some of the ships, men were repairing damage from storms, and there were other signs of the vast distances the ships had traveled. To Garrity, the ships symbolized a life of freedom, variety, and excitement, while he was trapped in the deadly monotony of an isloated sheep station in the outback.

The sailors backed water with their oars and brought the boat up to the end of a pier. Garrity climbed the ladder of boards nailed to a pile. Mabry followed him up, and they stood in silence for a moment. Then Mabry sighed, smiling. "It was uncommon good fortune that we happened to meet yesterday, Earl, and I've enjoyed seeing you again."

"I've enjoyed seeing you again, Tom, and I'm pleased that you're so well situated. Captain Spencer appears to be a most congenial man."

"He is indeed. If you decide that you want to go to

13

sea, he could find you a good berth. We're in Port Jackson every few weeks, so you might keep that in mind."

"Aye, I will, Tom."

"I'll be off, then," Mabry said, offering his hand. "Good luck."

"And good luck to you, Tom," Garrity replied, shaking hands with him. "Watch out those cannibals don't get you in a pot."

"No fear of that." Mabry went to the end of the pier to climb back down. "Goodbye, Earl."

"Goodbye, Tom."

The boat went away from the pier. It moved out into the harbor, bobbing on the swell, and Garrity stood and watched it. Mabry waved as the boat started through a line of ships. Garrity waved back. The boat disappeared behind a ship, and Garrity turned and walked along the pier.

Smoke from breakfast fires rose over the town. The waterfront and warehouses along it were deserted except for a few night watchmen who were leaving. Garrity walked to the end of the warehouses, and turned into a street leading up into the town. Vendors were making early morning deliveries. Their carts and wagons moved along the quiet streets. A murmur of livestock sounded through the streets as dealers drove cattle, sheep, and swine to the market by the common.

The street opened out, with a stable and small stockyard on one side, a wainwright's shop on the other. The previous afternoon, Garrity had taken his wagons to the shop for minor repairs, and had left his horse and oxen at the stable. Garrity turned onto the narrow street by the wainwright's shop. The yard at the rear of it was enclosed by a tall wooden fence, and smoke from a small fire rose from inside it. Garrity pushed open one side of the wide gate, and went in.

The men Garrity had brought with him from the sheep station were cooking breakfast over a fire by the wagons. One was a grizzled oldster named Potter. Another was a half-breed aborigine called Jay. The other two were boys who had been brought to Wayamba Station from the Sydney Boys' Orphanage the year before. They were of uncertain parentage, and were called Tod and John.

Potter turned pieces of pork in a frying pan. "We wondered where you had got to," he said to Garrity. "I opined that you might have found a doxie to doss in with."

The others laughed. Garrity smiled and shook his head and looked at the wagons. "No, I spent the night on a ship in the harbor. It appears they fixed everything on the wagons, including the spare wheels."

"Aye, some of them stayed late last night to finish the job," Potter replied. "And that'll probably set the price up to half as much again, even though we helped them and did half the work. This is about the last of the rations. We didn't bring any to spare."

"We'll get rations from the market," Garrity said, sitting down by the fire. "The victuals there will be better than we can get from a chandler."

"Aye, they will and all," Potter agreed, moving a fire-blackened billy closer to the hot coals. "Mayhap we can get some fresh vegetables as well. I could use a good feed of greenery, because I've been bunged up

15

tighter than a parson's purse this past week or more. One of you jackaroos fetch the plates, and we'll eat."

Tod rose and climbed into a wagon, and Potter poured a measured amount of tea into the water boiling in the billy. Damper was baking in another pan, the thin, tough bread made of flour, salt, and water that was a staple of food of the outback. A mixture of peas, beans, and rice was boiling in a pot, and Potter stirred pork grease into the mixture to season it. Tod climbed back out of the wagon with the box of dishes, and Potter filled the plates and pannikins and passed them out.

The boys washed the dishes when the meal was finished, and the owner of the shop arrived. Garrity paid for the repairs to the wagons, and went across the street to the stable. The others had put the bedrolls and other things into the wagons, ready to leave when he returned with the animals. They yoked the oxen to the wagons as Garrity saddled his horse. The lumbering wagons followed Garrity out into the street, the boys leading the oxen and Potter and Jay riding in the wagons and pulling on the brake levers to keep the wagons from building up speed on the sloped street.

The waterfront bustled with activity, wagons and drays rumbling along the street, men moving cargo and supplies between warehouses and piers. Garrity tied his horse as the wagons pulled up to the loading dock in front of the Cummings' warehouse. Potter and Jay followed him in. The warehouse foreman met them at the door, and took them to the corner where the cargo for Wayamba Station had been stored.

There was a pile of bar iron, cases of axeheads and

sheep shears, jute for baling wool, and other things. Potter lifted the end of an iron bar, feeling the weight, and shook his head as he put it down. "Those oxen are going to earn their fodder on the way back," he commented.

"Aye, they will," Garrity agreed. "I'll go up to the office and see them. You can get this loaded and meet me at the market. On your way up there, you might stop in at the postal office and see if there's any mail to be delivered along the way. And you could also stop in at that stationer and get some old newspapers." He took out his purse, and gave Potter a florin. "That should buy plenty."

Potter nodded, and he and Jay picked up a case of axeheads and carried it toward the door. The foreman called to men working on the other end of the warehouse, and they walked over and began carrying the cargo out to the wagons. Garrity went with the foreman to his small cubbyhole of an office to sign for the cargo, then he went back out and got on his horse.

He turned onto a winding street that led up into the town. Neat plaster and beam buildings with leaded windows lined the street, and carriages rattled along the cobblestones. Owners of inns and shops scrubbed their steps and gossiped, and men lifted their hats as women passed, their faces shaded by their sunbonnets, their skirts sweeping the street. A crew of convicts was replacing cobblestones on a curve in the street. The transportation of convicts to New South Wales had all but ceased. Most of them were now sent to Western Australia, but they were still seen in the town.

17

The office of the Cummings Brothers, traders and shipping factors, was on the other side of the curve. The firm had been the purchasing and shipping agent for Wayamba Station for decades, and there was a distant relationship by marriage between the Cummings and Garrity families. Garrity's mother had been married to a Cummings before she married his father, and an Infant Cummings was buried in the graveyard at Wayamba Station. She never discussed her past, but he had heard from many sources that it had been an unhappy marriage.

The office was cluttered with shelves filled with ledgers and sheafs of paper, and it had a hushed atmosphere. The head clerk sat at an elevated desk facing the door, a thin man with pale, drawn features. Two apprentices sat at table desks by the wall, and they darted glances at Garrity as they leafed through bills and made entries in ledgers. The head clerk nodded gravely in greeting as he put down his quill and stepped down from his stool and crossed the office to a door. He looked inside, exchanged words with someone, then beckoned Garrity.

The man in the office was Isaiah Cummings, one of the three brothers who had inherited the firm from their father. Jeremiah, another of the brothers, was disfigured by a facial birthmark that was an inherited characteristic in some of the family. Isaiah's complexion was clear, but Garrity had seen the man's children and two of them had the birthmark. All three of the brothers had the same solemn, deliberate bearing and manner.

A periodic financial account for the station had been

prepared, and Cummings went over the papers with Garrity in tedious detail, explaining each line. Garrity knew nothing about the accounts, but he nodded, murmured, and patiently waited for Cummings to finish. Cummings wrapped the sheaf of papers in oilskin for Garrity to deliver to his mother, and invited him to his house that evening. Garrity politely declined the invitation, explaining that he had to return to the station as soon as possible.

It was midmorning when Garrity left the office, and he rode on through the busy streets to Fort Macquarie, near the edge of the town. The market was on one side of the spacious common around the weathered stone buildings and walls of the fort, and it was a scene of noisey confusion. Cattle lowed, sheep bleated, and swine squealed as men haggled over them. Vendors and farmers with wagons filled with produce shouted their wares. Housewives milled about among the carts and wagons.

The wagons from Wayamba Station were parked at the side of the street leading away from the common. Garrity went to the market and bought provisions for the return journey, and the men carried his purchases to the wagons. The boys looked longingly at jars of boiled sweets in a vendor's cart, and Garrity bought each of them a bag of candy. Then the wagons rumbled on along the street, wheels bumping over cobblestones, chickens squawking in crates tied to the rear of the wagons.

The buildings became scattered, and the street curved around one side of the long, gentle slope where the town lay. The harbor came into sight, and Garrity reined his horse to one side and let the wagons pass as he looked down at the harbor. A ship was moving out to sea, its sails filling as it entered the long sound between the harbor and the headlands. Garrity sat and looked at it for a long moment, then reluctantly nudged his horse with his heels and caught up with the wagons.

The last scattered buildings disappeared behind, and the street became a track leading away from the town. The boys climbed into a wagon and ate their candy as the oxen trudged along the track. It wound through rolling hills, with small farms and selections on each side and the hazy bulk of the Blue Mountains to the west. Cattle grazed between outcroppings of gray rock on the hillsides, and farmers worked in the crop fields around the small houses. Towering ghost gums shaded the track in moist valleys, their thick, gray-green foliage blotting out the sunlight. Chattering red and green parrots darted between the trees.

The sun passed its zenith and began its descent, and the stifling heat of the summer afternoon settled in. The oxen tossed their heads and slashed at flies with their tails, and the folds of the Blue Mountains became more distinct. A junction came into sight, one track leading toward the mountains and the vast stretches of the outback beyond them, and the other to selections along the Georges River. The boys jumped down from the wagon and turned the oxen onto the track along the river.

Most of the selections were enclosed by rail fences, and narrow tracks turned off on each side and led through gates. The houses were widely scattered, and people working around them and in the fields stopped what they were doing to watch the wagons pass. The long, hot afternoon slowly dragged by. The wagons creaked and rattled along the rutted track. A sultry breeze stirred near sunset. The breeze freshened, breaking the intensity of the heat, and the selection that belonged to Wayamba Station came into sight as the wagons crossed a low hill.

Garrity's mother had bought the selection through the Cummings Brothers several years before. She had maintained a forbidding silence about her reasons, as she did about many things, and the ostensible purpose had been to provide pasture for sheep being sold in Sydney. But sheep were rarely sold in Sydney, pasturage could be rented, and the amount of money that had been spent on the selection was completely out of proportion to its usefulness. Then Garrity had found out by accident that his mother had lived on the selection when she was married to Cummings.

Beyond that fact, her reasons for buying the property remained obscure. Usually frugal, she had spent lavishly on the selection. She never left Wayamba Station, but she had dictated every detail of what was to be done. New fences and a luxuriously large house had been built, and she specified that a vegetable garden was to be located on the site of an old garden of years before. Alfred Mayhew, an employee who had lost a leg in an accident, was paid full stockman's wages to tend the garden and maintain the place.

One of the boys ran ahead to open the gate, and Garrity rode along the track toward the house. The selection was two-hundred acres divided into four small

21

paddocks. The rolling land sloped down to the Georges River, a narrow, wooded stream that marked one boundary of the property. The grass was tall and thick, with only a few scattered sheep grazing on it, and the garden behind the house was flourishing. Aborigines were living along the river and had built a half dozen *wiltjas* in the shade of a copse of trees.

Mayhew was on the wide veranda in front of the house, and he scrambled down the steps and stumped along the track on his wooden leg. He was an old, wiry man with a gray beard, and exuberantly pleased at having visitors. "How are you, Mr. Garrity?" he shouted. "What brings you all the way to Sydney this time of year?"

"We had to pick up some things we'll need before shearing. Are you all right, Alf?"

"Aye, rain can't rust me and the sun can't melt me." He looked at the wagons following Garrity, and waved his hat. "And there's old Potter and Jay. By God, it's good to see them again. Do you want to bed down in the house? There's room for an army, and it's clean."

"No, it'll be cooler outside. We can park the wagons by the house and bed down by them."

"Right you are," Mayhew replied, turning back toward the house. "And it'll be cooler to cook, won't it? I'll go open the gate, then."

He hobbled back along the track on his wooden leg, and opened the gate surrounding the trampled area around the house and outbuildlings. The oxen sensed they were near the end of the day's trek, and picked up their pace. The wagons trundled through the gate and swung around by the house, and Mayhew greeted Potter and Jay boisterously as they climbed down.

Potter and Jay unyoked the oxen. Garrity unsaddled his horse, and the boys led the animals to one of the paddocks. Mayhew was anxious to keep his sinecure, and he wanted Garrity to look around. They walked around the house, and he pointed out repairs he had made on outbuildings. Garrity looked at the garden and complimented him on it, then they went into the house.

The sun was deep in the west, and the trees along the river cast shadows far up the slope. The house was dark and retained the heat of the day. It still smelled of new wood. The thumping of Mayhew's wooden leg and Garrity's footsteps echoed through the rooms, but the sounds failed to dispel the static, lifeless feel that gripped the house.

"This is a big house, and grand for the likes of me," Mayhew said as they walked out onto the veranda. "I clean everything good at least once a week, but I only use that one room in the back."

"It's certainly clean enough to satisfy anyone," Garrity said.

"Well, I'm glad to hear you say that. I'm sure you saw those few sheep in the paddock, and you might have wondered how they got here. A man down the river gave up and moved into town, and he sold them to me for sixpence each. But if they're any bother, I'll get shot of them."

Garrity shook his head as they walked down the steps. "No, nobody will get their wind up about your grazing a few sheep."

"Well, I'm glad to hear you say that. That lot of

abos moved in down there by the river a few months ago, and I've left them be. I remember that Mistress Garrity always said that abos were to be left alone and to be helped if they wanted anything."

Garrity looked at the huts by the river. "Aye, that's right. They don't seem to be bothering anything."

"No, they've been no bother, and I haven't had more than ten words with them since they've been there," Mayhew replied. He sniffed and smiled as they walked around the corner of the house. He called out. "By God, that smells good, Potter."

Potter was cooking over a fire by the wagons. "It'll taste as good as it smells when it's done, Alf. Sit you down, and we'll have a drink of tea while we're waiting."

Garrity and Mayhew walked over to the fire and sat down. There was the good smell of slices of gammon sizzling in a pan. Potatoes and vegetables were cooking in pots, damper baked in a pan, and tea boiled in the billy. Potter filled pannikins with tea and sweetened it with spoonfuls of treacle, then he passed out the pannikins and refilled the billy to make tea to drink with the meal.

Potter and Mayhew talked as they drank their tea, exchanging stories about events of past years. Some of them were improbable yarns about the Garrity family in the early years of the outback, a fertile source of tales among oldsters. Dusk fell and darkness closed in, and the sky became a canopy of stars. Fires blazed up in front of the *wiltjas* by the river, and they silhouetted the aborigines as they moved back and forth around their shelters.

The food finished cooking, and Potter filled tin plates and passed them out. Garrity ate, then filled his pipe and smoked it and drank his tea. The boys gathered up the dishes and washed them, then took the bedrolls out of a wagon. Potter had picked up a bag of mail and a roll of old newspapers in the town, and got them out. He and Mayhew looked through the mail, examining and discussing the letters. After that they looked through the newspapers.

Garrity knocked the ashes out of his pipe. He unrolled his bedroll and lay down. The boys and Jay lay down and wrapped their blankets around themselves, and Potter and Mayhew continued looking through the newspapers. Their voices were a soft murmur as they talked, and the night was alive with sound; frogs croaking, insects chirping, night birds uttering their mournful cries.

The dirge-like, grinding groan of digereedoos came from the *wiltjas* by the river, a rising and falling drone accompanied by the clatter of rhythm sticks and soft chanting. The primitive music of the aborigines blended with the other sounds of the night, a harmonious part of the Australian night. Garrity lay and looked up at the stars, thinking about the ship he had seen leaving the harbor and wondering what distant, exotic places it would visit during its journey.

─────────────Chapter 2

BLISTERING, BREATHLESS, HEAT ENVELOPED GARRITY like a heavy blanket as his horse cantered slowly along the dusty track. A house, shearing sheds, and other outbuildings were by a sparsely-wooded creek three or four miles ahead. The sun glared down from the brassy sky, reflecting off the heat waves rising from the bare ground around the buildings and trees, that seemed to float in a shimmering lake.

Foam from the horse's mouth spattered its chest, and its neck and shoulders were black with sweat. The horse stumbled. Garrity reined it back to a walk. Rolling hills covered with brush, wallaby grass, and outcroppings of stone stretched away to the horizon. The air was motionless, birds and animals were in shelter until the heat broke in late afternoon, and the silence was as intense as the heat.

The horse panted heavily, tossing its head and mouthing the bit, and its hoofs raised puffs of dust as it walked along the track. Garrity saw a movement through the heat waves ahead, someone walking from one of the other buildings to the house. The tiny figure stopped, looked back, then ran toward the house. Others came out of the house. Garrity's horse began breathing more easily, and he urged it into a canter again.

The buildings were the home paddock of Henshaw Station, and the shimmering gleam of the heat reflection around them gradually diminished as Garrity drew closer. Henshaw, his wife, and their son and daughter stood in the deep shadow of the porch. They shaded their eyes, looking at Garrity. Henshaw was a burly man with a thick, dark beard, and he waved and stepped off the porch as Garrity approached.

"Are you all right, Earl?" he called. "What did you do with the wagons and men you took to Sydney?"

"I left them back at that billabong in your east paddock!" Garrity shouted back. "A 'roo jumped out of the grass in front of a wagon, and the oxen stampeded and sprung the bed on the wagon!"

Henshaw shook his head in sympathy. The others came down from the porch. Henshaw's wife was a heavyset, motherly woman of forty, the boy was sixteen, and the girl was pretty, precociously mature, and buxom at fourteen. She looked at Garrity with a wide, staring smile. He reined up in front of the porch and dismounted, nodding to the boy and girl, and touched his hat as he looked at Henshaw's wife.

"Are you all right, Mistress Henshaw?"

"Aye, I'm all right, Earl, and we're sorry to hear what happened," she said. "I trust nobody was hurt."

Garrity shook his head. He took off his hat and wiped his face with his sleeve. "No, one of my jackaroos was tossed around, but it didn't hurt him. The wagon doesn't seem to be damaged all that bad, but I didn't want to try to fit it there."

"No, you couldn't do anything out there," Henshaw said. "The flies would eat you up, and it might take several men. Both of my stockmen are in the north paddock, but I have two swagmen in the bunkhouse and they can help. Rob, roust those swagmen out, and hitch a yoke of oxen to the wagon. Emma, saddle me a horse, and get Earl a fresh one from the pens. We'll get that wagon in here, and we'll set it right soon enough."

"I'm much obliged," Garrity said. "You had a letter in the mails we picked up in Sydney. I brought it along with me."

Garrity took the thick packet out of his pocket and handed it to Henshaw. Henshaw turned it over in his hands, feeling it and looking at it in illiterate incomprehension, then handed it to his wife.

She squeezed it and felt it, holding it at arm's length and squinting at it, then turned to the porch. "I'll fetch my spectacles out and see who it's from."

"I'll tell you, Ma," Emma said, reaching for the letter. "Give it here."

"No, I'll see who it's from," her mother insisted, holding the letter tightly and stepping up to the porch. "It won't take me but a minute."

"That's right, Maud, you go ahead and get your spectacles," Henshaw said. "And you leave your ma be, Emma. She'll tell us who it's from." He smiled at his wife affectionately as she crossed the porch and went into the house. He turned to Garrity. "We're

29

much obliged, Earl. You say a 'roo made your oxen shy?''

"Aye, it jumped out directly in front of them," Garrity said, unfastening the girth on his saddle. "We've seen a lot of 'roos the past three or four days."

"I don't doubt that," Henshaw sighed, shaking his head. "They've been like a plague these last few months. I wish the dingos would start killing them and leave my sheep be."

Garrity took the saddle off his horse and put it on the edge of the porch. Henshaw and his children were silent, looking at the door, waiting for the woman. She came back out with her spectacles, small, thick lenses in a wire frame, and put them on. The others waited while she adjusted them and examined the letter, then she looked at Henshaw over the top of her spectacles.

"It's from the cousins in Durham, and it was only last autumn that we wrote them the last time. If this is an answer, it got here very quickly indeed. But they might have decided to just write us again, even though we owed them a letter."

Henshaw pursed his lips and stroked his beard as he pondered the question. "I expect it could be either one, Maud. There's been enough time for a letter to get back, if everything happened just right. On the other hand, they are good about writing and telling us all the news."

"Why don't you just open it, Ma?" the boy suggested. "Then you'd know, along with everything else they wrote about."

The woman looked at the letter again, turning it over in her hands, then looked back at Henshaw. "I'd like to wait for a while, Luke. Do we have to open it now?"

"Of course we don't, Maud," he said fondly. "If you want to wait for a while and think about it, there's no reason at all why you can't. A few hours or a few days won't break the back of months, so you wait as long as you like. Just put it away. I expect Earl could use a drink of water. And you two run on and do as I said."

Mrs. Henshaw nodded gratefully and went back into the house. The boy grumbled as he walked away. Emma had forgotten the letter, and her attention returned to Garrity. She stepped toward him to take the reins from him, gazing up at him with a smile. Her hand brushed his with a lingering touch as she took the reins, and she accentuated the movement of her hips and smiled over her shoulder as she led the horse away.

Henshaw's wife brought out a bucket of water and a pannikin, and Garrity sat on the edge of the porch with Henshaw and talked with him as he drank. Emma returned with a horse for Garrity and one for her father. She made token motions of helping Garrity saddle the horse, plucking at the saddle blanket, smiling all the time. Henshaw ignored her and kept on talking to Garrity. Emma's antics made it hard to listen.

The boy came back around the house, leading a team of oxen yoked to a wagon. Two swagmen, footloose wanderers of the outback, were in the wagon. They were bearded, ragged, and sunburned, and they had their small bundles of belongings with them in case they decided to continue on their way instead of

31

returning to the station. Garrity and Henshaw mounted their horses and rode away from the house. The wagon followed at the slow, deliberate pace of the oxen.

The accident had happened on a billabong—an ox-bow pond in a dry riverbed—called Booloroo by the aborigines. The name meant "many flies," and the smoke from the smudge fire the men had built to drive away flies was visible for miles. It rose straight up in the motionless air, gradually becoming more distinct, then the wagons and oxen emerged from the heat waves.

The fire was in the center of the track, and the two men and boys stood in the billowing smoke. The oxen were tethered in the shade of a mulga grove across the track from the wagons, lashing their tails and tossing their heads to drive away the flies. The flies descended in swarms as Garrity and Henshaw approached the wagons, settling all over them, trying to crawl into their eyes and nostrils. Their horses began shaking their heads and whipping their tails.

They dismounted as the men and boys walked over from the fire, and Henshaw crawled under the damaged wagons. The bed was several degrees out of line with the frame, and he moved around under the wagon and looked at it. Then he slid back out, slapping at flies, and climbed to his feet. "Well, she's sprung, Earl, and there's no doubt about that," he said. "But it looks like the frame is all right."

"Aye, it appears that way to me," Garrity agreed. "It looks like the bolts that hold the bed on were pulled through the frame beams without splitting

32

them. That being so, we can just straighten the bolts and make washers to keep them from pulling loose again."

Henshaw nodded. "It won't take us long to do that, once we get the wagon back to the home paddock. The wagon is going to pull to one side even when it's empty, but there's a good-sized mallee over there. We can cut it down and make us a pole to shove the bed over into line."

"We'll do that," Garrity said. "Jay, we'll need the axe out of the other wagon. You jackaroos can get back over there in the smoke. We won't need you."

The boys trotted back to the fire and stood in the edge of the smoke. Jay got the axe out of the wagon and followed the other men to a solitary mallee tree a few yards off the track. The men took turns chopping. They felled the tree and dragged it onto the track and trimmed off the limbs. Then they piled the green limbs on the fire, and stood in the edge of the smoke and waited for the wagon from Henshaw Station.

The wagon came slowly, and the swagmen were prepared for Booloroo Billabong. They had tied short lengths of twine through holes an inch apart around their hat brims, and small corks dangled at the end of the strings. The corks were in constant motion, bouncing with the slightest movement, driving away the flies from the swagmen's faces. They got down from the wagon, silent and withdrawn, and helped the others transfer the cargo from the damaged wagon.

Tod and John carried buckets of water from the billabong and extinguished the fire, and the men levered the bed of the damaged wagon into line with the frame. Then the swagmen stood at one side and talked quietly as the oxen were yoked to the wagons. Garrity and Henshaw mounted their horses and rode away at a walk. The wagons followed. The swagmen decided to remain at Henshaw Station for the present, and they caught up with a wagon and climbed into it.

The sun was sinking into the west, and the heat was easing up when they reached the home paddock. The boys led the animals away, and the men pushed the damaged wagon into the repair shed. Henshaw built a fire in the forge and fashioned large washers out of a piece of bar iron. Garrity and the others removed the bent bolts and positioned the bed on the wagon with a block and tackle. They straightened out the bolts, put them on with the washers, and transferred the cargo back to the wagon.

The station was a relatively small one, and Henshaw's wife cooked for everyone. At sunset, she and Emma carried trays of food out to a trestle table by the back door. The meal was a welcome change from the hurriedly-cooked food on the track. A large beef pie covered with flaky crust and filled with rich gravy and tender, tasty beef was flanked by bowls of vegetables. The vegetables were seasoned with onions and traces of mustard, treacle, and curry. There was apple pie for dessert.

The swagmen ate quickly and silently, and went to the stockmen's barracks. Dark fell as Garrity and the others finished, and Emma cleared the table, made more tea, and brought out a lamp. Jay went to the wagons for the remaining newspapers, and the Henshaws chose the ones they wanted. The boys became sleepy and went to the barracks, then Potter and Jay left. Garrity remained and talked with the Henshaws far into the night, telling them about his trip and all the news he had heard.

They left before dawn the next morning. Garrity took the lead and the wagons followed in the dark. Dawn broke, gray light spread across the sky and the vast miles of savannah, and the sun rose. The horizon to the north was lined with black clouds, and the mutter of thunder in the far distance was a sound more felt than heard. At midmorning the fence dividing Henshaw Station from the adjacent station came into sight, and one of the boys ran ahead to open the gate as they approached it.

The sun rose higher, and the oppressive, sweltering heat of midday settled in. The dark, threatening clouds to the north covered more of the sky. Lightning flickered in the bulging mass of the clouds, and a rumble of thunder carried across the miles. The air was motionless, and the calm had a steely, gripping quality, a tense atmosphere of powerful, violent forces gathering strength.

They were on Phelps Station, and the track crossed it several miles south of the home paddock. A small package and a letter for Phelps were in the mail, and Garrity took them and several of the newspapers to the house while the wagons continued along the track. Phelps pointed out the approaching storm and tried to persuade Garrity to stay for the night, but he declined. He talked with Phelps and his wife for an hour, telling them about the trip and all the news he had heard, then he rode back to the track and caught up with the wagons.

The storm inched closer, and the sun touched the black clouds with crimson highlights as it set. Garrity picked a high spot in the terrain to camp for the night, choosing the danger of lightning over that of a flash flood in a low place. Lightning broke the darkness with brilliant flashes and thunder roared during the night, and the animals moved about restlessly. At dawn, the storm was still several miles to the north. They moved on.

Clouds were heavy in the northern sky, and there was heavy rain up that way. The sunlight, thin and weak, seemed to shrink from the storm. Lightning crackled, and the air and ground vibrated with rolling thunder as the wagons moved along the track. A breeze stirred, carrying with it the smell and feel of rain, and it abruptly turned into gusty wind.

The trees and brush thrashed, and the tearing wind whipped up clouds of dust from the track. Kangaroos bounded wildly about on both sides, and emus darted back and forth across the track. The day was suddenly dark, and bruising hail began pounding down. Garrity stopped and tied his horse to a wagon, and helped the others keep the panic-stricken oxen from bolting. The hail turned into rain, and he mounted his horse again and rode along the track ahead of the wagons.

The rain was a downpour that blotted out everything more than a few yards away. The track turned into a quagmire within minutes, and the oxen threw their weight into the yokes as the wagon wheels sank into the mud and Potter and Jay cracked stock whips.

A rivulet in a shallow valley had turned into a wide, rushing stream, and the water rose rapidly and swirled up around the beds of the wagons as they crossed it. The track went up a slow incline and past a grove of ghost gums, and Garrity led the wagons into the shelter of the trees.

When the oxen and horse were tightly tethered, Garrity and the other men stood around the wagons, oilcloth covering the locks on their muskets. Kangaroos still leaped about, drawn by instinct to the higher ground, where wild boars and poisonous snakes also sought refuge when floods threatened. Flashes of lightning silhouetted the ghost gums and thunder shook the ground as the torrential downpour continued. Then it began to diminish.

When the rain slackened, Potter dug through the piles of bark the trees had shed, and found dry pieces to start a fire. He built the fire by the wagons to keep wild boars at a distance. He sheltered it with slabs of bark, and it dried out fast and began to blaze. The wind and rain continued as early dusk fell, and the boys gathered bark and piled it by the fire to dry. During the night, Garrity and the others took turns standing guard and keeping the fire built up.

There were intermittent showers on the day after the storm, but the danger of flash floods in creeks and gullies had passed. The storm had broken the heat, and the air was cool as the oxen pulled the wagons along the muddy track. Then the arid heat returned and quickly dried the ground, and the animals' hoofs and the wagon wheels stirred dust on the track the day after that.

The day after the last of the mail was delivered, a fence that stretched from the northern to the southern horizon came into sight. Potter and Jay cracked their whips and whooped, and the boys cheered. The fence marked the boundary of Wayamba Station, the vast sheep empire that Garrity's grandfather had established. It was one of the largest sheep stations in the outback, larger in area than many European kingdoms, and the fence continued far beyond the horizon.

One of the boys ran ahead and opened the gate, and Potter and Jay urged the oxen into a lumbering trot. Garrity rode his horse through the gate and rode into Wilcannia East, the easternmost section of the easternmost paddock. Potter and Jay let the oxen settle back into their plodding walk after the first moment of excitement. Days of travel still remained before they reached the home paddock.

A dark blot appeared on the horizon ahead and to the north, and Garrity and the other men looked at it apprehensively until dusk fell. It was larger the next day, and their fears were realized. It was smoke. A grassfire, the terror of the outback, was raging in one of the northern paddocks. The stockmen in Wilcannia also had seen it and driven their flocks south. There was no sign of sheep along the track.

The track went through another gate, and into Wilcannia West. The smoke was miles to the northwest, gradually shifting to the north as Garrity led the wagons across the section. The smoke thinned out to become a vague discoloration of the sky, evidence that it was being extinguished. When the wagons reached Penong Paddock, the smoke was almost directly north, and air currents carried its smell south to the track.

Garrity picked a camping place near the edge of the paddock, and the wagons went through a gate and into Penong East early the next morning. Near midday, Potter shouted to Garrity and pointed back along the track. Garrity reined up and looked. Five riders were approaching at a canter, and when they came closer, he recognized them as his younger brother Colin, and four stockmen.

Colin took off his hat and waved it. Earl Garrity and the others shouted and waved, and the four stockmen reined up by the wagons and exchanged boisterous greetings with Potter and Jay. Colin rode ahead to meet Earl. He was tall, like Earl and their older brother Dennis. All three of them resembled their mother and had blue eyes and brown hair, and they all had olive toned skin from their aborigine grandmother.

"Are you all right, Colin?" Garrity called.

"I am now," Colin laughed, reining up. "But we've had a bloody bad time of it for the past three days, I'll tell you."

"Aye, we've been watching the smoke. Where was it?'

"Windorah North, and it almost got away from us and spread across the whole section. But a lot of swagmen happened to be up that way, and some of the men from Tibooburra Station saw the smoke and came down to help. We lost five or six thousand head, I'd say."

Garrity winced and shook his head. "That'll put Ma

39

in a foul mood for a long while.''

"She's not in a good mood, and you can wager what you will on that,'' Colin said glumly. "And I'd best be on my way, Earl. Some dingos scattered a flock in Maralinga Paddock, and I had men over there gathering it back together when the fire started. We'll have to begin all over again if I don't get back over there by tomorrow or the next day.''

"Do you have to go now?'' Garrity asked. "I plan to camp at Mullewa Creek, and you could ride along while I tell you about the trip.''

"And mayhap have Ma come along and find me tarrying with wagons when I should be at Maralinga?'' Colin said. "She's looking over the loss in Windorah, but that won't take her long.''

"That's true,'' Garrity laughed. "I'll see you at the home paddock in a few days, then.''

"Aye, I'll be back there by the time you get there,'' Colin replied, turning his horse. "It's likely that Ma will come along this way, so you might keep an eye open for her.''

Garrity nodded, and his brother shouted to the stockmen. They turned away from the wagons and urged their horses into a canter, nodding to Garrity as they passed.

Garrity rode at the head of the wagons again and thought about Colin's hurry to be on his way. Their mother often expressed a blunt lack of satisfaction in him and his brothers—particularly in him. On a few occasions, he had tried to discuss his dislike of life on Wayamba Station with her, and she had become enraged each time he approached the subject.

40

Mullewa Creek was the halfway point between the eastern boundary and the home paddock, and Potter killed and cooked the last of the chickens to mark the occasion. The wagons were moving again at dawn the next morning. Stockmen in the paddock were spreading their flocks back to the north, and Garrity saw a flock in the distance near midday. The mass of sheep poured over a rise, dogs darting around them, and a stockman cracked his whip as he rode behind them and herded them along.

An hour later, Potter shouted at Garrity and pointed back along the track. A solitary rider approached at a rapid canter, two dogs scampering along behind the horse. And even from a distance, Garrity immediately recognized his mother by her bolt upright posture in the saddle and the way she held her head as she looked around.

The problems that had beset Wayamba Station had been as enormous as the station itself. Patrick Garrity, the founder of the station, had used heroic means to deal with the problems. Sheila Garrity, his daughter, had been no less famous. And they had been joined by Elizabeth Garrity, who exercised dominion over the vast sheep station with resourcefulness and a ruthless, unrelenting will that had made her a legend during her lifetime.

Garrity reined up and turned his horse around, and the boys scrambled out of the wagons and halted the oxen. Potter and Jay climbed down, and they stood with the boys by the wagons as Elizabeth Garrity approached. They lifted their hats. She nodded as her gasping, sweaty horse pounded past the wagons, the

41

two dogs running behind it.

An old double-barrel musket was tied across the bedroll behind her saddle, and the stock whip coiled on the horn of the saddle was black with age. Her features were composed in neutral lines in the shadow of her hat, and they were as ageless as the rocks on the rolling hills of Wayamba Station. Garrity started to lift his hat as she passed, but she reined up.

"Get off that horse and unsaddle it."

Garrity hesitated, surprised. Then he stepped down from the saddle and began unsaddling his horse. His mother dismounted and jerked at the girth on her saddle. Foam dripped from her horse's mouth, and its legs trembled. The two dogs collapsed in the shade of a clump of brush by the track, panting breathlessly.

The only visible sign of her anger over the grassfire and loss of sheep was a tension in her lips that made a white line around her mouth, but it was enough. She rarely showed any emotion except anger. Garrity pulled his saddle off his horse, and his mother put her own saddle in its place. Garrity started to help her, but she stopped him with a searing, sidelong glance thrown over her shoulder.

Her movements were quick, economical, and expert. She settled the saddle on the horse's back and tightened the girth. Then she mounted up, light and lithe in spite of her years and the hard, grueling miles she had traveled, and nudged the animal with her heels. The horse broke into a canter, and the dogs leaped up and ran after it. A haze of dust hung in the air, and the drumming hoofbeats faded rapidly as she rode away.

Garrity looked at the horse she had left. Its head dropped, and it was caked with dust and sweat. He picked up his saddle, took the horse's reins, and walked back to the wagons. Potter climbed into the first wagon, and he looked down at Garrity with a smile as he tossed his saddle into the wagon and tied the horse to it.

"It'll be a while before that horse is fit to ride," he chuckled. "So it looks like you'd best get used to riding in a wagon."

Garrity laughed ruefully. "I expect I'd best, and now I can understand why Colin was in such a hurry. He didn't have a wagon to ride in, and it would be a hell of a long walk."

───────────────Chapter 3

THE HOME PADDOCK CAME INTO sight as the heat was beginning to fade near the end of a desperately hot afternoon. The track ended by the low, wide shearing shed and its adjacent holding pens, the focus of the sheep station. Mustering yards and stock pens for horses and cattle spread away to one side of the shearing shed. The storerooms, barracks, smithy, repair shops, and other dark, weathered wooden buildings were clustered on the other side of the track.

The houses were along a creek, and separated from the outbuildings by a barren, trampled expanse. The main house was set apart from the others and shaded by ancient ghost gums and pale green pepper trees. Massive water tanks were on one side of it, and flower beds and the station graveyard were on the other side. The station vegetable gardens were along the creek near the houses occupied by the head stockman and other married employees, and past there, at some distance, was the aborigine village.

Someone saw the wagons and spread the word.

Stockmen, wives, aborigines, and children gathered by the shearing shed. Garrity saw his mother crossing the expanse between the houses and the outbuildings to meet him, evidence that her mood had improved. She was wearing one of the gray broadcloth dresses she usually wore while at the home paddock. The others waved and shouted, and she stood silent to one side of them and waited.

Potter and Jay cracked their whips, urging the oxen into a lumbering trot. Everyone but Elizabeth Garrity rushed forward and gathered around the wagons when they stopped, exchanging greetings with Potter and Jay. Garrity rode his horse over to where his mother stood. He dismounted, lifting his hat.

"Are you all right, Ma?"

"I am, and I can see you are," she replied, smiling faintly. "You returned with the same wagons and oxen you left with, so the trip must have been easy enough. Did you get the shears and everything?"

"Aye, everything's in the wagons, and nothing out of the ordinary happened." He took out the sheaf of papers Cummings had given him, and handed it to her. "There's the station accounts. Isaiah Cummings talked to no end about them, but it meant naught to me. But at least it wasn't Jeremiah I saw. I find it hard to talk with him because of that mark on his face. One doesn't want to be rude, but it's hard not to stare."

She was silent for a long moment, her features inscrutable as she held the sheaf of papers and looked into the distance, then she sighed and shrugged. "Well, it isn't his fault, Earl. Get finished here and clean yourself up for dinner. Colin and Dennis are about, and we'll all have dinner together."

"Aye, I'll like that, Ma. I'll be in directly, then."

She nodded and walked away toward the house. Garrity led his horse to the harness shed. The wagons were by the storerooms, and Potter, Jay, and other men were unloading them in a hubbub of voices. Everyone wanted to know about the trip. Garrity put his saddle in the harness room, led the horse to a pen and released it, and went to the house.

A heavyset, middle-aged woman named Martha Appleby was married to a stockman and lived in one of the smaller houses, and she worked as the cook and housekeeper in the Garrity house. She gathered up towels, a pot of soap, and clean clothes for Garrity. He got his razor from his room and went to the bathhouse to bathe and shave.

The bathhouse was shaded by the trees behind the house, and the water in the barrels was refreshingly cool. Garrity bathed, then lathered his face and stood in front of the small mirror on the wall to shave. He was putting on his clean clothes when he heard Colin and Dennis talking close-by as they entered the house. He finished dressing and went to join them.

Martha was putting the food on the table. Colin and Dennis were waiting in the dining room for their mother. Earl Garrity and his brothers greeted each other boisterously. They became quieter when their mother came in. They sat down and began eating, and Garrity talked about his trip to Sydney. When he told them about taking the damaged wagon to Henshaw Station for repairs, Colin and Dennis exchanged an amused glance.

"I'm surprised you're back so soon," Dennis commented, smiling widely. "Emma Henshaw is still there, isn't she?"

"Aye, she's still there." Garrity grinned at Dennis. "And I left the next day. Those oxen would have broken that wagon to bits if it hadn't been for Tod. He held onto the lead rope until Potter and——"

"What's this about Emma Henshaw?" his mother asked, interrupting him. "Who is Emma Henshaw?"

She had been eating with a preoccupied air, only half listening to him, and now her eyes were fixed on him in keen interest. He shrugged and shook his head. "She's Luke Henshaw's daughter."

His mother's face became tense with impatience, then she controlled her temper and she gave him a wintry smile. "Well, I didn't think her father's name would be Jones or something." Colin and Dennis laughed. Elizabeth Garrity's smile grew wider. "What's she like, Earl? Is she pretty?"

He took a bite of food and chewed, glowering at Colin and Dennis and their back country humor. "Aye, I suppose so."

"Well, there's naught wrong with a man having a look at a pretty woman," his mother said in a pleased tone. "But as well as a pretty face, she should have——" She broke off as Colin and Dennis made sounds of suppressed amusement. Her genial manner abruptly faded. "What the bloody hell's wrong with you two?" she demanded irately. "Here I am talking to your brother about a woman, and yea two are giggling like silly bloody schoolgirls! Now I'll have an end to this!"

Colin and Dennis busied themselves with their supper, but Elizabeth Garrity continued to glare at them, her face flushed and taut with anger. She sat back in her chair, cleared her throat, pushed at her hair, and tried to control her temper.

"Now there's no need for rancor," she said in a calmer voice. "No more than there's call for making fun of Earl. If he's cast his eye on a girl, then well and good. Moreover, I'm pleased by it. And yea two would be better advised to spend more time in looking for a wife and less in sniggering at your brother. Even a jackass knows his situation with a mare, which is more than yea two seem to know. Earl, did you go by the selection on the Georges?"

Garrity hesitated. For some time, his mother had been actively and bluntly encouraging him and his brothers to marry, hoping they would find wives with ability and interest in the station. She wanted to people the station with Garrity children. He thought about correcting his mother's misunderstanding, and decided against it. She had changed the subject, and it was at least possible that her interest in the matter was less keen than it had been.

"Aye, I did," he replied. "Mayhew is grazing a few sheep, and I told him no one would mind. He's taking good care of the house and keeping it clean as a pin, and the vegetable garden is flourishing better than ours."

His mother took a drink of tea. "Aye, there's no harm in his grazing a few sheep. As long as he keeps the place in order, he may do as he wishes. And I'm not

49

surprised about the vegetable garden, because he's always been more of a farmer than a stockman. When that ram mangled his leg, I daresay it happened because he mistook the ram for a ewe." She looked at Colin and Dennis. They got the joke, and she smiled and pushed her plate away. "It's cool now, so let's sit outside, shall we? We don't have the opportunity that often for all of us to sit together, and there's no point in loitering here and keeping Martha all night."

Garrity and his brothers pushed their chairs back and got up before their mother. Dennis went into the kitchen to get a light for their pipes. Garrity went outside with his mother and Colin. Her favorite place for sitting outside was on the wooden benches by the graveyard.

The gravestones were in neat rows, many of them mossy and weathered by the years. Patrick Garrity was buried by his aborigine wife, Mayrah. Sheila Garrity was buried by them, and there was a vacant space by Colin Garrity's grave. Frank Cummings was buried on the far side of the graveyard, his untended grave among those of several stockmen and swagmen who had died on the station. Infant Cummings was buried among the Garritys, as were several aborigines—Doolibah, Bahal, Narine, and others.

Garrity sat down on a bench and pushed pieces of Irish tobacco into his pipe. His mother sat by him, looking at the gravestones with a distant musing expression. Colin sat on another bench, busy with his pipe. Soon Dennis came around the house with a burning sliver of wood. He lit Garrity's pipe, then sat down by Colin. Garrity puffed on his pipe, and his mother smiled up at him.

"I enjoy the smell of a pipe," she said. "It takes me back to the time when your father was alive, and we sat out here when it was cool." She sat back on the bench, looking at the gravestones again. "What I was about to say to you at the table, Earl, is that it takes more than a pretty face to make a wife. And most especially a wife for a Garrity."

"Aye, I know, but——"

"No, hear me out, Earl. This has come upon me without warning, but I'm most pleased. At the same time, I won't have a flock on this station without looking to see if they have foot rot. Now the woman can come here for a week or two, and I can tell in less time than that if she's got the wind for the course. And Martha or one of the other women can go in the wagon that fetches her here. I don't know the Henshaws, but I shouldn't think they'd object to that."

Garrity squirmed uncomfortably, looking away. "Ma, there's been a misunderstanding about the situation. I have no intention of marrying Emma Henshaw."

Her face reflected perplexity, then anger. "You mean you've been trifling with her?" she demanded. "If you have, by God, then you'll marry her whether you wish to or no!"

"No, I've had naught to do with her," he said. "Emma Henshaw is only a bit of a girl, and her father has kept her on that sheep station until she's mad for any man who passes. Dennis was funning me about that, and you misunderstood. That's the long and the short of it, and I'll own fault for not setting it aright at once."

The color drained from her face, and she stiffened with rage. She rose and walked away from the bench, her hands clenched behind her, her fingers white. Garrity puffed on his pipe, looking at his brothers. They weren't sure what was going on. Elizabeth Garrity turned around and looked at them. She seemed to be angry at all her sons.

"I have here three great, strapping men," she said coldly. "Three healthy, hearty louts, and not one of them has any more interest in women than a wether has in a ewe. Colin, you're not yet old enough to concern me, but you're old enough to get married. But you show every sign of becoming just like your brothers. I'd dismiss it without a thought if any of you showed promise of being able to take my place, but the best of you will never be more than a stockman. And you'll never even be that, Earl." She drew in a deep breath, and shrugged in resignation. "Didn't Isaiah Cummings invite you to his house?"

"Aye, he did," Garrity replied. "But I thought I'd best be getting back instead of tarrying."

"Best be getting back," she sighed sarcastically. "I suppose it didn't occur to you that he might have intended to introduce you to a likely woman or two, did it? Or perhaps it did, and you feared one might smile at you and make you wet your breeches in fright." She stepped back to the bench and sat down, sighing again. "So you went all the way to Sydney and back without seeing anyone."

"I saw Tom Mabry." His mother glanced up at him sourly and looked away, her anger faded into weary disgust, and he looked at his brothers. "Tom's an officer on a cargo ship now, and he's been to cannibal country several times. His captain has a cannibal's head in a box."

"A cannibal's head in a box?" Dennis laughed as Colin echoed his surprise and amusement. "Does he carry it about to show people?"

Garrity laughed, shaking his head. "No, Tom and I tippled a few, and I spent a night on the ship. I met his captain the next morning, and he showed it to me then. The cannibals have a way of preserving heads and keeping them as souvenirs of tasty meals they've had, and the captain got it from one of them."

"If you'd been tippling, I daresay you spent an uneasy night on the ship," Colin chuckled. "With all that rocking about, you probably chundered more than you slept."

"No, it didn't bother me at all," Garrity replied, shaking his head. "In fact, I found it quite to my liking. It made for a cozy night's sleep, and the ship is very comfortable. Tom's more than satisfied with his situation, and I can readily understand why. An officer on a ship has a very pleasant life indeed."

"Aye, you've said as much before," his mother commented quietly. "And more than once. Do you fancy that yourself, then?"

Her tone and expression were dangerous, and Garrity cleared his throat uncomfortably. "I only remarked that Tom Mabry's contented, and he has reason to be. I don't want to argue with you, Ma."

"Nor do you wish to answer me, apparently," she said in the same quiet voice, rising again. She walked

53

a few steps toward the gravestones and stopped, her back to him. "Do you remember the pups that spotted bitch whelped a few weeks before you went to Sydney?"

"Aye, but I haven't seen them about."

"No, and you won't. I took them down to Tanami North and none of them had any interest in the sheep, so I knocked them on the head. And that's the third litter that bitch has dropped that had no interest in sheep, so I knocked her on the head as well."

"Ma, Earl only ventured a comment about Tom Mabry," Dennis said placatingly. "That's certainly no——"

"You hold your tongue!" she hissed, wheeling on Dennis. "When you have the mettle to deal with matters, then you can have your say! Until you do, you hold your tongue!" Her eyes moved back to Garrity, glaring at him, and she stabbed a finger in emphasis as she snarled. "This is a sheep station! Sheep! Sheep! Sheep! There's nothing here that doesn't have to do with sheep! If I let time and effort on this station spread out to anything else, then the first year would be the end of Wayamba Station! Do you understand that?"

He nodded. "Aye, I understand."

"And nothing comes in front of Wayamba Station," she said. "A settler with a sick wife and ten hungry children who ventures over the borders of Wayamba Station will be dealt with like a bushranger. And they know it. A government surveyor who tries to change our boundaries will get a short walk under a long rope. And they know it. When it comes to Wayamba Station, I have feelings for naught or no one else."

She drew in a deep breath, then hesitated. Garrity knew that she was on the point of asking him for a direct, unequivocal answer on what he wanted to do. Her face reflected an inner struggle, wanting the answer but fearing a rift between them that would never heal. And he shared her fear. She was dictatorial and overbearing, but he was proud to be her son. And he loved her.

The sun had set, and dusk was settling. The gray at her temples was more pronounced in the dim light, and she was tall and slender in her gray broadcloth dress. She suddenly turned and walked toward the gravestones. Colin breathed an audible sigh of relief, and he and Dennis rose and went around the corner of the house to go back inside. Garrity knocked the ashes out of his pipe. His mother knelt by Sheila Garrity's grave and began searching for weeds among the flowers on it.

Garrity could barely remember his aunt, a tall woman with the dark hair, eyes, and skin of her mother's people, but the finely-etched features of her father's. He remembered her as a woman of mercurial moods, quick to kiss and caress, and quick to spit out a tirade of blistering profanity. Through the years, he had heard about the close bonds between his mother and his aunt, and he had a vague understanding of those bonds.

His mother had come to Wayamba Station, the daughter of a minister, born and reared in Sydney, and the victim of an unhappy marriage to Frank Cummings. She had found a friend and an anchor in life in

Sheila Garrity, and some old swagmen darkly hinted that Sheila had killed Cummings. And Sheila had molded his mother, shaping her to take her place as the monarch of Wayamba Station. Garrity watched his mother as she pulled at weeds, whispering softly. She was talking to Sheila.

He rose and went into the house, and went to bed. Darkness fell, and the moon rose. The pale light of the moon came through his window as he lay awake, looking up at the ceiling and listening for his mother's footsteps. Hours passed, but she still remained outside. He dozed off.

Then he woke abruptly as his door vibrated from a hard knock and his mother called to him from the hall. He sat up in bed, blinking and trying to collect his thoughts. "What is it, Ma?"

"Do you fancy going to Sydney and joining the crew of a ship, then? And just answer me yes or no."

"Aye, I do, Ma. But at the same time, I don't want to——"

"You gather your swag and saddle a horse, and you leave by sunrise. And you're never to set foot on Wayamba Station again. Do you understand?"

He hesitated, then replied. "Aye, I understand, Ma."

She walked on along the hall, and her door slammed. He lay back down. Her voice had almost broken with emotion as she ordered him to leave, and he knew she was probably weeping. And he also knew he had to leave and never return. Elizabeth Garrity, the monarch of Wayamba Station, always had precedence over Elizabeth Garrity, his mother.

Sleepless, he lay and looked up at the ceiling. Hours passed, and the thick darkness dissolved. Gray light filtered through the window. He rose and dressed, and began gathering up his belongings.

PART TWO

Chapter 4

HEAVY SHOES SHUFFLING ALONG THE hallway outside the workroom was a rumble over the whirring of the spinning wheels. Meghan looked up from the carding table. The noise of the spinning wheels died away as women working at them looked at each other and at the door. The footsteps in the hallway became louder, and the wooden bolt on the outside of the door rattled and slid aside. The door opened, and a guard looked in and rapped his truncheon against the doorjamb.

"Everyone outside! Everyone out for assembly!" he shouted.

"Who've you got for us today?" a heavy set woman called out. "Mayhap some handsome farmer looking for a wife?"

"Not for the likes of you!" the guard snorted. "You'll be well off if you get a bachelors' hut to look after!"

"Aye, I'll take that," the woman laughed. "As long as there's a dozen or more bachelors in the hut, and they're well set up and in good fettle."

The guard roared with laughter, and reached out to pinch the woman's thigh. She shrieked, pushing at his hand half-heartedly, and let him pinch her. Other women laughed and went outside. Meghan put down the bundle of raw wool she had been carding and followed them. The guard stood in the doorway, and some women laughed and brushed against him as he pinched and fondled them.

Meghan avoided the guard with her eyes, pushing through the doorway. A petite, attractive woman with light brown hair and blue eyes, she was always singled out by the guards. And on the edge of her vision, she saw him reaching for her. She twisted to one side, trying to evade his hand, but his hard, grasping fingers pinched her painfully through the thin, rough fabric of her shirt. He chuckled in sardonic satisfaction, and reached for another woman, who was trying to evade him as Meghan walked out into the hallway.

The hall was dark and narrow, and crowded with women walking along it in a noisy babble of conversation. Meghan's cheeks burned with outrage at what the guard was doing. The workroom door slammed, and his heavy footsteps came along the hallway. A woman squealed in mock indignation, hoping to humor him. Meghan edged to the right.

His footsteps slowed, and Meghan glanced over her shoulder. He was reaching for her, a taut, eager smile on his coarse face, and she took a quick step and slapped at his hand. He laughed and knocked her hand aside, and he grasped her thigh and moved his hand up, fondling her. She beat at his hand and tried to get away from him, suppressing the angry cry that rose in her throat. He laughed again and he walked on past her, pushing women aside, still mauling them.

"What are you making such a bloody fuss about?" a woman behind Megan demanded, tugging her hair. "It wouldn't bloody hurt you to give him a bit of what he wants, you know."

Meghan glanced back. The woman was one of the trouble-makers in the prison, one much feared by the other women. Her name was Margaret Wilson, and she was a large, powerful woman, her prison shift taut with bulging rolls of flesh. Her features were thick and ugly, and her tiny, beady eyes glared down at Meghan. Meghan looked up at her, then silently looked ahead again, following the other women along the hall.

"I spoke to you, pox pimple!" the woman barked, grasping Meghan's hair and jerking painfully. "And I'll not be ignored by the bloody likes of you!"

Conversation died away, and the others turned to stare. Meghan looked over her shoulder. The woman was large and strong, and it would be futile to try to fight her. And it would be foolish. Those who started fights were confined with the incorrigibles, who were never considered for release from the prison, and all the women would testify that Meghan had started the trouble. "Leave me alone," she said.

"Leave me alone," the woman sneered, mocking Meghan, then she glowered down at her. "I'll box your bloody ears until your bloody eyeballs knock together if you give me any bother, you poxy whore's whelp!"

"Oh, leave her be, Maggie," another woman laughed. "She'll come around soon enough."

"It had better be soon," the woman growled. "She

might think what she has is for lords and such, but she's no bloody better than any bugger else here. And her flaming sort makes it hard on the rest of us in this bleeding, swining arse of the earth." Her voice faded into a sullen grumble.

Meghan's eyes stung with tears of humiliation as she walked on along the hall. The guard had reached the door of the workroom near the top of the staircase, and he opened it and called the women out. They began filing out, crowding into the hall, some laughing and squealing at the guard.

Another guard stood at the top of the stairs, leering, fondling, and pinching. Meghan pressed her lips together and struggled to hold back her tears as she pulled away from him and walked down the stairs.

The guards were former convicts, crude and brutal. They prowled the hallways of the dormitories at night, and women who went out to them and were chosen were rewarded with extra food and easier work. Women who refused them were subjected to intense pressure, both from the guards and from other women. A complaint could be made to the superintendent, but Meghan had heard stories about torment inflicted on women who complained.

The long voyage from England had been a nightmare. The tiny compartment had been crowded with women, and several had died. The pumps on the aged, leaky ship clattered constantly, and it had almost foundered during storms. The meager portions of gray, rancid pork and wormy ship biscuit had barely been sufficient to stave off starvation. Meghan and the other women on the ship had been destined for

Western Australia, because no more convicts were being transported to New South Wales. But the ship had barely been able to reach Port Jackson. And Parramatta Prison was much worse than the voyage.

The guards followed the last woman down the stairs, laughing and talking with some who hung back to curry favor. A third guard stood at the foot of the stairs. He unlocked and opened a heavy door that led outside. He walked out ahead of the first women, leading the column out into the prison courtyard. On the far side of it, the prison superintendent stood with three other men. The guards immediately fell back from the women and became silent as they came through the doorway.

It had rained during the night, and the breeze was damp and chilly. But it was also fresh and clean, sweeping the stench of sweat and unwashed bodies and clothes away from Meghan's nostrils. It was reminiscent of the fragrance of parks after rain, stirring poignant memories of much happier times. It smelled of the sunshine and green, growing things, of the fields and forests beyond the prison walls. The scent was one of freedeom, stirring an agony of yearning within her.

The punishment building for incorrigibles was at the opposite end of the courtyard from the workhouse. Women stood in the windows and shouted obscenities at the superintendent and other men through the thick wooden bars. Dormitories for women with children were along one side of the courtyard, and stained, ragged clothing that had been washed hung on ropes between the buildings. Babies cried, and women holding children stood listlessly in windows and watched.

All of the buildings and the high wall around them were made of rough, unpainted wood. The superintendent and other men stood in front of the long, low building that housed the offices, storerooms, and prison chapel. The guard at the front of the column stopped a few yards from the superintendent and began forming the women into four ranks. Meghan was in the last line next to a woman named Mary Whittacker.

Meghan had learned to be cautious about forming acquaintances, but she and Mary had much in common. Mary was a tall, attractive woman, and like Meghan, she was enduring the same pressure for refusing to give in to the guards. And when the guards found out they were friends, they had been separated, sent to different dormitories and work groups.

Mary smiled at Meghan, taking her hand and holding it. "I heard Maggie Wilson," she whispered. "Give her no mind Meghan. Perhaps we'll be chosen this time, and be finished with her and her kind."

Meghan nodded, standing on tiptoe to see the men with the superintendent. Many men in Australia were either convicts or former convicts who had found employment or taken a land grant, but one of the men in the yard looked like a prosperous free immigrant or a government official. He wore a wool suit, stock, and a tall hat. A caped greatcoat was draped around his shoulders against the spring chill. He was a tall, slim man with streaks of grey in his neatly-trimmed beard and mustache.

One of the other two men wore canvas trousers

tucked into heavy boots, a short coat, and a work-man's cap. He appeared to be the foreman of a crew of laborers, and probably in need of women to attend to bachelors' huts. The third man was a seaman, wearing a tricorn and a long frock coat with large pockets and brass buttons. Whatever his purpose in coming to the prison, his first glance at the women appeared to have disgusted him. He stood and looked away with a dark scowl, his hands clasped behind him.

All three of the men represented the possibility of freedom. Meghan had heard that some women who left the prison were treated harshly, which was easy to believe, but at least they were free. Other men had come during the six weeks that Meghan had been in the prison—former convicts searching for wives, a man in need of workers for a small net factory in Sydney, and others. Each time, Meghan had stood in line with the other women, then returned to the drab misery of the workhouse.

The superintendent talked to the man in the great-coat, who appeared to be someone of importance. The guards walked along the ranks, barking officiously for silence as they motioned the women into straight lines. The murmur of whispers faded and the women stood quietly and waited, their shifts moving in the breeze. The superintendent folded some papers and turned to the women.

"Let me have your attention," he said in a loud voice. "This is Mr. James Wyndham, the Secretary of the Land Board. He requires a maid for his house in Sydney, and he has come here to see if he can find someone who might be suitable."

A stir of interest passed through the women, and Meghan and Mary exchanged an excited glance. It seemed almost too good to be true, by far the most advantageous situation that had become available while Meghan had been in the prison. The surroundings in the large house would be congenial, the work would be easy, and there would be ample food and clothing. Marriage brought automatic remission of sentence for a female convict, and there would be opportunities to meet men at leisure instead of standing in line and waiting to be picked for marriage by a stranger. Most of all, there would be release from the torture of prison.

The superintendent and Wyndham walked slowly along the first rank of women, and Meghan pushed at her hair and tugged her shift straight as she watched them. Wyndham appeared to be a pleasant man. He had the bearing of a man who was accustomed to the exercise of authority, but he was courteous when he stopped to talk to a woman in the front rank. Meghan's heart sank as he stopped, then her hopes began building up again as Wyndham and the superintendent walked on.

Their progess along the second rank was tediously slow, and they stopped again to talk to a woman in the third rank. Meghan waited breathelssly, listening to the murmur of Wyndham's voice and the woman's replies. The two men walked on. They reached the end of the third rank and started along the fourth, and Meghan clenched her hands to keep them from trembling. She looked straight ahead, feeling Wyndham's eyes on her as he approached, and her heart pounded furiously.

He stopped in front of her, looked at Mary Whittacker, then looked back at Meghan. "What is your name, please?"

Meghan tried to speak, and couldn't. She swallowed, then replied in a thin, quavering voice. "Meghan Conley, sir."

The superintendent rustled his papers, thumbing through them, and found her name. "Meghan Ann Conley," he said. "Sentenced to three years of penal labor for conspiracy to spread sedition. She has had no bad marks against her while she's been here, Mr. Wyndham."

"It was for handing out broadsides, sir," Meghan blurted. "I meant no disloyalty to the queen."

The words came out almost of their own accord, and she immediately regretted them. Anxiety had made her tone servile, and several women snorted and grunted derisively. The superintendent frowned. Wyndham had started to speak to Mary, and she had interrupted him. He turned his attention back to Mary.

"What is your name, please?"

"Mary Whittacker, sir."

The papers rustled again, and the superintendent found Mary's name. Mary Genevieve Whittacker. Sentenced to five years of penal labor for perjury in connection with forged banknotes. And she has no marks against her, Mr. Wyndham."

Wyndham nodded, looking at Mary. "Have you had any experience working as a maid?"

"No, sir."

"But I daresay you've worked in a household,

haven't you?''

"Yes, sir. At home, and I kept house for my sisters from time to time when they were ill."

Wyndham nodded musingly and looked back at Meghan. "Have you had any experience working as a maid?"

Meghan tried to lie, thinking rapidly of some story to tell him, but she was unable to force the words out. The hesitation was another error, Wyndham waited, with the superintendent frowning impatiently, and she shook her head. "No, sir. But I did help and do some cooking in my father's household."

Wyndham hesitated for an agonizingly long moment, then he looked at the superintendent and pointed to Mary. "I believe this young woman will do excellently well."

"Very well, Mr. Wyndham," the superintendent replied. "If you'll go to the office, my clerk will give you her papers." He looked at Mary and motioned to the dormitories. "Get your things, and step lively."

Mary made a small, involuntary sound of happiness. She squeezed Meghan's arm, and she turned and walked rapidly away. Wyndham and the superintendent walked along the line of women. Meghan sagged in dispair, struggling to hold back the tears of bitter disappointment that welled up in her eyes.

Wyndham went to the office, and the superintendent introduced the next man. He was the foreman of a gang of convicts, and he had come to choose women to attend the the men's huts. The superintendent walked along the front rank of women with him, thumbing through his papers. Wyndham came back out of the office with the clerk, and waited for Mary. Mary returned from the dormitory with her bundle of belongings, smiling happily and walking with a quick, eager stride.

The clerk went to open the gate for Wyndham and Mary. Mary looked back and waved to Meghan in farewell. Meghan felt wrenched, knowing she should be pleased over a friend's good fortune, but she was envious and miserably ashamed of her envy. And in a way she even hated Mary, because she knew that Wyndham would have chosen her if Mary hadn't been there. She forced a smile, returning Mary's wave.

The change in status that had occurred between her and Mary during the past moments was immense. Mary could wave, but a guard pointed his truncheon threateningly at Meghan for returning the wave. Meghan dropped her arm and faced to the front, and watched Mary and Wyndham from the corners of her eye. As the gate opened, she saw the magnificent, gleaming carriage at the side of the road in front of the prison.

Wyndham and Mary went through the gate, and walked toward the carriage. A driver came around it, and he took Mary's bundle and opened the door of the carriage. Wyndham took Mary's arm and helped her into it. Then the clerk closed the gate and locked it, and walked back toward the office. There was a faint sound of hoofs and rumble of wheels outside the wall and the carriage moved away from the prison.

The superintendent followed the convict foreman along the lines of women, still looking through his papers. The first few times men had come to choose women to cook, clean, and wash for laborers, Meghan had been apprehensive and afraid of finding herself in a situation that was no better than the prison. Then she found out that only large, sturdy women were selected, and women who were attractive enough to cause trouble among the men were rejected. Many leered at her, but none chose her.

The foreman picked five women, then went to the office as the women went back toward the dormitory. He had chosen wisely, because the women were all more or less good-natured, women who had been indifferent or even occasionally pleasant to Meghan. All those who contributed to making her life barely endurable remained in the prison. The superintendent introduced the last man. His name was Buell, and he was the master of a whaling vessel. He was contemplating marriage, and his wife would accompany him on his voyages and cook for the ship's officers.

To Meghan the way Buell was dressed was poignantly reminiscent of far happier times. Her father and two brothers had been in the Royal Navy, as had the men of her family for generations, and her earliest memories were of seamen who had been frequent visitors in their house. But it appeared that Buell thought he had made a mistake in coming to the prison. He walked rapidly along the lines of women, barely glancing at them.

Meghan looked into the distance, in an agony of self-recrimination over the mistakes she had made while Wyndham had been talking to her, mistakes that had probably kept him from choosing her. The five women chosen by the convict foreman returned with their bundles, and stood in front of the office and chatted happily while waiting for the clerk to finish with their papers. Buell and the superintendent walked along the third line of women, and Buell suddenly stopped and looked at Meghan. He stepped between two women and stood in front of her.

"What's your name, then?" he snapped impatiently.

Meghan blinked, startled, then replied. "Meghan Conley, sir."

The superintendent followed Buell, looking through his papers. "Meghan Ann Conley," he droned in a monotone. "Sentenced to three years of penal labor for conspiracy to spread sedition. And she has had no bad marks against her here, Captain Buell."

Buell looked at Meghan, then he shrugged and sighed heavily. "Aye, well, she'll do."

"Very well, Captain Buell," the superintendent said, folding the papers. "Is it agreeable with you, girl?"

Meghan hesitated, looking at Buell. Things had happened rapidly, before she had examined her reactions to the possibility that he might choose her. He was a stocky man of about forty, with a thick beard and mustache, a gruff, unpleasant man. His face reflected a quick, vicious temper, but at the same time, he was a means of release from the prison, possibly the only one for months to come.

Buell frowned. "Well, what do you say?" he barked. "I didn't come here to stand about all day! And if I can make do with a seditious wench from a prison, you should be able to tolerate a ship's master! I daresay that few would debate that you've the best of the bloody bargain, and by far!"

73

Meghan cleared her throat, struggling to decide, then she nodded. "Aye, I agree," she murmured quietly.

"Go get your things and come to the chapel," the superintendent said. "Please come with me, Captain Buell."

Buell grunted and nodded, turning and following the superintendent. Meghan turned and walked toward the dormitory. She felt numb, struggling to grasp the full implications of what had happened to her. But one single, overriding fact of the situation rose far above the muddled tangle of her thoughts—she was leaving the prison.

The guards shouted at the other women, forming them into a column to return them to the workhouse. Women in the dormitories for those with children stood in the windows and stared dully at Meghan as she crossed the courtyard. The stench of the dormitory reached out to her from yards away, thick and foul after being in the fresh air.

Her cot was on the upper floor of the dormitory, and she climbed the stairs and walked along the center aisle between the cots. Erratic, fragmentary thoughts flitted through her mind. Someone else would have to finish the bundle of wool she had been carding. She was hungry, a constant state, and she would miss the noon meal of thin soup and ship's biscuit.

An extra shift and a canvas coat hung on pegs by the cot, and a worn pair of extra shoes was under the cot. Meghan put them on the cot, and rolled them in her blanket. The road outside the prison was visible from the window by her cot, and she had often looked at it yearningly. She looked at it now.

The foreman and the five women he had chosen were walking along the road. A cart that Buell had brought was outside the gate, a rawboned, sagging horse hitched to it. The cart was very small and shabby in comparison to Wyndham's carriage, and it was a bitter reminder of the difference between her situation and Mary's. She picked up the bundle and walked back along the aisle between the cots.

Chapter 5

THE CEREMONY WAS A SORDID travesty of a wedding. Women were cleaning the other end of the chapel, and their conversation and the thudding of heavy wooden benches being moved about filled the bleak, cavernous room with loud echoes. The superintendent and his clerk were the witnesses, and they discussed some detail of prison affairs as the chaplain perfunctorily read the service. Then it was over, and the superintendent told Buell about the charge for the wedding.

"Three bloody shillings?" Buell snarled angrily. "This is the first I've heard about that, or I might have bloody thought again!"

"You came here of your own free will, and no one here made any attempt to inveigle you, Captain Buell," the superintendent replied firmly. "If you had asked, as many do, you would have been informed. The ministry here at the prison is self-supporting."

"To what bloody ends?" Buell demanded. "If the Church is loath to provide a vicar here, then do without. I see no reason why a scurvy lot of convict wenches need a parson, and less still why I should pay for it. What can a parson do for them?" He wheeled and glared down at Meghan. "What has he done for you?"

All of them looked at Meghan. She shrank and shook her head uncertainly, apprehensive that the dispute would turn into an argument and she would remain in the prison. The superintendent frowned testily, looking back at Buell. "Regardless of your attitude on the matter, Captain Buell, a self-supporting ministry is maintained here. And for those who can pay, a charge is levied for services performed by the ministry."

"An ample bloody charge it is, and all," Buell growled. "I'd be well off if I could earn as much with as little effort, but mine comes through the sweat of my brow and at risk of life and limb."

"I'm sure it does," the superintendent said indifferently. "But conducting a ministry in a prison isn't the easiest of undertakings. That aside, the charge must be paid in order to conclude our business."

Buell grunted sourly and took out his purse. "Aye, well, I know when I'm between tide and wind, so I'll bloody pay and be done with it. But no thanks go with it, and you may be bloody assured of that."

Meghan relaxed, breathing a soft sigh of relief. Buell counted out coins, and the superintendent took the money and gave him the papers. The men turned and walked out of the chapel in silence, a raw atmosphere of conflict remaining between them and Buell who was still glowering angrily. Meghan picked up her bundle and followed them.

The superintendent and chaplain went into the office, and Meghan followed Buell and the clerk to the gate. The distance to the gate and to freedom and release from the abuse, humiliation, and degradation of the prison diminished from yards to feet. Then the clerk unlocked the gate and opened it, and Meghan followed Buell through it.

The sunshine seemed brighter outside the dark walls, the breeze fresher and more invigorating. Meghan put her bundle in the cart, and climbed up to the seat. Buell untied the horse, and picked up a whip from the bed of the cart and climbed up beside her. He slashed the whip across the horse's bony, scarred back, and the cart jerked into motion.

He was still fuming with anger, frowning darkly and muttering under his breath, and he glanced at Meghan as he snapped the whip across the horse's back. "Taken up for sedition, were you?" he growled. "If they didn't get your willfulness out of you in prison, you'll wish you were back in there before I'm bloody finished with you. You'd best get that in your mind here and now."

His voice and manner were intimidating, and he was large and burly on the seat beside her. Meghan clenched her hands together, trying to keep from showing fear. "I'm the queen's loyal subject," she replied quietly.

"Aye, the pure innocent," Buell sneered. "And these papers I have in my pocket concern someone else, no doubt. The prisons are full of rogues and wenches who never did anything, to hear them tell it."

"I was helping my father, who was pressing for

79

more generous treatment for pensioners from the Navy. Some ministers were opposed, and my father said the matter came to trial only because of his association with Thomas Buxton, the reformer."

Buell shrugged and looked away. "More fool him, then," he grunted. "He found out that trouble follows a trouble-maker like fleas do a dog, which is something I found out when I was no more than a boy. Was he transported as well?"

"No, he was sentenced to prison in England. At last I heard, he was on a hulk in the Thames."

"Aye, well, that's doubtless the last you'll ever hear," Buell chuckled sardonically. "An ordinary prison is a stroll through a garden compared to a hulk."

"That's a most unkind thing to say, true or not," Meghan replied. "My father is a good man, and I love him."

Buell's temper flared abruptly, and his eyes blazed as he glared at her. "You curb your bloody sauce when you talk to me!" he barked. "I've spent a good part of my life dealing with dogs who could start more mischief in a minute than every slut in that prison back there could think of in a month! I'll have little trouble in dealing with you, and you'd best remember that!"

His bearded face was ugly and twisted with anger. Flecks of spittle shone on his lips as he shouted at her. He seemed to become larger, more a vicious, brutal animal than a human being. Meghan dropped her eyes and looked away. Buell growled wordlessly, venting his anger on the horse, and the whip hissed through the air. The horse leaned into the harness and trotted heavily for a few paces, then slowed to a plodding walk again.

The cart bumped along the road, approaching the outskirts of the village of Parramatta, and tiny farms were on both sides of the road. Most of the houses were made of rough, weathered wood, with thatched roofs. A few were made of clay and wattle. Small outbuildings and pens for animals were scattered behind them, and there were clearings planted in grain and vegetables. The gardens became smaller, and the houses closed together on both sides of the road.

The villagers resented the close proximity of the women's prison, even though many of them were former convicts or descendants of convicts. The road turned into a street through the village, and men and women walking along it stared stonily at Meghan in her prison shift. The village square was paved with a corduroy of logs and surrounded by houses and shops, and people in the square turned to watch the cart pass.

The cart trundled along the street on the other side of the square, and the houses thinned out again. The village disappeared behind, and Buell looked straight ahead in silence, ignoring Meghan. The man was repugnant, and Meghan felt ill at ease with him. But she was married to him, and she wanted to make peace with him and establish an amicable relationship if possible. She cleared her throat, looking up at him.

"I'm grateful that you took me out of the prison."

"I can do without your gratitude as long as you do as you're told."

"I'll do my best. Are the horse and cart yours?"

"What would I be doing with a bloody horse and cart?" I'm a ship's master, not some bloody farmer or mechanic. No, they belong to the cooper who's making my oil casks."

"He loaned them to you?"

"So he said, but I'll pay dearly for their use, no bloody fear. By the time I finish paying for the casks, I'll probably wish I'd bought a horse and cart to use."

"What sort of vessel do you have?"

"You'll see it when we get there," he replied curtly. "And you'll have your fill of seeing it and then some before you see the last of it."

His tone ended the conversation, but it had served its purpose and he appeared less irritated than before. The road wound through rolling hills covered with thickets of trees and clearings where deep, coarse grass grew. Aromatic trees along the sides of the road filled the air with a fresh, clean scent, and parrots and other exotic birds with bright plumage flew back and forth between them.

Everything was fascinatingly strange, far different from England. The hollows between the hills were dotted with the brown squares of cleared crop fields, with small houses here and there, but elsewhere it was a wilderness. The colors were rich and vibrant, spring foliage was sprouting, and brooks ran, by the road. And in spite of Buell, life was exciting once again. The prison was behind her, and she was free.

The horse toiled up a gradual incline in the road, and the foreman and five women came into sight a mile ahead as the cart reached the top of the rise. They were straggling along the road in single file, and they disappeared behind some trees. The horse walked more rapidly, the cart pushing it downhill. The foreman and women came into sight again, waiting by the side of the road.

"Will you give us a ride, Captain?" the foreman called as the cart approached.

"No, I bloody won't," Buell replied brusquely. "I'll sell you a ride for tuppence each, though."

"You can keep it, then," the foreman said in disgust, and he beckoned the women and went on ahead. "I don't have a shilling to throw away on transport."

"And I didn't come up here to provide transport for those who didn't provide their own," Buell retorted.

The foreman muttered, and the women fell into line behind him, and the cart slowly overtook them as they walked along the road. A large women at the front of the line looked up at Buell as the cart passed, and she smiled lewdly.

"Give us a ride, Captain, and I'll give you something worth more than a shilling," she chuckled. "I'll give you such a tossing as no man has ever had before."

"Aye, and doubtless a huge, great clap to match it," Buell growled scornfully. "You can keep both of them for someone else."

"Then take your cart and go to buggery with it!" the woman shouted, shaking her fist, and she snatched up a stone and threw it. "And take that with you, you stingy sod!"

The stone slammed into the back of the cart, and the horse flinched and began trotting. Buell sprang to his feet in fury, looking back and bracing himself against the jolting of the cart as he pointed with the whip. "I'll flay the skin from your poxy arse, you swining slut!" he roared. "And you, you take that scurvy lot in hand, or I'll have them sent back to where they came from for public disorder!"

"Take them in hand yourself," the foreman laughed. "You're the bugger who incited them, so don't look to me to settle them."

All of the women began picking up stones, laughing shrilly, and Meghan reached for her bundle to protect her head. Stones sailed through the air and pattered down around the cart, another one struck the back of the cart, and one clattered into the bed. The horse lurched into a lumbering canter, and Buell was almost thrown from the cart. He sat down and looked back, bellowing profanely while the women shrieked and pelted the cart with stones.

The foreman and women disappeared behind as the cart jolted rapidly along the road and went around a curve. The horse slowed to a trot and then to a walk, its bony sides heaving. Meghan put her bundle back in the bed of the cart. Buell sat in glowering silence, seething with anger. Then he lashed the horse and glanced at Meghan. "By God, if I had that lot of flaming whores in my charge, I'd soon teach them how to bloody act."

"They had no cause to be so unruly," Meghan agreed. "And those five were among the more orderly of the women, so you may well imagine how the rowdy ones are."

"Aye, well, you're one of them as well," Buell grumbled. "So don't set to putting on bloody airs."

Meghan knew it was obvious that she was completely different from the convict women, a fact that had caused much of the abuse she had suffered in prison. The remark was gratuitously cruel, and it hurt. And it also stirred her temper. For months, survival had been the paramount consideration, and anger a luxury that could endanger her. What she had been unable to escape by melting into the crowd, she had meekly borne and tried to ignore. She had kept her temper under tight rein for so long that the smoldering anger felt almost strange as it swelled within her.

The cart trundled along a stretch of road like an avenue, lined with towering eucalyptus trees. The air was fragrant with their scent, and spots of sunlight dappled the road. A family of aborigines was camped by a brook a few yards off the road, and the scene had a wild, primitive beauty. The aborigines, virtually naked, sat around a fire in front of a small shelter made of saplings and bark. Their skins were dark and dusty, but the two small children had strangely bright blonde hair.

The road went up a long, gradual incline. The hills fell away to the west, and a range of mountains came into sight across miles of wilderness, blue and hazy in the distance. The breeze was from the east, and it carried the damp, tangy scent of the sea. Then they could see the long, wide sound leading into the harbor, and the sunlight glinting on the waves. The cart reached the top of the rise, the trees thinned out, and Sydney lay below.

The town was on a deep curve in the shoreline, spreading up a slope from long piers reaching out into the harbor. Warehouses and other sprawling buildings stretched along the street fronting on the piers, then there were streets of buildings two and three stories tall. An old fort was on a knoll at one side, and parks and the larger structures of churches and government buildings were scattered through the town. Away from the center of town, streets of houses turned into roads wandering across the slopes overlooking the bay.

The streets of the town bustled with activity— drays, carriages, wagons, riders, and the tiny figures of people moving about. Boats moved back and forth in the harbor, and rows of ships at anchor made a bristling forest of masts and spars on each side of the roadstead at the center of the harbor. Buell's ship was easy to identify, the only one with long, slender whaleboats hanging on davits forward of the waist. It was a large, three-masted vessel, a full-rigged ship.

The scent of the sea blended with the smell of woodsmoke as the cart rumbled along the road winding and twisting down the slope to the town. Meghan felt self-conscious in her prison shift, but the people were intent on their own affairs and few looked at her.

Buell turned onto a street of small warehouses and repair shops near the waterfront. The street was busy and noisy, a clamor of activity. Odors of tar, rope, hot metal, and other smells came from the buildings. A tall, brawny man in a leather apron stood in the doorway of a cooperage and talked with two other men. The two men walked away and the tall man started to go inside, then he stopped when he saw the cart approaching.

He waved to Buell, smiling amiably, then his smile faded, and his eyes opened wider as he stared at Meghan in surprise and curiosity, before he took the horse's bridle. "You're back soon, Captain Buell, and I see that you were successful."

"Aye, I got what I went for," Buell replied, climbing down from the cart. "Her name's Meghan."

The man's smile became wide, and he went around to the side of the cart to take Meghan's arm. "I'm Jim Dunhill, and I'm pleased to meet you," he said, helping her down from the cart. He laughed and looked back at Buell. "By God, I might make a trip up there myself. I didn't know they had any of her sort at Parramatta, Captain Buell."

Buell looked at Meghan peculiarly, as though he were seeing her for the first time, and he appeared pleased by Dunhill's emphatic compliment. Then he grunted and nodded and looked away. "Aye, she'll do. Do you have my casks together for me yet?"

"Give me a chance, man," Dunhill chuckled. "I'll be another day or two seeing what I have and what I need, then I can tell you when you'll have them. But it'll be less than a fortnight, in any event."

Buell winced and shook his head, sighing heavily. "Very well, if that's the best you can do. I'll go by Palmer's and see about my try pots while I'm here, and doubtless I'll hear the same from him."

"Like as not, Captain Buell," Dunhill replied mildly. "He's hardly had time to get sorted out on them, has he?"

"That may be, but he'll still be getting sorted out a month from now if I don't liven him up," Buell said morosely, turning away. "I'm obliged for the use of the horse and cart."

"It was my pleasure, and I'm glad you had such good fortune in the use of them. Good day to you, and to you, Mistress Buell."

The form of address sounded strange to Meghan. Dunhill gave her a wide, admiring smile and touched his forehead. Meghan murmured and nodded in reply, taking her bundle out of the cart. She felt Dunhill's eyes on her as she walked away, following Buell across the street and into the alley.

The light in the narrow alley was dim, with buildings on both sides blocking the sunlight, and the ground was muddy and littered with debris. The air was thick with the stench of urine and decaying refuse. Rats rustled in the piles of garbage. Meghan lifted the hem of her shift, picking her way around the puddles while Buell strode ahead. The light brightened near the end of the alley, and they came to a storage yard.

Men talked and moved about inside the yard. Buell stopped at a gate in the wall. He put his eye to a crack, then thumped the gate with his fist. "Is that you, Palmer?"

"Aye, it's me," a man replied. "Who's there?"

"Captain Buell. When am I going to have my try pots back?"

Footsteps approached the other side of the gate, and a heavy wooden bar slid back. The gate opened, and a man in greasy, sooty clothes looked out. "We've just finished cleaning them, and——" He broke off, looking at Meghan, and smiled. "Who's this, Captain Buell?"

"My wife. I've just fetched her from Parramatta."

"From Parramatta?" Palmer exclaimed in astonishment, and he looked at Meghan's shift. "Aye, I see she's from there, but it's hard to believe." He laughed heartily, looking at Buell. "You don't think they'd take mine in trade, do you?"

Buell stroked his beard, unsmiling but appearing pleased by Palmer's reaction. "Even if they would, trading would be a waste of time and effort. One's much the same as another."

"In many instances I might agree, but not in this one," Palmer chuckled, and he touched the peak of his grimy cap and bowed to Meghan. "I'm most pleased to meet you, Mistress Buell."

"And I'd be most pleased if I could find out about my try pots," Buell snapped. "Every day I spend in port costs me money."

Palmer looked back at Buell, unperturbed by his tone. "We've just finished cleaning them, and I can have them ready for you in a week. And from the looks of one of them, you've got something wrong with one of your furnaces."

"I don't need you to tell me that." Buell sighed gloomily. "I have men taking the bricks loose now, and it'll doubtless cost a king's ransom to repair. And if it'll take you a week to see to the pots, then that'll have to do. I need to go out to my ship, and it would save me trying to signal someone aboard if I could use your boat."

Palmer smiled and nodded amiably. "You're more than welcome to use it. It's where I usually keep it at the pier. The oars are in it."

"I'm obliged, and I'll return it as I find it," Buell said, turning away. "And I'll have it back directly."

"Use it for as long as you like, Captain Buell. Good day, Mistress Buell, and it was a pleasure meeting you."

Meghan followed Buell back along the alley. Palmer stood in the gate and looked at her as they walked away. When they reached the end of the alley, Meghan heard Palmer close the gate and slide the locking bar back into place. He called excitedly to other men, and she knew he was telling them about her.

The piers were to the left of the crowded street, but Buell turned to the right. Lodgings, inns, taverns, and other places where men congregated were scattered among the shops and other businesses. Seamen were everywhere. Buell fell back until he was almost walking beside Meghan, and he nodded in reply as men looked at Meghan and spoke to him.

They went through an alley along another street. The smell of food came from some of the inns, and Meghan was ravenously hungry. She wondered if Buell intended to stop for food, but they went on, passing the inns. Then Meghan knew the reason for all this apparently aimless walking. Buell was proud of her and wanted to show her off.

They walked the slope to the waterfront. Buell walked ahead of her again, leading the way through the clutter and confusion. Barrels, crates, and hogsheds were stacked on the pier, and men were taking them to a warehouse across the street. Buell and Meghan stopped at the end of the pier and he asked,

"You don't need any necessaries or anything, do you?"

His tone discouraged an affirmative reply, but Meghan felt painfully self-conscious in the prison shift. "I could well do with some clothes, or fabric to make them," she said hesitantly.

"Clothes?" he replied brusquely. "What do you call that you have on, and what's in that bundle?"

"This is a shift and I have another one, but they scarcely serve the needs of decency."

He scowled fiercely, looking at her shift. Men passed looking at Meghan, and Buell sighed heavily and nodded in resignation. "I daresay you'll live until tomorrow with what you have, and I'll see what I can do then."

Meghan followed him onto the pier, and he walked along it looking down at boats tied to the piles. He stopped where a rowboat was tied, rocking in the low swell rolling across the harbor, and he climbed down to the boat on boards nailed to the pile. Meghan dropped her bundle into the boat, and climbed down the boards as he untied the boat and put the oars in the locks.

The smells and bustle of the town faded behind as Buell rowed the boat out into the harbor. The foliage along the shoreline and on a large island in the harbor was different from that of England, but the ocean was universal and unchanging, the same as the ocean that washed the shores of England. When Meghan had been a child, her oldest brother had owned a wherry and had often taken her sailing, and the moment evoked Meghan's childhood memories of the sailing trips with her brother.

And from the time of her earliest memories, she had constantly heard that a seagoing life was the highest attainable goal. That point had been reinforced all through her life by everything her father and brothers had said and done, and through force of circumstances she had achieved that goal. She was going to live on a ship.

The sun was deep in the west, tinging the fleecy clouds overhead with a warm tone of approaching sunset. Gulls wheeled and swooped over the glinting waves, and the breeze sweeping across the harbor stirred Meghan's hair. The prison seemed far behind her as she looked around, breathing deeply and savoring the fresh, tangy fragrance of the breeze.

The masts and rigging on Buell's ship were sooty from whale oil being rendered on the deck, but it was more tidy than many of the other ships. Sails were furled and tied with precision, and all the rigging was taut and neat. The bow of the ship was gracefully curved, the long bowsprit and the foremost stays thrusting far out over the water, and it was named the *Baleen.*

Buell hailed the ship, and a blond youth of fifteen or sixteen came to the rail at the waist of the ship. He opened a hinged section of the rail, and unrolled a ladder made of wooden slats and rope over the side. Buell backed water with the oars as the rowboat approached the towering, weathered hull, and stopped the boat by the ladder.

He tied the painter at the bow of the boat to the ladder, looking up at the youth. "Is Mr. Tench aboard?"

"No, sir, Captain Buell," the youth replied, knuckling his forehead. "Mr. Tench and the bosun are still ashore."

Buell climbed up to the ship. The boy knelt and leaned down from the edge of the deck to take Meghan's bundle, and she climbed too. The ladder swayed back and forth with her weight, and the boy stood up and glanced between her and Buell, his bright, guileless face reflecting eagerness to help her mixed with uncertainty about the proprieties.

Two large furnaces for rendering whale oil were on the deck forward of the mainmast, mounted on firebricks to insulate them from the deck. Several men were around the one on the starboard side, removing the bricks. Most of them looked at Meghan curiously, but a few older ones looked at her in disapproval. And she knew why. Sailors were superstitious, and one of their most deeply-rooted superstitions was that a woman would bring misfortune to any ship except a passenger vessel.

The men resumed their work and chipped industriously at the bricks as Buell looked at the furnaces in dissatisfaction. The youth was handsome, with large blue eyes and features that were almost girlishly pretty. He grinned and flushed furiously, handing Meghan her bundle. Buell glanced at Meghan and beckoned her forward with a jerk of his head.

They crossed the deck to a door in the center of the bulkhead below the quarterdeck. It opened into a dim, narrow passageway, and Buell pointed to doors as they passed them. "That's the officers' galley and pantry, and that's the wardroom. Mr. Tench is the mate and that's his cabin, and this is mine."

He opened the door at the end of the passageway, and Meghan followed him into the cabin. It was spacious, as wide as the stern of the ship, and as neat as the rest of it. Books, charts, and navigational instruments were on shelves fitted with boards across the front to keep things from falling off during heavy seas. Clothes hung in a corner, and the brass lanterns hanging from the overhead beams were brightly polished. Portholes overlooking the water under the stern of the ship were open, and a breeze and sunlight came into the cabin.

Meghan glanced around. She looked at the bunk, then she looked at Buell. It was the moment she had dreaded. Guards had glared at her, their eyes burning with lust, and only the presence of others had restrained them. The single time she had been caught alone with a guard, he had pushed her against a wall and tore at her shift to pull it up, thrusting at her in savage passion. And she expected the same from Buell. He had been hostile, but she expected him to satisfy himself.

But he remained cold and withdrawn. He stood with his hands folded behind him, his tricorn tilted over his forehead and the brass buttons on his long coat gleaming dully. His expression was inscrutable, but he seemed to regard her as an intruder. And strangely, there was a hint of uncertainty in his gaze, betraying unease similar to hers. He abruptly turned, stepping back to the door.

"I've business ashore, and I'll sup there," he said gruffly, jerking the door open. "The pantry's been victualed, if you're hungry."

The door slammed behind him, and his heavy footsteps went back along the passageway. Meghan realized she had been holding her breath, and she released it in a sigh of relief and put down her bundle. She was puzzled by Buell's behavior, then she dismissed it and went back out to the passageway, to look around.

The atmosphere of the ship was comfortable, and she had a feel of being at home, in her natural environment. The thick beams and shiny oak walls were sturdy and solid, and the smells were pleasant. The names and functions of all the sails, spars, and pieces of rigging towering above the deck had been familiar to her from childhood, and she had a sense of belonging. It seemed to have a personality, one that was warm, cheerful, and amiable, and one that welcomed her aboard.

The galley was a long, narrow room, with a small stove and table against the far wall. Utensils hung on the wall above the stove and table, and the long walls were lined with deep cabinets with strong latches to keep them closed during rough seas. Meghan opened cabinets and looked in, gasping in delight at the great store of food.

One cabinet was filled with bags of potatoes, onions, and vegetables. Kegs of salt pork and beef were in another, and another contained ship's biscuit, flour, peas, beans, and rice. Others contained delicacies that were only a memory to her—dried apples, treacle, pickles, cheeses, tea, a wide assortment of spices, and other things. She looked around and found a knife, and cut a thick slice from a cheese.

She ate ravenously, taking a handful of ship's biscuit and fishing pickles from an earthenware jar. She cut another slice from the cheese. The spicy pickles and rich cheese made a twinge of nausea stir in her stomach, and she ate more slowly as she finished them. Then she ate a few slices of dried apples, and put a ship's buscuit on a pewter plate and poured the thick, sweet treacle over it.

She was breathlessly full when she finished the biscuit and treacle, leaning against the table and holding her stomach. She took a cannister of tea from a cabinet and put it on the table, and put the kettle on the stove. A box under the table was filled with wood for the stove, but the stove was cold and the kettle and water buckets were empty. She picked up a bucket, and went up onto the deck.

The sun had set and the light was starting to fade, and the spring evening had a penetrating chill. The men were still around the furnace, and they stopped working and looked up as Meghan walked toward the water butt by the mainmast. An older man among them spoke to the blond youth and nodded toward Meghan, and napped an order to the others. The youth sprang to his feet and trotted toward Meghan, and the others resumed working and darted glances at her.

The youth grinned and knuckled his forehead as he approached. "I'm Dickon Muir, Mistress Buell. I'll fetch you some water."

"That's very good of you, Dickon. I also need a flint and steel to kindle a fire in the galley."

"If you wish, I'll get a shovelful of coals from the

forecastle galley and bring it with the water, mo'm."

"I'd be most grateful."

He took the bucket, and Meghan walked back across the deck and into the galley. She shook down the ashes in the stove, and broke up sticks from the box under the table and put them in the stove. Dickon knocked on the door a moment later, and brought in the bucket of water and a shovel heaped with glowing coals. He was awkwardly silent until Meghan began talking to him, then he talked in a flood of words. He was from an inland village, and he had joined the ship's crew only a few days before.

The boy was obviously homesick, missing the comfort of a family around him, and the butt of practical jokes among the crew because he was young and inexperienced. His situation was far less cataclysmic than Meghan's had been, but she could understand his feelings. And while he was only a few years younger than her, she felt ancient and wise in comparison with him. He filled the kettle, built up the fire in the stove, and did other things to prolong his minutes with her. Finally, he left.

Darkness fell, and Meghan took a lantern down from an overhead beam and lit it. The water in the kettle boiled, and she brewed a cup of tea and sat on the stool by the table and drank it. The tea was the first she had tasted for months, and it was delicious. The stove made the galley cozily warm against the evening chill, and the lantern cast a cheerful yellow light. The galley was comfortable, and more.

For months, she had been constantly in the presence of other women, most of them disagreeable, their noise and smells surrounding her. The privacy and the quiet of the galley were luxurious. There was no need to be constantly on guard, watching and listening to everyone around her. The sounds around her were soothing, the fire murmuring in the stove and heavy timbers creaking and groaning as the ship tugged at its anchor ropes in the low waves rolling across the harbor.

The ship's bell gonged, and bare feet padded across the quarterdeck above the galley as the anchor watch changed. Bells rang on other ships anchored nearby, their chiming notes carrying through the night. Meghan washed the dishes she had used, and took the dishwater outside. Fog had risen a few yards above the water, and the anchor lights on the yardarms were faint spots of luminescence. The fog was clammy, and Meghan shivered as she threw the water over the rail and hurried back inside.

The thought of going to bed in Buell's bunk was unpleasant, but she was weary and drowsy from the heavy meal. She banked the fire in the stove, and went to the cabin. The damp chill had crept into the cabin through the open portholes, and she closed them and locked the dogs on them. The bedclothes were frigidly cold when she undressed and got into bed, and she curled up and shivered. Then the warmth of her body took the chill off the bedclothes, and she relaxed and fell asleep.

She was awakened abruptly and rudely. A strong reak of rum surrounded her, the night air was cold against her naked skin, and powerful hands roughly gripped her thighs and dragged them apart. The darkness was thick and for an instant she thought she was back in the prison and was being attacked by a guard. Panic exploded in her mind, and she began fighting back furiously, ready to scream.

"Try to deny me, will you?" Buell snarled in a thick voice. "By God, I'll have my rights with you whenever I wish!"

Memory of her surroundings returned as she recognized his voice, stopping her scream at the last instant. Buell knelt over her on the bunk, this thick, hairy body brushing hers, and he grasped her shoulders, lifted her, and shook her viciously. Her head snapped back and forth, her teeth cracking together, and he threw her back down on the bunk. The world seeming to spin dizzily around her, and she lay limp.

Buell pushed her thighs apart and crouched between them, and probed at her. He was flaccid, ineffectually pushing at her. And he was drunk, weaving as he leaned over her. He breathed heavily and grunted with effort, thrusting, and his breath was a thick cloud of rum fumes in her face. Then he grumbled in frustrated anger, trying to force himself into her, and Meghan gasped in pain and bit her wrist to keep from crying out.

"You're no bloody help," he growled drunkenly. "You're no bloody help and no bloody good."

Meghan lifted her wrist from her lips, swallowing dryly. "What do you want me to do?" she whispered.

"Bloody nothing!" he barked. "Just lie there like the bloody dead sow that you are!"

He dug his fingers into her savagely and he snarled

at her. Meghan smothered her wail of protest with her arm. She struggled to relax, lifting herself to accommodate him and to ease the pain as he continued thrusting. After a moment, the physical stimulation of the contact overcame the effects of the rum. She felt him becoming firm against her, then rigidly hard.

Meghan opened her thighs wider, and moved her hips and positioned herself to receive him as he continued thrusting blindly. Then he entered her, and made a sound of satisfaction in his throat as he stopped moving. The entry was shallow, and Meghan held herself motionless as he weaved drunkenly over her. He put his hands around her waist, gripping her tightly, and penetrated deeply.

The pain was agonizing, and Meghan bit her lips and tried to pull away from him. His hard, grasping fingers dug into her waist, holding her and lifting her, and he moved in a rapid, driving rhythm and pushed deeper. The stabbing pains became almost unbearable, then they began diminishing. Then she became numb, lying limply on the bunk as he bent over her and clutched her, thrusting harder all the time.

He finished quickly, lifting her higher as he lurched in a convulsive flurry of movement and grunted, then he collapsed on her. His heavy body crushed her into the bunk and he lay on her and panted hoarsely. Then he lifted himself off her and lay beside her. He pulled the covers around himself and began to snore.

Meghan lay without moving for several minutes. The cold of the damp night air against her naked skin made her shiver, and she turned away from him and pulled the covers over herself. Her eyes filled with tears, then the tears flowed over and and she silently wept.

Chapter 6

IT WAS STILL DARK IN the cabin when she woke.
Buell was dressing by the light of a lantern. He froze
and looked at her as she pushed her hair back and sat
up, holding the blanket around her. Then he looked
away and continued dressing, his eyes not meeting
hers. His bearded face was in shadow from the light of
the lantern, and it was difficult to see his expression.
But he was uncomfortable in her presence, and he appeared to be ashamed of what he had done the night
before.

Meghan pulled the blanket closer, moving to the
edge of the bunk. "I'll prepare breakfast."

"I don't have time for that," he muttered, pulling
his hair back and tying it. He crossed the cabin to the
desk, and picked up a sheaf of papers and stuffed
them into one of his wide coat pockets. "I have business to attend to ashore."

"Then I'll heat water for tea. I'm sure you can well
do with that, after the rum you had last night."

Her tongue was involuntarily sharp, but it failed to

stir his anger. His eyes moved toward her, then without meeting her eyes he put on his tricorn and walked toward the door. "I said I have no time. I'm going ashore, and I'll get what I want there."

He took the lantern and went out. The cabin was thrown into darkness, the portholes gray with the first light of the foggy morning. Buell's footsteps thumped along the passageway, and he shouted for the mate. Tench replied from the quarterdeck, his voice deep and resonant, and his footsteps crossed the thick boards above the cabin to the steps leading down to the main deck.

Dull pain throbbed from Buell's savage assault the night before as Meghan slid off the edge of the bunk. She held the blanket around her, and crossed the cabin to a side porthole. Sharp pains stabbed with the first few steps she took, then faded away. She opened the porthole and stood looking out it, the floor of the cabin cold under her bare feet and the fog damp and cold against her face.

Other ships anchored nearby were dark shadows, their anchor lights still burning. A boat thumped against the hull of the ship, and oars splashed and squeaked as the boat moved away from the ship. Buell and Tench's voices carried from the boat, muffled by the fog. Meghan closed the porthole and walked back across the cabin. She dressed, then walked along the passageway to the galley.

Coals glowed in the ashes in the stove, and Meghan broke splinters from a stick and dropped them on the hot coals. Buell's brutality cast a pall of depression over everything, and she forced it out of her mind.

Few marriages were based on love and none were idyllic, and the way he had acted while dressing gave her hope that it wouldn't happen again. And her situation was still much better than the misery of the prison, even with Buell included.

The fire roared in the stove, warming the galley, and the light coming through the porthole brightened. Meghan mixed a small bun of bread and put it in the oven, and made tea. She sat and sipped tea until the bread began baking, then she sliced thin pieces of salt pork and put them in a pan. The pork crisped in the pan, an appetizing aroma rising as it hissed and popped. She took the bun out of the oven and ate.

Sounds of activity came from the deck by the time she finished eating and washed the dishes. She used the last of the water to wash her face and hands, then she tied her hair back and carried the water outside. The sun was burning off the fog, and the light was bright and diffuse. Men worked around the furnace and others scrubbed the deck, and their attention became divided between Meghan and what they were doing as she carried the bucket to the rail and emptied it.

A man wearing a bosun's small, low-crowned hat and neat, clean canvas trousers and coat stepped from behind the furnace. He walked toward Meghan with a purposeful stride and air of authority, men glancing at him and working more industriously as he passed, and he lifted his hat as he approached. "Good day, Mistress Buell. I'm Porter, the bosun."

"Good day, Mr. Porter, and I'm pleased to meet you."

"I'm pleased to meet you, mo'm," he replied tersely, unsmiling. "When would it suit your convenience to have the hands clean the wardroom and the officers' quarters?"

"Whenever you wish, Mr. Porter, but I can do it myself."

He pursed his lips and shook his head briskly. "There'll be no need for that. Captain Buell requires a clean and orderly ship, and it's our practice to go from stem to stern daily. And in passing, I'd like to mention that it's customary for women aboard ship to remain abaft the mainmast, in event you don't know."

"I do know, Mr. Porter. The men in my family have been seamen for generations to no end, and I've heard about little else from when I was a baby. I'm familiar with customs on shipboard."

He nodded and started to lift his hat and turn away. Then he looked at her again, his cold gray eyes moving over her face, and he frowned musingly. "Might you be a Conley, mo'm?"

"Aye, I'm Captain George Conley's daughter."

Porter thawed visibly, his brown, weathered face creasing in a faint smile. "Aye, I should have known as soon as I saw you, because you favor your brother Amos markedly. He was the third officer on *Ajax* when I was in the Navy and aboard her."

"You saw him later than the last time I did, then. He was at home for a time after he left *Defiance*, then he went to join *Ajax*."

Porter's smile faded, and he nodded and looked away. "I was sorry to hear about it when *Ajax* was lost, because I had a lot of friends on her. And I was sorry to hear about what happened to Captain Conley. It's a widespread feeling that he got short shrift, considering the service he rendered while he was an active officer."

"He often told me that service is its own reward, and I trust that is sustaining him now and keeping him in a good frame of mind."

"Aye, let us hope so," Porter replied. "And it's a curious turn of events that you should end up here, but you're on shipboard and that should suit the disposition of a Conley. If there's aught I can do to ease things for you, you only need let me know."

"That's very good of you, Mr. Porter. At the same time, I expect to accommodate myself to the ship rather than the other way about, so please let me know if I go amiss."

"I don't look for that," Porter chuckled, lifting his hat and turning away. "I'll send the men to clean the wardroom and officers' quarters."

Meghan smiled and nodded, crossing the deck to the passageway door. Porter walked toward the men scrubbing the deck, and he shouted to two of them and beckoned. One of the men was Dickon Muir, and he and the other men filled the wood box and all the buckets in the galley, then began dusting and cleaning the other room. Meghan found where Buell put his dirty clothes, and carried them to the galley to wash them. Dickon went for buckets of seawater to wash the floors, and he stopped in the doorway of the galley before he carried the buckets along the passageway.

"Mistress Buell, I'll be at liberty to go ashore directly. Is there anything I can bring you from the town?''

Meghan straightened up from scrubbing a shirt and started to shake her head, smiling. Then she thought again. "I have a friend who's a maid in Mr. James Wyndham's house, and I'd like to send her a message. Do you know where he lives?''

"No, mo'm. But I've heard of him and I can find his house, no fear. Am I to just hand it in the back door?''

"Aye, that's right. Are you sure it won't be too much trouble?''

Dickon shook his head emphatically. "I'll be most glad to do it for you, Mistress Buell.''

Meghan dropped the shirt back into the water and wiped her hands on her skirt. Dickon grinned over his shoulder, and carried the buckets into the wardroom. Meghan went back to the cabin, and looked for writing materials, and found them in a cabinet in a corner by the desk. She sat down to write.

Pride made her want to make the most of her situation in the message to Mary, and she found it easy when she began writing. She was on a ship, and being married to a ship's master was a situation most women would envy. The only undesirable factor was Buell's disposition, and she skipped over that.

The other man was working in the wardroom when she stepped back out of the cabin. Dickon was scrubbing the floor in the passageway. He silently grinned and nodded as he took the folded sheet of foolscap and put it in his pocket. Meghan returned to the galley and finished the washing, then she found a length of twine in a cabinet and tied it across the galley to hang the wet clothes.

Dickon and the other men finished their work and left. Meghan carried a bucket of water to the cabin and took a sponge bath. She changed into her clean shift, and washed the other one and hung it to dry. Buell had an extra coat hanging with other clothes in the corner, and she sponged it and brushed it, and shined the brass buttons on it.

Then she had nothing to do. Since childhood, moments of leisure had been rare, and some useful activity had always been waiting. She felt almost guilty as she looked around in the cabin. Buell's telescope was on a shelf, and she took it down and looked at the other ships through a porthole. Then she looked at the navigational instruments and the other things on the shelves, fascinated by them as she had been as a child.

Footsteps came along the passageway while she was reading the ship's log, and she hastily closed it and replaced it on a shelf. There was a knock at the door, and she opened it. A tall, angular man with thin, hawkish features stood outside the door, holding a bundle of clothes. A patch covered one of his eyes and his face had a piratical cast, but his expression was amiable and a wry sense of humor twinkled in his single eye. He wore a frock coat and tricorn, and a cockade on his tricorn indentified him as an inactive naval officer.

He lifted his tricon, bowing. "Mistress Buell, I'm Gershom Tench."

Meghan bobbed in a curtsey, opening the door wider. "I'm pleased to meet you, Mr. Tench. Please come in."

Tench ducked his head and stepped into the cabin,

and he carried the clothes to the bunk. "The captain bought these for you at an oddments and salvage store, Mistress Buell. I had to return to the ship to take some of the men on liberty ashore, and he asked me to bring these clothes to you."

"I'm most grateful, Mr. Tench, and it appears a fair assortment."

"Aye, the owner of the shop had his wife in for advice on what was needed." Tench chuckled. "The captain was somewhat uncertain as to the proportions they were to fit, but now that I see you I believe they'll do well enough. I understand from Mr. Porter that you're Captain George Conley's daughter."

"Aye, that's correct. Do you know him?"

"No, I haven't had the pleasure, but I know several who have met him and who have served with him. I might also add that I know many who are dismayed over what befell him, none moreso than me. I did know your brother Timothy, and I met him a few months before he was killed. It appears that your family has had more than its fair share of misfortune, and I'm sure you're more than pleased to be free of Parramatta."

"Indeed I am, Mr. Tench. It was a dreadful experience."

Tench nodded sympathetically, then smiled. "But it's over now, and it's best that you put it behind you as soon as possible. I must confess to some misgivings when the captain announced his intentions, but I'm delighted with the outcome. Now I can look forward to having pleasant company to lighten the dreary moments of our voyages."

"That's very kind of you, Mr. Tench."

"I mean it most sincerely," he replied, walking back to the door. "It appears that the captain and I will be aboard for tiffin, in event you like forewarning."

"I do, and I'm grateful for the advice. And for your trouble in bringing the clothes."

"It was my pleasure, Mistress Buell."

He went back out, and Meghan stepped to the bunk and untied the string around the clothes. It was a large bundle, and the clothes had cost a substantial amount of money. There were muslin pantaloons and chemisettes, grosgrain stockings, two dresses made of sturdy, durable madras, and scoop bonnets to match the dresses. The clothes had been worn, but they had been carefully laundered and folded. All of them were in good condition, and they would fit.

The fog was gone and the sun was shining through the portholes. The day was bright and cheerful, and Meghan's mood matched it as she dressed in the clothes, feeling as though she had finally left the prison completely behind her. She hung up the other dress and found room in drawers under the bunk for her shift and the other clothes, then walked along the passageway to the galley.

A fresh breeze came through the porthole in the galley, and kept it from becoming too hot while she cooked. She mixed a pan of bread and put it in the oven, then put slices of salt beef in water to soak out part of the salt. When the bread was baked, she put on pots of peas, beans, and rice, and rolled the slices of beef in flour. She fried a slice of pork to make grease to fry the beef, then shredded the crisp pork and put it in the peas and beans.

The rice became soft and tender, and she took it off the stove and put cinnamon and treacle in it to make pudding. She added mustard to the beans and bits of onion to the peas, then put them on the back of the stove and let the fire die down so the beef would fry slowly and become tender. Then she sat down on the stool, waiting, and she heard a boat thump against the hull of the ship.

A murmur of voices carried into the galley as Buell and Tench crossed the deck, talking quietly. They entered the passageway, and Buell stopped in the galley and looked at Meghan. Whatever diffidence he had felt during early morning was gone, and his attitude was similar to that of the day before. "Well, at least you don't look like some prison doxy fleeing the warders now," he growled.

"I'm most grateful for the clothes."

He grunted sourly, nodding. "But not so grateful that you won't be able to think of something else you want, I daresay."

Prudence dictated silence, but Meghan's reply came almost without conscious volition. "In fact, I do need some combs to pin up my hair. But it isn't a matter of pressing urgency."

Buell stiffened, his face flushed, and he wheeled and stamped across the passageway to the wardroom. Tench passed the door and looked in at Meghan. He bowed and lifted his tricorn, his lips twitching in a dry smile, and followed Buell into the wardroom. Meghan filled pewter plates with food and gathered up silverware and the plate of bread, and carried them across the passageway.

The two men sat at the table and talked as Meghan put the things in front of them. Tench nodded in thanks, but Buell ignored her. Meghan returned to the galley and made tea, and filled pannikins and took them to the wardroom. Tench looked up at Meghan and smiled as she put the pannikins on the table.

"This is very tasty, Mistress Buell. I must say that you have a rare talent for cooking."

"It's only a bit of seasoning here and there, Mr. Tench, and nothing more than most do. Who cooked before?"

Tench hesitated a long second, then picked up his pannikin and took a sip from it. "We've had cabin boys from time to time."

"More than one? Did they leave, then?"

"Aye."

The reply was uncharacteristically terse for Tench, and his smile was gone. He looked down at his plate as he continued eating, subtly indicating that the conversation was finished. Buell frowned at his plate as he ate. The silence was tense, and Meghan realized that she had broached a subject that for some reason was to be avoided. She turned and left the room.

The men began talking again, discussing the preparations for the coming voyage, and their voices carried across the passageway. Meghan sat on the stool in the galley and ate, listening to them. They repeatedly mentioned two men named Drexler and Suggs, and the references to them were perplexing until Tench made a comment that explained what they had to do with the ship. The men were financiers who invested in shares in ships, and they owned the controlling share of the *Baleen.*

Buell had to keep the confidence and good will of the two men, or he would lose his berth as the ship's master. But he made several comments that indicated the profits from the last voyage had been poor, and Meghan perceived the problems that faced him. The new casks for whale oil, the ship's stores, wages for the crew, and all the other expenses had to be financed by Drexler and Suggs, and during the past year they had realized less profit from their investment in the *Baleen* than they had from other whalers in which they owned controlling shares. And the difficulty with the starboard furnace would be a further expense.

"I'll go ashore this afternoon and talk to Drexler and Suggs," Buell said. "There's no point in letting the matter hang forever."

"They'll want to know the expenses on the next voyage to the penny, Captain," Tench replied. "And it's anyone's guess what it'll cost to repair the furnace."

"I know what it'll cost," Buell growled. "It'll cost five or ten guineas for a few dozen bricks."

"It could cost a lot more," Tench said doubtfully. "That furnace might need rebuilding from the deck up, and it should have it if it needs it. We'd be in a sad situation if we were trying out blubber in a running sea, and that furnace fell in and spilled whale oil into the fire."

There was a momentary silence, then Buell's voice was a morose rumble as he replied. " And I'd be in a sad situation if I were beached, Mr. Tench. You're accustomed to the Navy, where you draw what you like from naval stores and hang the cost. Here we answer to the owners. We could use new pumps, the foremast wants restepping, and I could find a dozen other ways to spend money. When you get your own ship, you'll find that a master's tasks include making do on coppers instead of guineas. The furnace will have to suffice with a few bricks until we have an exceptionally good voyage, and there's the end of it. You go on out and see how far they've got with it, and I'll be out directly."

The chairs scraped against the floor as they rose from the table. Tench passed the galley door, nodding to Meghan, and he walked on along the passageway and went out. Buell stepped into the galley doorway and looked at Meghan. "Hold yourself in readiness to go ashore this afternoon. It could be that I'll be seeing some men I know, and I'll take you with me if I do."

"Aye, very well," Meghan replied.

He turned and left, and Meghan frowned worriedly as she went across the passageway to gather up the dishes. During the conversation between the two men, there had been hints that the owners simply disliked Buell for some reason or other, creating a further problem. It appeared he wanted to establish himself on a more personal basis with the owners by taking her with him to meet them. That implied he was deeply concerned, which disturbed Meghan. Her situation would be much worse if he lost his command of the ship, and it had already become like a home to her.

The afternoon passed slowly after Meghan washed the dishes, worry making the hours drag. She glanced

through the books in the cabin, but she was too restless to read and she went out and climbed the steps to
the quarterdeck. The expanse of the ship was in full
view from the prominence of the quarterdeck,
hatches, boats, masts, and other features cluttering
the deck as it stretched away to the bow. She paced
back and forth on the quarterdeck, watching for the
boat to return from the piers.

It was late afternoon when Buell and Tench returned to the ship, and Buell was in an ugly mood. The
two men sat in the wardroom and talked as Meghan
cooked, and she listened to Buell's profane, vitupera-
tive snarls and pieced together what had happened.
Drexler and Suggs had refused to see him, and they
were coming to the ship the next day to look at the furnace. Buell regarded it as encroaching upon his authority, and he seemed to think they were searching
for a reason to remove him from command of the ship.

The ship's bell rang the second dog watch and dusk
settled while Buell and Tench were eating, and
Meghan lit the lanterns in the galley and wardroom.
Men who had been on liberty ashore returned to the
ship, some singing drunkenly. A few minutes later,
Dickon Muir came to the galley with an armload of
wood, and he handed Meghan a folded sheet of paper.
It was a note from Mary Whittacker.

Most of the note was excited congratulations over
Meghan's marriage to the captain of a ship, and there
were a few lines about what Mary was doing in the
Wyndham household. There was also a suggestion
that they meet at the church on High Street on Sunday afternoon, when Mary would be free. Meghan

read the note, and listened to Buell's angry voice in the wardroom. She folded the note and put it in her pocket. She would have to ask Buell's permission to go ashore, and this was not the time to ask.

Buell and Tench finished eating, and went out on deck. They summoned the men out of the forecastle, and began work on the furnace by the light of lanterns. Meghan washed the dishes, and carried the dishwater outside to throw it over the rail. Fog had risen and was swirling across the deck, and the men working on the furnace were wraith-like figures as they moved about in the dim glow of the lanterns.

Meghan went to bed, and the distant, muffled sounds of the men working continued until the ship's bell rang the midwatch. Then Buell came into the cabin, and Meghan lay on her side of the bunk and waited, her mouth dry and her heart pounding with apprehension. But he avoided touching her as he lay down and pulled the covers over himself. She slowly relaxed, listening to him moving restlessly and muttering to himself. It took her a while to get to sleep.

Buell dressed by the light of a lantern the next morning, awakening Meghan. She had put out a clean shirt for him, and he was looking at it suspiciously as she sat up, holding the blanket around herself. He glanced at her, then looked away as he put the shirt on. "My coat wants brushing," he growled.

"Your spare coat has been brushed, and the buttons are polished."

He pulled his cravat under the wide collar of the shirt, and folded it as he crossed the cabin to get the coat. Meghan moved to the edge of the bunk. Her

117

chemisette was open, and the blanket fell down and exposed her breasts. Buell shrugged into the coat and walked back across the cabin. Meghan snatched up the blanket, but all Buell did was to stamp out of the cabin and slam the door. Meghan got dressed.

The ship seethed with activity as dawn broke, men still working on the furnace, and others cleaning the ship. Meghan sprinkled nutmeg on bread left over from the day before, heated it in the oven and poured treacle over it, but Buell had no appetite for breakfast. He drank a pannikin of tea, then went back out to watch the men working on the furnace.

It was difficult for Meghan to feel anything but aversion and hate for Buell, but there was an element of pathos in his anxiety about losing command of the ship. Her welfare was also involved, and she thought about ways she might be able to influence the situation. As a girl she had learned how to achieve her purposes with her father, brothers, and their friends. And she had learned that tasty pies, puddings, and pastries were effective in inducing a receptive and congenial mood.

She picked slices from the bag of dried apples and put them in water to soak, and mixed dough to make apple pastries. The hours of the morning passed, and Meghan could hear Buell's heavy footsteps on the thick timbers overhead as he paced restlessly back and forth on the quarterdeck. When lunch was ready, he came in and sat in the wardoom for a few minutes, picking at his food, then he left. Meghan washed the dishes after Tench finished eating, then began baking the pastries.

Men called out on deck during the afternoon as a boat approached the ship. The last of the pastries were finished, the flaky crust glazed with treacle and the juicy filling oozing thickly through slits in the crust, and the blended scents of ginger, cinnamon, and apples filled the galley. Buell's footsteps thumped across the quarterdeck and down the steps to the main deck as Meghan put the last pan of pastries on the table. She tugged at her dress and straightened before she went to see what was going on.

Drexler and Suggs were portly, older men, with gray hair and clean-shaven faces, and dressed in the latest London fashions. Both of them wore buff nankin trousers that were tight around the lower portions of their bulging stomachs, with straps at the cuffs that went under the insteps of their shiny, high-heeled shoes. Their waistcoats were made of bright damask that contrasted with their dark swallowtail coats, and they had on tall hats and flowing, snowy cravats.

They were in a sour mood, prepared for an unpleasant meeting, and it appeared they had suffered a loss of dignity in climbing the rope ladder. Buell was talking with them, unsuccessfully attempting to hide resentment. Tench was cordial and urbane, but with his sardonic features and the single bleak eye peering down at the two pudgy men he appeared more suitable to a quarterdeck under the Jolly Roger. Porter stood by Tench, stiff, alert and respectful. Meghan pushed at her hair, tugged at her dress again, and walked out on deck.

The men were walking toward the furnaces, and they stopped as she crossed the deck toward them.

Buell frowned, then looked at Drexler and Suggs. They were surprised, exchanging a glance and looking back at Meghan. Then Buell spoke, introducing her perfunctorily. "Gentlemen, this is my wife Meghan."

The two men tipped their hats and bowed, introducing themselves, and Meghan curtsied. There was a momentary stiff silence, the men still looking startled, and Meghan smiled brightly and glanced around. "I beg pardon for interrupting, but I've just taken some apple pastries from the oven. I'll have them ready for you when you come to the wardroom."

Drexler smiled, then chuckled and rubbed his ample stomach. "Apple pastries? Now there's a sweet sound to these ears."

"And to these," Suggs chortled, and he laughed and looked at Buell. "Captain Buell, you old sea dog, where did you find this utterly delightful young woman? I didn't know you were married."

"Nor did I," Drexler said. "When did this happen, Captain?"

"Since I last returned," Buell replied, smiling thinly. "I fetched her out of Parramatta."

"Parramatta?" Suggs gasped as Drexler gaped in astonishment. "'Pon my word, the judges in England must be going mad! Whatever could possess them to send a young woman of quality to Parramatta? I was wondering how you expected her to endure a whaler, but I'm certain she can manage after having been in Parramatta."

"She could in any event," Buell said. "She's a Conley, and she has seawater in her veins. Her father is Captain George Conley, who came afoul of some ministers and ended up charged with sedition. She was involved, and she was sentenced to transportation."

"That was as much a crime as ever been committed!" Drexler exclaimed in disgust. "The judge who did that should be removed from office! And Conlcy, you say? Conley? Yes, I'm certain I've heard that name many times."

The atmoshpere among the men had been transformed, becoming cordial. Meghan stepped closer to Drexler and Suggs, smiling up at them. "If my credentials for being on shipboard are established, I'd now like to establish my credentials for being in the officers' galley. The pastries are fresh from the oven, and you won't delay until they're cold, will you?"

Drexler beamed down at her, slapping his stomach with both hands, and looked at Suggs. "Would we do that, Suggs? Would we let apple pastries get cold?"

"Never!" Suggs shouted, roaring with laughter. "Bother the furnace, I say, and let's go see to the pastries."

"And I agree," Drexler laughed. "The good captain here knows twice as much as we do about furnaces, and he can tell us about it. Show us to your wardroom, Captain Buell."

Buell nodded, a wintry smile on his face, and motioned toward the wardroom. Meghan crossed the deck ahead of the men, perplexed by the abrupt reversal in the situation. At best, she had hoped the men's judgment would be influenced, but it appeared they had largely dismissed their purpose in coming to the ship.

Tench went to the lazarette for a bottle of port, and

Meghan took plates and pannikins for the port into the wardroom. The men talked and laughed noisily as they ate and drank, Meghan sat in the galley and listened. Most of the conversation was about other ships and mutual acquaintances, but it touched on the next voyage of the *Baleen*. Drexler and Suggs agreed with Buell that the winter season was always poor for whalers, and the next voyage should be more profitable than the last.

The conversation continued for an hour, then chairs scraped as the men rose to leave. Drexler and Suggs stopped in the doorway of the galley to talk with Meghan for a moment, commenting emphatically on how delicious the pastries had been, then they walked on along the passageway with Buell and Tench. Meghan went to the wardroom, and gathered up the dishes to take them to the galley.

Buell and Tench came back in after seeing Drexler and Suggs off in their boat, and they talked with satisfaction about the outcome of the visit. They walked into the wardroom as Meghan was cleaning the table, and Buell poured the dregs from the port bottle into his pannikin. "I'm well pleased to be done with foolishness," he said, taking a sip from the pannikin. "Now we'll have a clear road to see to the affairs that should properly concern us."

"Aye, it's good to have that behind us, Captain," Tench replied. "And with as favorable an outcome as one could wish, and all. Mistress Buell and her pastries had a hand in that, to say the least."

Buell nodded indifferently. "Aye, I suppose so. Those two should have a care about how they eat, or there'll come a time when someone will think they're whales and start heaving harpoons at them."

"I wasn't far behind them, because I can't remember when I've had a pastry that would compare with those," Tench chuckled. "I do hope there's some left for later, Mistress Buell."

Meghan smiled and nodded. "Aye, there's plenty left, Mr. Tench, and I can always make up more when those are gone." She hesitated, thinking about the note from Mary Whittacker, and looked at Buell. "I received a message from Mary Whittacker, who was a good friend of mine at Parramatta, and she would like to meet me at the church on High Street on Sunday. Would it be agreeable to you if I went?"

He was lifting the pannikin again, and he put it back down as he frowned at her. "A message? When did you receive it?"

"She sent it to the ship yesterday. She's a maid in Mr. James Wyndham's house, the gentleman who came to Parramatta when you did, and she knows we're married."

Buell hesitated for a long moment, then he grimaced sourly and shrugged as he drained the pannikin and put it on the table. "I see no harm in it, but be back aboard before the first dog watch. Mr. Tench, let's go and start seeing about our stores."

"It's late in the day, Captain," Tench replied. "Do you think we'll be able to get enough done to make it worthwhile going ashore?"

Buell grunted and nodded emphatically. "Aye, even if I have to drag some of those sods from their houses. I want to get the hooks out of the mud, and get to sea where we belong." He walked toward the door, looking at Meghan. "We'll sup ashore."

Meghan nodded, picking up the bottle and pannikins from the table. Buell and Tench went out and along the passageway, and Meghan carried the bottle and pannikins to the galley. She took out the note from Mary and read it again, smiling in anticipation, then she put it back in her pocket and piled the dishes in a basin.

It was quiet after Buell and Tench left. The ship settled into its late afternoon routine, and the sounds of the men moving about were lost under the groaning of timbers as the ship moved gently in the swell. Meghan heated food left over from lunch, and ate. The sun dipped into the west and the light in the galley became dim while she ate. She lit the lantern and washed the dishes.

The sun was below the horizon and the last light of day was fading when she took the dishwater out and tossed it over the rail. Thin clouds in the west glowed red, still touched by sunset, and stars twinkled in the east. Meghan climbed the steps to the quarterdeck. A thin, wiry old sailor was on anchor watch, standing by the binnacle in his loose, shapeless canvas shirt and trousers. His gnarled feet were bare and his old-fashioned tarred queue stuck out in back, and he knucked his forehead in bashful greeting. Meghan nodded to him and crossed the deck to the taffrail.

It was a quiet, peaceful moment, and Meghan savored it. The ruddy light in the west gleamed on the waves in the harbor, dying away as dusk fell. Anchor lights on ships dotted the harbor, and spots of light outlined the waterfront and streets in the town. The moon rose, its pale light shining on wisps of fog rising in the harbor. Then the chill of night settled, and Meghan walked back across the quarterdeck to go below. She went into the galley and banked the fire for the night, then walked to the cabin and went to bed.

The cabin door closed, awakening her from a deep sleep. She stirred drowsily, listening to Buell's movements, and slid over to her side of the bunk. He stumbled and muttered drunkenly, and a strong smell of rum wafted across the cabin. Meghan became wide awake, a chill of fear racing through her. She edged farther over and pressed against the bulkhead by the bunk and waited.

He undressed, breathing heavily. The smell of rum became thick as he weaved to the bunk and bent over it, jerking at the covers, and the bunk creaked under his weight as he lay down. He pulled the covers over himself, and he grunted and sighed as he settled himself. A moment passed, and Meghan began relaxing. Then he turned and reached for her.

She shrank from him, revulsion mixed with her fear, and pushed his hands away. "Am I so loathsome to you that you can bring yourself to touch me only when you're mindless with drink?" she hissed.

He growled angrily, seizing her shoulders and shaking her. "You're my wife!" he snarled thickly. "You're my wife, and I'll not be denied my rights with you!"

"I won't deny you," Meghan whimpered in pain as his powerful fingers dug into her shoulders with crushing force. "But must you be so harsh? Does it give you pleasure to inflict pain on me?"

125

He released her and propped himself on an elbow, swaying drunkenly as he leaned over her. "You'll do as you're told, or I'll take a rope's end to your arse," he grumbled. "I'll have my rights with you when I wish, and not at your bloody convenience."

"I said I won't deny you," Meghan replied, opening the front of her chemisette. "But do be more gentle."

Buell grunted, lifting himself over her, and he grasped her thighs to drag them open. Meghan started to protest, and his fingers dug into her thighs. She lay back and opened her thighs wider, positioning herself for him as he crouched and probed at her.

The stink of rum eddied around Meghan, and she felt faint. He slowly became aroused and probed harder, panting hoarsely. Meghan put an arm over her face and bit her wrist to keep from crying out in pain.

Chapter 7

MEGHAN HELD A COIL OF hair in place on top of her head and pushed a comb into it to hold it, then ran her hands over her hair and pushed at the other combs. The combs were expensive, made of carved bone and edged with forneyware, and Buell had sent Porter to the ship with them and two more dresses on the morning after he had assaulted her for the second time.

Two combs were left over, and Meghan put them in a drawstring bag she had made out of a piece of material from the ship's slop chest. She put on her bonnet and tied the ribbons, and tucked the strings on the bag over her wrist as she left the cabin and walked along the passageway. Stores were being lightered from a pier in a boat and stowed in the holds, and the clatter of blocks, shouting voices, and thumping of bare feet on the deck carried through the door at the end of the passageway.

Buell and Tench were at the table in the wardroom, pouring over the bills of lading for the stores and annotating ledgers, and they looked up as she stopped in the doorway. Buell frowned, his eyes moving up and down her. "Where are you going?" he demanded.

"I'm going ashore to meet my friend."

"Going ashore?" he snorted, sitting up straight. "To meet a friend? What gives you leave to go ashore and meet someone?"

"You told me I had leave to do so, on the day that Messrs. Drexler and Suggs visited the ship."

He frowned darkly and pursed his lips, thinking. Then he remembered the conversation, and he nodded grudgingly. "You'll have to go in the lighter," he grumbled. "I don't have anyone at leisure to unship and row a boat. And you be back aboard before the first dog watch."

"I shall," Meghan replied, nettled by his tone and attitude. "And I'm capable of unshipping and rowing myself, if need be. But I'll be content to go in the bumboat."

"That's not a bumboat!" Buell barked angrily, looking up again. "That's my ship's longboat!"

Meghan shrugged nonchalantly, plucking at her sleeves and straightening them. "I refer to the boat alongside the ship just now, and to me it has the appearance of a bumboat. But bumboat or longboat, it'll do to fetch me ashore."

Tench put his quill aside and stood up. "I'll have a word with Porter and see who's cocksun on the boat, Captain," he said, his lips twitching with suppressed amusement. "You'll want someone who'll keep the men's tongues in check while Mistress Buell is being taken ashore."

"Very well, then," Buell said irritably. Tench took

128

his coat from the back of his chair and picked up his hat from the table, and followed Meghan out on deck.

The deck was cluttered with piles of stores, and it bustled with noise and activity. The cover was off one of the main hatches, and men carried kegs and boxes and passed them down to men in the hold. A spar had been rigged out from the mainmast to hoist heavier containers out of the boat by the ship, and a large hogshead dangled from the rope on the spar. Blocks clattered as a line of men holding the other end of the rope eased forward and lowered the hogshead to the deck. Porter watched the men, supervising their work.

Tench crossed the deck to Porter. Meghan walked around the edge of the deck to the rail, and looked down at the boat. Two barrels remained in it, and the men in the boat were moving them into position to be hoisted aboard ship. Tench finished talking with Porter and walked over to her.

"The cocksun is a good man, Mistress Buell, and he'll belay any offensive talk while you're in the boat."

"Thank you, Mr. Tench. Could you tell me how to find the church on High Street?"

"Aye, go up the street directly across from the pier until you see the sign of a ship broker and refitter named Poage. That'll be High Street, and the church is about half a mile along it to the right."

"That sounds easy enough to find."

"I'm sure you won't have any difficulty. On the last trip the men make with the boat before the first dog watch, they'll remain at the pier until you arrive to make sure you get back on time."

"Thank you very much, Mr. Tench."

He smiled, lifting his tricorn, and walked back toward the wardroom. The hogshead settled to the deck with a heavy thump, the rope on the spar going slack. The men swarmed around the hogshead, and untied the rope. They swung the end of the long spar around toward the rail, and Porter came over to Meghan.

"We'll be finished with this load directly, Mistress Buell. Shall I have a bosun's chair rigged for the boom?"

Meghan shook her head, laughing. "No, not for me, Mr. Porter. I've been skinning ladders since I could walk."

"Aye, I expect you have," Porter laughed, turning away. "We'll have those last two barrels up and have you on your way in a moment, then." He pointed to a man as he walked away. "You, go fetch the rope ladder."

The man knuckled his forehead and trotted away, and Porter walked along the rail and looked down as the end of the spar swung out over the boat and the rope dropped into it. The men in the boat tied the rope around one of the barrels, and the blocks squealed as the men on deck hauled in the rope. The barrel lifted out of the boat, turning lazily as it dangled, and the spar swung ponderously around over the deck.

The man returned with the rope ladder as the last barrel was being hoisted out of the boat, and he unrolled it over the side of the ship. Men in the boat picked up oars, and they fended the boat off the hull and held it steady in the water. Meghan climbed cautiously down the ladder, feeling for the rungs with her toes. Then other men climbed down into the boat, and gathered up oars.

The boat turned away from the ship and skimmed across the water, picking up speed as the men stroked with the oars. The wind whipped the ribbons on Meghan's bonnet, the sun glinted on the emerald waves, and scattered, fleecy clouds drifted across the sky. The day was very bright and cheerful, alive with vibrant color, and Meghan smiled in anticipation as she thought about seeing Mary again.

Buell had prevailed upon the chandlers who dealt with him to work their men on Sunday. All the piers were quiet except one, and it was piled high with stores for the *Baleen*. The cockswain in the stern of the boat bawled out orders, and the men backed water with their oars as the boat approached the pier. They slowed the boat, and brought it alongside a pile with boards nailed crosswise on it.

Meghan climbed the boards, and picked her way along the crowded pier. A dray was parked at the end of the pier, and men were unloading it and stacking more barrels and crates onto the pier, surly and cursing because they had to work Sunday. Meghan stepped off the pier and crossed the street.

The sounds of activity faded behind, and the twisting street leading up into the town was virtually deserted. The quiet street had something of the feel of sleepy Sunday afternoons in England, the buildings crowded together on each side and many of them with leaded windows and familiar designs of beams and plaster. But the atmosphere was different, and the patina of age was missing. The stone thresholds were not grooved by the footsteps of generations, and there was no timeless feel of heavy beams settled into place by the weight of centuries.

Three men sat with their pipes and tankards on a bench in front of an inn, and they rose and doffed their hats as Meghan passed. Sailors stared. Meghan approached a cross street, and a large sign with the name Poage on it.

High Street was wider, and it was busier. It appeared to be the promenade where the nubile and eligible met, groups of young women eyeing and being eyed by groups of young men. Couples strolled with children in tow, and apprentices stood in doorways and watched the passers-by. Carriages and horses moved along the street, and peddlers selling shellfish and sweetmeats trundled small carts and shouted their wares.

The church was a large, sprawling building that was being rebuilt, stone replacing wood. It was surrounded by wide, grassy grounds shaded by scattered trees, and the graveyard was in the rear. People lounged and strolled in the shade, and Meghan's eyes were drawn to a young woman who was alone on a bench under a tree.

The woman wore a bright cotton dress with flounces on the bodice and lace at the cuffs and throat, and a matching bonnet. She was tall and young, with nothing of the sordid misery of Parramatta about her. And yet she was hauntingly familiar even with her face averted. She turned her head and looked at Meghan, and smiled as she rose. Meghan ran as Mary ran to her.

Mary laughed in delight, holding Meghan close and

132

kissing her, then she stepped back and held her at arm's length. "Meghan, I hardly recognized you! My word, you're lovely!"

"And you are, Mary. That's such a lovely dress, and for a moment I thought you were some wealthy merchant's daughter out for a stroll."

Mary chuckled, her eyes shining with tears of pleasure. They looked at each other in silence, and tears of happiness suddenly welled up in Meghan's eyes. She choked back a sob, her lips trembling, and Mary leaned over and kissed her again, patting her shoulder. "Let's go and talk, Meghan. We can go to the Wyndham house, and sit in the kitchen."

"Aye, let's," Meghan said, wiping her eyes as she turned toward the street with Mary. "Are you certain it'll be all right for us to go to the house?"

"Yes, the family is away for the day, but it would be all right in any event. They permit all sorts of liberties. And Mistress Beasley, the cook, is a friendly soul. When I told her I might be meeting you today, she straightaway told me to bring you and sit in the kitchen to talk. She wants to meet you as well." She smiled at Meghan, taking her hand. "But wasn't it such good fortune for you that you were chosen by a ship's master? I was beside myself with happiness when I read your message."

"Aye, being on shipboard suits me well."

"Yes, you above all people. I remember seeing a man who appeared to be a ship's officer on the day we left Parramatta, but I scarcely took notice of him. What is he like?"

Meghan stared ahead as they walked. She was silent for a moment, but pride was overcome by the need to talk about it. "He isn't a kind man, Mary. Ship's officers are often hard men, as they often need to be. My father and brothers were, but they had their kind side. My husband doesn't."

Mary sighed and shook her head sympathetically. "I'm very sorry to hear that, Meghan. Does he make you work hard?"

"No, the work is nothing," Meghan chuckled wryly. "It amounts to no more than a bit of cooking and washing, and I'm at leisure much of the time. The mate and bosun are very congenial, and they knew my brothers. I also find being on the ship pleasant beyond words, and the food is in abundance and variety that would please a lord. The only thing amiss is that my husband treats me like a slothful crewman. And worse, when abed. On balance, though, I'm far better off than I was at Parramatta."

"And that's how you should see it, Meghan," Mary said, patting her hand. "Husbands can be cruel, but in time they can often be brought to rein. And being married to a ship's master makes you the envy of most women, doesn't it? Being master of a ship is a most respectable position. So it's best to endure, and at length do what you can to alter things. What sort of ship does he have?"

"A whaler of a thousand tons dry burthen, square-rigged and built on Bristol lines."

"Is it indeed?" Mary laughed. "And now I know precisely as much as before, because you wrote in your message that it was a whaling ship. I wasn't born to the sea as you were, Meghan, and you'll have to explain in much more detail than that."

Meghan laughed, and described the ship. The pedestrians and carriages on the street gradually diminished, and the buildings along the street became smaller. Meghan and Mary turned onto a side street leading away from the center of town. The street turned into a wide, smooth road leading around the slope overlooking the harbor, and large, widely-separated houses were set back from the road.

The Wyndham house was a stately structure of stone in country manor style, with a clutter of chimneys on its slate roof. Parakeets chattered and darted through the eucalyptus trees around it in flashing spots of bright green, red, and yellow. Ivy struggled to gain a foothold on the house and the fieldstone walls on each side of the carriage drive. Meghan turned onto a flagstone walk that led to a side entrance at the rear of the house.

Mary stepped ahead at the end of the walk, and opened the door and looked inside. "Are you there, Mistress Beasley?"

"Aye, is your friend with you, love?" a stout, gray-haired woman replied as she came to the door. She looked at Meghan, a beaming smile on her round, friendly face, and lifted her eyebrows in surprise. "Is this her? Mercy, she's hardly more than a sweet little girl, is she?"

"She is lovely, isn't she? Meghan, this is Mistress Beasley, the cook. Mistress Beasley, this is my friend Mistress Meghan Buell, wife of the master of the *Baleen*."

"Just call me Alma, love," the woman said, patting

Meghan's arm. "And give me no mind, because any-one smaller than an ox is little to the likes of me." She turned away, motioning toward the table. "Go ahead and sit down. I've made some scones, and the water's ready for tea."

Meghan and Mary crossed the kitchen to the long, heavy table. The kitchen was expansive, with a smooth stone floor, thick beams across the ceiling, and a large fireplace and iron oven at one end. It was fragrant with the scent of clusters of herbs hanging from the beams, and a breeze blew through the open windows and brought the fresh feel of the flower gardens into the room. Alma bustled about, taking a plate of scones from the oven and making tea. She looked over her shoulder at Meghan.

"Do you look forward to going on the ship, love?" she asked. "Mary tells me that yours has been a sea-faring family for generations beyond counting, and you like ships and such."

"That's true, and I am looking forward to it. The ship has quite become my home already, and I enjoy it very much."

Alma smiled as she brought the scones and teapot to the table, then she pulled a chair back and sat down. "Better you than me, then. My husband took me out in the harbor in a boat years ago, when he was still alive, and I was chundering before the boat was prop-erly untied." She poured the tea, and pushed the scones toward Meghan and Mary. "When will you be leaving, love?"

"Within a day or two," Meghan replied, taking a sip of tea and reaching for a scone. "We're loading stores now, and that'll soon be done. Whales run off the coast of New Zealand during late spring and summer and we'll be there waiting for them."

Alma was taking a drink of tea, and she almost choked. She swallowed with a gulp, her eyes wide in horror. "New Zealand?" she gasped, and shuddered. "I trust your husband will keep you well protected from the savage heathens who inhabit that place. They're cannibals, you know."

Meghan smiled and nodded. "Aye, I know, but we won't be going ashore. We'll stand well off the coast, and fill our casks and return here. We won't be in any danger."

"Of course you won't, love," Alma said apologetically, reaching over to pat Meghan's hand. "Here I am nattering on about the place, and all I know about it is what I've heard. It's only a tiny patch of a place, I've been given to understand, so there'd be no reason why you'd want to stop there. Do you cook on the ship, then?"

"Aye, for the officers. We have only one mate, and cooking for two men is little enough to do. I have ample leisure."

Alma nodded, and bit into a scone. "And well you should, love. A young woman like you should have time to yourself, even though many are married to men who work them like bullocks." She swallowed and smiled reminiscently as she took another bite of the scone. "My man was a good sort, a good, settled man who worked hard and provided well. The same sort as the one who's been lurking around here after you, Mary."

"Has someone been calling on you, Mary?" Meghan asked. "Why didn't you tell me about him?"

Mary shrugged. "He hasn't actually been calling on me, Meghan. He's only been coming around, that's all."

"Listen to her." Alma snorted in amusement. "He's been mooning over her ever since he first saw her, and that's all."

"Tell me about him, Mary," Meghan said. "What's his name?"

"Joshua Venable," Mary replied quietly, looking down at her cup. "He served as apprentice to Jubal Poage, the ship broker and refitter. He now works at full wage, and he hopes to become a partner."

"Aye, I saw the Poage office on High Street," Meghan said. "And it appears a thriving firm. Did you give up an afternoon with him to meet me? I wouldn't have asked you to do that."

"You wouldn't have had to," Mary replied quickly, reaching over and putting her hand on Meghan's. "I so wanted to see you, Meghan, and I would have gone to any ends to talk with you for only a moment. But he's working today, as he does every Sunday."

"That's what you want in a man, love," Alma said, picking up the teapot and rising. She refilled the cups and carried the teapot toward the fireplace, talking over her shoulder. "Sweet words and smiles make thin gruel, and you want a man who'll work hard to provide for you."

Mary smiled faintly and nodded, then glanced at Meghan and looked back down at her cup. As their eyes met, Meghan saw the wistful light in Mary's eyes, and she understood. Joshua Venable was practical, dependable, and hard-working. Mary was a creature of laughter and gaiety, the daughter of a prosperous merchant, and her life had been destroyed because she had tried to protect an errant brother who had passed counterfeit currency. She yearned for the excitement and merriment she had once known.

Alma made more tea and brought it to the table, talking about her husband and their life together. She had been born in Australia, her parents some of the first convicts sent to the penal colony, and her husband had been a seaman who had come to Australia and remained. Her life encompassed the development and growth of New South Wales during the years it had become self-sustaining, and her attitude toward life had a bleak, austere aspect that was rooted in that struggle.

The hours fled, and the sunlight coming through the windows took on the warm tones of late afternoon as Meghan talked with Alma and Mary. The time came when she knew she should leave, and she put it off minute by minute. Then it could be deferred no longer. She moved her chair back from the table during a pause in the conversation. "As much as I regret it, I must leave."

Alma's expression became sad. "Aye, pleasant times must end, musn't they? One can grasp at an hour in any way one wishes, but it won't make the difference of the smallest part of a second."

Meghan smiled at Alma as they rose and went to the door. "It's been a pleasant time, and I'm most grateful to you for your hospitality. It was kind of you to allow Mary to invite me here."

"I thought it would be a way to pass the time," Alma replied. "Time hangs heavy when the family's gone. There's so little to do. But as it turned out, meeting you has made it an afternoon that I'll always remember." They stopped at the door, and she took Meghan's hand. "It's easy to see why Mary values your friendship so highly, because you're a rare sort. And you have rare courage, because you're setting out to sea and you regard it as lightly as most would a walk along a road."

Meghan laughed and shook her head. "It has its dangers, Alma, but accident or illness can befall anyone at any time."

"And you prove what I said, because there speaks your courage," Alma said, smiling sadly. "We all know the perils of the sea, but you dismiss them out of hand. It's easy to believe that you come from brave ship's captains." She put her arms around Meghan and pulled her close, kissing her. "Do be careful, love."

Meghan patted Alma's cheek. "You may be certain of that. And I'll think of you often, because I feel we've become friends."

"And I do, love," Alma replied, her voice quavering. She kissed Meghan again, and sniffled and wiped her eyes. "God bless you and keep you safe on your voyage, love."

"And God bless you and keep you, Alma. Goodbye."

"Goodbye, love."

Mary waited on the path as Meghan and Alma embraced again. At the end of the path, Meghan looked back and waved. Alma waved, wiping her eyes, then closed the door.

Smoke from evening cooking fires hung over the town, and the shadows grew longer as Meghan and Mary walked back into the town. They talked desultorily for part of the way, then fell silent. Commonplace comments were painfully inane, and their feelings about the uncertainty of when they might meet again was a subject too vast to encompass with words. Mary took Meghan's hand, and they laced their fingers together walking in silence.

High Street was still busy, with people urgently wringing the last moments of pleasure from their day of rest. Meghan and Mary walked along the street to its intersection with the winding street that led down to the waterfront, then stopped. They looked at the Poage office across the street, then at each other. Meghan read Mary's thoughts in her eyes. Joshua Venable was somewhere in the building, pouring over large sheets of foolscap covered with small figures.

"I had to get married to be free of Parramatta, Mary," Meghan said. "You have a choice in what you do."

"You had no choice, nor do I," Mary sighed despondently. "Choices are ever a matter of picking the path that seems less stony and less strewn with thistles, and that is no choice."

"Life is dreary, but it has its pleasures," Meghan replied. "We met, and we've had pleasure in each other's company. Now we part for a time, but we'll meet again."

Mary looked down at Meghan, her eyes shining

with tears. "If I truly had a choice, I'd have your sweet face with me always. You're the dearest friend I've known, and I'll not rest until I see you again." She pulled Meghan to her and kissed her. "Godspeed on your journey, Meghan."

"And God keep you safe and in good health," Meghan replied, kissing Mary, and she turned away. "Goodbye, Mary."

"Goodbye, Meghan."

Meghan hurried down the street, averting her tear filled eyes from two men who lifted their hats. Others passed, blurred on the edges of Meghan's vision. She stopped at a curve in the street and looked back. Mary stood at the corner, looking at her. She waved, and Meghan waved. Then Meghan dropped her arm and walked away.

The street winding down toward the waterfront was almost deserted. Meghan was lost in her thoughts and suddenly there were two men in front of her. The men were sailors, wearing ragged slop chest clothing. They were dirty and disheveled, and had been drinking heavily. They leered at Meghan as they stood blocking her way. She moved to one side then the other, and they weaved on their feet and jostled each other as they laughed jeeringly, keeping in front of her.

Heavy, rapid footsteps crossed the street, and a booming voice rang out. "You louts stand aside, or I'll bloody skin you alive! I said to stand aside, you scurvy dogs!"

Meghan turned and looked. The man was a ship's officer, wearing a tricorn and frock coat with brass buttons. He was a young man, but he was large and determined-looking, his bold, strong features stiff with anger and his blue eyes blazing. The two men backed away from Meghan, suddenly subdued and much less drunk. Apprehension replaced their leering smiles.

"We meant no harm, sir," one said. "We were only having a lark."

"You meant harm enough!" the young man barked. "And you did harm enough! Now get out of here before I swipe the pair of you!"

The two men trotted away, and the young man turned to Meghan and lifted his hat. "Are you all right, Mistress?"

Meghan looked up at him and nodded, starting to reply, the words somehow became lost, dying into silence on her lips. He was an extremely handsome man, and his brown face was so smooth it almost shone in the sunlight. His wide blue eyes had been sparkling with anger, and now they were kind and gentle, attractive eyes.

And he was more than handsome. Some compelling quality about him started a throbbing glow swelling within her and spreading out through her body. There was a magical, thrilling tension between them that Meghan had never experienced before, and he felt it too. His smile faded, and his eyes searched hers intently. Seconds passed as they stood looking into each other's eyes.

Meghan suddenly realized what she was doing, awareness of her surroundings returning in a rush, and she felt color flooding her cheeks. He blushed too, and seemed at a loss for words. Meghan looked away in confusion.

"Aye, and I'm most grateful for your assistance," she said.

"It was my pleasure. Do you live along here, then? I think it best that I see you to your door."

"No, I'm going to the piers for a boat out to a ship, and I'm sure I'll have no further misadventure."

"That may be, but I'd not be at ease in my mind if I let you go alone. Please allow me to walk to the piers with you."

Meghan wanted to run from him, frightened by her reaction to him. And at the same time she felt a tantalizing, blissful pleasure in his presence. She silently nodded, and he adjusted his long stride to hers. He was silent, towering over her as he walked beside her, and she searched for some polite comment. She remarked on the weather, interrupting him as he said something.

He apologized, their words running together again as she apologized, then he laughed. It was a pleasant, hearty laugh, like everything about him. His teeth were very white and the corners of his eyes crinkled. "I was only going to say something about the weather," he said. "What did you say?"

"Nothing of any greater moment," she replied, laughing. "but I do hope I'm not taking you away from friends or anything."

"Not any who'll notice my absence. I came ashore with my captain, and there are others with him. I'm on the *Pamir.*"

Meghan searched her memory for the names of ships she had seen in the harbor, and recalled the ship.

It had entered the harbor the day before, its decks piled high with lumber. "Aye, that's a brigantine, and you're loaded with lumber and naval stores, aren't you?"

"Aye, that's right, we just came in from New Zealand. And as soon as we're unloaded, we'll be on our way again."

"Did you have any bother with the cannibals?"

"No, those at the settlement in the Bay of Islands appear accustomed to white people. But judging from those, I'd not want to make landfall anywhere in New Zealand other than the Bay of Islands."

Meghan smiled in response to the note of wry humor in his voice. They walked around the last curve in the street. Most of the stores on the pier had been taken to the ship. Stacks of crates, barrels, and kegs were at the far end of the pier, and two seamen with clubs and lanterns were on the pier to guard the stores that would remain when night fell.

They stopped on the corner across the street from the end of the pier, and he looked at the stores. "Someone said that the whaler in the harbor was taking on stores. Is that the ship you're going to?"

"Aye."

"I'd consider it a privilege if you'd allow me to see you out to the ship. Failing that, I'd be most pleased to remain here and await your return so I can see you home. If you're at the ship long, it'll be dark when you return."

"I'm grateful for the offer, but I'll remain on the ship."

He looked down at her in perplexity, shaking his

145

head. "Remain? But surely you're not going with her when she puts to sea."

Meghan hesitated. Something precious had come to life between them in the minutes they had been together. A moment out of time had occurred, golden, ecstatic, and it was difficult to return to the sordid realities of life. She cleared her throat, tugging at her bonnet. "Aye, I am. Captain Buell, the master of the *Baleen*, is my husband. I'm Meghan Buell."

His features reflected crushing disappointment for an instant, then he hid it and looked away. "I see. Shall I wait with you until the boat comes from the ship, then?"

"No, two of the men from the ship are there, and it'll return shortly. Perhaps it would have been better if I'd made myself clear at once, rather than permit a misunderstanding."

"No, no," he protested quickly. "If there was misunderstanding, it was of my making. It would be beyond reason to expect a woman such as you to be without attachment. Common sense would tell anyone that. We probably won't meet again, will we?"

"I expect not. They say all ships eventually speak in the roads of the Thames. But that seems unlikely for a whaler and an antipodes trader, doesn't it?"

"Indeed it does," he replied, forcing a smile. "I'll be on my way, then. Our meeting has been a pleasure I'll always remember."

"And I."

He bowed and touched his hat, and walked away. Meghan started to cross the wide street to the pier, then stopped and looked back. The young man walked

146

dejectedly along the deserted street with his hands folded behind him, looking down at the cobblestones. She called after him.

"May I know your name?"

He stopped and turned, smiling apologetically. "Please forgive my discourtesy. I'm Earl Garrity."

"Goodbye, Mr. Garrity."

"Goodbye, Mistress Buell."

He turned and walked on. Meghan again started to cross the street to the pier, and again she hesitated. She looked at Garrity as he walked on up the street. He reached the first curve in the street, stopped and looked back. They both waved and went their separate ways.

Meghan crossed the street to the pier. The two men rose, touched their foreheads and bowed. She nodded to them, and walked on to where the boat would come in. The boat was still alongside the ship, the spar hanging out over it, lifting a barrel, but an hour or more remained before the first dog watch. She would reach the ship in plenty of time.

She walked and turned a keg on end and sat down on it. A jarring combination of heavy depression and breathless excitement possessed her as she sat looking at the ship, thinking of Earl Garrity. A boat approached the other side of the pier, its oars squeaking. The boat bumped against a pile with a heavy thud, and the oars clattered as they were dropped into the boat.

Two men climbed up to the pier, hidden from sight by the stores, and they puffed with effort as they talked. "What the bloody hell's all this?" one asked.

147

"Who's taking on stores on Sunday?"

"Buell of the *Baleen,*" the other man replied. "He doesn't know the meaning of Sunday, and he's the sort who'd rave like a madman until the chandlers would be glad to accommodate him on Sunday just to be shot of him."

"Aye, I know Buell, and I know him well." The first man chuckled. "I hear he got himself a doxy from Parramatta, and a comely-looking wench and all. And that puts to rest something I heard of him."

"Indeed? What would that be?"

The first man lowered his voice, replying, and Meghan was unable to hear what he was saying. Their footsteps faded along the pier and Meghan frowned, puzzled by the conversation. Then she dismissed it with a shrug and looked back at the ship still thinking about Earl Garrity.

PART THREE

Chapter 8

THE WATER IN THE BASIN rocked as Meghan washed the breakfast dishes, and she stood with her feet apart and automatically balanced herself against the motion of the ship. The galley was filled with a constant clatter of things on shelves and in cabinets, and heavy timbers groaned in a soft undertone. She finished the dishes and put them away, and emptied the basin into a bucket.

Fresh water had become precious, and the water would be used to wash the lunch and dinner dishes before it was thrown out. The danger of fire was a constant concern with the ship in motion, and Meghan looked in the stove before she left the galley. The fire had burned down to glowing coals. She latched the stove door securely and went out.

The wind stirred her dress and hair as she climbed the steps to the quarterdeck. The sun was a few degrees above the horizon, rising from the sea into a rich blue sky. The day was sparkling clear and bright, a few large clouds scattered across the sky, and the sea was moderate. The ship heaved slowly along under light sail and ahead of a gentle wind, rocking with a steady motion as the waves hissed past the hull.

The men on watch were washing down the decks, and those who were off duty lounged on hatch covers instead of going to the forecastle to sleep. During daylight hours, most of the men remained on deck to listen for a cry from the crow's nest. They were tense and restless, fearing the dangers that lay ahead, but caught up in the excitement of the search.

Tench and Porter stood a few feet in front of the helmsman, talking quietly. Buell had been on the quarterdeck since midnight the night before, and his eyes were red with fatigue as he stalked about. Tench and Porter lifted their hats and nodded to Meghan. Buell ignored her. During the first part of the voyage, Meghan had taken advantage of the routine of watches and avoided sleeping with him. But he had shown no interest in her. All of his attention was on the ship and the search for whales.

Meghan smiled at Tench and Porter. "It's a lovely day, isn't it?" she said.

They murmured in agreement, and she walked to the binnacle and looked at the course on the compass. Buell's telescope was on the binnacle, out of the field of the compass, and it was a constant temptation. But he had ordered her off the quarterdeck the single time she had picked it up while he was on deck. She walked back to Tench and Porter.

"Mr. Tench, I see we have only the mains and foresail aloft. We could make better use of this puff of wind if we had more canvas up."

"Could we indeed?" Buell barked, wheeling toward her as Tench started to reply. "Do you want to go aloft to make more sail, then?"

"La, no," Meghan laughed, completely accustomed to his ill temper and unruffled by it. "The only time I've had to do with sails was when I crewed my brother's wherry as a girl, and more than once I fouled the halyards and put us on beam's ends. But I am curious as to why we coursed along for a time, and now we dally."

"Your curiosity about things that don't concern you knows no bloody ends," he growled, stamping toward the steps. "Mr. Tench, awaken me at the end of the forenoon watch."

"Aye, aye, Captain," Tench replied. He waited for Buell to go down the steps before he spoke to Meghan. "If you'll remember, it was hazy when we had up more sail. The lookout couldn't see as far off the beams, so we covered more sea. Now it's clear, so we've slowed down for the lookout to search thoroughly off the beams."

Meghan clicked her tongue and nodded. "Aye, of course, and I should have thought of that myself. He can probably see a blow at twenty miles now, can't he?"

Tench nodded, looking out over the waves. "That, or more. There's very little white on the water today, so it's a good day for sighting. If you want to know how far you can see just now, try to find a dark spot on the horizon there."

He pointed to the east, and Meghan shaded her eyes with a hand and looked. A faint smudge was on the ho-

153

rizon. "Aye, I see it. What is it?

"It's a mountain on the coast of North Island, New Zealand. And it's over forty miles away."

Meghan took Buell's telescope to the rail, and Tench and Porter chuckled as they watched her. She had an extensive academic knowledge of ships taught to her by her father and brothers, and Tench and Porter had taught her many of the practical aspects of operating a ship. During the weeks they had been at sea, she had learned the rudiments of navigation and how to read charts, and Tench had let her use the sextant to take bearings when Buell was below.

The telescope was a powerful one, but the view of the mountain through it was disappointing. It remained a faint shadow on the horizon, swimming up and down in the field of the telescope from the motion of the ship. Meghan closed the telescope and took it back to the binnacle. Porter started to say something to her, then broke off as a faint cry came from the crow's nest.

"She blows! She blows!"

The effect was electrifying as the cry echoed all over the ship. Porter and the helmsman stiffened, their attention riveted on the crow's nest. Tench cupped his hands around his mouth and shouted.

"Whereaway does she blow?"

"Six points off the starboard bow!" the lookout voice replied. "And at twenty miles!"

Tench turned to the helmsman, harsh sounding and brusque. "Port the helm six points!" he ordered. "Mr. Porter, all hands on deck! Set the jibs and all sails up to t'gallants, and haul up the braces! Mistress Buell,

154

kindly fetch the captain to the quarterdeck!''

The spokes in the wheel were a blur as the helmsman spun it, and the bow of the ship began turning ponderously to starboard. The deck canted to the left, blocks in the rigging clattered, and timbers groaned and creaked. Porter ran toward the steps, shouting at the top of his voice at men on the deck, and Meghan ran after him.

Bare feet pounded on the deck, and it was alive with men racing about, leaping into the shrouds, climbing fast. Porter bounded down the steps, and Meghan ran down the steps and to the passageway door. It opened as she reached for it, and Buell almost knocked her off her feet as he ran out, shrugging into his coat and putting on his hat.

"How far and whereaway, Mr. Tench?'' he shouted.

"Twenty miles, Captain!'' Tench replied. "Six points to starboard, and we're coming to bear!''

"No, no, man!'' Buell bellowed angrily, trotting up the steps. "You want to come downwind to a whale, not across the wind! Now port the helm another bloody ten degrees and get upwind of the bugger!'' He hesitated on the steps, looking at the sails, then roared at Porter in a voice that carried over the commotion on the deck. "Mr. Porter, when you're quite through mucking about on the flaming deck, will you kindly have the sodding, bleeding braces hauled up before this ship comes to a standstill!''

Porter shouted and pushed at men on the deck, and they ran to the rail and unfastened the ends of the braces, the long ropes that adjusted the angle of the spars. They formed into lines and began hauling on

155

the ropes, stamping and chanting, and the spars slowly turned and trimmed the sails to the wind. The men climbing into the rigging spread out, crawling out on spars and unfurling sails.

Meghan walked back up the steps to the quarter-deck. She stood by the rail and watched Buell. Tench and Porter were experienced seamen, but Buell had experience in whaling that exceeded theirs. And while he was a cruel, brutal man, he was also a highly-skilled seaman. Under his command, the crew was a cohesive, coordinated unit.

The sails on the masts fell into place, and the triangular sails in front of the bowsprit unfurled. The chanting stopped, the spars turned at a sharp angle off the keel of the ship, the sails taut and bulging with wind. The ship gradually picked up speed, the deck canted to the left in a starboard tack across the wind. Buell looked up at the sails, and stepped to the edge of the quarterdeck overlooking the main deck.

"Mr. Porter, set the staysails, skysails, and royals!" he shouted. "There's no point in loitering about here!"

"Aye, aye, Captain," Porter replied.

Buell clasped his hands behind him and paced the deck restlessly, his fatigue forgotten. Porter shouted to the men in the rigging, and they began climbing higher. Tench was by the binnacle, watching the compass, and he turned toward Buell.

"Captain, I'm concerned about the loose stepping on the foremast, with the fore royal and skysail set. The stays might not hold."

"And I'm concerned about a hold full of empty oil casks, Mr. Tench," Buell said curtly. He cupped his hands around his mouth and shouted to the lookout. "Ahoy, the crow's nest!"

"Ahoy!" the man answered, his voice carrying faintly over the other sounds of the ship.

"Whereaway does she lie now?" Buell shouted.

"She sounds!" the man replied.

Buell looked at Tench. "Mr. Tench, you might go see how the fore backstays look when the fore royal and skysail are set."

Tench touched his tricorn, and walked rapidly toward the steps. Buell began pacing again. Meghan looked up at the sails. The men in the rigging were tiny, climbing along the upper spars on the masts. The royals and skysails fell into place on the upper yards and filled with wind, and the staysails opened between the mainmast and the foremast.

The ship picked up more speed under the mountain of canvas, heeled sharply to the left from the pressure of the wind. It pitched and rolled heavily as it plowed across the waves, crabbing through the water between the pressure of the wind and that of the rudder. Spray burst into the air at the bow. The men climbed back down from the rigging, and Tench trotted up the steps to the quarterdeck, Porter behind him.

"The stays are tighter than a publican's purse strings on almsday, Captain Buell," Tench said. "I wouldn't trust them in any more wind than we have now, but I think they'll hold."

Buell nodded brusquely, pacing back and forth. Tench and Porter stood near the binnacle, their feet wide apart as they braced themselves against the surging motion of the ship. The burly helmsman was naked to the waist, and the muscles in his back and arms were rigid as he gripped the wheel and held the rudder steady. Buell stopped and turned as a cry rang out from the crow's nest.

"She blows! She blows! Two points off the port beam!"

Buell ran to the binnacle for the telescope, then ran to the port taffrail. Tench and Porter followed him, trotting with short steps down the slant of the deck. Meghan crossed the deck, leaning back and balancing herself, and stood at the rail near the three men. Buell peered through the telescope, scanning with it. Then he stiffened and leaned forward, holding the telescope steady.

"Do you see it?" Meghan asked excitedly, moving closer to him. "Do you see it?"

"Aye, I see it," he answered, squinting through the glass. "It's a single big blow, so it's a lone bull. And he'll fill enough casks to——" He broke off, his head snapping around, and he glared at her. Then he looked through the telescope again. "Mr. Porter, get set to haul in the braces athwartships when we come into the wind."

Porter turned and ran toward the steps. Tench walked back up the slant of the deck to the binnacle, and Meghan moved along the rail toward the stern, scanning the horizon. Porter shouted at the men on the main deck, and there was a flurry of activity. Men ran to the rails and unfastened the brace ropes, and formed into lines to haul them in.

Several minutes passed as the ship knifed through the hissing waves. Buell scanned with the telescope again. The whale was sounding. The lines of men stood by the rail and held the brace ropes and waited. Porter stood on a hatch cover and looked up at the quarterdeck. Buell leaned forward and held the telescope steady. He looked, then he lowered the telescope and turned, barking orders.

"Down the helm! Mr. Porter, haul in the braces!"

The helmsman spun the wheel. Porter shouted, and the lines of men surged into motion. They burst into a roaring chant, stamping their feet. Blocks in the rigging squealed and chattered as the ropes slid through them. The ship shuddered and groaned, slowly turning downwind. Ropes snapped and jerked in the rigging, and the spars twitched around to a right angle to the keel of the ship.

The deck became level again, and the ship rocked sluggishly as it turned into the wind and waves. It began pitching with an even rhythm, traveling in the same direction as the low waves, and the chant stopped as the men secured the brace lines on the rails again. The ship began picking up speed, then it seemed to come alive.

The ship ran before the wind and the following sea, the towering mass of sails bulging. Spray exploded and foam boiled under the bow and along the hull. The rigging hummed softly, and a quivering vibration ran through the deck under Meghan's feet as the ship raced through the water. She leaned against the taffrail and held her hair away from her face, smiling in exhilaration.

Tench and Porter stood near the binnacle again, and Buell stood by the taffrail on the port side of the quarterdeck and looked ahead through the telescope. Porter looked at Meghan, and nudged Tench and laughed. Tench looked over his shoulder at Meghan and smiled. "There's nothing like running before the wind under full sail, is there, Mistress Buell?" he called across the deck. "This is like rolling down to St. Helena, with stunsails aloft and alow."

"I'll ask you to remember that we're onto a whale, Mr. Tench," Buell called, lowering the telescope. "Kindly see to the boats, if you would. Mr. Porter, sort out the boat crews."

The two men touched their hats and went to carry out their orders. Buell glared at Meghan. She averted her eyes and looked up at the sails, afraid he would order her off the quarterdeck. But Buell lifted the telescope and looked ahead again. Meghan relaxed, watching Tench and Porter on the main deck. Porter stepped up onto a hatch cover and began pointing to men, motioning them into a line. Tench took several men forward to the whaleboats.

The two long, slender boats hung on their davits by the rails, forward of the mainmast. They were kept covered with canvas, and the harpoons, lances, tubs of rope, and other equipment was kept stowed in them in a precise arrangement dictated by custom so there would be no hesitation or groping during the deadly process of harpooning and killing a whale. The men pulled the canvas off a boat, and Tench climbed into it and began checking the equipment.

The men Porter picked waited by the boat. Others stood by the rails and climbed into the lower shrouds. Tench finished checking the boats and returned to the quarterdeck with Porter, and the sun inched higher in the sky. For the moment, there was no sign of a whale.

The lookout shouted again, and men on the deck crowded forward and pointed. Meghan narrowed her eyes and looked where Buell was pointing the telescope. Then she saw it, a tiny spot of white against the blue water. Buell closed the telescope, and went across the deck to Tench and Porter. "It's a sperm whale," he said. "And a big bull. He'll try out to a thousand gallons, or better."

"And he hasn't changed course, has he?" Tench added. "It appears we're well onto him."

"Aye, we are," Buell replied. "He's running straight down the wind and blowing five or six times each time he surfaces, so we have a good chance. I'll take the first boat, and you'll take the second, Mr. Porter. You take the quarterdeck, Mr. Tench, and try to keep us in sight. Mr. Porter, get set to strike the sails, and I'll have the boats run out."

Porter trotted toward the steps, shouting at the men. Buell put the telescope on the binnacle and followed him. A new sense of urgency gripped the men as they scrambled about on deck and climbed into the rigging, silently intent on what they were doing. Buell hurried along the main deck to the whale boats, and the boat crews cleared gear out of the way to lower the davits out over the rails.

The plume of spray was clearly visible ahead when the whale surfaced again. It rose, ebbed, and rose again as blocks chattered and the long, slender whaleboats swung out over the water rushing past the ship. The whale sounded into the depths, long minutes

161

passed, then the spray burst into the air less than two miles ahead of the ship. Porter shouted orders, and the men began clewing up the sails.

The ship slowed, closing on the spout rising from the water ahead. Two sails on the mainmast remained open to maintain headway. The spray rose five times, and the whale sounded again. Then the ship crawled through the water, pitching gently in the long, low waves, and the crews climbed over the rails and into the boats. Meghan moved along the affrail, watching Porter's boat as it was lowered into the water.

The long oars dug into the water and moved in unison, pulling the boat away from the ship. Buell's boat came into sight, sweeping around the bow of the ship, with Buell standing in the stern and the harpooner in the bow. Porter's boat fell in behind it, and the harpooners readied their harpoons and long lances as the boats pulled ahead of the ship.

The ship was still and quiet, and even the rattle of blocks in the rigging and the creaking of timbers seeming muted. Meghan almost jumped when Tench tapped her shoulder and handed her the telescope. "I'll ask you to exercise care not to drop the captain's glass over the side, Mistress Buell."

Meghan opened the telescope. "It should be coming up again just any moment now, shouldn't it?"

"Aye, unless it's found food."

"A school of fish or something?"

"Sperm whales have teeth, and they feed mostly on squid and such. It it's found a squid to chase, we might not see it again."

Meghan lifted the telescope and looked through it.

The boats had pulled well ahead of the ship and were a hundred yards apart. The waves stretched ahead of the boats to the distant, unbroken horizon. Then the water several hundred yards in front of the boats swirled, furiously, a large area turning white and boiling. An island of glistening black emerged, and a geyser of spray erupted from it with a distant, roaring buzz.

Compared with the giant mass of the whale, the boats were frail things tossing on the waves. The men in Buell's boat leaned into the oars, straining to reach the whale before it sounded again, and the boat pulled away from the other one. The long oars flexed as the men threw their weight against them, approaching the whale from the rear and out of its line of vision.

The spray rose again, breaking into a cloud that drifted over the water, and the waves lapped against the immense bulk of the whale. The boat sped across the water, a hundred yards from the whale, then it slowed. The men shipped the oars, and picked up paddles and began paddling. The boat closed the distance rapidly, and the harpooner stood in the bow and held the harpoon as he looked back at Buell.

"He's going wood to skin," Tench said quietly.

It was a figure of speech among whalers for ultimate daring, drawn from approaching a whale until the boat brushed it before the harpoon was thrown. The harpoon could be thrown from a distance of four or five fathoms, but wood to skin assured that the harpoon head would penetrate the blubber and bury itself firmly in flesh. And it was also perilously dangerous.

The harpooner lifted the long, heavy harpoon. He

was a powerful man, the bulging muscles in his wide shoulders and thick arms rigid as he held the harpoon poised, the rope trailing back from it. Spray rose again, and drifted over the boat. The boat glided into the massive creature's shadow. It touched. The harpooner uncoiled, his body snapping around as he plunged the harpoon deep into the whale.

The water by the boat exploded, and the men paddled frantically and backed away. The giant flukes of the whale lifted from the water, a huge, black cliff rising from the sea and hanging over the boat. The enormous mountain of flesh was suspended over the boat for an instant, a vast bulk that dwarfed the frail craft. The boat slid from under the flukes, and the whale's tail crashed back into the water as it sounded.

A foaming wave picked up the boat and skidded it sidewards, and it tilted and teetered on the point of rolling over. Then it righted itself in the churning water, and the rope jerked and snapped as it spun out of the first tub and through the bow chocks. The men in the boat bailed frenziedly and paddled to turn the boat in the direction in which the line was running, and they dodged to avoid the rope as it whipped out of the tub.

The water settled and the boat floated in the waves, moving forward from the force of the rope sliding through the bow chocks. The first tub of rope emptied, and the rope began snapping out of the second one. Porter's boat moved closer, the men in it preparing to pass another tub of rope to those in Buell's boat. Then the rope spun out more slowly, and the whale surfaced a hundred yards in front of the boats.

The whale's massive head came all the way out of the water, blunt and gleaming black. The harpoon was a tiny dart high on its side, the rope snaking back from it. Its flukes struck the water with a resounding splash, then it surged into motion and swam just under the surface. Buell took a turn of the rope around the loggerhead in the stern of the boat, and the boat skimmed and slapped across the water behind the whale.

The boat became small in the distance, and the men in Porter's boat rowed rapidly to keep it in sight. Tench started to order men aloft to make sail, then the boats turned back toward the ship. The water far ahead of Buell's boat swirled from the churning of the whale's flukes, and the rope rippled through the water. The boat sped past the ship, the men in it throwing water on the smoking loggerhead as the rope dragged around it.

The whale slowed, tiring, then stopped and lay on the surface. The men pulled in rope and coiled it, and the harpooner lifted one of the long lances as the boat approached the whale. The men quietly paddled the last few yards, and the harpooner drove the lance into the whale's side. An instant passed before the whale reacted, and the harpooner churned the lance, searching for an artery or some other vital organ.

The whale stirred, and the harpooner jerked the lance out by its long lanyard as the men quickly paddled the boat away. The flukes lifted lazily and the whale sounded, dragging coils of rope back off the boat. Then it surfaced again and towed the boat downwind. Porter's boat was returning from the first run, and it turned and followed.

The whale stopped again several miles downwind. Porter's boat caught up, and the ship closed the distance. The whale was on the surface and blowing as the ship got close enough for Meghan to see it clearly, and the spout had lost its high, arching lift of before. The boats were taking turns at darting it for the harpooners to stab with lances, and the whale was trying to swim away, too weak and too weary to sound again.

Tench ordered men aloft to furl the sails on the foremast, and the wind slowly pushed the ship past the whale and the boats. The sun shone down brightly and glinted on the waves, and made a rainbow in the mist of the whale's spout as it blew again. Then the spout turned into a shower of pink, and the men on the ship cheered. The pink deepened into red, blood gushing and staining the emerald seawater.

The whale made a last effort, thrashing and rolling as it swam blindly in a circle and tried to escape the stabbing lances. The boats pursued it, and continued darting in. The whale left a wide path of red in the sea behind it, jerking and splashing in convulsions that rocked the boats. Then a fountain of blood poured from it, and it rolled onto its side.

Men lowered other boats to help tow the whale to the ship, and they cheered as they rowed away from the ship. Others kindled fires in the furnaces, and smoke eddied across the quarterdeck. The boats reached the whale, swarming around it, and the men passed ropes around the whale's flukes and began towing it to the ship.

Tench crossed the quarterdeck to the rail, and stood

by Meghan. "Well, there's our first whale of the voyage, Mistress Buell."

Meghan sighed. "Its agony seemed as great as its huge size, didn't it?"

"Aye, with rivers of blood pouring, it always seems so. But dying is a painful undertaking for any creature, and a flea's might be as great in its own way. A few like that one will make a good voyage though, and if it's good enough we can get the foremast restepped, the starboard furnace rebuilt, and other things that we need."

"So we can go in search of more of the same."

"Aye, well, that's the nature of things, Mistress Buell." Tench shrugged. "Everything eats, and is eaten. It's true, though, that a close view of the nature of things can be distressing."

Meghan looked at the boats towing the whale toward the ship. A wide swath of red spread out behind the huge mass, and she nodded. "Aye, it can be distressing indeed, Mr. Tench," she said quietly.

Chapter 9

THE PRISON SHIFT WAS CREASED from the weeks it had been in the drawer under the bunk, and Meghan tugged at it and tried to pull out some of the creases as she put it on. She hung up her dress and tied back her hair, and tugged at the shift again as she walked back along the passageway and out to the deck.

The men were gathered at the waist of the ship on the port side, and they had finished putting the flensing platform in place over the whale in the water by the ship. Several were standing on the platform and cutting on the whale with boat spades, wide blades fixed to long handles, and others were rigging out a heavy spar from the main mast to use as a boom. Buell, Tench, and Porter moved among the men and directed the work.

Meghan walked over to the port rail and looked down at the whale. The water at the side of the ship was red with blood, and alive with sharks. The men on the platform were severing the head, chopping through the tough skin, thick layers of blubber, and

169

flesh and bones with the keen, heavy boat spades. The water boiled round the whale and sharks lunged and wriggled violently to tear mouthfuls loose.

"You be careful, Mistress Buell," Dickon Muir said behind Meghan. "Anybody who fell down there wouldn't last long."

Meghan smiled at him. "I shall, Dickon, and you be careful as well."

"Oh, I will, Mistress Buell. It would take ten men to put me out on that platform, and twenty to keep me there."

Meghan looked down at the whale. The men on the platform had cut a deep fissure across the whale's back behind the head, and the spar rigged to the main-mast was hanging out over the whale. A sharpened cargo hook was on the end of the rope on the spar, and the men dragged it along the side of the whale to snake the skin. It caught, and men pulled on the rope. The whale turned in the water, and the men on the platform took up their boat spades again.

The whale rolled onto its side, sharks clinging to it by their teeth. Most of them slid off, but one held on. Its long, sleek body thrashed as it tried to rip loose a piece of skin and blubber, and a man on the platform stabbed at it with a boat spade. The sharp blade slashed a deep gash down the shark's back, and it re-leased the whale and rolled off. Men on the deck whooped as the shark tumbled into the water, blood gushing from the gaping wound in its back.

The men on the platform chopped with boat spades, extending the fissure down the whale's side. The glossy black on the whale's back melted into bluish-

170

gray along its sides, then into white on its belly. Its large eye was dull and glazed under the bulging overhang of its brow, and its mouth was standing open. The mouth was enormous, long and slender, with teeth in the lower jaw.

The blades cut rapily through the soft underbelly, and the whale was rolled on over. It was traditional to ask for a volunteer to fasten the hoist chain onto the whale's head when flensing in shark-infested waters, "What? No volunteer?" Buell called out. There was silence, the men shuffling their feet and eyeing the sharks swarming around the whale. Then a small, wiry old man named Gibbs volunteered.

Gibbs had a reputation among the crew as a comic, and his age and the situation permitted him to be waggishly impudent. He exploited it, arguing with Buell about his payment as the other men listened gleefully. The whale's jaw had no commercial value, but the sailors used the teeth to make scrimshaw and Gibbs demanded the lower jaw and one crown as his payment for chaining the head.

"A crown?" Buell snorted indignantly. "For less than a penneth of work? There's plenty of teeth in that jaw, and that's bloody payment enough! I'd do it myself before I'd pay you a crown!"

"Ahoy, there!" Gibbs barked officiously, turning and stretching to look over other men as he beckoned. "Fetch that rope over here! The captains's going to chain the head!"

Splutters of suppressed mirth broke out among the men, and Tench turned away to hide his smile. Buell flushed, and shook his fist at the old sailor. "You saucy

171

bugger!" he bellowed. "I'll take a rope's end to your sodding back, then I'll throw your scurvy arse down there to those sharks if you don't check your flaming tongue!"

"What did I say, sir?" Gibbs asked in innocent surprise, looking up at Buell. "I thought you wanted to chain the head. But if you don't want to, then I'll do it for the jaw and a crown."

"I'll give you the jaw and one bloody shilling!" Buell roared in Gibb's face. "And not a bleeding farthing more!"

Gibbs looked up at Buell with polite attentiveness and without flinching, undaunted by Buell's anger. He looked away, twisting his face into a droll expression of intense concentration, and a stir of amusement passed through the men. Then he leaped into the air and waved his arms, shouting . "I'll bloody do it! I'll do it for a shilling and the jaw! I'll chain the head for a shilling and the jaw!"

The men roared with laughter, pushing Gibbs back and forth in boisterous horseplay. A man brought a long coil of rope and a heavy cleaver, and the men warned Gibbs of what the sharks would do to him. He put the thong of the cleaver handle over his wrist and adjusted the rope around his waist, telling the men how indigestible the sharks would find him. Then he walked out onto the platform.

The laughter among the men died away as the old man slid over the edge of the platform and dangled from the rope. Gibb's grin became sickly, then faded. The sharks thrashing around the whale churned the water to foam, and the carcass of the whale was pocked with deep holes where sharks had ripped aways pounds of blubber. The side of the whale was only inches out of the water, easily within reach of a shark if one leaped out of the water in its feeding frenzy.

The men let the rope out slowly, lowering Gibbs onto the whale. Gibbs reached for the flipper sticking out stiffly from the whale's side, and grasped it. He clung to it, his bare feet sliding on the whale's slippery skin, then he balanced himself and began creeping toward the whale's head. The men continued to let out the rope and kept it taut over the edge of the platform, breathlessly silent as they watched his progress.

Gibbs crossed the deep fissure the men had cut to separate the head from the trunk of the whale, and eased out onto the head. His feet slipped from under him, and the men pulled on the rope. The rope snapped around the corner of the platform, sliding from the front and along the side, and it went slack. Gibbs slid down the sloped head of the whale toward the water, clawing frantically. Then he slammed the cleaver into the blubber and held onto the handle, his feet inches from the water.

The men pulled the rope taut again, and Gibbs dragged himself higher on the whale's head. He lifted the cleaver out and dig it in higher, and pulled himself farther up. The bulge of the brow was just out of his reach, and he lifted the cleaver out again and threw himself at the bulge. He caught it with his fingers and pulled himself up onto it, then he turned on his stomach and slid toward the whale's mouth.

He clung to the slippery skin, cutting through the

173

blubber and flesh with the cleaver, and digging a hole behind the thick ridge of bone around the upper part of the whale's mouth. The men lowered a heavy chain on the cargo hook, and Gibbs pushed the chain through the hole and put the end links over the hook. Then the men pulled on the rope, lifting Gibbs off the whale's head, dragging him back up to the platform.

The men were laughing again by the time they had Gibbs up to the platform, and they joked with him about his antics when he had fallen. The color was returning to his blanched face, and he clowned and contorted his face in comical expressions of fear. Buell's anger had faded, and he chuckled as he took out his purse and gave Gibbs a shilling. Porter barked orders, and the men began hauling in the rope to hoist the whale's head.

The rope was doubled through a set of heavy blocks, and they squeaked as the men took in the slack in the thick rope. The rope became taut, the men formed into a line and chanted as they heaved on the rope, and the whale's head stirred in the water. The spar flexed and groaned from the tons of pressure on it, and bones broke with dry, snapping cracks as the whale's head began to lift.

The men knelt on the platform and chopped at the thick spine and the smaller bones. The head separated, and the water boiled with sharks savagely attacking it as it lifted out of the water. One clung to it, fifteen feet of gleaming, muscular body wriggling furiously, its wide mouth gorged with a flap of skin and blubber. A man stabbed the shark with a boat spade, and slashed its stomach open. The men cheered as the shark tumbled into the water, its bloody entrails spilling out.

The spar sagged and creaked ominously as it swung around with the whale's head, and the wide expanse of the deck was small in comparison with the huge mass. Tattered shreds of flesh and skin dangled, bloody seawater poured from it, and it brought with it a strong smell of fish, a fatty stench of blubber—the odor of death. It collapsed on the deck, inert and flaccid, seeming never to have possessed life, and the men swarmed around it with knives and boat spades on short handles.

The men cut in straight lines through the tough black skin and the inches-thick layer of fondant-white blubber. Large blocks peeled away and flopped to the deck, and the men threw them into a greasy, quivering pile near the furnaces. The huge, domed skull was carefully opened. It contained quarts of the finest oil and spermaceti, a wax used to make costly candles, and men brought small oak kegs from the hold and filled them with the precious stuff.

The men on the platform loosened a flap of skin and blubber where the whale's head had been severed, and snagged it with the sharpened cargo hook. With other men hauling on the rope and keeping it taut, they cut a line up the whale's body and extended the flap into a long strip of skin and blubber two feet wide. The whale's body slowly turned in the water. The men peeled the skin and blubber from it in a continuous strip. Then they cut the strip into ten-foot lengths as it reached the deck.

Meghan looked around for where she would be most

useful, and joined the men working on the piles of blubber near the furnaces. Several of them were trimming away bits of flesh from the blubber, and cutting it into blocks one foot square. Others took the blocks and turned them into what they called books, slicing the blubber into thin leaves so it would render more quickly, with the skin still attached.

The stench from the mounds of blubber was nauseating, and touching it made Meghan feel queasy. And at first, the men left a wide space around her, then she overcame her nausea, and the men became more accustomed to her prescence and nodded in approval as she sliced the blocks into books with quick slashes. Buell walked by, looked at her, and walked on.

The fires burned hotly, and men stirred the huge iron pots with long paddles to keep the blubber from burning and discoloring the oil. The penetrating, queasy stench of a smoky oil lamp eddied around the furnaces, becoming almost overpowering. Blubber surfaced in the pots, crisp and rendered of oil, and the men dipped it out and threw it into the furnaces. It burned hotly, and clouds of black smoke belched from the furnaces as the fires roared.

Buell, Tench, and Porter frequently passed by the starboard furnace and examined it, and the men put less blubber in the iron pot over it than in the one on the port side. Men brought casks up from the hold and put them in lines by the furnaces, and funneled the thick, pale brown oil into them. The men on the platform finished stripping the blubber from the whale carcass and cast it loose, and the grotesuqe, shapeless mountain of flesh, what was left of the head, made a gigantic splash when the spar swung out and dropped it into the sea.

The men dismantled and stowed the flensing platform, and scrubbed down the deck where the head had been. Buell dismissed those on the off-duty watch, and the activity settled into a routine. Men took full casks to the hold and returned with empty ones, and piled blubber into the pots. Meghan continued slicing the blubber and throwing it into a pile, the men working around her. The sun set, and the breeze carried the thick cloud of greasy black smoke away from the ship as it moved slowly through the waves under light sail.

Dusk was falling when Meghan finished slicing a last piece of blubber and went to the galley. The food she had left cooking slowly was almost ready to eat, and she built up the fire in the stove and carried a bucket and rope out on deck. She dipped up a bucket of water and scrubbed the greasy blubber off her hands and arms, then went back into the galley to finish preparing the meal.

Buell and Tench came in and sat in the wardroom over a bottle of rum from the lazarette, and Meghan filled the plates with food and brought them in. Buell was in an ebullient mood from the successful day and from the rum, laughing and talking with Tench about the whale. Meghan put the plates on the table, and returned to the galley and listened to the conversation between them as she ate.

The subject changed. Buell talked about searching for whales in the waters between the two islands of New Zealand. "You'll remember that the best days we had on the last voyage was just outside the entrance to Cook Strait," he said. "And I've been giving that some thought. It could be that we'd find rich whaling grounds in there."

"And it could be that we'd find something else, Captain," Tench said. "I'm eager to find whales to cook, but loath to find a place where I might be cooked. I know of no one else who goes there, and that could very well be the reason. I don't like sailing closed waters when there's something like those Maoris about."

"Closed waters?" Buell sneered. "How much water do you need about you to have open waters? There's more than a hundred miles of clear water at the north end of the opening between those islands, and it's wider than that in some places before the narrows in the Strait."

"Those Maoris think nothing of a hundred miles of water with the canoes they have," Tench replied. "I certainly wouldn't enjoy being off a lee shore or becalmed with such as that lot about. And I always think twice about any danger when a woman is involved."

Buell dropped his spoon on his plate with a clatter, and his voice became impatient. "I've combed these coasts, Mr. Tench, and the only Maoris I've seen was when I called at the Bay of Islands a few years ago. It wouldn't be dangerous, particularly if we keep on the south side of the opening. It's well known that the Maoris on South Island aren't nearly as savage as those on North Island."

"Aye, I've heard that," Tench said doubtfully. "I've also heard that freezing to death is to be greatly preferred over drowning, and I wonder how anyone could know. I'd prefer an end in ripe old age with grandchildren around me to either. You're the captain, though, and it's your decision as to where we go."

Buell grunted, and the two men were silent. Tench continued eating for several minutes, then his spoon rattled on his plate as he put it down and pushed the plate away. Meghan had finished eating, and she rose and crossed the passageway to gather up the dishes. Buell was pouring rum into his pannikin, and he gulped it down and pushed his chair back.

"Well, we've work to do, Mr. Tench."

"You've been up for the best part of twenty-four hours now, Captain," Tench said as he rose from the table. "Mr. Porter and I can take the quarterdeck and keep it through the morning watch, and you can get some sleep."

Buell shook his head as he picked up his hat. "No, a drink of rum now and again keeps me going, and I want to watch that starboard furnace for a while longer. Let's go see how it looks now."

Tench followed Buell out, and they went back out on deck. Meghan finished collecting the dishes, and carried them across to the galley. She washed them and put them away, thinking about the conversation between Buell and Tench. And she thought about what she had read and heard concerning the fierce, warlike natives who inhabited New Zealand.

The thick column of black smoke reached far into the sky at one side of the ship, soaking up the moonlight and obscuring the stars. The men around the furnaces were dark silhouettes against the ruddy glare of the roaring fires as they stirred the pots and ladled oil into casks. The sounds of the ship and the breeze masked the noises they made, and they looked like silent shadows moving about in a grisly ritual.

Meghan banked the fire in the galley for the night, then went to bed. The events of the day kept her awake. She thought about the conversation about the Maoris, and the memory of the dying convulsions of the whale continued to haunt her. The ship's bell rang the midwatch, and footsteps moved back and forth across the quarterdeck as the watch changed. She drifted off into a shallow, restless sleep.

Sound and movement around her partially awakened her, and the memories of the day's events had turned into a nightmare. Rivers of blood were gushing from the giant body of the whale and turning the sea into a thick, putrid liquid, and the ship was sinking in it. The dull eye in the hideous mountain of flesh of the stripped whale's head was staring accusingly at her. Sharks were gnashing their teeth and waiting for the ship to go down.

She emerged slowly from sleep and the nightmare, impressions vague and dream-like as they registered. Buell was getting into bed beside her. The strong smell of rum triggered a warning in her mind, and she became completely awake. His breathing was labored, as it always was when he had been drinking heavily, and his movements were clumsy. He jerked the covers off her, and she opened her eyes.

The moon shone through the porthole and dimly illuminated his bearded face and thick, hairy body as he crouched over her, naked. The last time had been

180

weeks before, and in the interim her resignation had weakened. His hands pulling at her thighs stirred revulsion and outrage, and in her mind it became comingled with the fading shadows of her nightmare. She almost pulled away from him, crying out.

Then she caught herself, and smothered the outcry in her throat. He began moving, and she struggled to relax. The moon shone on her, but his eyes avoided her and there was no contact beyond that essential to his purpose. It was strangely like the attack on the whale—brutal, implacable, methodical, and without even hate to impart a degree of human emotion. He moved more rapidly as he penetrated, and she closed her eyes and put her arms over her face.

———————— Chapter 10

THE SMOKE BOILED UP FROM the furnaces for three days, and the huge whale yielded more than a thousand gallons of oil. The cliffs along the west coast of South Island were occasionally visible on the horizon as the ship continued south during the three days, the lookouts watching for whales. At the end of the three days, Buell ordered the ship put about, and it sailed back to the north.

Other whalers were sighted in the distance, the victory flag of black smoke rising from some of them as blubber was rendered. A storm swept out of the north and the ship ran before it for a day, all fires extinguished and everything secured as the wind screamed through the rigging. Rain pounded down, and towering waves tossed the ship. Then the storm passed, and the ship turned back to the north.

It was during the midwatch and Meghan was asleep when the ship turned to the east. She had become completely attuned to the ship, her mind subconsciously monitoring its sounds and movements, and the groaning of timbers and the shifting of the bunk awakened her. Buell was on the quarterdeck, and she sat up and looked around in the darkness of the cabin, momentarily puzzled by the heavy list to starboard.

The ship had been sailing across westerly winds for two days, and occasionally tacking upwind at night to stand well off the coast. The list to starboard meant the ship was turning downwind and running in toward the coast, which was dangerous at night. Then she remembered the conversation she had heard between Buell and Tench. The ship was turning into the waters between North and South Islands.

Blocks rattled as the braces were hauled in and the sails trimmed to the new course. The bunk became even again, and the ship pitched with a steady, even movement. Meghan lay down and went back to sleep, and the ship's bell awakened her when it rang the morning watch at four o'clock. She rose and dressed, and went to the galley.

Buell wasn't ready to eat breakfast. Meghan made tea and ate a piece of bread left over from the day before, and went out on deck. The thick darkness before dawn had settled, making the light of the lanterns in the forecastle and by the binnacle seem feeble. The sky was bright with stars, and green phosphorescence swirled in the wake of the ship.

The ship was quiet, with no one moving about on deck, and Porter stood in the faint glow of light from the binnacle. He lifted his hat and spoke as Meghan climbed the steps to the quarterdeck, and crossed the deck to the taffrail. She leaned against the rail and held her hair back against the breeze, and looked around as dawn broke.

A blush of light touched the eastern horizon, then the stars dimmed as the purple sky brightened. The waves near the ship were gray and oily in the flat, first light of dawn. Dawn came, and a mottled mass off the starboard side of the ship dissolved into a shoreline. Waves washed against rocky points and stretches of shingle beach. The sun rose, touching the tops of towering inland mountains miles beyond the shoreline.

Waves stretched away to the northern horizon. The coastline to the south was less than ten miles away. Flocks of gulls dotted the morning sky, and they wheeled and glided around the ship. Meghan took the telescope off the binnacle and looked at the shore. Waves lapped deserted beaches, and the hills were an unbroken wilderness of ferns and other exotic growth. It appeared to be uninhabited, but the stillness had an eerie quality, a feeling of furtive movements just out of the line of sight.

The sun rose higher, and the helmsman rang the forenoon watch on the ship's bell. The watch changed and the men were more subdued than usual, looking at the shore and muttering to each other. Meghan replaced the telescope on the binnacle, and went down to the galley and built up the fire to cook breakfast. Buell and Tench came out of the cabins and sat in the wardroom, yawning and talking sleepily.

Buell and Tench went up to the quarterdeck after they ate breakfast. The ship turned a degree or two to port, angling away from the shoreline, and men bustled about on deck, washing it down. Then Meghan heard the lookout shout shrilly, and pandemonium exploded on deck.

The ship veered to port as Meghan ran along the passageway. The turn tightened, the ship listing heavily, swinging into the wind. Sails boomed as they came aback of the wind, and the ship shuddered from the violent maneuver. Meghan was thrown to one side of the passageway, but she regained her balance and ran out onto the deck.

Men were scrambling about in the rigging and clewing up the sails, and others were working frantically around the whaleboats and preparing to launch them. Buell and Tench were at the boats, bellowing and pushing at the men as the davits swung out over the rails, and Porter stormed at the men aloft from the quarterdeck. Meghan ran to the rail and looked. The ship had rounded the headland of a vast bay, and dead ahead was a school of whales, dozens of them.

Spouts shot up over a wide area in the bay. Meghan climbed the steps to the quarterdeck, and walked along the rail to the stern. The ship wallowed in the water, slowly swinging back into the wind as it seethed with frenzied activity. Buell got his crew into his boat, and blocks chattered as it lowered into the water. Tench's boat came next.

The two boats moved rapidly away from the ship, fanning out toward opposite sides of the whales. The men finished clewing up all of the sails except the main topsails, and the ship turned back into the wind and regained headway. Meghan took the telescope from the binnacle and watched the boats as they approached the whales.

Buell's boat fastened a whale first, and Tench's had

one a moment later. The two boats skidded about as the whales sounded and ran, and the spouts from the other whales disappeared and began appearing again miles to the east. The whales that had been harpooned tried to follow the others, towing the boats to the east. The boats became tiny in the distance, moving back and forth as the whales ran, and the ship slowly followed.

The sun rose to its zenith, and the other side of the bay became a dark line on the horizon as the ship crept through the water, two miles from Tench's boat. The whale towing Tench's boat had tired more quickly than the other one, and the boat made runs at it for the harpooner to stab it with a lance. The whale spouted blood and rolled over in the water. Tench signaled the ship. Men lowered boats and rowed them out to help tow the whale to the ship.

It was a baleen whale, with tons of blubber, hundreds of pounds of valuable whalebone in its mouth. Buell's boat was several miles away, making runs at the other whale. Tench led the other boats out to help Buell after the baleen whale had been towed to the ship.

Men began putting the flensing platform into place over the first whale, and Meghan went to the cabin and changed into one of her old shifts. There were fewer sharks around this time, but enough to make the men cautious. The whale's head was hoisted onto the deck, and men began peeling off the blubber and chopping the whalebone out of the mouth. Meghan worked with the men preparing the blubber for rendering. Smoke from the furnaces rose in a dense column and drifted away on the breeze.

The boats returned to the ship during late afternoon, towing the other whale, and Meghan went to the galley to prepare dinner. The boats thumped against the hull of the ship, settling the whale into place. Blocks squeaked as the boats were hoisted back aboard. Buell and Tench came to the wardroom a few minutes later. Buell was laughing and talking exuberantly.

"By God, there's a fair day's work finished, Mr. Tench," Buell said. "I've passed through here before, and I remarked to myself that whales might feed through here and down by the narrows in some seasons."

"I'll defer to you on that, because you know more about whales than I do, Captain," Tench replied. "We might be able to loiter hereabouts and fill every cask we have to brimming."

"Damn right we'll be able to," Buell said confidently. "And it appears we might be able to do it without having other whalers mucking about alongside of us and getting in our way."

Meghan filled plates with food and took them to the wardroom, then returned to the galley. She ate, listening to their conversation. Soon Buell changed the subject, talking about the captain of a whaler who had sold a cargo of whale oil at the settlement in the Bay of Islands.

"The owners were all set to beach him when he put back into Port Jackson," Buell said. "But that got him out of it. He sold the cargo there, had the funds credited to the owners through the bank in Sydney, then revictualed and had good luck again. Then when he put back into Port Jackson, the owners paid him a premium to stay with the ship."

"Drexler and Suggs would certainly be pleased to have the profits of two voyages out of one," Tench said. "If we put in at the Bay of Islands, could we get something done about the loose stepping on the foremast and that starboard furnace? Drexler and Suggs wouldn't be disposed to argue about the cost if we got two cargoes of oil."

"Bugger that pair," Buell growled. "But I doubt if we could get much in the way of refitting at the Bay of Islands. It's only a bit of a settlement, with a few traders, missionaries, and such. But if we can fill our holds here and sell the cargo at the Bay of Islands, I see no need to return to Port Jackson. We've hardly done more than touch our stores, and we wouldn't need to get much from the Bay of Islands. And if we can take as many as three cargoes before we return, that'll cure all of our worries."

"It would cure mine," Tench laughed. "The mate's share of three full cargoes of oil would more than satisfy me, and your share would be a goodly amount indeed."

"Aye, it would," Buell agreed. "And then Drexler and Suggs could do as they wish, because I could buy shares in a ship and command it, and not have to bother with the likes of them."

Meghan sat up on her stool, listening. Those who lived on land coveted land, acres they could possess as their own, and the goal of any seaman was to own a ship. Her father and brothers had discussed it constantly, and they had invested in cargo shares to try to accumulate capital. Their investments had never produced enough profit to buy shares in a ship, but they had never become discouraged.

She had a feeling of possessiveness toward the *Baleen,* but she also knew that Drexler and Suggs owned the ship. Her father and brothers had included her in their discussions, and even indirect involvement in owning a ship had always been a dream to her. It had been a dream that seemed unattainable, but suddenly it was at least within the realm of possibility. And the discussion about putting into the port at the Bay of Islands was also fascinating, because the ship that Earl Garrity was on went to the Bay of Islands to load lumber.

Buell and Tench finished eating and went back out. The sun was setting when Meghan finished washing the dishes and went out on deck. Men were dismantling the platform and washing the deck, and Meghan joined those preparing the blubber for rendering. At dusk the ship changed course and stood away from the shore for the night, and the off-duty watch went to the forecastle. Meghan dipped up a bucket of seawater and washed, then she went to bed.

Two whales were sighted at dawn the next morning. By early afternoon one of them had been harpooned and brought alongside the ship. The mounds of blubber on the deck were replenished, and the furnaces roared through the night. The narrows of Cook Strait were on the horizon the following morning, and Buell ordered the ship put about. Whales were sighted again, and one was harpooned and towed to the ship by nightfall.

Days passed as the ship continued sailing slowly back and forth through the wide stretch of water west of Cook Strait, smoke constantly boiling from the furnaces. The weather remained fair, and the winds were steady and light. The blubber occasionally diminished to scraps, then the hunt began again. The crew was caught up in the excitement of the rich bounty of whales, and their fears of the Maoris were forgotten.

Clouds gathered in the north, and the sea became heavier. The starboard furnace remained a constant concern, the rendering pot on it always filled with less blubber to reduce the pressure on the bricks, and even less was put in it when the pitching of the ship increased. The threatening clouds gradually covered more of the sky over a period of days, the storm line slowly moving south, and the waves became higher and more broken.

The storm front passed at night, while Meghan was in bed, and it awakened her. Buell was in the bunk with her, and he rose, dressed quickly, and went out. Meghan lay in the bunk, listening to the rain pounding on the quarterdeck as the ship rolled and pitched. The thought of the hot, highly-flammable whale oil washing around in the huge pots just above the roaring fires in the furnaces kept her awake. In a while, she rose and dressed.

The rain had passed when she went out on deck. Darkness was thick, and the wind whipped flames out of the openings in the furnaces, and the wet deck gleamed ruddily. Buell and Tench were looking at the starboard furnace. The level of oil and blubber in both pots was low, but oil still occasionally spilled over the edges and made flames lick up the sides of the pots. Several of the men working around the furnaces had tied crude bandages over burns where scalding oil had spilled on them.

Dawn broke slowly under the dark clouds, and light spread over the green, foaming waves buffeting the ship. The main force of the storm line had passed to the west, behind the ship, but rain showers hung down from the clouds within a few miles of the ship. The ship was angling back in toward the shore, and the shoreline ahead was a broken mass of fiords and rocky islands jutting out of mist and fog.

Meghan prepared breakfast out of cold leftovers from the day before, and Buell and Tench came to the wardroom and ate. Three days had passed since whales had been sighted and the pile of blubber on the deck was small. Buell was considering having the fires in the furnaces extinguished until the stormy weather passed. He and Tench discussed it as they ate, then they went back out on deck.

A rain shower swept down on the ship while Meghan was washing the dishes. Buell and Tench came in to get their oilskins from the cabins, and went out again. Meghan finished the dishes, and stood in the doorway at the end of the passageway and looked out. Buell had decided against extinguishing the fires in the furnaces. The fires still burned, and the men working around the furnaces were vague shadows through the downpour of rain and swirling clouds of smoke.

The rain slackened and left behind an airy freshness

as it moved toward the shore. Low clouds and rain drifted away in front of the ship, and the lookout shouted from the crow's nest. Buell and Porter ran down from the quarterdeck, shouting orders, and men scrambled to launch the boats. Meghan crossed the deck to the rail. Whale spouts were lighter spots in the murky gray of the thin mist ahead of the ship.

A rain shower drifted in, and the boats disappeared as they pulled away. The rain passed, and the boats were barely visible in the distance, through the haze. They were several miles from the ship, and one had harpooned a whale. It was moving rapidly through the water, and the other boat followed it. The boats vanished into another rain shower.

The rain showers ended during the afternoon, and the sun broke through the clouds. The boats came into sight north of the ship, both of them on the harpoon line to tire the whale more quickly. The ship followed the boats north, away from the storm, and the clouds became more scattered. The boats took turns closing in on the whale for the harpooners to stab it with lances, then the men in them signaled the ship.

It was late afternoon by the time the boats towed the whale to the ship, and the men worked hurriedly to flense it before darkness fell. The waves had become a high, steady swell in the wake of the storm, and the men working around the furnaces were able to put more blubber into the pots. Meghan prepared dinner and washed the dishes after Buell and Tench had eaten. Then she went out on deck to help with the blubber, working until the off-duty watch was dismissed.

Hours later, she was jolted from sleep by an outburst of hoarse screams and panic-stricken shouts on deck. Buell leaped out of the bunk and pulled on his clothes, and left the cabin door open. Tench ran out of his cabin at the same time. The bedlam on deck carried down the passageway, along with a glare of raging flames. Meghan sprang out of the bunk, struggled into her shift, and ran out on deck.

The deck from the starboard furnace to the rail was a mass of liquid fire, and flames were leaping up and licking around the shrouds and rigging. Bricks under one end of the furnace had crumbled. The furnace and the rendering pot on it were tilted sharply, and more oil gushed from the pot with each roll of the ship. Men raced about around the flames and others poured out of the forecastle. Three or four who had been burned were screaming in pain.

Porter and others were pulling a burned man out of the oil, and Tench bellowed at men to get buckets and rope to dip up seawater. Buell ran to men who were milling about, and he roared at them and shoved them toward the water butt. Men ran into the forecastle and brought out buckets and ropes. Those with Buell gathered around the water butt and pushed on it.

The water butt toppled lazily, and a wave of water poured across the deck, sweeping the burning oil ahead of it, washing it into the scuppers. The burning oil flowed over the side of the ship, still burning as it spilled down into the waves, and the ship left a trail of fire behind it. Scattered spots of oil still burned on the deck and flames raced up the tarred rope of the rigging. Men dipped up seawater and dashed it on the flames.

Meghan joined the men dipping up seawater, working in silent, furious desperation. They tossed water into the rigging and doused the flames licking up into it. They threw water on burning pools of oil along the edge of the deck to wash it overboard. Darkness closed in as the flames were smothered, and men brought lanterns out of the forecastle.

The injured men were clustered in front of the forecastle, their faces pale and drawn with pain. Dickon Muir's left hand and arm, and Gibbs's legs and feet had been severely burned. A man named Hites had fallen in the burning oil on the deck, and his head, chest, and shoulders were ghastly in the dull, yellow light. Others had less serious burns. A man named Johnson had a broken arm. Meghan took them to a corner of the deck below the quarterdeck, and went to the cabin to get the medicine chest.

The decking had almost burned through in places. Some planks were too charred and weak to support a man's weight. The main backstays had burned in two, and they dangled in the breeze as the mainmast leaned forward at a dangerous angle. The starboard main rigging had been damaged, and braces and other rigging was ruined.

The ship was a living entity to Meghan, and she felt crushed by the devastation. Buell was somber and brusque as he sent men aloft to furl the sails on the mainmast and to rig out temporary stays to support the mast. He surveyed the damage with Tench and Porter. The men cautiously climbed along the spars on the teetering mast, furling the sails. They dropped ropes from the mast table. Men on the deck snubbed the ropes to the rails, and pulled them taut to hold the mast steady.

Meghan looked at the injured men, busying herself to take her mind off the ship. Hites appeared to be beyond help. His hair was burned away, his face was blistered and swollen, and glistening liquid oozed from blisters on his chest and shoulders. He appeared to be unconscious, and a keening sound came from his throat as he breathed. Large blisters covered Dickon's left hand and arm, and Gibbs's legs and feet. Johnson's arm appeared to have an extra joint in the forearm, and the skin bulged outward from the pressure of the end of the broken bone.

A set of lancets and cups for bleeding was in a leather case in the top of the medicine chest, with two books on medicine and a Book of Common Prayer under it. Another leather case contained pliers, punches, and a small mallet for extracting teeth. Vials of emetics, purges, and various popular remedies were nested in cotton tow and bandages to keep them from breaking. Several of the bandages were stiff with dried blood and pus, of proven effectiveness because of the wounds they had bound had healed.

Most of the men with minor burns had rejoined the others, but two with blistered feet remained. The men waited and watched Meghan as she leafed through the books, trying to appear confident, but inwardly quaking with uncertainty. She found nothing useful in the books, and she put them aside and took a pewter spoon and vial of tincture of opium from the medicine chest. Gibbs and Dicon winced from the bitter taste of the liquid.

Meghan put the vial back in the chest, and looked through the others. The woodcut label on one proclaimed it as a healing unguent for cuts, burns, and bruises, as well as a sovereign remedy for hair loss, unwanted hair, itch, boils, sores, and other diseases of the skin. She poured a liberal amount on the three men's burns, spreading it carefully with a wad of cotton tow, then daubed it on the other two men's blistered feet.

The two men with burned feet limped away, and Meghan gave Johnson a large spoonful of the tincture of opium. Dickon and Gibbs had become drowsy from the effects of the powerful narcotic, and Johnson dozed off after a moment. Meghan went to the galley for pieces of firewood to use for splints, and she straightened Johnson's forearm and bound it firmly between the pieces of wood.

Buell, Tench, and Porter went down into the hold to examine the damage below the deck. They came back up a few minutes later, and Meghan could hear their conversation as they walked away from the hatch. The mainmast stepping had been loosened when the mast had tilted forward, and some of the main beams under the decking had been damaged by fire. Buell intended to anchor somewhere along the coastline and have the men cut lumber to make temporary repairs. They would repair the foundation under the starboard furnace with spare bricks that had been brought along.

"There's no question that we're not seaworthy," Tench said with no real conviction. "But we need to put in somewhere for repairs. Perhaps we could make do with patching the rigging, and go to the Bay of Islands. We'd be in a sad state indeed if Maoris found us at anchor in a cove along here."

"All the Maoris I've seen will fit into my pocket, with room left over," Buell replied impatiently. "We're here to take whales, and we have empty casks. In any event, we've no fresh water, and there's no sign of rain. I'll take the longboat and search along the shore for a good anchorage. You keep the ship hereabouts till I return."

Tench nodded and said nothing more. Buell shouted and men crossed the deck to the boat, and began clearing gear out of the way to lower it into the water. Porter and Tench walked toward the steps to the quarterdeck, and Tench looked at Meghan and the injured men lying on the deck. He turned and crossed the deck and came to her.

"How are the men, Mistress Buell?"

"Johnson's arm should heal easily enough, and Dickon and Gibbs should be all right in time so long as their burns don't become septic. As for poor Hites, though, it's in God's hands."

"Aye, I didn't think he'd have much of a chance. When someone is burned about the head like that, they rarely recover." He looked back at Meghan. "I suppose you heard what the captain said, and I trust you're not too alarmed at the prospect of putting in along the shore. It's commonly said that the Maoris on South Island aren't a mark as savage as those on North Island. Beyond that, we have a goodly number of men and arms for all of them."

Meghan shrugged. "I'd as lief keep well away from the shore, but we must do something about poor *Baleen*, mustn't we? The very sight of her state fills me with despair."

"There speaks a Conley," Tench said. "If it would make you feel better about being at anchor, I'll teach you how to load and fire a pistol."

"Teach a dog how to bark, Mr. Tench," Meghan laughed. "My brothers taught me to shoot when I was no more than eight or nine, and I can snuff a candle with a pistol ball at ten paces."

"Can you now?" he exclaimed in amusement. "You are a rare one indeed, Mistress Buell." He chuckled and shook his head, looking at the men again. "Shall I have these men taken to the forecastle? Some of the others can look after them."

"No, I've little enough to do, Mr. Tench, and I believe they'll do better in the fresh air. The sun will be warm soon, though, and it would be good if you'd have a spare sail put up as an awning."

"Yes, I'll see to it immediately," Tench promised. The men went to get the sail, and Meghan closed the medicine chest and stepped to the rail. The men were lowering the boat, and it thumped against the rail as it settled in the water. Buell and four men climbed over the rail and jumped down into it, and the boat went away from the ship.

Meghan looked at the boat, then at the shoreline beyond it. The shore was five miles away, a broken line of cliffs and rocky points reaching out into the water.

Morning mist was still rising from the densely-forested hills that ran back from the shore. Everything was so peaceful—and so threatening.

Chapter 11

THE BOAT DISAPPEARED, THEN RETURNED during early afternoon. Buell ordered men aloft to make sail on the foremast and mizzenmast, and the ship sailed several miles along the coast. Then Buell ordered the ship put about, and it tacked slowly back and forth across the wind, waiting for the onshore tide to run. Meghan scanned the shoreline, but she could see no sign of the cove that Buell had found.

The ship turned toward the shore, and Meghan could still see nothing more than cliffs and rocky points foam-washed. Then she saw a narrow opening in a cliff. The ship sped toward it, pushed by the wind and carried along by the tide. Men climbed into the rigging and out on the yards, ready to rapidly clew up the sails.

The cliffs on each side of the entrance drew closer, towering above the ship, and the sound of the breaking waves became a drumming roar. The winds became erratic, and the ship started through. Waves washing around the foot of the cliffs made treacherous eddies that threatened to wreck them.

The entrance opened out into a small cove, a sheltered stretch of water a few hundred yards wide. Forested slopes on the west side of the cove rose up to a mountain, its upper reaches obscured by veils of mist. A shingle beach was on the east side, and the hills above it were covered with ferns, copses of trees, and outcroppings of rock. On the south side of the cove, a wide creek rushed around boulders and poured across the beach and into the cove.

The ship yawed to one side as the waves pushed it to calm water. Buell shouted at the men on the bow to cast the forward anchor, and it splashed into the water. The line snaked out and became taut, and the stern of the ship slowly sung around the bow pointed toward the entance as the anchor caught and held. Buell nodded to the men holding the stern anchor, and they let it go.

The roar of the waves faded to a background noise, and the cove seemed very quiet and still. The ferocity and cunning of the cannibal Maoris was the subject of tales told among seamen from Liverpool to Calcutta, and the men looked around apprehensively. Buell barked orders, and the men lined up on deck. Tench and Porter went down into the lazarette, and came back with muskets and cutlasses for the men.

Buell led a heavily-armed party ashore, and explored the hills above the beach. They returned, having found no sign of Maoris, and took the fresh water casks to the creek to fill them. Tench and Porter set other men to dismantling the starboard furnace. Still others built up the fire in the port furnace, and began rendering the remainder of the blubber.

Thick smoke arose from the furnace in a black column that could be seen for miles, and some of the men worried about it. The wind became stronger near sunset, scattering the smoke. Clouds moved from the land and covered the coastline. Soft rain began falling as Buell and the men returned with the casks of fresh water. Meghan adjusted the sail over the injured men so it would keep the rain off.

She built up the fire in the galley and prepared food for the injured men. Hites was still unconscious, moaning softly with each breath. Meghan gave Dickon and Gibbs a spoonful of the tincture of opium after they had eaten. She went to bed very tired, but worry about the Maoris and the pacing of the guards on the quarterdeck over the cabin kept her awake most of the night.

Hites was dead the next morning, and men wrapped the body in sail cloth and lowered it into a boat. It was still raining, a gentle downfall that pattered on the hood of Meghan's oilskins as she sat in the stern of the boat by the body and the men rowed to the beach. The men carried the body up the hill above the beach and dug a grave. Buell read the service. After the funeral, they began to cut lumber to make repair to the ship.

The ship teemed with activity. The carpenter and a crew of men took up the burned decking, while another work gang got drums of spare cordage from the hold to repair the rigging. The last of the blubber had been rendered during the night and the fire in the port furnace was extinguished. The men finished dismantling the starboard furnace and began taking the brick foundation apart. The solid crack of axes on wood came from the hill above the beach, echoing across the cove.

Johnson rejoined the other men, with his broken arm in a sling. Dickon and Gibbs were in more pain than the day before, and their burned limbs were massively swollen and covered with blisters. Meghan looked at the medical text again, finding obscure and conflicting advice, and she did what she could. She bled both of them and gave them large amounts of liquid, as well as tincture of opium to allay their pain.

The rain stopped during late afternoon and the sky began to clear. Next morning was bright and sunny. The carpenter and his crew had removed most of the burned decking, and heavy beams showed through the gaping holes. Men sat around the rails and tarred and spliced rope. Porter and Tench looked through the bricks men were removing from the foundation of the starboard furnace, and those that were cracked from the heat were discarded. Trees had been felled in a thicket on the hill above the beach. Buell had men digging a saw pit.

When the saw pit was finished, logs were rolled down the hill and set in place. Pairs of men used whipsaws to cut boards from the logs, with one man in the pit, the other on the log over the pit. More trees were cut down to saw into beams and braces, and the lumber was floated across the cove to the ship. The ship's carpenter picked boards to replace the decking, grumbling and cursing the green wood that he trimmed and shaped to fit the gaps in the deck.

Anxiety about the possiblity of a Maori attack

faded as one peaceful day followed another, and Buell reduced the guards at night to an armed anchor watch at the bow and stern of the ship. Meghan's apprehension also faded, and she began going ashore to take walks. At first she walked back and forth along the beach in sight of the ship, then she began taking walks in the hills.

The vining plants, ferns, and trees were different from any she had ever seen before, and they grew in luxuriant profusion. It was also the first time in her life that she had been without other people very close to her. Away from the sounds of the work on the ship, she experienced a deeper peace than any she had experienced in the past amid the stillness of a wilderness that had been undisturbed for centuries.

Tiny, beautiful flowers grew under the lacy, delicate fronds of the ferns along the creek, and the lofty heights of the mountain west of the cove was majestic. Meghan walked up the creek to bathe and wash clothes, and spent warm, sunny afternoons walking across the hills above the beach. The trees on top of the hills were stunted and gnarled by storms that raged along the coast, and the coastline itself was wild and rugged.

Buell glared at her when he happened to be where he could see her when she rowed a boat to or from the beach, but he said nothing to her about it. Tench insisted that she carry a firearm when she went ashore, and she took a long, heavy flintlock pistol with her to satisfy him. She settled into a routine, cooking, caring for Dickon and Gibbs, and rowing a boat to the beach for a walk every afternoon.

Dickon and Gibbs improved, the swelling subsided in their burned limbs, the dead skin sloughing off. When the vial of unguent from the medicine chest was almost empty, Meghan discovered that it was whale oil mixed with tea, and she prepared another batch. The two men regained their strength and went back to work.

The last of the lumber was cut and smoothed, and the repairs were rapidly completed. The rigging went back up, looking much as it had before the fire, and the ship vibrated with resounding thuds as wooden wedges were driven into place to tighten the mainmast stepping. Buell and Tench watched the men closely as they rebuilt the foundation for the starboard furnace with extra bricks from the hold, and the furnace was reassembled.

The last adjustments were made to the rigging during the afternoon on a clear, warm day. Tench took men in a boat to refill the fresh water casks that had been emptied while the ship was at anchor, and Buell walked about and looked at the repairs once more. Meghan had seen by reading the ship's log that he had been closely watching the tide, and an ebb tide would occur at sunset. At the same time, the water cooled more rapidly than the land at the end of a warm day, which could produce an offshore breeze that would carry the ship out to sea.

Tench and the men returned to the ship with the casks, and the casks and boat were hauled aboard. The ship was quiet after the bustle of noise and activity. All over the ship there was an atmosphere of expectant waiting.

Discarded boards were scattered around the abandoned saw pit. Raw stumps jutted up in the gaps in thickets on the hill. Brush had been trampled and crushed where the men had worked and dragged logs, and there were other signs of the brief occupancy of the cove that would disappear within a few seasons. Meghan looked at the hills and at the creek, remembering the beautiful hidden nooks and glades she had found, and she felt a nostalgic sense of leavetaking.

Tench came up the steps to the quarterdeck. "We'll soon be on our way, Mistress Buell, and far more shipshape than when we arrived."

Meghan looked up at the rigging and at the dark patches of the green wood on the main deck. "Aye, there's no question about being more shipshape. How long will the mainmast stepping remain firm?"

"Well, that green wood will shrink as it seasons," he replied cautiously. "But we have a goodly number of casks filled, and it won't be long until we have a full cargo if our good fortune holds. It should last long enough for us to get where more permanent repairs can be made."

Buell, Porter, and the helmsman came up the steps. The helmsman went to the wheel. Buell glanced at the sun and looked around at the cove as he crossed the deck to the binnacle. The sun was deep in the west, and the ship bobbed in the low swell. The tide was beginning to run out, leaving a wet line on the beach above the reach of the lapping waves.

"Set the rudder amidship," Buell said. "Mr. Porter, we'll go out under the fore tops and main t'gallant and tops. Put the starboard watch in the rigging and the man the windlass."

The helmsman spun the wheel and centered the rudder, and Porter shouted at the men as he went down to the main deck. Men leaped into the rigging and scrambled up. Others gathered around the windlass. Then the ship was quiet again, men clinging to spars and standing around the windlass, waiting.

The sun was below the cliffs by the entrance to the cove, and the light had the warm tones of sunset. The trees around the cove stirred as an offshore wind began blowing. Waves churned into foam in eddying currents, and the ship tugged at its anchor ropes as the tide ran out more rapildy. Buell stepped to the edge of the quarterdeck above the main deck.

"Mr. Porter, make sail and hoist anchor!"

Porter bellowed at the men, and the ship came alive. The men at the windlass stamped and chanted as they heaved their weight against it and marched around it. It groaned as it turned. Sails rumbled and spilled down into place, and the men in the rigging climbed about among the spars, trying to outdo each other in speed and daring.

The line on the bow anchor tightened and snapped with strumming vibrations that quivered through the ship. The anchor pulled free of the bottom with a jerk, and the men ran around the windlass and turned it rapidly. The sails rippled and filled with the breeze, becoming taut as, one after another, they unfolded.

The stern anchor began dragging, and the men on the windlass secured the bow anchor and seized a turn on the stern anchor line around the windlass. They threw their weight against the spokes on the windlass again, stamping and chanting. The line hummed with tension, then the stern anchor pulled free from the bottom and the ship urged toward the entrance to the cove.

The ship picked up speed, pitching in the higher waves near the entrance, and the tall, formidable cliffs loomed clear. Then the cliffs were on both sides, almost blotting out the fading light, and the ship yawed from side to side in the currents. The ship nosed on through the entrance, the light brightening into a golden sunset, and the men climbed higher in the rigging and unfurled more sail.

The coastline was far behind when darkness fell, and the ship stood off the coast for the night. A whale was sighted north of the ship at dawn the next morning and the ship followed it through the day, tacking slowly back and forth across the wind. The whale was lost when night fell, but a school of whales was sighted to the north the following morning.

The wind was favorable, blowing from the west, and the south coast of North Island rose above the horizon as the ship closed on the whales. The boats were lowered into the water, and a whale was harpooned. The coastline to the north became more distinct as the hours passed and the whale grew weaker and more fatigued. Then the whale was killed and towed to the ship.

The coastline was still within sight when darkness fell, and it remained in sight at daybreak the next morning. A whale was sighted and the ship closed on it, and again the boats were lowered. The whale was harpooned, and the spouts of another school of whales were sighted in the far distance.

The proximity of the ship to the coast of North Island caused grumbling among a few of the men, but the uneventful stay in the cove had allayed fears of Maoris. And the crew had reason for satisfaction. Most of the casks in the hold had been filled, and the area teemed with whales. The voyage promised to be unusually short and highly profitable, and the crew would receive a bonus wage and have liberty as soon as the ship put into a port.

The furnaces belched smoke the day and night, and lines of casks on the deck were filled with oil and taken back to the hold. The ship sailed back and forth along the coast, finding whales every few days, and it occasionally came close enough to the coast for Meghan to see details of the bay, rocky points, and other features through the telescope. She once saw a faint haze of gray on a hill that looked like smoke, but Tench looked through the telescope and was unable to see it.

Then she distinctly saw smoke early one morning when Buell was asleep in the cabin and she was on the quarterdeck with Tench. The sun was just above the horizon and the coast was less than fifteen miles away, its details distinct even to the naked eye. A wide river gushed into the ocean and made a semicircle of lighter color against the emerald green, and a cloud of gray woodsmoke rose into the clear morning air from a fold in the hills overlooking the river.

Tench took the telescope and looked where she pointed. He lowered the telescope and closed it, his lips pursed and his brow creased in a faint frown. "Aye, there's no doubt that it's smoke, Mistress

210

Buell," he said. "It could be from a small forest fire, but that doesn't seem likely. It's probably from a cannibal village in those hills."

"If we can see that smoke, they can certainly see the smoke from our furnaces as well as our sails."

"That's true," he agreed quietly. "The sun is just right to outline our smoke and our sails, and they could be seen clearly from the coast in any event."

Meghan turned and looked up at the sails. The ship was on a port tack, sailing close to the wind and angling slowly away from the coast as it crabbed through the water. "We'd get a better bit on the wind if we put about, and that would take us away from the coast more rapidly."

"No, we're in a bight of sorts along here," Tench replied. "There's a point of land over the horizon behind us, and another ahead. The one behind reaches out much farther, and we couldn't clear it if we came to starboard now. But we'll be able to within an hour or two, and perhaps that's what the captain will do. He'll be up on the forenoon watch."

He lifted the telescope and looked again, and Meghan crossed the deck to the steps. The lookout was watching for whales, looking out to sea instead of landward, but he glanced around and saw the smoke. He shouted down to the quarterdeck about it, and men crowded to the rail and looked for the smoke, frowning with worry.

Meghan went to the galley and built up the fire, and prepared breakfast. The ship's bell rang the forenoon watch, and Buell came out of the cabin a few minutes later and sat in the wardroom. Tench came in and

211

spoke to him quietly, and they went out on deck together. They returned, and from the conversation Buell was less than alarmed by the smoke.

Meghan filled plates with food and took them in. Back in the galley, she listened to Buell and Tench as they discussed the few remaining empty casks in the hold. It was clear that Buell wanted to fill them.

The lookout shouted, and a babble of voices rose up on deck. Porter ran into the passageway, calling for Buell.

"Captain Buell! Three canoes full of cannibals have put out from the shore, and they're overhauling us!"

Tench and Buell leaped up and ran out. Meghan went up the steps to the quarterdeck and scanned the shoreline. The mouth of the river was now barely visible to the naked eye, and the hills where she had seen the smoke were a blur in the distance. And she could see no canoes off shore.

Buell scanned with the telescope, then held it still. Meghan looked where the telescope pointed, and saw them. They were miles away, but their canoes looked much larger than she had expected. She had thought of canoes as comparable as small rowboats, but these appeared to be as large as small ships.

She moved along the rail to Tench and plucked at his sleeve. "They seem quite large, Mr. Tench."

He glanced down at her and nodded as he looked back at the canoes. "Maori canoes run to forty or fifty feet, and they can have up to sixty or eighty men in them. And they're fast."

Buell lowered the telescope and closed it. "All hands on deck, Mr. Porter. Man the braces to take the starboard tack. Mr. Tench, secure the ship to wear the wind."

Wearing across the wind to the starboard tack took much less time than letting the ship fall off the wind and come about, but it was a violent maneuver. Tench shouted at men and pointed to boats and the furnaces as Porter bellowed at the men in the forecastle. Meghan ran into the galley.

A bedlam of noise carried along the passageway from the deck. Voices shouted hoarsely and bare feet pounded back and forth. Meghan closed cabinet doors, latched them and the stove door as well. Then she held onto the table and braced herself.

Timbers groaned as the bow of the ship began swinging to the left. A quivering shudder gripped the ship, becoming a forceful shaking as the bow continued turning into the wind. Things tumbled and rattled in the cabinets, and the lantern hanging from the ceiling danced wildly. Sails came aback of the wind with thunderous booms, and the ship slowed with a forceful jerk. A cabinet door banged open and dishes went flying. Then the vibrations began to die away as the bow continued to turn. The deck canted and the ship took the starboard tack.

Blocks were rattling as men hauled on the braces to trim the yards. The men were worked in grim, silent haste, no longer stamping and chanting. Others climbed in the rigging and unfurled more sail. The ship heeled sharply to the left as the sails filled. Meghan climbed the steps to the quarterdeck and looked at the canoes. They had changed direction, and were following the ship.

The ship picked up speed, and waves burst into spray at the bow. The men climbed back down from the rigging, and Tench and Porter returned to the quarterdeck. Buell stood at the stern taffrail and looked at the canoes through his telescope. They were closer, and Meghan could make out details. A high, carved prow and tall sternpost jutted up on each canoe. They were filled with warriors, far outnumbering the men on the ship. Moving in unison long lines of twenty or more paddles flashed up and down on both sides of each canoe. And they were slowly closing on the ship.

Buell lowered the telescope and turned away from the rail. "Lash the helm. Mr. Porter, break out cargo nets and have them hung along the waist. Mr. Tench, open the lazarette and issue arms. You'll command the port watch on the main deck, and I'll have the starboard watch up here on the quarterdeck."

The helmsman took a length of rope from the binnacle to tie the wheel. Meghan followed Tench and Porter as they went back down to the main deck. Porter called to men and pointed to a hatch cover. Tench beckoned men and opened the door to the lazarette. Meghan went down into the small, cramped space with Tench. Cases of port and rum were stacked there and racks of muskets and cutlasses and long, steel-tipped boarding pikes lined the walls. Meghan gathered up an armload of weapons and carried them up to the deck.

Porter had taken the cargo nets out of the hold and men were stretching them along the waist of the ship, tying them to shrouds and braces and draping them over the rails. Meghan helped the men carry up weapons, shot, and gunpowder. The men finished hanging the cargo nets and armed themselves. Tench went to his cabin for his sword. Porter picked out two pistols and a cutlass for Buell and led the starboard watch up to the quarterdeck.

Meghan loaded two pistols and pushed them under her belt. She remained on the main deck and resisted the impulse to go to the quarterdeck for another look at the canoes. Tench came back out, adjusting his sword belt, and he assembled the men of the port watch. He arranged them in two ranks in the center of the deck, ready to defend either or both sides of the ship. Dickon was among the men, holding a boarding pike in his right hand. Old Gibbs was just as ready to fight.

Meghan thought Tench was going to ask her to go to her cabin. But he changed his mind, and he smiled encouragingly. He appeared nonchalant about the situation, his saturnine features composed and reflecting no fear. Meghan tried to control the shrinking fear she felt, forcing a quick smile in response to his, and she stiffened her legs to stop the trembling in her knees.

A distant, rhythmic sound carried over the hum of the wind and the noises of the ship and the waves. It was a melodic, throbbing noise, pulsing the air. Then Meghan realized it was the Maoris, many deep voices joined together in a triumphant, ringing chant as they drew closer to the ship. And the chant seemed to strike a chord within her, awakening some primitive, deep-seated fear.

The men looked at each other, color draining from their faces. Tench laughed. "Well, they're not the only ones who can sing, are they? Let's have a verse or two of 'Tar the Bosun's Queue,' shall we? It won't offend you, will it, Mistress Buell?"

Meghan swallowed, and tried to keep her voice steady. "If you know a chantey more saucy than those my brothers were accustomed to sing, Mr. Trench, you'd blush yourself when you sang it."

Tench's booming laughter rang out again. "Well said, Mistress Buell! Well said indeed! All right, let's see if we can make them hear us, lads!"

He started the chantey, and the men began to join in. Their voices were weak and uncertain at first, stark fear showing on many faces, then they took heart. The men on the quarterdeck also picked up the chantey, and men stamped and tapped boarding pikes against the deck as they sang. Meghan was a few yards from the men, and at first their singing drowned out the sound of the Maori warriors. Then she heard it again, a pounding, ominous roar that grew louder as the canoes approached.

The ship was heeled sharply under the heavy spread of sail, and the port rail was much lower than the starboard. It was the logical side for the Maoris to attack, and Tench slowly moved to the port rail as he kept the men singing. He glanced behind the ship when he reached the rail, then he beckoned the men to the rail and deployed them in a line, still keeping them singing.

The Maori chant thundered, the air seeming to vibrate with it. Now the canoes were only yards behind the ship. Tench kept the men singing, walking back and forth behind them slapping their shoulders. The chantey clashed with the chant. Meghan checked the priming in her pistols, her hands shaking, and moved closer to the men. The Maoris stopped chanting and began to shriek.

A canoe struck the stern of the ship with a resounding thud, then another struck it. The popping of muskets on the quarterdeck was a thin sound over the bedlam of bloodthirsty whooping. A canoe swept alongside the ship by the port rail, its tall, carved prow and sternpost as high as the rail, and iron grappling hooks slammed into the rail and caught. Then the Maoris swarmed onto the net draped over the rail.

A few had spears, but most of them hacked at the net and the men with sharp hardwood swords and heavy axes. Their faces were covered with lines of deep, dark tattooing, each a mask of savagery, and their bronze bodies were large and muscular. Muskets popped, and the men jabbed and hacked with pikes and cutlasses. Two warriors seemed to take the place of each one that fell. Tench was everywhere, shouting encouragement, pulling at men to fill gaps in the thin line, thrusting with his sword.

Meghan was numb, beyond fear. She blindly fired, reloaded, and fired again without looking for or seeing any effect the shots made on the seething confusion in front of her. Then she saw that a warrior had almost cut through the net in a gap between two men. She stepped closer to the rail, and aimed the pistol.

Tench also had seen the warrior, and thick drops of blood dripped from his sword as he ran to stop him.

217

The warrior froze, his keen axe lifted. His eyes met Meghan's as she looked down the barrel at him from a distance of six feet. Smoke puffed from the pan as the hammer fell. The sound of the pistol was lost in the pandemonium.

A large red spot appeared in the mass of tattooed lines on the warrior's forehead. His mouth opened, an expression of astonishment on his face, and he tumbled backwards and disappeared. Tench stopped beside Meghan and said, "Good shot, Mistress Buell!" before he ran a Maori through with his sword.

Meghan's fear faded into grim determination to fight for her life and her ship. She lifted the other pistol and aimed at a tattooed face. The warrior fell. A pike rolled at her feet, and she peeled it up and drove the sharp steel tip into a brown chest, and the pike was almost jerked from her hands as the warrior dropped. She backed away, looking around, then charged at a warrior who was fighting a wounded sailor.

The hardwood sword seemed to come from nowhere, and the blow on her forehead felt like little more than a tap, but she was suddenly on her back, looking up at the sails. There was a numbness in her forehead, but no pain. Then a twinge on the left side of her forehead turned into a searing agony.

Tench bent over her. He took her arm and helped her to her feet. He shouted and pointed to the cabin, then ran back to the rail. Blood flowed from Meghan's forehead and into her left eye. Choking, suffocating rage swelled within her. She wiped the blood from her eye with her sleeve, and began reloading her pistols.

Tench backed away from the rail, pointing to two men and shouting.

"You two there! Fetch some hot oil over here, and let's give them a taste of that! Hold them, lads, and we'll see how they like hot oil!"

The two men ran to the water butt and snatched up buckets, and ran toward the furnace. Meghan pushed her pistols into her belt, following them. Her vision in her left eye blurred, and she wiped her eye with her shoulder as she snatched up the ladle the men used to funnel oil into casks. The men stood aside as she leaped onto the step by the furnace, and dipped the ladle into the pot, and ran to the rail with it.

The ladle sagged on its long handle, oil splashing all over it, and she shouted at men to move aside. One failed to hear her, and he yelped in pain and leaped to one side as the oil spattered on him. Meghan slung the oil through the net, and it caught three warriors full in the face and splashed on others. The warriors fell, their savage, tattooed faced twisted in agony. Tench whooped in delight.

"By God, they don't like that! You two step lively with those buckets! Stand fast, men, and we'll teach them a lesson. Mistress Buell, please do retire to your cabin!"

Meghan ignored him, wiping her eye with her shoulder as she ran back to the furnace. The two men with dripping buckets of oil passed her, grimacing with pain from burned fingers. They tossed the gallons of hot oil through the net in a wave that swept across the warriors and poured down into the canoe. Screams of pain and rage rose up and the noise of battle ebbed.

Fewer warriors were clinging to the net, and the men attacked them furiously.

The rest of the warriors began jumping down into the canoe. The sternpost of the canoe turned away from the ship as the warriors cut the ropes on their grappling hooks. Seething with fury, she dropped the ladle and picked up a fire shovel. She opened the furnace, and scooped up hot coals.

She ran toward the rail with the shovel. Coals spilled from it, falling onto oil spilled on the deck. Flames sprang up. Tench pointed and shouted in alarm, and men ran to stamp out the flames. Meghan reached the rail and heaved the fire and coals through the net. Flames burst up in the net as the fire rained down on the canoes, and men began chopping at the net with their cutlasses.

The canoe turned away from the ship, fire racing along a third of its length. Warriors who had been doused with oil were human torches, flames streaming back from them as they leaped into the sea. Meghan stepped back from the rail, wiping blood from her eye. The men chopped the burning net loose and dropped it into the sea.

"To the quarterdeck, men!" Tench shouted. "You three there, help the others bring oil! Mistress Buell, please go to your cabin! Follow me, men!"

Three other men ran for buckets, and the rest followed Tench. Some were wounded, but they cheered, knowing they had won. Meghan's anger had faded, she felt weary, and throbbing, burning pain enveloped the side of her head. But she gathered strength, and rejoined the fight.

Only part of the Maori force had been able to climb the high stern of the ship, but they vastly outnumbered the men on the quarterdeck. The battle raged, and Tench and his men joined those at the rail. Meghan pushed in among them, firing her pistols. The Maoris began to jump into the sea.

Meghan's strength left her suddenly, and the pain in her head became a dull, throbbing ache that blurred her vision. She crossed the quarterdeck and strumbled down to the cabin to look at herself in the mirror. Her knees almost folded under her when she saw the wound. The tip of the hardwood sword had cut a four-inch gash over her left eye. Blood still oozed from it, and her face was caked with blood.

The cabin spun around her, and she teetered on her feet. Then she gripped herself, drawing in a deep breath and fighting the surge of nausea and dizziness. She opened the drawer under the bunk, found a strip of cotton cloth, and staggered to the galley.

Up on the deck the men were cheering. They had met the dreaded Maoris and defeated them. Meghan filled a basin with water and sat at the table, washing the blood from her face and hair. She felt an intense relief, but she also felt depressed in the aftermath of the battle.

Tench came in with a bottle of rum as she was folding a piece of the cloth to tie around her head. He looked at the cut. "Aye, that's not so bad, Mistress Buell. I'm sure it's painful, but it will soon heal."

"No doubt, but it will leave a large scar, I fear."

"It'll take more than that to spoil your pretty face. Conleys have fought in many battles and have acquitted themselves well, but none better than one did to-day. You helped turn the tide of the battle."

Meghan's melancholy faded, and she smiled. "I ran amok, and I could have burned the ship to the waterline."

Tench dipped water from a bucket with the pannikin and poured rum into the water. "Aye, fire and oil on a ship are dangerous, but all's well that ends well. The cannibals were defeated, we'll soon have a full cargo of oil, and we'll be putting into the Bay of Islands to sell it."

"It's certain we're going there, then?"

"Aye, the captain just said so," he replied, handing her the pannikin. "Drink that, and it will make you feel better."

Meghan took the pannikin, and he went back out. She sipped the rum and water, and her despondent feeling disappeared. A sense of hopeful anticipation replaced it. There was at least a remote possiblity that Earl Garrity would be at the Bay of Islands.

Chapter 12

GULLS CIRCLED THE SHIP IN a noisy clamor as it moved through the low waves inside the headlands of the Bay of Islands. The numerous islands that had given the bay its name were scattered across the wide expanse of deep blue water. The shoreline was an irregular, broken maze of inlets and coves. Some islands were no more than bare, black rocks jutting up from the water, surrounded by the foam of the waves breaking against them. Others were low, furry mounds of foliage etched against the dark hills of the mainland, and a few were large, sprawling masses covered with trees.

Tench climbed the steps to the quarterdeck, lifting his tricorn to Meghan and nodding to Buell. "Good morning, Mistress Buell, and a lovely morning it is and all, isn't it? Well, we had a tolerable passage after all, didn't we, Captain Buell?"

Buell grunted, his eyes red with fatigue from being on the quarterdeck since the midwatch. "It took long enough. Where's Mr. Porter? I believe he was to be on deck for the forenoon watch, not to mention the fact that we're coming into port."

"The forenoon watch has only rung, Captain," Tench replied. "And here he comes now, in fact."

Porter crossed the deck and climbed the steps to the quarterdeck, and lifted his hat as he glanced around and nodded. "It's a fair day to make port, isn't it? And standing off for the night was well advised. Threading these islands in the dark would be hazardous."

"No more so than putting into Port Jackson at night," Buell grumbled. "If we'd had a moon, we'd be at anchor now. And if we were, I should think you'd be ashamed to show your face ashore, Mr. Porter. The state of the rigging wouldn't do credit to a Malacca trader's scow."

Meghan pushed her hair back and leaned against the taffrail, watching the men. Storm damage or temporary repairs were viewed as honorable and unavoidable disorder on a ship entering port, but any other disarray reflected on the officers. The men in the rigging adjusted the folds of furled sails and looked for loose ends of rope to tie up, and those on deck straightened gear and scrubbed the planking.

The ship was moving slowly through the low waves under light sail, and the breeze was coming directly over the stern. A large island with a broken shoreline of rocks was two miles away off the port side of the ship. Meghan looked at it more closely when she saw smoke. Then she saw a cluster of huts in the edge of the trees above a stretch of shingle beach.

The morning sun made deep shadows under the trees, but she could see vague, indistinct figures of people and children moving around the huts. She glanced at the telescope on the binnacle and looked at Buell as he stood talking quietly with Tench. Then she looked back at the island, shading her eyes with a hand, trying to see the people.

The ship passed the island, and a stretch of water between it and a long, low island came into view. Two canoes a hundred feet apart were between the islands, moving slowly through the water as lines of men along the gunwales paddled. Tall, wide frames for drying fish were on an open, sunny beach on the smaller island.

Women and children worked around the fish racks, and the canoes were towing a seine. The canoes were large and looked much like those that had attacked the ship, with tall, ornately carved gunwales and sternposts, and from a distance the men in them appeared the same as the warriors. The canoes looked warlike and threatening, and their use as fishing boats seemed incongruous.

Buell frowned darkly. "If those buggers were off my bow, they'd either get out of my road or they'd find themselves arse over teakettle in the water."

"They look peaceful enough now," Tench commented. "But one wonders how peaceful they'd be on a dark night."

"Night or day, I don't trust the scurvy sods," Buell growled, and he turned and looked at Meghan. "If you can bestir yourself to do something useful, I'd like to breakfast sometime today."

The ship had passed the last of the large islands, and was crossing a wide stretch of sheltered water inside the bay. A line of rocky cliffs lay ahead, the inland hills rising behind them. Wide inlets opened on the north and south sides of the bay. Meghan had studied the chart of the bay when Buell had been out of the cabin, and she knew the anchorage was in the inlet to the south.

The view of the inlet was blocked by a long point that reached out into the bay, and men lined the port rail and waited for the inlet to come into sight. The rigging and the ship were tidy, sails tightly furled, loose ends of rope tied up, deck gear neatly stowed. The deck boards that had replaced the burned decking had curled and cracked as they dried and seasoned, but they had been scrubbed along with the rest of the deck.

Smoke rose from clearings on the inland hills, and there were other signs of habitation. Seines hung on poles on shingle beaches, canoes were crossing the inlet on the north side of the bay, and a large cluster of huts was at the mouth of a river that flowed into the inlet on the south side of the bay. A yawl came out of the inlet, passing through the lighter color of the fresh water, beating up the wind to avoid the cliffs.

Tips of masts became visible over the point at the side of the inlet, and the men shouted and pointed. Breakfast had improved Buell's mood, and he grunted in satisfaction as he looked at the masts and turned to Tench and Porter. "Well, here we are, then. Mr. Porter, prepare for a port tack, and let's show these lubbers how a well-ordered ship enters port."

"Aye, aye, Captain. Port watch into the rigging! Starboard watch man the braces for tack to port!"

The men along the rail scattered, some of them climbing into the rigging, others unfastening the ends of the braces. Buell folded his hands behind his back and stepped to the port taffrail. He watched the point at the side of the inlet as the ship passed it, then turned. "Up helm and bring her across smartly! Haul up the braces, Mr. Porter!"

The helmsman spun the wheel, and the bow of the ship turned toward the inlet. The men stamped and chanted, pulling on the brace lines, and the spars turned and kept the sails on the wind. The yawl was passing on the starboard side, a hundred yards from the ship, and Meghan crossed the deck to the rail and looked at it. Two men crewed the yawl, and a woman sat in the stern sheets of the small vessel. She looked at Meghan in astonishment, then returned her wave.

The ship crabbed through the water on a port tack, and entered the inlet, which opened out into a wide body of water surrounded by beaches and low, wooded hills. Its upper end disappeared into a finger of water winding into the hills. Dozens of vessels were on the east side of the inlet, anchored in random positions rather than in lines, and they ranged from yawls and ketches to large, full-rigged ships.

Buell grumbled about the scattered arrangement of the ships, and barked orders to the helmsman and to Porter. Meghan looked as ships came into view from behind others, searching for the barque she had seen loaded with lumber in Port Jackson. The settlement was a disappointment, a small collection of buildings spreading up the hill from the beach and around a shallow cove.

Buildings were scattered along a single street. Most of them looked like taverns. A church and a few small houses were up on the hill, with small gardens and animal pens around them. Several small, spindly piers jutted out into the water, but it appeared that the beach was also used to load and unload stores and cargo. Maori canoes were pulled up onto the beach, along with rowboats and other small boats.

The ship approached the perimeter of the anchorage, and the men rapidly furled the rest of the sails. The anchors splashed into the water, and as the ship came to a stop, Meghan saw another ship that appeared to be the *Pamir*. It was several hundred yards away, almost hidden behind other vessels. Only its stern and part of its quarterdeck were visible, but it was a brigantine and it looked like the *Pamir*. And a tall, well-built man was by the rail on the quarterdeck.

The men secured the ship and looked at the settlement, the rest of them questioning the few who had been there before. Buell went down to the main deck, and a boat was lowered. Tench climbed down into the boat with Buell and a man rowed them toward the beach. The ship became quiet again after the excitement of arrival. Porter posted anchor watches and put other men to work on the endless small repair tasks. The men on the off-duty watch lounged by the rail and thought of going ashore.

Meghan waited until the rowboat disappeared among the ships, then she returned to the quarterdeck and ran to the binnacle to get the telescope. As she stepped to the rail, the man on the ship lifted his arm and waved. She lifted the telescope and looked at him.

Then she lowered it and waved. The man was Earl Garrity, and he had recognized her across the distance between the two ships.

During the months since she had seen him, a vivid image of his features had remained firmly imprinted in her memory. And she could remember the timbre of his voice, the way he smiled, and other things about him. But she wanted to look at him, to reassure herself, to reinforce her memory. The breeze shifted and ships swung on their anchor ropes, blocking her view of the *Pamir*. She wondered how she would get to see him, to talk to him again.

Several of the ships were large merchantmen, and one appeared to have stopped at the Bay of Islands while enroute between England and Australia. It had gray, weathered sails and storm damage to its bowsprit and yards, and other evidence of a long voyage.

Maoris walked about along the street and among the houses of the settlement. Some of the men wore a native costume that was similar to a long skirt. Most of the women wore garments from the settlement, and many had children with them. Several Maoris were walking along a wide path from the settlement to a fold in the hills above it, indicating there was a village on the other side.

Buell and Tench were with a third man, and they walked down to the rowboat on the beach. They got into it, and the man pushed it into the water and rowed back toward the ship. The boat disappeared among the ships, then came into sight again. Meghan took the telescope back to the binnacle, feeling dispirited. Ships still blocked her view of the *Pamir*, and she

229

had thought of no way to be able to see Earl Garrity again.

The man with Buell and Tench was short and heavy-set, and dressed in a mixture of style that reflected the informality of an outpost of civilization. He wore the plain, heavy boots, trousers, and shirt of a workman, but he also had on a tweed coat and a hat. Meghan walked down to the main deck as he climbed aboard with Buell and Tench, and Buell introduced her perfunctorily. The man lifted his hat and bowed.

"Elmo Hensley at your service, and it's a pleasure, Mistress Buell," he said, and he glanced around as he put his hat back on. "It appears you had a fire as well as an attack by Maoris, Captain Buell."

"Aye, that starboard furnace caused it," Buell replied. "I could use some new bricks in the foundation under it, as well as decking and such. And my main-mast stepping is loose."

"You've had an eventful voyage, haven't you?" Hensley said. "Well, I have bricks. And I'm not set up to pull a mast, but my men can see to the tenon if its loose. I also have good, seasoned wood for your deck, and cordage or whatever else you might need. And I can provide you with plenty of empty casks, solidly built of good wood."

Buell grunted. "I'm more interested in talking about my cargo first. If we can strike a bargain, then we'll talk about the ship and what it needs."

"I'm ready to discuss whatever you wish," Hensley said amiably. "But when we discuss price, do remember that this entire settlement won't use twenty gallons of oil a month and I'm betwixt and between when it comes to disposing of cargoes. I don't have a ready market."

"You don't?" Buell growled skeptically, pointing to a ship. "What's that? And those others? Did they put in here just to rest their sails?"

"No, no, they didn't." Hensley laughed. "And I can dispose of good oil, but I'm not in the position of a London trader. You'll have to remember that when we discuss price."

"I'm sure you'll keep me reminded," Buell growled sourly. "And I don't have anything but good oil, along with plenty of case oil, whale bone, and spermaceti." He turned to Porter. "Mr. Porter, have the main hold opened, and get a bung starter so he can check the oil."

Buell, Tench, and Hensley walked over to the hatch as the men removed the cover. Someone handed Porter a bung starter, and they all went below.

Hensley opened three casks to smell and taste the oil, then drove the bungs back in and looked at the whale bone as he discussed the cargo with Buell. Tench got a bottle of rum while Buell and Hensley walked to the wardroom. Meghan took pannikins into the wardroom, then sat in the galley and listened to Buell and Hensley. Buell shrewdly used the damage on the ship to his advantage, suggesting that he was half-decided to return to Port Jackson for repairs, and he gradually forced Hensley upward in price.

The men agreed on a price for the cargo, with the remainder of the money, after the repairs were made, to be credited to Drexler and Suggs through a bank in Sydney. They briefly discussed the work to be done on the ship, then Hensley left in the boat and Buell and Tench came back to the wardroom, chuckling in satisfaction over the bargain.

Meghan thought she had found a way to see Earl Garrity again. It depended heavily upon luck and Buell's mood, but it was at least a possibility. She knew Garrity was watching the *Baleen,* and if she could convince Buell to allow her to go ashore, Garrity would see her and come ashore.

She carried plates of food into the wardroom. "Dealing with landlubbers would try Job's patience," Buell was saying. "They can never do anything within a reasonable amount of time, but I'll keep after them. And to that end, I'm going to quarter ashore while the repairs are being done."

"Quarter ashore?" Tench said in surprise. He glanced up at Meghan. "It's your affair what you do, of course, but it appears what you'll find there in the way of quarters will leave much to be desired."

"I'll find something, and I'll be situated to keep after Hensley night and day if he lags. And I don't fancy being aboard when all the work and knocking about is being done." Buell took a bite of food and said to Meghan, "Staying ashore wouldn't be proper for you, though, because there's naught but cannibals and seamen. You'll stay aboard the ship."

It was a perfect opening, and Meghan nodded quickly. "That more than suits me, because I'm not sure I could sleep elsewhere but on *Baleen.* I would like to go ashore and get a few things for the pantry, though.

"For the pantry?" Buell exclaimed, frowning. "We

should have ample victuals left!"

"We do, but we're out of dried fruit and I'd like to get some to make pastries. I'd like to get the wherewithal to make small beer for a change from either water or tea. Also, the salt pork is also going a bit off, and I've heard they have many pigs hereabout. If I could get some fresh pork, I could cure it properly myself."

Tench took a bite of the pork and chewed reflectively, and looked up at Meghan. "You know how to cure pork, Mistress Buell?"

"Aye, with treacle, salt, saltpeter, and smoke. It keeps much better, and it's far more tasty than salt pork. The port furnace would do very nicely for the smoking, once it's cleaned out and the try pot is removed.

Buell took a bite of the pork and chewed it, then shook his head. "I've lived on much worse than this, and that settlement is no place for you to be wandering about."

"I'd be glad to take her, Captain," Tench said quickly. "And I'd like some small beer, as well as more of Mistress Buell's pastries."

Buell hesitated, but gave in at last. "Very well, but I'll charge you to see that she doesn't spend the best part of the profits we've accumulated."

"Aye, I'll see to that." Tench promised. "We'll go tomorrow morning, Mistress Buell."

Meghan nodded agreement. Having Tench go with her was an unexpected complication, and an intrusion. But at least she would be near Garrity if he saw her go ashore and followed her. And other opportunities to see him might arise while the *Baleen* and *Pamir* were in port together.

Buell had been up since the midwatch the night before, and Meghan waited for him to go to bed. She looked at the anchor lights on the ships in the harbor as she waited, wondering which of the glowing spots of yellow light were those on the *Pamir*.

She lay and listened to Buell snore as she looked up into the darkness, thinking about Earl Garrity and unable to sleep. Even across the distance between the ships, his personality seemed to reach out to her. She formulated interesting and amusing things to say to him, and she speculated what his reaction to them would be. And she wondered if a young woman in Sydney was waiting for him to return.

The ship's bell rang the midwatch, and the distant sounds of bells came from other ships. Bare feet crossed the quarterdeck above as the anchor watch changed. She dozed but it seemed only moments later that Buell was climbing out of the bunk and dressing. She felt weary and dazed from too little sleep, but she had to get up.

Everything seemed to go wrong. She burned her hand while preparing breakfast, and the nervous fluttering in her stomach made her nauseous when she tried to eat. Her hair kept falling down, and her prettiest dress was wrinkled. Tench kept a boatload of oil casks waiting while she got ready, and Buell was furiously angry over the delay.

Then her confusion was suddenly gone as she sat in the stern of the boat beside Tench and the men rowed it ashore. The day was bright and sunny, and she felt the same way. She felt beautiful. Tench was interested in how she planned to cure the pork, and she had to fight to keep her mind off Garrity as she told him.

Hensley owned two of the piers and one of the warehouses, but Tench had the men beach the boat so she could get off more easily. Most of the men working around the warehouses were Maoris, some with the dark lines of tattooing on their faces and some without.

A lot of them were slovenly and dissipated from drunkenness, and all of them stared at Meghan. Tench glanced at them threateningly, taking her arm as they passed. Drunken singing came from some of the taverns. Two seamen, and a short, stout Maori woman lay in drunken sleep between two buildings. The woman's dirty dress was pulled up to her thighs.

"The captain was right," Tench commented, shaking his head in disapproval. "There's only wanton and riotous conduct in this place, and it isn't a proper place for you to be."

"If he can live here, I'm sure I can endure a visit, Mr. Tench."

Tench blinked in surprise, then pointed to a building. "Aye, perhaps so. This is the chandler's place here, Mistress Buell."

The building was one of the larger structures on the street, with sheds and a wall-enclosed yard behind it. Tench opened the door, and followed Meghan in. It was dim and cluttered inside, and filled with a blended odor from the stacked barrels, kegs, and crates of ship's stores. Three Maori men sat on kegs in a corner and looked at Meghan with silent, intent curiosity. A small white man with thin, sharp features came from the back of the store, smiling and bowing as he approached.

"Good day, and welcome. I'm Horace Dobbins, the proprietor."

"I'm Mr. Tench, mate on the *Baleen,*" Tench replied. "This is Mistress Buell, the captain's wife, and she wants to buy a few things for the pantry. You're to render your accounting to Mr. Hensley for settlement."

"Very well, Mr. Tench. And what would you like to see first, Mistress Buell?"

"Do you have any dried barley that has been kept dry and in good condition?"

"Indeed I do, Mistress Buell. Come this way, please."

Dobbins led the way to the back of the store, and lifted the lid on a barrel of malt barley. Meghan felt and tasted the grain, then ordered a peck and asked about dried fruit. Dobbins opened barrels of dried apples and peaches, and Meghan examined them. She ordered a bushel of each, then asked about the saltpeter, treacle, flour, and the other things she wanted.

For the first time, she had serious doubts about whether things would go as she had planned. She could barely see the *Pamir* from the *Baleen,* and Garrity would be able to see the *Baleen* no better. Even if he had seen her leave the ship, it was possible that he was on watch or some other reason would keep him from coming ashore. What had seemed a logical course of action suddenly appeared to be wishful thinking.

Live pigs were in a pen in the yard behind the building, and Dobbins called one of the Maoris out to drive the pigs around the pen while Meghan looked at them. She studied the pigs and delayed her decision, giving Garrity as long as possible to get ashore, then she chose two pigs when Dobbins and Tench began to betray signs of impatience. Dobbins bowed Meghan and Tench to the front door.

"If possible, I'd like everything delivered in the forenoon tomorrow," Meghan said. "And the pigs must be slaughtered and drained no earlier than an hour before they're delivered."

"I'll see to it myself, Mistress Buell," Dobbins replied. "And you may be assured that everything will be completely to your satisfaction. If you need other things while you're here, I trust you'll return. In the meantime, it was a pleasure meeting you. And you, Mr. Tench."

They walked back along the street. Meghan was crushed with disappointment. Her vision of seeing Garrity again had wilted into a gray, drab emptiness inside her. Tench talked to her, and she tried to follow the conversation.

They reached the end of the buildings and the beach came into sight. And Meghan felt her heart pound. Earl Garrity was stepping out of a boat on the beach. Tench looked down at her, murmuring interrogatively. A flush was rising to her face, and she ducked her head to hide her face.

Tench offered her his arm, and they walked down the path. Garrity approached, lifting his tricorn and bowing. "Good day, Mistress Buell."

Meghan stopped and bobbed in a curtsey, looking

away and swallowing to control her voice. "Good day. Mr. Garrity, isn't it? This is Mr. Tench, the mate on the *Baleen*. Mr. Tench, this is Mr. Earl Garrity. He was good enough to drive away two ruffians who were being rude to me while I was ashore in Sydney."

Tench bowed. "Indeed? Then you have my thanks, Mr. Garrity, as well as the captain's. Garrity? I've heard that name many times. Doesn't your family own a very large sheep station in Australia?"

"Aye, but that wasn't for me," Garrity chuckled. "I'm on the *Pamir*, and that suits me better."

Tench laughed and nodded. "Aye, I know how you feel. My family is in trade, and I signed on with the Navy to get away from that. But I've never regretted it, and everyone must choose his own way. The *Pamir*, you say? I'm well acquainted with Captain Johnson, and I'd say you have a very good berth."

The two men talked about the ship and the captain. Tench was favorably impressed by Garrity, and the reasons were easy to see. Garrity had a candid, forthright manner, and an amiable disposition. At the same time, his bold, manly features suggested that it would be unwise to cross him. Tench was a tall man, but Garrity was even taller. And he was very handsome as he stood with his hands clasped behind him and talked with Tench.

"I've always been interested in whalers," Garrity commented casually, changing the subject. "But I've never had a good opportunity to see one properly. Would it be possible for me to visit the *Baleen*?"

"Of course!" Tench answered. "Of course it would, my good man. I'd be most delighted to have you visit.

We're unloading now and things are in disorder, so it would probably be best to wait until that's done. Will you be in port that long?"

"That long, and longer," Garrity said. "Taking on lumber here is a tediously slow affair. When you're through unloading, then, I'll pay you a visit.

"Let's plan on Friday next," Tench said. "We'll finish unloading on Thursday, and we'll be sorted out again by the next day. We'll be making some repairs, but that won't interfere with your looking around. And if you'll come in the late afternoon, perhaps we can persuade Mistress Buell to set us a good triffin. I'll guarantee you that will remain in your memory longer than seeing the ship, because amongst her other sterling qualities, Mistress Buell has unsurpassed talent in the galley."

"I'm sure she has, and I'll be there in late forenoon on Friday," Garrity said, and he bowed. "It was a pleasure meeting you, Mr. Tench, and to see you again, Mistress Buell."

Garrity's eyes met Meghan's for an instant, creating a breathless, glowing warmth inside her, then he turned away. Tench offered Meghan his arm, and she put her hand on it as they continued down the path to the beach.

"Now there's a most pleasant young man," Tench said. "I know Captain Johnson well, and he's a cordial fellow and a good seaman. So Mr. Garrity has a good berth, and at the same time it appears that Captain Johnson has a fine officer from a good family. I'm looking forward to his visit."

Meghan nodded, feeling Garrity's eyes on her as she

walked down the path by Tench. "Aye, so am I, Mr. Tench."

Chapter 13

THE NOISE OF THE WORK on deck suddenly stopped, and Meghan turned to the galley doorway and listened. She had helped clean the furnace, to start the pork smoking, and she was scrubbing the soot and grease off her hands and arms. Voices carried along the passageway, Tench saying something and Buell replying in an angry growl. Meghan picked up a cloth and wiped her hands and arms and went to the door. Just then Tench called out, "Mistress Buell, a boat with a woman aboard is coming alongside, and the men are rigging out a bosun's chair. If you want to see to your toilet you'll have a moment to do so."

"Thank you very much, Mr. Tench."

A boat thumped against the hull as Meghan was hastily changing into one of her good dresses. She pulled a comb through her hair and tied it back and went up on deck.

The men were unloading casks over the starboard side, and Buell and Tench were at the port rail with a man in a dark suit and clerical collar. He was a small man, but he had the self assurance of one accustomed to commanding respect. Buell looked annoyed.

A spar was over the port side and men were hauling in the rope on the bosun's chair. They lifted the woman over the rail as Meghan crossed the deck. The woman was a few years older and an inch or two taller than Meghan, and her features were familiar. Meghan looked at the woman, and remembered where and when she had seen her. She had been in the yawl that had passed the ship on the day it arrived in port.

The woman smiled at Meghan as she slid out of the canvas sling and stood on the deck. Her smile was pitiable, revealing agonizing loneliness in this isolated place and a frantic yearning for companionship. It was also a beseeching smile, begging for friendship, and Meghan smiled at her warmly as she walked across the desk.

The minister lifted his hat and bowed to Meghan. "And this is your good wife, Captain Buell? I'm John Cargill, Mistress Buell, and this is my wife Amanda."

"I'm pleased to meet you, Reverend Cargill," Meghan replied as she curtsied. "And you, Mistress Cargill. Did you enjoy your sail in the yawl the other day?"

"You remembered me!" Amanda exclaimed in delight, stepping to Meghan and taking her hand. "My word, you have good eyes, don't you? I was so astonished to see a woman on a ship that I nearly failed to wave!"

"Indeed she did," Cargill chuckled. "And since then I've heard of little else other than she must meet you, Mistress Buell." He turned back to Buell. "It's my custom to call on the masters of vessels that stop here, Captain, and I trust it hasn't discommoded you that I brought Mistress Cargill with me."

"No, having your wife with you makes little difference," Buell replied morosely. "If you felt you had cause to come aboard, it's one and the same that you brought her with you."

His attitude appeared to be more or less what Cargill had expected, but he was imperturbable, his religion a shield. But the comment created a strain in the atmosphere, and Meghan broke the silence. "I have some small beer in the galley, and perhaps you would enjoy a cup. It's still a bit green, but it's potable."

"It's more than potable," Tench said enthusiastically. "I had some with tiffin, and it would grace a lord's table. Would you care to come to the wardroom for a cup, Vicar?"

"Yes, and thank you very much," Cargill replied. "And perhaps I can have a word with you and Mr. Tench while our wives are visiting, Captain Buell."

Buell grunted and nodded, and they walked across the deck toward the wardrooms. Amanda took Meghan's arm as they followed the men, talking to her, telling her about the trip in the yawl. She had been enroute to visit the wife of another minister who had a church at a village on the other side of the bay. They were the only two white women in New Zealand, and they visited each other every few weeks.

The men went into the wardroom, Meghan and Amanda to the galley. Meghan filled a pitcher from the urn of beer. They took the beer to the wardroom, and Meghan asked Amanda if she would like some. Amanda smiled and shook her head, taking Meghan's hand.

"No, I'm so excited over meeting you that I couldn't sit still to drink it, dear Meghan. Could we just talk?"

"Of course, Amanda. Come, I'll show you around."

They walked back out on deck, and Meghan showed Amanda the pork smoking in the furnace. Amanda said, "That's very clever. I've heard of preserving meat in that fashion, but I've never tried it. Will any sort of wood do for the fire?"

"No, only hardwood, but the carpenter found several pieces of good oak for me. It must be soaked in water so it won't flame up, and the fire requires constant care. But we have anchor watches around the clock, so that's easily seen to."

Amanda nodded, glancing uncomfortably at Porter as he barked at the men wrestling with the heavy oil casks. Meghan led her back across the deck and up the steps to the quarterdeck. She had heard about the Maori attack on the ship and asked about it, her eyes lingering on the scar over Meghan's left eye. Meghan briefly described the incident. Then Amanda talked wistfully about her childhood home in England and how she had met her husband, and she asked Meghan how she had met Buell. Meghan told her about Parramatta, and her eyes grew wide with horror.

"My word!" she gasped when Meghan finished. "I'd have done away with myself. My exile here seems very dreary, but it's a veritable paradise compared to what you've endured. But I must say that your misfortune failed to injure your sweet and kindly nature, so you must be very strong."

"No, I'm not," Meghan sighed. "It had me on my knees, Amanda. I endured it, but no better than most would have. Didn't the vicar say he visits the masters of all ships that call here? To what ends does he do that?"

Amanda glanced around, and lowered her voice. "Some of the men from ships have been venturing over to the village to disport themselves. So the vicar has been visiting the captains in an effort to have them order their men to stay away from the village. But he's met with little success thus far."

Meghan lifted her eyebrows and shook her head doubtfully. "Captain Buell has a taut ship, but the men are on their own when they're ashore. And so are men on other ships, except the Navy. I fear the vicar has hold of a loose handle."

"How would you say it could best be done?"

"By establishing a constabulary. That would remove many evils. And from what I saw during my brief visit in the settlement, I'd say a constabulary would more than pay for itself in fines."

Amanda sighed hopelessly, shaking her head. "This isn't a colony, Meghan, and we have no governor or government here. The mood in England is against establishing more colonies, and it doesn't seem likely that we'll ever have a government. And without a government, we have no way to establish a constabulary. Warships call and their captains do as little or as much as their conscience dictates, but they're not here all the time. And the Maoris are much like children in many ways. A good girl can be enticed with a scrap of cloth, and the men are mad for rum.''

''Aye, the little I saw bears that out. But they don't appear to be as murderous as what one hears.''

''Not those immediately about us here, but elsewhere they're like those who attacked your ship. And we've made a number of converts among them, but the seamen who come here make our task much more difficult. I'm not as strong as you, Meghan, and things are very discouraging at times. If it weren't for my visits with Julia, I'd fear for my state of mind. And my letters from home are also a help, of course.'' She smiled. ''There's something I can do for you, dear Meghan. Would you like to send a letter to England? Ours go free, and I could send it with mine.''

Mailing a letter to England cost almost a guinea, and Buell had adamantly refused when Meghan had asked him if she could write to a relative. She gasped in delight. ''Could you, Amanda? I have an uncle in the Admiralty in London, and he favored me as a child. I'd most earnestly like to write him so he can tell my father about my situation and write back to me about my father's welfare.''

''Yes, I'll gladly forward it,'' Amanda replied, pleased that she could do something for Meghan. ''A ship in the harbor is collecting the mails, so you should let me have it within the next day or two. In fact, you could bring it, couldn't you? Then we could visit again.''

Meghan hesitated, then shook her head doubtfully. ''Captain Buell doesn't like me to go ashore. I don't think I'll be able to, but I'll ask if I may.''

"Do try and persuade him," Amanda begged. "And if you can't, then send the letter and I'll see that it goes with mine." She turned and looked down at the deck as the men came out of the passageway. "How time has flown. I've enjoyed our visit so much, and you will try to come and see me, won't you?"

"Of course I will, Amanda. I've enjoyed our visit very much indeed, and I regard you as my good friend."

Amanda smiled and took Meghan's hand as they walked down the steps to the deck. Buell was even more glum than he had been before and it appeared that the minister had talked both Buell and Tench out of a contribution to charity. They stood by the rail, and Cargill turned and smiled at his wife.

"It appears you enjoyed your visit, Amanda."

"Indeed I did," Amanda sighed. "And I truly hope that Mistress Buell will be able to return the visit."

"That should be easy enough, shouldn't it, Captain?" Cargill asked Buell. "When you bring Mistress Buell to church on Sunday, you'll stay for supper so they can visit, won't you?"

Buell shook his head obstinately. "I'm engaged Sunday, and I won't be able to come to church. And I won't have my wife go ashore in this place without an escort."

"As you wish," Cargill replied mildly. "I'm sure you know the consequences of what you do, and this isn't the time and place for me to dwell on the subject. But I must be more insistent that your good wife be afforded the opportunity for worship." He looked at Tench. "Didn't you say that you took Mistress Buell to buy provisions, Mr. Tench? If you did that, surely you can bring her to church on Sunday. Then you can stay for supper, and you'll be back on your ship shortly after dark."

Tench tugged at his cravat and nodded reluctantly. "Aye, I suppose I can, Vicar."

"Excellent, excellent," Cargill said briskly. "We'll expect you on Sunday, then. Thank you again for your contribution, Mr. Tench, and thank you for yours, Captain Buell."

Buell grunted sourly and beckoned Porter. Porter brought three men over to lower Amanda into her boat in the bosun's chair. Amanda smiled as the men hoisted her and turned the spar out over the rail, and slowly lowered her into the boat. Cargill climbed down the ladder. Tench was wryly amused and Buell was angry as they walked away from the rail. Meghan waved to Amanda until the boat went out of sight.

Meghan was overjoyed at the chance to go to church the following Sunday. It had been well over a year since she had been able to attend any church service except those at the grim, dismal chapel at the prison. She had always enjoyed going to church. And it would be another opportunity to see Garrity, if the circumstances were favorable.

He would go to church if he knew she was going, and she thought of ways of introducing the subject when he came to the ship on Friday. She also thought about the letter to her uncle. Buell begrudged her anything that cost money. There was foolscap in the cabinet by the desk and she took several sheets. She searched and found an extra quill and bottle of ink, and took

248

them to the galley to write the letter.

The past months had been eventful, and she sat at the table in the galley and wrote slowly, organizing the sentences in her mind. She brushed over her experiences at Parramatta with a sentence or two about the prison, and she made the most she could of her marriage. Night began falling when she put the letter away and prepared dinner. She worked on it until after Buell had gone to bed.

The letter was finished the next morning, and Meghan made an envelope from another sheet of foolscap and flour paste. Porter and Tench did things for her without Buell's knowledge, and she wrote a note to Amanda and took the note and letter to Porter. Porter sent them by Dickon Muir on the next boatload of casks, and he returned with a note from Amanda. Most of the note was about Amanda's plans for their visit on Sunday. Meghan's letter had been put with hers for dispatch to England.

The unloading of the ship was progressing rapidly, and it rode higher in the water and bobbed more heavily in the waves in the bay. Meghan mixed another urn of beer and put it aside to brew, and turned the pork on the skewers in the furnace. The treacle was forming a shiny glaze on the pork. Meghan picked out a choice piece of shoulder to cook on the day of Garrity's visit.

The men had been promised liberty as soon as they finished unloading, so they finished it a day early. Hensley returned to the ship with another white man and two Maoris, and they conferred with the ship's carpenter on the repairs. Porter flipped a coin to determine which watch would have liberty first, and the starboard watch won.

Buell also went ashore. The reasons he had given Tench for wanting to stay ashore were obviously false, but Meghan had no idea of the truth. She knew that it wasn't for the Maori women, because the few comments he had made about them had been in terms of disgust. She was idly curious about it, but more gratified by his absence than curious. He returned to the ship the next morning to talk to Tench for a few minutes and look at the repairs in progress. Then he left again.

Meghan was up before daybreak the following morning to prepare for Garrity's visit. She put the smoked pork roast in the oven to start it baking. Buell came to the ship while she was polishing the table in the wardroom, and she had a few anxious minutes when it appeared that he might stay and cast a blight over Earl Garrity's visit. But he went back to the settlement.

The thought of cooking for Garrity was pleasant. The galley smelled of roast pork. She put on pans of beans, potatoes, and peas, then she made the pastries.

When most of the cooking was done, she went to the cabin and changed into one of her good dresses. She combed her hair and piled it on her head, pinning it up with combs, then returned to the galley. Everything had gone right, the food was perfect. The pork was tender and coated with a crisp crust, the pastries were light and flaky. She decided her beer was perfect.

A boat thumped against the hull as she was setting the table in the wardroom, and she heard Tench greet Garrity. She was suddenly breathless, her heart pounding, and she pulled nervously at her dress. And she thought about the shiny, four-inch scar on her forehead. Her bonnet had covered it before, and she wondered if it would detract from her appearance. She waited for him to come in.

His eyes hesitated on the scar. Then he looked into her eyes, and what she saw in his eyes banished all her fears. And he was magnificent, in nankin trousers, shiny knee boots, a buff shirt and cravat. His frock coat had shiny brass buttons and patch pockets. His thick hair was combed and his smooth brown face shone in the sunlight.

"Good day, Mistress Buell," he said. "It's a pleasure to see you again."

"And you, Mr. Garrity. Mr. Tench, please don't tarry in showing Mr. Garrity about so that the food will go cold."

Tench stroked his chin and glanced from Meghan to Garrity. "I'd as lief delay looking around the ship until after tiffin. I had a good breakfast this morning, but the smells from that galley have made me hungry. What do you think, Mr. Garrity?"

Garrity smiled. "I smelled the food before I was near the ship. I'm ready to eat."

"Then let's eat." Tench laughed, gesturing toward the wardroom.

Tench took a bite of the pork and chewed. There was a blissful smile on his face as he swallowed. "Mistress Buell, I've never tasted anything like that. You said it would be tasty, but that didn't tell a tenth part of the story."

Meghan smiled and nodded. "Thank you, Mr.

251

Tench, but it wants a bit more curing yet. Another week in the smoke will make a difference."

"Then I'll look forward to that," Tench said. "But I don't see how it could be improved upon. What do you think, Mr. Garrity?"

"It is delicious," Garrity agreed. "And I can see that these are beans and peas, but they're more than that. How did you flavor them, Mistress Buell?"

"Only bits of mustard, onions, a spoonful of the pork grease, and such as that, Mr. Garrity."

"She has a marvelous talent in the galley," Tench said. "She can take the most common food and turn it into a meal fit for the queen."

"You'll turn my head, Mr. Tench," Meghan chuckled. "What sort of fare is served on the sheep stations in Australia, Mr. Garrity?'

"Plentiful and plain," Garrity replied. "It's usually baked mutton and boiled potatoes, or boiled mutton and baked potatoes."

Meghan smiled and poured more beer for them. She watched Garrity without seeming to. He ate the way she had anticipated, with a natural grace that seemed to be a part of everything he did. The story about the Maori attack on the ship had spread, and he asked Tench about it. Tench related what had happened, then nodded toward Meghan as he finished.

"But the best part of the story is that Mistress Buell did as much as any man on the ship," he said. "She's as good a shot with a pistol as I've seen, and she has spirit that would put many men to shame. A savage gave her that nick on her head and I tried to get her to retire from the battle, but she was in the very thick of it until the end."

Garrity looked at Meghan with a thoughtful smile. "One can tell that much by looking at her," he said quietly. "At least so far as her spirit goes."

"Aye, one can," Tench agreed. "She's a Conley, from a long line of seamen, and she lived up to her name that day. If I had a dozen men with her spirit, I'd take on that many savages again."

"You exaggerate, Mr. Tench," Meghan chided. "In fact, I was quite beside myself with terror, and you may have a choice of apple or peach pastry whether or no you boast about me. And do remember before you stray too far from facts that you'll have to repent on Sunday." She looked at Garrity, smiling brightly. "Mr. Tench is escorting me to church on Sunday."

Tench nodded. "Aye, I am indeed. That vicar was too quick for me, and he had me trapped before I knew it."

Garrity took a drink of beer. "I'll see you there, then, because I plan to go myself."

Tench stopped chewing and looked at Garrity. "You do? Then perhaps you wouldn't mind taking Mistress Buell with you, because I have others things I'd rather do on Sunday. Captain Buell hasn't met you, but I know he'll offer no objection. I'll see him tomorrow and speak with him about it. The vicar and his wife have asked Mistress Buell to supper, but that shouldn't keep you too long."

"I'd be most pleased to, as long as Mistress Buell has no objection."

"Aye, I didn't mean to overlook your feelings, Mistress Buell," Tench said apologetically. "Please for-

253

give me if I left that impression."

Meghan took a sip of beer, looking down at her plate to hide what was in her eyes, and she shook her head. "No, I took no offense, Mr. Tench. And I have no objections at all, Mr. Garrity."

─────────────Chapter 14

A FEW DEVOUT SEAMEN WERE at the church service, but most of the congregation in the small, primitive church were Maoris. The building, benches, and pulpit were made of unpainted wood, and the windows were without sashes and panes. But the church had a homely charm. And with Garrity sitting on the bench by Meghan, for her the church was transformed into something more significant than the most stately cathedral.

He was immaculate, as he always seemed to be. A faint odor of tobacco and what she thought of young masculinity clung to him. The effect he had on her was devastating.

Amanda Cargill sat on the other side of Meghan, but her presence was not an intrusion. The three of them used the same hymnal, and Garrity's large, warm hand touched Meghan's as he helped her hold it. During the sermon, his hand rested on the bench between them. Meghan slowly moved her hand off her lap and let it slide down to the bench. He moved it with his.

When the service was finished, they went to the parsonage. Cargill and Garrity sat on a bench under a tree behind the house and smoked their pipes, and Meghan helped Amanda prepare dinner. The men's voices carried through the open kitchen window, and the atmosphere was pleasantly domestic. It provided the mood for a daydream in which she and Garrity were married and were visiting the Cargills, a daydream that made it difficult for her to keep her mind on the conversation with Amanda.

The meal was a great success. Meghan felt proud of Garrity. He was so entertaining, with a seemingly endless store of amusing and interesting stories, but he could be serious, too. The hours flew, and it was suddenly dark. Amanda and her husband pressed Meghan for a commitment the following Sunday, and she knew at least part of the reason was because they had enjoyed having Garrity visit them.

Meghan had wondered if she would see Buell while passing the settlement, and possibly endure an awkward moment if he were drunk or in a particularly surly mood. But Garrity had found a path from the beach to the church that avoided the settlement and curved around the side of the slope. Cargill offered Garrity the use of a lantern, but he said the moon was bright enough to illuminate the path.

Maori women squealed and laughed shrilly in and around the taverns. Seamen laughed, sang, and fought in a drunken hubbub that drifted up the slope. Meghan and Garrity walked in silence. The daydream was slipping away and reality was taking its place, producing a jarring mixture of feelings. She had so much to say to him, and at the same time—nothing.

His mood seemed similar, but there was no tension in the silence between them. Already there was no need for words. He knew when she was finding the footing unsteady, and he held her arm more firmly. She knew when he wanted her to step ahead of him and be guided by his strong, gentle hand on her elbow.

The tide had gone out, leaving the rowboat several feet above the waterline. Garrity lifted the bow of the heavy boat and pushed it into the water. Meghan gathered up the hem of her dress and started to tiptoe across the wet pebbles, but Garrity stepped back to her and carried her to the boat. The effortless way he lifted her left her breathless, and it was more than a means of getting her to the boat. He stopped and held her for a moment, then put her in the boat.

She sat on the seat facing him as he slowly rowed the boat out among the ships. The riotous noise from the settlement faded behind, and was replaced by the quiet lapping of the waves against the hulls and the soft creaking of heavy timbers. The ships were silent and dark except for the bright glow of their anchor lights, and their masts and spars were silhouetted against the starry sky.

"This has been a day I'll long remember, Meghan," Garrity murmured quietly, breaking the silence between them.

"So will I, Earl," she whispered.

He rested the oars, looking at her in the moonlight, then laughed softly as he began rowing again. "My mother would be surprised out of her wits. She's been trying to get me to marry since I turned eighteen, and I've had the sharp edge of her tongue more than once at that. Now I can't eat or sleep for thinking of you."

"I'm sure there's a pretty girl or two in Sydney who's caught your eye, and who'll do at least for company if not for marriage."

"No."

His tone was firm, flat, and definite. It was a subject of intense interest to Meghan, one of frequent speculation. She had been prepared for jealousy, even while acknowledging that it was illogical, and she felt keenly pleased and relieved that an undefined threat had been removed. The light dimmed as the moon went behind a cloud, turning it into a gleaming mass of incandescence. Meghan looked up at it.

He rested the oars again. Then he leaned toward her, reaching for her. She had wondered if he would want to kiss her, hoping he would and knowing she should avoid it. She felt paralyzed, unable to move. His hands touched her shoulders, and something within her took control. She responsed without willing herself to move, melting into his arms and lifting her lips to his.

His arms closed around her, and his lips covered hers. The touch of his lips and his strong arms around her kindled a glowing warmth that spread through her, turning into a fiery throbbing. Their embrace became more passionate, his lips moving over her face and down to her throat. He murmured broken phrases of love. She whispered her love as she kissed him, touching, and caressing his face. He lifted her hand, squeezing it and kissing it, sighing heavily.

"If you were mine, I'd ask no more of life, Meghan."

She pulled herself closer to him. "I truly wish our way were clear, Earl."

"Then say the word, and I'll clear it. There are sloops and yawls all about us, and I can get provisions so we can be on our way to Australia tomorrow night. And once we reach Australia, no one will ever find us."

She looked up into his eyes. He was serious, and she pulled away from him and sat back on her seat and shook her head. "No, that would be the worst sort of folly, Earl."

"It would be what we both want, and no one would find us."

"We couldn't escape our conscience, or the judgment of God. Apart from the crime of stealing a boat, I'm a married woman. And I don't take my vows lightly, whatever the circumstances in which they were given."

He groaned and rubbed his face with his hands. "It isn't fair, Meghan. I love you and you love me. We belong together."

"I do love you and I know you love me, but there's the end of it, Earl. Human beings have no covenant with God for life to be fair or just, and only knaves and children rush pellmell to what they want."

"Suddenly it sounds as though I were talking to my mother, Meghan. If you deny yourself what you want, then how do you bring yourself to face life?"

"Through courage. When I was at Parramatta, each night I faced a decision on whether or not to make a rope from my bedsheet and hang myself. It would have been an easy escape, and it would have been wrong. It would be easy to flee with you, but it would be wrong. So one summons the courage to do what is right, and one goes on."

"You sound more and more like my mother," he sighed, picking up the oars and rowing again. "Would it be wrong for us to see each other again?"

"Aye, but that's a wrong of a lesser order," she said. "So I'll happily see you at every opportunity, and pray for forgiveness."

The moon came out from behind the cloud, and the *Balleen* came into sight through the ships ahead. Garrity glanced over his shoulder, pulling harder on one oar and turning the boat.

The anchor watch coughed on the bow of the ship, a reminder that others were nearby. Garrity backed water with the oars and stopped the boat by the ladder. Meghan put her hand on his as she rose. He took her hand and squeezed it in a quick embrace, smiling up at her, then she climbed the ladder.

The boat disappeared into the darkness, and Meghan went to the cabin. The seething confusion of happiness and melancholy that churned within her made her restless, and she put her bag and bonnet away and went to the galley. Tench stirred in his cabin as she lit a sliver of wood on the coals in the stove to light the lantern. Tench came out of his cabin to speak to her.

"Did I disturb you, Mr. Tench?" Meghan called.

He stopped in the galley doorway, yawning and shaking his head. "No, I can never sleep soundly when in port, Mistress Buell."

"There's some pastries left, and I could make a cup of tea to go with them if you like."

"Indeed I would, and I'd enjoy it even more if you'd join me. I'll have a look about and check the anchor watch while you're making the tea. I'll be back in a moment."

Meghan took a plate of pastries from a cabinet and filled the kettle. The water boiled and she took tea, pastries, and the lantern to the wardroom.

Tench came in and sat down. "Did you enjoy the service today, Mistress Buell?"

"Aye, it was very pleasant."

Tench took another bite of pastry. His single wise, keen eye lingered on her, studying her face, and Meghan wondered if something in her features or manner betrayed what was between her and Garrity.

They ate in silence for a few minutes, and Meghan thought about the repairs to the ship. She wanted to know how long she would have opportunities to see Garrity. At the same time she was reluctant to think about it. But she might as well know what she had to face.

"How much longer will it take to complete the repairs, Mr. Tench?"

"It's hard to say just now, but it'll be a few days yet. And even at that, there's only so much they can do. The mainmast footing is cracked, and we can't lift it out here to replace it. They can't do much for the foremast either, or for the furnace. But when we leave we should be in more or less the same condition as when we left Port Jackson."

"That was well short of truly shipshape."

"Aye, it was." Tench agreed. "But we should be able to make do. If we can fetch in another cargo like the

261

last, the owner's won't begrudge anything we need. And if we can fetch in two more cargoes like that, then we'll be in an excellent situation indeed. Anyway, we'll be here long enough for you to go to church again, if that's weighing on your mind."

The yellow glow of the lantern highlighted his craggy features. His smile was warm and kindly, but his eye seemed to be looking into her and reading her thoughts. She took a sip of her tea, looking away into the darkness of a corner of the room, saying nothing.

Tench sat back in his chair. "That was a most delicious repast, Mistress Buell, and I'll be able to sleep like a baby now. I'm not an unreligious man, but I've always had far more use for my Bible and for God than I do for parsons. So I'm most grateful to Mr. Garrity for taking you to church today. He's a very congenial man and I enjoy his company, and I was thinking about asking him to visit again. Would it be an imposition upon you to ask you to set tiffin for him again?"

His smile was gentle and understanding—and he knew. Meghan felt a flush rising from her throat to her cheeks, she looked away in confusion and silently shook her head. Tench got up and prepared to leave. He stopped at the door and looked back.

'Did I ever tell you that I have three sons? I do, and the oldest is about your age. They're fine men and I've always been proud of them, but I've always wished I had a daughter. And if I had one, I'd want her to be just like you. But it's just as well I don't, because I'd want her to stay with me and keep me company instead of getting married."

"Thank you, Mr. Tench."

After he left, Meghan went to her cabin and quickly settled into the bunk. Hours passed as she relived every moment with Garrity, and she slowly drifted off to sleep. The ship's bell woke her when it rang the morning watch, and she was on the quarterdeck and looking toward the *Pamir* when dawn broke. Ships arrived, left, and changed position every day, but the *Pamir* was still there. Earl Garrity was on the quarterdeck, and she knew he was smiling at her.

Buell came to the ship during the forenoon watch, as he usually did each day. He walked around with Tench for a few minutes, and growled irately at the carpenter and Hensley's men. After he left, Tench put on a clean shirt and cravat, brushed his coat, and rowed a boat over to the *Pamir*. He returned an hour later, and told Meghan that Garrity would visit the *Baleen* again on Wednesday.

Another ship arrived during the afternoon and completely blocked the view of the *Pamir*. It was a clipper, one of the greyhounds of the oceans. It was long and sleek, with a gracefully raked bow that jutted far out over the water, and its mast towered above all others.

Law and order arrived during late afternoon in the form of HMS *Viper*, a frigate armed with thirty-six guns. The captain of the warship went ashore with a squad of marines at nightfall. The first ten drunken seamen the captain found were impressed to fill vacancies in the crew of the *Viper*. Then the captain singled out the most unruly of the taverns and had it burned.

The next morning, Buell came back at the usual time, grumbilng and cursing about the highhanded methods of the captain of the frigate. He mustered the crew. None of his men had been impressed, and he left again. During the day, word spread through the ships of the intentions of the warship's captain. The warship was there in response to French interest in New Zealand, and would remain for the duration.

Garrity arrived the next morning shortly after Buell left, and he and Tench walked about on the ship while Meghan prepared lunch. A warm friendship had developed between the two men. Tench found a reason to go out on deck after lunch, giving Meghan and Garrity a few minutes alone in the wardroom, and they kissed until she was breathless.

He remained another hour, talking with her and Tench on the deck. The hours of the afternoon dragged on after he left, and Sunday seemed very far away.

The atmosphere in the settlement had became more satisfactory to Tench, and he went ashore after dinner. It got late, but Meghan felt too restless to go to bed. She went up to the quarterdeck and stood, looking out at the ships in the moonlight, then she went back to the galley to make a pot of tea before retirng.

There was a knock and she moved the kettle to the back of the stove and went to the door. It was Dickon Muir with an armload of wood. "Come in, Dickon. I was almost out of wood and I thought I'd have to ask for more, but you remembered, didn't you?"

His large, blue eyes were red and his smooth, boyish face was pale, and he looked as if he had been crying. He tried to smile, then he averted his face as he stepped in with the wood and walked toward the box under the table.

"What is it, Dickon? What's happened?"

Dickon put the wood in the box and straightened back up, turning to her. He started to speak, then color rushed into his face. His features twisted and he almost burst into tears.

Meghan stepped to him and put a hand on his arm. "Come, Dickon, tell me. Whatever's amiss, I'll see that it's put right. Now tell me what's happened."

He shook his head again, keeping his face averted. "I can't, Mistress Buell," he choked. "I can't tell anyone. I'm so ashamed."

Meghan looked up at him. He had obviously brought the wood to the galley in the hope that she would be there and he could talk to her about whatever was bothering him. She thought rapidly, wondering if he had got drunk and had been with a Maori woman, and was stricken with boyish shame and contrition. But it seemed more than that.

She leaned back against the table, tugging on him and pulling his head down to her shoulder. She patted and stroked his hair. "Of course you can tell me, Dickon. I'm your friend, aren't I?"

"Aye, I hope so, Mistress Buell," he murmured, his voice muffled against her shoulder. "But I can't tell anyone."

"You can, Dickon. In times past, when I had something I couldn't talk about, my father would have me put my head on his shoulder thusly. Then I didn't have to look at him, and I could tell him anything. And you can do the same, can't you? Now tell me about it, Dickon."

He trembled and swallowed, then spoke softly. "It

265

was the captain."

"And he was cruel to you?" she replied, patting his head. "He's a hard taskmaster and unduly so at times. Her voice faded as he shook his head. "It wasn't that, then? What was it, Dickon?"

He hesitated again, then replied in a quavering whisper. "I was on liberty tonight, and I met him in the settlement. He told me to come to his room in the tavern for a drink of rum. So I went to his room, and when I got there, he made me take off my breeches, and he——"

Meghan was perplexed for an instant, then chilling shock gripped her as she realized what the boy meant. She held him close, thinking of things that suddenly had meaning. Two men on the pier in Sydney had talked about rumors concerning Buell. He had displayed her on the street the day he had brought her from Parramatta. Cabin boys had been on the ship and had left. Drexler and Suggs had been on the point of severing ties with Buell, evidently having heard the rumors, and their attitude had changed when they met her.

Anger replaced her shock. "I'll see that it won't happen again, Dickon," she said. "Try to put it aside and forget it, if you can."

"Perhaps it would be better if I just left the ship and hid ashore," he whimpered. "I don't want to face him again."

"Desert your ship?" she replied indignantly. "No one will force you to do such a dishonorable thing. I'll see to that! And you won't have to face him. Do your duty and stay out of his road, and I'll see to the rest of it."

She opened the door and let him out, then closed it and walked back to the table. Her anger returned, a fiery rage swelling within her. She undressed and went to bed.

Revulsion blended with her anger as she thought about the times that Buell had taken her while in a drunken stupor, trying to make her pregnant and himself more secure. The thought occurred to her that what she had learned was a potential way to be free of Buell, and a potential means to happiness with Earl Garrity. But her remission of sentence had been through marriage, and she was uncertain of the legal ramifications. More than that, Dickon Muir's shame would be made public, and everyone associated with Buell would be touched by the scandal. The problem was hers alone, and she would have to deal with it alone, and then live with the situation.

Hours passed. Tench returned to the ship, and went to his cabin. Another boat thumped against the hull as some of the men returned to the ship. The ship's bell rang the midwatch, and the anchor watch changed. Meghan remained sleepless, looking up into the darkness, listening to the quiet sounds of the ship, waiting for dawn. The morning watch rang, and the anchor watch changed again. Then the portholes turned gray as first light came. She got up and dressed.

Tench saw something was wrong when she took his breakfast into the wardroom. He asked her about it, then dropped the subject when she shrugged off the question. Tench finished and went out on deck. And she washed the dishes and sat at the table in the galley again. The ship's carpenter and Hensley's men started the day's work, hammering at the base of the mainmast. A boat came alongside and a moment later she heard Buell's voice on deck.

He was standing with Tench by an open hatch and discussing the work on the mainmast when Meghan walked out on the deck. "I'd like a word with you."

His brows drew together in an impatient frown. "Well, have it then!" he snapped.

"I will, if that's what you wish. But I believe it would be best seen to in the cabin."

His eyes narrowed, and his frown became uncertain. Meghan turned and walked toward the passageway. Buell muttered something to Tench in a tone of forced amusement, and followed her. He came in behind her, and slammed the door.

"Now what the bloody hell do you want?" he demanded.

She turned and faced him. "You're to leave Dickon Muir alone. Except in connection with his duties, you're to have nothing at all to do with him."

Consternation, fear, and embarrassment flashed across his face. He was stupified for an instant, then he recovered and took the offensive. "What the bloody hell are you talking about?" he bellowed. "You don't tell me what to do!"

"You know full well what I'm talking about!' she snapped. "I can see it in your scurvy, piggish eyes, you vile creature! And I'm telling you to cease befouling this good boy with your evil, unholy desires."

His face turned red, and he raised his fist threateningly. "You don't talk to me like that, woman!" he roared. "I'll teach you your place!"

"If that blow falls, I'll destroy you!" she hissed, stepping toward him. She stopped inches from him. "I'll spread this to the ends of the earth! Wherever you go, from Calcutta to the roads of the Thames, every ship's master in every port where you drop anchor will salute you with a pair of pantaloons from the tip of his mainmast! If you still command a ship, that is, which is beyond imagining!"

"I don't know what the bloody hell you're talking about," he growled defensively. "It could be that I said or did something that was taken wrong, or——"

"Have done with lies and evasion!" she interrupted him impatiently. "We both know the fact of the matter, and it's what was rumored abroad in Sydney. One would think you'd have taken warning and mended your depraved ways, but that's neither here nor there. At issue here is your abuse of a good boy, and I'll not stand idly by for that." She leaned toward him, pointing at him. "And further, you've put your foul hands on me for the last time!"

"By God, I took you out of the prison in Parramatta, and I can send you back there," he muttered.

"Aye, perhaps you can," she replied. "But until you do, you're brought up short against the fact that I'm a Conley. There's a name known to most of the ship's masters in this harbor, and I daresay it's also known to the master of the frigate in the harbor. And if I undertake to broadcast this, I've no doubt I'll get a fair hearing. Now you know what's to be done, and it's no more than discretion would dictate to one less ruled

269

by degenerate and loathsome desires. Do it and be done with it."

He stood with his back to her. "I want naught to do with the swining brat, nor with you for that matter. But I'll not have him spreading lies about me."

"You may be assured of his silence, if that's your concern. His shame is as great as the odious indignity you inflicted upon him."

He turned and walked to the door, and looked back at her. "By God, you might think you can call me down like a schoolboy and get away with it, but you'll pay for this."

"I wouldn't attempt to do it to a man."

"The day will come when you'll rue saying that," he grated. "You can mark my words, you scurvy wench. You'll live to regret your loose tongue."

"Aye, I've no doubt you'll seek revenge," she said quietly. "I knew that when I undertook this. But you've killed the albatross, and you'll proceed with caution unless you wish to have it hung about your neck for all the world to see."

He snatched the door open and stamped out, slamming it behind him. Meghan felt drained, weary from lack of sleep and exhausted by anger. Tears burned in her eyes, and she blinked them away and sat and waited for Buell to leave the ship.

But Buell was still on ship, barking and ordering men about, and he had several more men helping the carpenter and working on the starboard furnace. It was a long time before he left. Tench came in for lunch a few minutes later. While they were eating, he told her Buell wanted to sail as soon as possible.

Hensley sent two additional men to the ship during the afternoon, and they stripped up the temporary decking and cut seasoned boards to replace it. Tench curtailed liberty for some of the men, and put more of them with the ship's carpenter and those working on the furnace. When Meghan went to bed, the men were still working by the light of lanterns. The noise kept her awake for hours.

Work on the repairs started early the next morning. Hensley again sent additional men to the ship. Buell arrived earlier than usual, and Tench hurriedly finished breakfast and went out on deck. Meghan went up on the quarterdeck to watch the men working. Hensley arrived with two of his men who were delivering bricks for the furnace, and he and Buell got into an argument about the repairs. When Hensley threatened to take his men off the ship, Buell controlled his temper and the work went on.

Buell left shortly after Hensley. Work on the mainmast stepping was completed during the afternoon, and boats loaded with the new casks pulled alongside the ship. The last of the casks were stowed and the hatches were closed, and the repairs to the decking were finished before nightfall. Work on the starboard continued by lantern light.

On Saturday it became evident that the ship would be able to leave no sooner than the morning tide on Monday. Buell spent only a short time on the ship, grumbling as he looked at the disassembled furnace. Meghan steamed the wrinkles out of a dress and prepared to go to church the next day.

Sunday was a bittersweet, poignantly enchanting

day. The sun seemed brighter than usual, and the air was sparkling clear. The foliage on the hills and the blue of the sky were rich and vibrant. Meghan shrugged off all thoughts of Buell, and the day was keenly enjoyable for her. Time seemed to be suspended. But time did pass, and the knowledge that a happy time was coming to a close added a haunting, melancholy overtone to each moment of the day.

The sun set in a blaze of colors as Meghan and Garrity sat at the table with the Cargills in their house. Dusk gathered. Amanda Cargill and her husband talked about when the *Baleen* might return to the Bay of Islands, and Meghan could visit with them again. But the uncertainties of the sea and of life were an undercurrent in all the cheerful conversations. The time to leave came, and Amanda burst into tears and clung to Meghan as they were saying goodbye on the doorstep.

Meghan and Garrity were silent as they walked down the path to the beach, and as he rowed the boat out into the bay. He rested the oars and reached for her at the same instant she reached toward him, and she flowed into his arms. She crushed herself to him, kissing him passionately and grasping for all she could wring from the moment.

"If you ever need me, Meghan, I'l turn heaven and earth to come to you. All I need is word from you, and nothing will stand in my way."

"I know, love," she whispered. "And it's my most earnest wish that a moment will come when I can send for you or come to you."

They kissed once more, and the boat moved on out

to the *Baleen*. She stood on the deck and watched him go. That night she cried herself to sleep.

Buell was aboard the ship at dawn the next morning, barking orders as the men prepared to weigh anchor. Meghan stood by the taffrail looking at the *Pamir* as it came into view from behind the clipper. Garrity was on the quarterdeck, watching the *Baleen* leave. They waved their farewells.

Chapter 15

THE STORM DESCENDED ON THE ship at night with sudden, devastating fury. The abrupt change in the motion of the ship awakened Meghan, and she struggled out of the bunk. The wind grew stronger as she dressed.

The motion of the ship threw her from one wall to the other as she stumbled along the passageway to the galley. She felt for the stove, burning her hand on it, then felt for the bucket of dishwater. She threw the water into the stove, then felt her way to the table and sat down.

The barometer had given a low reading the previous afternoon, and clouds were on the horizon at sunset. The indications had pointed to a change from the fair weather, but not to such a sudden and violent change. But a few old sailors had muttered warnings, looking at the sky and rubbing joints that were sensitive to the weather.

A bucket rolled back and forth on the floor. Faint sounds of running footsteps were audible over the screaming of the wind and the pounding of the waves as the men secured the ship.

A sail burst with a creak that was loud over the sounds of the storm. Meghan knew what the men were doing. They were putting out a sea anchor, a sail of long ropes, to let the ship ride with the storm. But she had no idea of which direction the wind was driving the ship. The coast was only a few miles away to the west.

The darkness was absolute, and Meghan had a sensation of plummeting through the night toward unknown perils. Her sense of the passage of time was confused, and many hours seemed to pass as she sat and listened to the tumult of the storm. Then the porthole in the galley began to turn gray. The light slowly brightened into dim twilight. Objects became visible. Meghan rose and returned to the cabin to get her oilskins.

A porthole cover in the cabin was loosening, and seawater ran down the wall as waves washed above the porthole. She tightened the dogs on the cover and put on her oilskins. Waves were breaking across the deck, and she waited for a moment when she could open the door without flooding the passageway. The ship pitched forward, sliding down a wave. She opened the door and stepped out.

Men were huddled along the bulkhead in front of the quarterdeck, their clothes soaked and their hair and beards plastered down by seawater and the driving rain. Life lines were stretched along the deck, and tattered shreds of sails that had burst fluttered from the yards. The rain limited visibility to a few yards.

The men reached up to help her steady herself. She gripped the knobby, calloused hands that were offered, and she loved them in her way. When she reached the steps, she waited for the ship to pitch upward. A wave broke across the bow, washing along the deck. The bow rose sharply. The steps were almost level, and she lifted the hem of her dress and ran up. Buell was by the binnacle with Tench and Porter, and he glanced at her and looked away. Tench crossed the deck, bracing himself against the motion of the ship.

"This is a very strong blow, Mistress Buell," he shouted over the wind. "You should remain inside."

"What is our heading, Mr. Tench?"

"Due west."

Meghan looked toward the bow, vainly trying to see ahead. "How far off the coast are we?"

"A few miles yet, and we should be able to hear the surf before we're on it. Our sea anchor is working well, so we're in no danger yet. And if this wind will slacken a little, we might be able to get up a sail or two so we can turn to the south."

Meghan nodded, moving back toward the steps. "I'll put up some cold breakfast whenever you're ready for it."

Meghan hung up her oilskins in the galley. She listened to the wind and pounding waves, visualizing the ship moving inexorably toward its doom on the rocks along the coast. The motion of the ship changed and it became more bouyant, and voices rang out as bare feet pounded up onto the quarterdeck. A rope on the sea anchor had broken, and several minutes passed as the ship tossed wildly. Then the ship settled again, pitching and rolling in the waves.

Buell and Tench came in, water streaming from their oilskins, and Meghan brought cold food and ship's biscuit to the wardroom. The men ate, then Buell went to the cabin for a chart. He and Tench sat in the wardroom and discussed it for several minutes, then he returned it to the cabin and they went out again.

Meghan had no appetite, but she forced herself to eat a little cold meat, a piece of biscuit. Then she waited again, listening to the storm raging around the ship. Voices carried into the galley, and she rose and hastily put on her oilskins.

The rain had thinned out ahead, and over the roar of the storm, there was a deeper, rhythmic thunder—surf washing against a shoreline.

Tench was coming back from the bow. He pointed as he made his way across the deck to her. "We have a river in sight a few hundred yards to the south. We're going to try to get up a sail or two to give us steerageway. If we can get in there we'll have shelter.

"Will we make it, Mr. Tench?"

"The river appears wide and deep, and the tide and wind are with us. But an ugly point of rocks reaches out along one side of the river, and we won't have much steerageway. I believe it would be wise for you to get your belongings together."

Meghan tried to keep her fear from showing on her face. A wave washed across the deck and boiled around her legs, pulling at her dress. Tench took her arm to steady her. The wave subsided, and Tench opened the door for her and closed it behind her.

278

She piled her clothes on the bunk, then looked around. Everything appeared valuable. The ship's log caught her eye. She ran to the desk for it and raced back to the bunk, throwing it with the clothes and rolled them up. Then she tied the bundle.

The ship began responding to the rudder. The bow slowly turned to port, and the ship rolled more heavily as it quartered into the waves. Meghan sat in the galley with her bundle on her lap. Each minute felt like an eternity as she waited. The ship continued rolling far to starboard as the waves broke over the port bow, then the bow gradually turned back to starboard and the ship was oriented downwind again.

Meghan detected a straining vibration as the ship moved forward under the conflicting pressures of the tugging sails and dragging sea anchor. The thunderous roar of surf drowned all other noises.

The ship quivered, touching something solid that dragged against the hull. Meghan stiffened, gripping the table. The ship vibrated harder. Something was dragging the length of the hull.

The ship collided with rock on the starboard side with a battering force that knocked Meghan flying. She rolled across the floor of the galley, the stool sliding with her. The ship struck again with a crash of splintering timbers. The stove fell over, and sooty seawater gushed through the flue. Flour, peas, beans, and other things mixed with the seawater on the floor, and Meghan's shoes slid in it as she dragged herself back to her feet. Her bundle was a few feet away, and she lunged for it.

The door burst open, and Tench and Dickon ran in

and dragged her toward the door.

The ship struck again, and all three of them fell in the doorway. Tench and Dickon leaped to their feet, and got her up on deck. Black, gleaming rocks towered over the starboard side of the ship, pressing in over the rail. The masts were canted, and the deck was buckling. Men darted about, dragging boats and lowering them over the port side.

Porter and other men were waiting by the rail with a rowboat, and they lifted it over the rail and lowered it on ropes as Tench and Dickon crossed the deck with Meghan. The men climbed over the rail and jumped down into the boat. Tench lifted Meghan, leaned over the rail, and dropped her. The hood of her oilskins covered her face, blinding her, and she plummeted. Her breath was knocked from her as the men in the boat caught her and set her down. She managed to hold on to her bundle.

They pushed her down into the bottom of the boat. She tried to sit up, tugging at the hood of her oilskins. Tench and Dickon jumped down into the boat. The rowboat slammed into the hull of the ship with a jarring crash, and bare feet tramped Meghan's legs as men stumbled about. Tench bellowed at them, and the boat swung away from the ship.

Meghan got her oilskin hood off her face and sat up in the boat. It was crowded with men, blocking her view, but she glimpsed tall, dense trees along the banks of the wide river ahead. Waves tossed the boat and rolled far up the river on the flood tide. They broke over the stern of the boat. Water gushed into the boat from cracks that had opened in the bow when it struck the ship, and the men with oars rowed hard while others bailed.

She looked back at the ship. Cold, icy shock gripped her, her mind struggling to comprehend what she saw. The massive beams and thick timbers had seemed invincible, but the ship was in its death throes. Waves were lifting it and battering it against the rocks at the mouth of the river. The hull had been smashed under the waterline. Masses of emply oil casks, timbers, and other debris swirled in the waves.

Men clung to casks, and a rowboat was floating upside down. Another rowboat and one of the whaleboats were a few yards behind the boat Meghan was in, both of them crowded with men.

Meghan sat in watcr up to her waist in the bottom of the boat. It was almost swamped. Men bailed frantically, but the boat was gradually sinking. She glimpsed the longboat ahead, Buell standing in the stern. The far bank of the river was barely visible through the heavy rain.

The near bank was a sheer wall of earth several feet high, with towering trees down to the edge of it and tangles of roots hanging out over the water. The whaleboat passed and threw them scoops and buckets. Meghan caught a scoop, and began dipping up water and tossing it out. The other rowboat lingered behind, picking up men clinging to debris, then caught up. All three boats followed the longboat toward a stretch of river bank that tapered back into a gentle slope above the water.

Water rose higher in the boat, and Tench shouted at men not bailing or rowing to jump out. They leaped out and clung to the gunwales, swimming alongside the boat. The longboat touched the bank ahead, and the men in it jumped out and pulled its bow up onto the bank. A rowboat nosed into the bank. So did the whaleboat.

The boat Meghan was in continued to settle in the water, and the men threw their weight against the oars. It was yards from the bank, then feet. The men swimming by the boat found footing. Other men waded into the water and dragged the boat up onto the bank. Tench helped Meghan to her feet.

It was darker under the thick, towering trees above the bank, and there was a strong smell of wet earth and foliage. The men milled about, looking back down the river at the ship. Meghan clutched her bundle and held Tench's arm. Her feet sank into the mud as she walked up the bank with him.

The Maoris appeared suddenly. It was quiet, the babble of voices around Meghan almost smothered by the rainfall, and the trees were dark and silent. In the next instant Maoris were on all sides, whooping and shrieking. Canoes filled with warriors shot down the river and pulled up to the bank. Dozens rushed out of the trees. Their savage, tattooed faces were exultant as they surrounded the survivors.

They were close to death when a tall warrior bellowed orders and pushed through to the front. A steely silence fell. The sailors and the savages looked at each other, and a man near Meghan groped in his shirt for a knife. Tench touched the man's shoulder.

"Belay that," he warned quietly.

The tall warrior pointed toward the ship and

shouted. There were four Maori canoes, all much smaller than those that had attacked the ship, with twenty to twenty-five warriors in each one. The Maoris surrounded Meghan and the men, herding them up the bank.

"Men with knives gather around Mistress Buell," Tench said quietly. "And keep your weapons hidden unless they try to mistreat her."

"There'll be no resistance in any event, Mr. Tench!" Buell snapped. "I'll remind you that I'm in command of these men!"

"I'll point out that we're ashore and we've been taken captive, Captain Buell," Tench replied firmly. "I'll follow your orders, but not beyond the point where they collide with the dictates of my conscience."

Buell glared at Tench, but remained silent. The men climbed the bank, and they gathered around Meghan. There they stood and waited, the rain drumming against the trees overhead, dropping down onto the path and the wet undergrowth. The Maoris seemed fascinated by Meghan. Their tattooed faces and chests gleamed wetly in the rain.

Tench squeezed Meghan's arm, and she pushed back the hood of her oilskins and looked up at him. He smiled encouragingly and patted her arm. She forced a smile and nodded, and looked back at the warriors. The taller warrior stood to one side of the others and looked down the river. One of the canoes came back up the river, and four sailors who had been picked up along the bank and from the ship were huddled in the center of it. Warriors went down to the edge of the river and herded the four men up to the others, and the canoe went back down the river.

The tall warrior shouted and beckoned, and the other warriors closed in around the survivors. The group began moving along the path, and the men around Meghan fingered their knives. The path led around the side of a low bluff above the river, and turned into a wide, trampled road as the trees opened out. There was a village ahead.

It was on a low, bare incline overlooking the river, and other canoes were at the edge of the river below it. A high palisade wall surrounded the village, enclosing an acre or more. A horde of men, women, and children streamed out of the wide gate in the wall and rushed down the slope. They waved their arms and danced, shouting and cheering in a deafening uproar as they crowded around Meghan and the men.

The villagers seemed more curious than blood-thirsty, but their frenzy of dancing and shouting indicated a dangerous potential for violence. And their savage, primitive appearance made them frightening. Men wore the skirt-like garment Meghan had seen at the Bay of Islands, and most of the women wore a similar garment with a cape around the shoulders. Some women wore nothing over their breasts, and some men were without facial tattoos. Women had dark tattoos on their chins and lower lips. Most of them were short and stout, and they had long, black hair.

The warriors tried to keep the villagers back, but Meghan and the men were jostled as the people pushed in on all sides. Children squealed and pushed through the adults to look, and dogs darted about through the crowd. The gateposts at the front of the village were ornately carved, and the wide gates were pulled back against the palisade walls. There was a tight squeeze at the gate, villagers crowding through on each side of Meghan and the men, and pushing in behind them.

A wide street led through the village, and low, sprawling houses with wood walls and thatched roofs were on both sides. Side streets had houses scattered along them, and the openings between houses were malodorous garbage dumps. The street inclined upward, and a larger building with open sides and richly carved roof beams was in the center of the village. The tall warrior, the chief of some kind, stopped at a house on a corner. He gestured and the Maoris pushed Meghan and the men toward the door.

Men filed into the house ahead of Meghan, ducking their heads because of the low doorway. Tench took Moghan's arm and guided her in ahead of him. The house was a single large, dim room, with a fire smoldering in the center of the floor. It was smoky from the fire, and the rafters supporting the thatched roof were barely high enough for Tench to stand erect. Grass mats were scattered about on the dirt floor, and the house smelled of dogs and wet, mildewed thatching. The rest of the men came in, and several of the warriors stood guard outside the door. Tench glanced around and spoke briskly. "Well, let's get settled down and keep in good spirits, lads. Some of you fetch a few of those grass rugs over to a corner. You can hang them from the rafters and give Mistress Buell a bit of privacy."

"Mr. Tench, I'll thank you to cease ordering my men about!" Buell objected angrily. "I'm in command of these men, and I'll give the orders!"

"And what are your orders, Captain Buell?" Tench asked imperturbably. "It would appear there are severe limits on what we can do."

"I'll study the situation and decide," Buell growled. "In any event, there are things of greater importance than providing privacy for her."

"Aye, I won't debate that," Tench said. "And I'm sure Mistress Buell would gladly dispense with privacy if she could be elsewhere. But it won't do any harm, and I don't believe it'll make the men so weary that they'll be unable to carry out your orders when you decide what you want them to do. That corner over there, men, away from the door."

Glowering at Tench, Buell stalked to the fire and sat down by it. Some of the men gathered up mats and carried them to the corner. They pulled strands of grass out of them and tied them to the rafters, partitioning off the corner. Meghan nodded thanks. She went behind the mats, took off her oilskins, and hung them on a beam in the corner. The men had dropped extra mats on the floor, and she spread them out and put her bundle down.

Chilling fear gripped her as she sat in the quiet corner. She had escaped death in the shipwreck only to be captured by cannibals whose ferocity was known to everyone. They were still alive, but for how long?

Buell, Tench, and Porter sat by the fire, and the men gathered around them. The men were silent and fearful. Tench talked to them cheerfully and speculated about the possibilities of a favorable outcome to the situation. He joked with the men, and started them laughing, talking, and ridiculing those who looked most frightened. Meghan sat in the corner and listened, trying to control her fear.

A chant came from somewhere in the village, the voices of men and women. It lacked the threatening cadence and ring of the chant of the warriors who had attacked the ship, but it still sounded ominous. The street outside the house was constantly busy, people rushing back and forth and calling to each other. It sounded as if preparations were being made for some kind of gathering.

The chant continued, and villagers still hurried back and forth along the street as the hours passed. The conversation among the men lagged occasionally. Tench always got it going. Darkness fell and the men found wood by a wall, and they built up the fire. The feeble light of the flames shone under the edges of the mats hanging around Meghan.

A babble of talk broke out among the warriors, then one of them came in and shouted. The men stirred and Tench called Meghan. The warrior inside the door was holding a torch, and the yellow light gleamed on his fierce, tattooed face. Tench took Meghan's arm, and men gathered around her.

It had stopped raining, but the dark sky was still overcast and a gusty wind was blowing. The warriors outside the house held torches. They smoked heavily and smelled strongly of resin as the wind whipped the flames. Villagers lined the street. They were dim figures on the edge of the torch light, and they chanted and danced as the warriors herded Meghan and the men along the street.

A blaze of light came from torches stuck into the ground around the large building in the center of the village. More villagers were gathered around it. The torches illuminated the center of the village and nearby houses, and the crowd became noisier as Meghan and the men approached. The sides of the building were open and the wooden floor was elevated above the ground. Four men were at the front of the building.

One sat and the other three stood behind him, and one of the three was the tall warrior who had been at the river bank. The one who sat was obviously the principal chief. His face was seamed with age under the dark lines of tattooing. His shock of black hair was streaked with gray, and he gazed around imperiously. The prisoners were brought to a halt in front of him.

Plunder from the ship was piled in the building behind the four men. Casks, sails, cordage, pieces of iron, and other things were in a huge, jumbled mass. Meghan saw one of her beer urns. The weapons from the lazarette were at one side, and arranged with more care. Muskets, cutlasses, pistols, boarding pikes were in neat rows on the floor.

The chief rose to his feet, and the villagers grew silent. The silence was abrupt and absolute, broken only by the crackling and fluttering noises of the torches in the wind. The chief stepped down to the ground and shouldered his way through the prisoners. The men moved aside uncertainly, not knowing what to do. The chief stopped when he got to Meghan.

The man was tall. He towered over her and his burly shoulders and deep chest were covered with the scars from many battles. His dark eyes were piercing, and the tattooes on his face were grotesque ridges of scar tissue. Meghan steeled herself, looking up into his eyes. He reached out, and Meghan fought for control as he squeezed her arm.

He turned away, shaking his head, commenting in a disparaging tone. Then he went to the edge of the crowd and patted a stout woman's fleshy arm with approval. Laughter broke out, swelling to a roar as the villagers howled their amusement and craned their necks to look at Meghan. The chief stepped back up into the building. His smile faded, and the laughter died away. He shouted a command to a warrior before he sat down.

The warrior stepped up into the building and picked up one of the muskets. He pointed to the men, sweeping his finger back and forth, shouting two syllables over and over in an imperative voice. As he kept repeating them, a frown formed on his face and became darker. Meghan suddenly realized he was shouting two mispronounced words in English.

"Who chief?" the warrior boomed. "Who chief?"

Buell turned and looked as Tench nudged him and pointed. Then he glanced around uneasily and stepped out in front of the men. "I'm the captain here," he said uncertainly. "My name is Captain Buell."

The warrior looked at Buell, and spoke to other warriors standing in front of the building. The warriors pushed a man without facial tattoos out in front of them and stepped back. The man glanced around fearfully, and started to move back among the villagers until the chief shouted at him. Then he froze in terror, glancing at the chief, looking for mercy. The warrior handed the musket to Buell, and pointed to the terrified man.

"You kill," he ordered.

Buell took the musket and shook his head. "The powder's wet." He pointed to a keg of powder among the loot from the ship. "Here, pass me that keg of powder, and I'll show you. Seawater's got to it, and it's no good now."

The warrior picked up the keg and carried it forward. Buell opened it and took out a pinch of the dark, gummy mass of wet gunpowder, and he explained in pantomime that it was useless. The three men standing behind the chief moved closer and watched. Buell explained several times. They finally understood and the warrior reached down to take the musket back.

"Hand me a cutlass if you want the bugger killed," Buell said, pointing to the cutlasses. "I'll do the job just as good, and I'll show you how to use it properly."

The chief was dissatisfied, and shook his head. He glared at Buell and the rest of them. Then he looked up at the three warriors standing behind him. They spoke in a murmur, and the chief pondered again. When he was finished, he bellowed an order. The warriors moved closer. But there was no killing—at least not yet.

The villagers were quiet. The silence seemed ominous as the group moved along the dark street, the light of the torches flickering on the front of the houses. The prisoners filed back into the house and built up the fire in the center of the floor, talking quietly. They looked up in surprise. Four Maori women had come in with baskets of food, cold baked fish and thin, gnarled roots similar to yams.

The men thought this was a good sign, and their spirits picked up. Meghan had no appetite, but she took a yam and ate it as she lay down behind the curtain of mats. The men became quiet after they finished eating. A few were able to sleep.

Meghan's clothes were damp and clammy, and the dirt floor was hard and cold under the thin mat. She stared into the darkness for hours, exhausted but sleepless. Finally she sank into a shallow, restless sleep.

The village stirred at dawn, awakening Meghan. Memory returned as she woke, and it brought a sense of despair. She summoned her courage, and tried to shrug off the crushing despondency. The men began moving about and talking. Meghan straightened her dress and pulled her hair back and tied it. Tench called to her, and she got up and came out.

A woman stood inside the door. She beckoned Meghan. Tench looked at the woman, then at Meghan. "We'll make a stand if you don't wish to go with her, Mistress Buell."

Meghan hesitated, then she shook her head. "No, thank you, Mr. Tench. I'm sure she means no harm."

Tench nodded reluctantly. The woman was large, with bare, pendulous breasts, an intricate pattern of tattooing on her stony face. Meghan followed her out.

The woman led the way to the gate, and down toward the river. Other women were walking to and from the river, most of them with children, and they stared curiously at Meghan. A large group of women and children were bathing in a pool to one side of where the canoes were beached, and the woman turned onto a path along the river and led Meghan up river to where others were bathing. Several children started to follow, then turned back when the woman shouted at them.

The splashing and shouting faded behind, and the path led past another shallow pool. The woman undressed and waded into the pool, motioning for Meghan to do the same. Meghan undressed and waded into the water. The woman glanced at Meghan without interest as she splashed water over herself. Meghan bathed, then followed the woman back out of the water and got dressed.

The woman led Meghan back to the house, but the men weren't there. She looked for her bundle, and it was where she had left it. The men returned a few minutes later, their voices carrying along the street. They had been taken to another pool along the river, and some of them were digruntled because they had been made to bathe.

Buell was not among them, and Tench told Meghan that he had been taken to see the chief again. The four women who had brought food the night before came in with baskets of shellfish and yams. The men gathered around and Tench divided the food. He gave Meghan three clams and pieces of yam, and she took them to her corner. When she finished eating, she untied her bundle and spread out her clothes to dry. Then she heard Buell come in, laughing and sounding confident.

"By God, they're going to turn us loose, Mr. Tench!" he yelled. "They're going to let us go!"

The men gasped in astonishment. Meghan stepped from behind the mats and looked at the men gathering around Buell. "They are?"

"How did you manage to get them to agree to that?" Tench asked.

"These buggers are forever warring with each other, and it appears this lot has a war going on with a nearby tribe," Buell said happily. "They want to kill them more than they want to kill us, so they've agreed to release everyone in exchange for ten kegs of gunpowder and teaching them how to use the muskets."

Tench nodded, stroking his chin. "Aye, well, that's more than fair, considering who we're dealing with. It's only a matter of a trip to the settlement and back."

Buell grunted and nodded in satisfaction. "They've said I can use the longboat and take a crew of four men with me, and I'll have ten days to get there and back. The weather's clearing nicely, and I should be able to do it in less than that."

"Aye, that longboat will go anywhere a ship can," Tench agreed. "Did you ask them if you could take Mistress Buell? It would be good to get her out of here as soon as possible."

Buell hesitated. "I didn't, but for now they'll only let me go with a crew of four for the longboat."

The men were silent for a moment. Meghan concealed her disappointment, forcing a smile. She knew Buell was lying, but it seemed likely that the Maoris

293

would have refused if he had asked. Buell sat down by the fire with Tench and Porter, and the conversation began again as he discussed the trip with them. He talked with them for several minutes, then he looked around and picked out the men who were to accompany him.

The four men followed him, and others crowded about saying noisy, boisterous farewells. At the door, Buell paused and turned back. He looked at Meghan with a faint, sardonic smile, then he went out. It was the first time he had smiled at her.

The men settled down around the fire, elated over the prospect of release. Meghan went back to see to her clothes.

The last of the firewood was used up during the afternoon. Tench spoke to the warriors who knew a few words of English and he allowed Tench to take five men out to gather wood. They came back during late afternoon, and the four women brought more food shortly after nightfall. The night passed, and the woman who had taken Meghan to the river to bathe came to get her again.

To pass the time, she looked through the ship's log she had wrapped in her clothes and read the entries from years before. The days became a routine. The woman came to take her to the river each morning. The rest of the day was without incident. Tench was summoned several times to explain the use of some article the Maoris had recovered from the wreck of the ship, and now and then he was allowed to take men out to gether firewood or to collect shellfish at the mouth of the river.

The woman who took Meghan to the river each morning was impersonal, performing a task that someone in authority had assigned her. The only reaction from the other villagers was curiosity. But Meghan was unable to overcome her constant fear of them, because they were a primitive people and placed no value on life. Even when they were placid, the threat of deadly violence was always there.

How could she forget the heavily-tattooed man who killed a man without facial markings? It happened near the pool where Meghan was taken to bathe. The man with tattoos suddenly lifted the club and split the other man's skull.

The killing attracted only passing interest among others who were nearby. The man with tattooed features wiped his club on a clump of grass and walked away, dismissing the incident from his mind. The woman with Meghan made a whimsical comment, smiling in amusement, and walked on along the river bank. Meghan followed her, numb with shock and terror.

The men's anticipation of their promised release began to fade after a week had passed, and Buell failed to return. On the tenth day, Tench was summoned to talk with the chief and the warrior who spoke some English. When he returned, he was quiet and thoughtful, vague about what had been discussed. He tried to take some of the men out to gather firewood the next day, and the warriors at the door refused to let them leave.

On the twelfth day, there was a disturbance in the village as Meghan returned from the river with the woman. Villagers along the river bank rushed up the slope to the gate, and smoke rose from a large fire in the center of the village. When Meghan reached the village, she saw warriors dragging Gibbs and another man named Hanks along the street. Villagers gathered around, chanting eagerly.

The woman forgot Meghan, and ran along the street to join the others. The chanting became louder, a frenzied, pounding beat of many voices joining together in a rising cadence. Meghan could hear Gibbs and Hanks screaming. The entire village was gathered around the fire, and the men Meghan saw had savage, ferocious smiles.

The prisoners were silent, glancing up at Meghan as she entered. Tench rose and followed Meghan to her corner, and spoke quietly. "Gibbs said he wanted you to have this, Mistress Buell."

He held out a large sperm whale's tooth, and Meghan took it. It was a tooth from the first sperm whale that had been taken during the voyage of the *Baleen,* and Meghan had frequently seen Gibbs working on it with his knife and a sharpened nail. The long, tapered piece of ivory was covered with scrimshaw, and she turned it in her hands and looked at it.

A large etching of the *Baleen* was on one side, painstakingly and expertly scratched into the ivory in perfect detail. Etchings of boats approaching a whale, men flensing a whale, and other small scenes were on the top and bottom. On the other side there was an etching of her standing on the quarterdeck of the *Baleen,* with Tench and Porter in the background.

"Thank you, Mr. Tench," Meghan said.

She went to her corner and untied her bundle. She put the whale's tooth in it and tied it again. Then she lay down and pillowed her head on the bundle. Tears filled her eyes and she smothered her sobs to keep the men from hearing.

She thought about Buell's faint, sardonic smile on the day he had left. It finally had meaning to her. He had left, never intending to return.

PART FOUR

Chapter 16

"I SAY THE BUGGER WAS headed for Australia," the bosun's mate insisted loudly. "That boat couldn't have got where it was unless he had been."

"To what bloody end?" the marine sergeant demanded. "What ship's master would go off and leave his crew and wife to the mercies of cannibals? And who'd try to sail from New Zealand to Australia in a small boat?"

The bosun's mate whooped with laughter, and leaned over and slapped the sergeant's shoulder. "Kemp, you keep to your bayonets and such, and leave seafaring to seamen. A ship's longboat is an ample craft to sail from New Zealand to Australia. And the way the winds were setting, that boat couldn't have been blown off course. Its bloody course was from New Zealand to Australia. As to why it was, the only one who'd know that is dead." He turned and looked Garrity. "Someone said you knew him, Mr. Garrity. Did he strike you as he sort who'd do that?"

Garrity shook his head. "I only saw him a time or

two, and I didn't know him. But Mr. Tench, the mate on the *Baleen,* is a good friend of mine. It does seem beyond reason, though, that a man would abandon his wife and crew to cannibals. Also, the master of the ship that picked up the boat and survivors was in doubt as to the exact position where he found them. He'd been having a lot of trouble with his compass. He didn't have a sextant, and he'd been blown off course several times."

"Aye, that's true," the bosun's mate agreed. He turned back to the sergeant. "Now there's a right one for you, Kemp. A lame compass and no bloody sextant, and somehow he found New Zealand. I'd as soon been in that longboat."

"And I'll take this warship over both of them, by far," the sergeant replied. "I'm a soldier, and I've no great fondness for ships of any sort. But I wouldn't be on some of the little cockleshells that I've seen plying back and forth across the sea."

The men crowded into the deckhouse laughed heartily at the sergeant's comical expression, and they continued discussing Buell and the longboat from the *Baleen.* Garrity smoked his pipe and listened. The deckhouse was the quarters for petty officers and noncommissioned officers on the frigate *Viper.* Buell and the longboat had been a constant topic of conversation among the men since the warship set sail from the Bay of Islands.

The boat had been picked up by a small trading ship that plied back and forth between Australia and New Zealand. Three men were in it. The three insisted that the boat had been enroute from where the *Baleen* had gone around to the Bay of Islands, and it had been caught in a severe storm. They told how Buell and another man were washed overboard during a storm. They had been attempting to find their way to the Bay of Islands when the ship found them.

When the ship had found the boat, it had been far off course from a direct line between where the *Baloon* had wrecked and the Bay of Islands. But it had been heading toward the Bay of Islands. The three men all related the same story and steadfastly insisted that they were telling the truth when the captain of the *Viper* and others questioned them. However, no other ship had encountered the storm they described. Two of the men had injuries that looked suspiciously like knife wounds, and their explanations about how they injured themselves were implausible.

Some, like the bosun's mate, thought that Buell had set a course for Australia. Few seamen could navigate, a fact which prevented mutiny in many instances, because the mutineers would be unable to find a port unless an officer joined or cooperated with them. But any seaman could tell directions by the sun and stars, and it would have been evident to the men in the boat that they were going in the wrong direction.

The bosun's mate and others speculated that at least some of the men in the boat had refused to abandon their shipmates and had mutinied, and Buell and another man had been killed during the ensuing fight. Then the remaining men had agreed on a story, and had remained unshakable on it. And for good reason, because a mutiny in which the master of the vessel was killed would result in summary execution of the mutineers, regardless of the motives involved.

Other explanations fit the facts, including the possibility that the longboat had been caught in a freak storm. But they were all irrelevant to Garrity. His single, overriding concern was that Meghan was a captive of the Maoris, and the ten day deadline the Maoris had given Buell to return from the Bay of Islands had been exceeded by more than two weeks.

The conversation in the deckhouse broke off as the door opened and a marine guard looked in. "The captains compliments to volunteer officers," he said. "And will they please repair immediately to the wardroom."

"Aye, we're starting to get set now," the sergeant said in grim satisfaction. "Those bloody buggers are going to get the shock of their heathenish lives when we get there."

Garrity and three other men stood up. The captain of the *Viper* had asked for volunteers to augment the marines on the warship, and most of the men on the vessels at anchor on the Bay of Islands had volunteered. A few from each ship had been selected, and Garrity and three other second officers from the ship had been selected to command the volunteer contingent.

The moonlight glinted on the waves, and the mass of bulging sails on the mast shadowed the deck and blotted out the stars. The warship was under full sail, speeding south through the night toward the river where the *Baleen* had wrecked. Lanterns glowed on each side of the door leading to the officers' cabins and wardroom, and the marine guard stepped ahead and opened the door. He held it for Garrity and the others, then followed them in and opened the wardroom door.

The lanterns hanging from the ceiling beams rocked gently with the motion of the ship, and cast flowing shadows around the room and along the long, gleaming table. The first and second officers of the ship were at the table with the commander of marines, Lieutenant Perry. Two Maoris from the Bay of Islands sat in a corner, cheerfully enthusiatic about leading a military expedition against an enemy tribe.

The door opened, and Garrity and the others rose as the captain entered. He was a stocky man of forty, brisk and neat in his uniform and gold epaulettes. He placed a chart on the table. "Be seated, gentlemen. Lieutenant Perry, did you have a look at the arms the volunteers were provided by their captains?"

"Aye, I did, sir," Perry replied. "They'll do amply well. Some of the men were short on shot and powder, and I had enough issued to give each man twenty-five rounds."

The captain unrolled the chart and pointed. "By daybreak tomorrow, we'll be here. Lieutenant Perry, you'll disembark with the volunteers, the marines, and a Maori guide, and you will proceed overland to the village. I'll stand offshore until the next morning, then I'll take the ship up the river on the morning tide. That should be just before you arrive, from what the guides say. I'll attempt to negotiate the release of the captives, and if that fails I'll open fire. I'll lift the cannon bombardment when I see you attacking. Questions?"

Perry stroked his chin, looking at the chart. "What if you don't have on onshore wind that morning, sir?"

"Then I'll lower boats and have the ship towed up the river," the captain said testily. "When I asked for questions, Lieutenant Perry, I referred to your undertaking and not to mine. Be assured that *Viper* will be in the river abreast of the village."

Perry was unruffled by the captain's acid tone. "Are you certain we have the right village, sir? It would be a disaster of no small magnitude if we were to end up fighting the wrong savages."

The captain lifted his eyebrows and shrugged. "We know how long the *Baleen* was enroute and her approximate speed, so we know the approximate area the shipwreck occurred. The guides say this is the only river in that area which fits the description the survivors provided us, and we must trust their judgment. They also say the village will have lookouts posted, but they think that *Viper* will draw the attention of the lookouts when we come upriver. That being the case, you should encounter none."

"Aye, the warship should draw everyone's attention," Perry agreed. "And our attack should come as a surprise, which will go far toward winning the battle. I have no more questions, sir."

"The stewards will issue cold rations for the shore party," the captain said, glancing around the table. "There will be no baggage porters, so each man will carry his own rations and blanket. Does anyone else have any questions?"

"What if all the captives have been killed, sir?" one of the volunteer officers asked.

"Then we will have done all we can," the captain replied. "But there will be no reprisals, regardless of what we find. A savage can't help being a savage, and those who have commerce with them or sail these waters would be well advised to keep that in mind. The village will probably burn if we fire on it, but I want no unnecessary killing. In that respect, Lieutenant Perry, you'll keep the men you command under control. Forces under my command will not engage in massacres."

"Aye, aye, sir," Perry replied. "There will be no massacre."

The captain rose and rolled up the chart. "Let's hope the Maoris will turn over the captives to us and be done with it. But if it comes to force of arms, I'm sure you and your men will acquit yourselves well. I wish you good fortune."

Garrity and the others rose as the captain turned to go. They moved away from the table and filed out the door. Perry and the two officers walked along the passageway toward their cabins. Garrity went back out on deck. He crossed the deck to the rail and leaned against it, looking out at the ocean."

The moon was a gleaming disc in the sky, and large, fleecy clouds drifted slowly across the stars and passed in front of the moon. The night was like the night he had brought Meghan back to the *Baleen* from the Cargill house. Each moment of that day and evening was engraved in his memory, as was every moment he had spent with her from the first time they met.

Images of her floated in his mind as he stood and

gazed out at the waves. He thought of how she had looked the first time they met, how she looked in church, and at other times. She was a small woman who gave an impression of a larger stature, a young woman who had a mature bearing. Her steady gaze and self-assured aplomb made him feel awkwardly boyish and gauche at times, and her radiant, sparkling smile took his breath away.

He thought about his trepidation the first time he tried to kiss her, and his rapture when she assented. Her indomitable will, rigid code of right and wrong, and other things about her made her strikingly similar to his mother in some respects, yet she was warm and loving and like no one else in the world. He loved her with an intensity that was painful, a love that permeated every fiber of his body. Without her, life had no meaning.

But she had been taken prisoner by the Maoris, and the time they had allowed for her to be ransomed had long since passed. Garrity sighed as he turned away from the rail and went back to the deckhouse. All the men had gone to bed and it was dark there, filled with the sounds of snoring and heavy breathing. He felt his way across it to the corner where he had left his blanket, pistol, and cutlass.

He unrolled his blanket, then he lay down and pulled it around him. Frustrated, helpless anger gnawed at him as he thought of Meghan living in constant terror in a Maori village. He forced it out of his mind, and willed himself to sleep.

Several petty officers got up to go on duty when the morning watch rang. The petty officers coughed and yawned sleepily as they dressed by the light of a lantern. Garrity rolled up his blanket and went out with them. He washed his face and hands at the water butt, then went to the forecastle galley. The cook passed out pannikins of strong, scalding tea and plates of steaming plum duff. Garrity went out to eat on deck.

The stars dimmed in the east as the sun came up. The ship angled in toward the shoreline. Orders rang out in the dark, men bustled about, and blocks rattled and squeaked as the sails were trimmed to the wind. The coastline was a dark mass to the west, gradually becoming more distinct as the light grew stronger.

The captain came out and went up to the quarter-deck. The ship bustled with activity as it moved in toward the broken, rugged shoreline. The Marines and volunteers formed on the deck, and Garrity lined up his men with the others. Stewards issued cheese and ship's biscuit to each man, and Perry walked through the ranks of the volunteers and once again examined the weapons their captains had issued them. A sheltered cove with a shingle beach came into sight ahead, and the ship turned in closer to the shore as sailors scrambled aloft to furl the sails.

The ship's boats made two trips to ferry all the marines and volunteers to the beach . And Garrity and his men went with the first group. Garrity sat on the beach with his men, watching the boats as they went back to the ship for the second group. He seethed with impatience. Everything seemed to be taking place at a leisurely pace. Perry and the Maori guide sat at one side and conferred over a chart. The men laughed and talked as they lounged and tossed pebbles into the water.

The ship had a satisfyingly martial appearance as it lay hove to a mile off the beach. The tiny figures of men swarmed over the side and down to the boats bobbing in the waves alongside the ship. The boats moved away from it. The long oars flashed in the sunlight as the boats climbed up and down the swells. Then they swept in to the beach on a wave. Perry shouted orders and the men formed a column. The boats went back toward the ship.

Perry knew the location of the river and the village, and the Maori guide was a presumed expert on finding a safe and easy route. The column left the beach, started into a dense growth of ferns, brush, and vines under the massive, towering trees. Some of the men sang as they marched, alarming the Maori guide, but Perry ignored it. After the first mile, the men were silently and grimly struggling through the thick tangle of growth. The route led up and down the coastal hills, through valleys and across the rocky slopes. Half of the marines were at the head of the column and half were at the rear, and they set a hard, driving pace.

Garrity relished the rapid pace. He fought through foliage, helped men who stumbled, and shouted at his men to keep up. The column spread out as the men became weary. Perry called a halt at a creek at midday. Men collapsed by the creek and splashed water on their faces. The Maori prowled up and down the creek and looked for shellfish. Garrity waited for the march to resume.

The ocean came into sight again during late afternoon. The column went over an inland mountain slope that had been denuded of trees by a forest fire. The ocean was on the far side of the rugged coastal hills that the column had painfully traversed. It melted into the blue sky on the horizon. The light began to fade. Some of the men were nearly exhausted, and Perry called a halt for the day.

Most of the men were stiff and sore when the column formed again at daybreak, and they hobbled along as the column marched south across broken hills and swampy lowlands. The coastline curved inward ahead, coming into sight as the column crossed the hills. Men spotted the ship and pointed to it. It was under full sail, heading for the mouth of a wide river a short distance along the coast. The column veered away from the coast, and the ship and the river were lost from sight.

Perry slowed the column, passing the word back to move more quietly. The Maori picked out a route that led through a winding valley between the hills along the river. The river came into sight again along a rushing creek that fed into it, and the column turned up the hill at one side of the creek. Perry halted the column and summoned all the marines to the head of it, then slowly led the way up the hill.

The top of the hill was covered with thick brush and old, rotting stumps where trees had been cut down years before. A haze of woodsmoke rose beyond it. Perry halted the column again and formed the men into squads on a line abreast, then led them forward again. Garrity and his men crept through the brush behind a squad of marines. He could see the village and the river from the top of the next hill.

The village covered a slope on the other side of a shallow valley, and it was three-hundred yards away. The ship was anchored in the river, but from where canoes were beached below the village. A boat from the ship was at the edge of the river and one of the officers from the ship was talking with warriors. The slope between the river and the village was filled with warriors, women, and children, all of them milling about in excitement.

The marines stopped on Perry's command. Garrity halted his men and told them to take cover. The arrival of the overland force, had gone unnoticed by the Maoris. All of their attention was focused on the warship. Garrity watched for several minutes, and the scene remained unchanged. The Maori who had come from the *Viper* translated what the warrior was saying to the naval officer. An impasse appeared to have developed.

Garrity crawled forward, working his way through the marines to where Perry lay in front of them. Perry was in a clump of brush, the other Maori at his side. Garrity pointed to the river bank, "There doesn't seem to be much happening."

"Aye, very little," Perry agreed. "My man here says the chief wants the officer from the ship to come to the village and talk. Naturally he's under orders to stay at the river. There's no point in giving them another prisoner."

"How long are we going to wait?"

"As long as it takes, but I'm sure it'll end directly. I'm sure we'll have a fight."

"You don't think they'll negotiate?"

"I don't think they'll have a chance to negotiate," Perry said, pulling a blade of grass and chewing it. He gestured toward the Maori guide. "You've got to remember that these people are enemies of those in that village. We've got one of them translating for us, and I don't think his translation will be very favorable to a peaceable settlement."

The Maori followed the conversation, his tattooed face intent and his eyes moving between Garrity and Perry. He grinned and nodded when Perry finished.

Garrity looked at the village. The palisade wall around the village was tall and strong. Thatched roofs were visible on the other side. He looked at the roofs, thinking about Meghan and wondering where she was. She might not even be alive.

Perry touched Garrity's arm. "It appears that might be the chief, Mr. Garrity. You'd best get back to your men."

Four men had come out of the village. One walked in front with a deliberate, measured stride and haughty bearing. The other three followed him. Garrity turned and went back through the brush, crawling around the marines. He reached his men, and looked back down at the river.

The four Maoris had reached the river, and all the other warriors had withdrawn to a respectful distance. The chief stood with folded arms, facing the officer as the Maori from the ship stood at one side and translated. Warriors were moving up the slope, ordering the women and children into the village. Garrity looked at the ship. The gun ports were open on the side facing the village and the guns had been run out, their dark, deadly muzzles looking like death itself.

The chief gestulated angrily as he replied to something. Warriors drew closer, fingering their weapons. The last of the women and children streamed into the village, and warriors began closing the huge, heavy gates. The marines in front of Garrity stirred, checking their weapons, and he turned and told his own men to check the priming in their muskets.

Sailors were holding a ship's boat in shallow water. The chief and the Maori translator argued furiously, shaking their fists. The officer turned and walked to the boat, beckoning to the Maori. He stepped into the boat and the Maori turned and ran to it, still shouting at the chief over his shoulder. The men pushed the boat into the water and jumped into it, lifting the oars. The Maori ran through the water and leaped into the boat as it swept out into the river.

The warriors surged to the edge of the water, brandishing weapons as they jeered and shouted in a roar of voices that echoed in the hills. The warriors were still dragging the massive gates shut.

The chief turned back to the warriors, shouting and pointing to the canoes. Several dozen of the warriors ran to the canoes and pushed three of them away from the bank, and jumped in. The men in the ship's boat threw their weight against the oars, pulling toward the stern of the ship. The Maori canoes pursued them.

The Maoris had obviously never seen cannon. A puff of smoke belched from the bow of the ship, and a waterspout rose high above a canoe. The slapping boom of the cannon rolled down the river. The Maoris stopped paddling, looking at the warship, then began paddling frantically toward the river bank.

Three cannon fired. A waterspout rose by a canoe, drenching the warriors in it. One ball tore lengthwise along another canoe, ripping through the warriors. The ornate prow exploded into splinters. A gunwale disintegrated on the third canoe, and it rolled over in the water. Warriors spilled out of it, and swam for the bank.

A hundred or more warriors remained on the bank, motionless as they looked at the ship. A single canoe reached the bank, broaching in the current as the warriors abandoned it and rushed to rejoin the others. That seemed to galvanize the entire group into motion. They all turned and ran.

The cannon on the warship fired in sequence, puffs of smoke blossoming along the side of the ship from bow to stern. The reports of the cannon ran together like thunder. Cannonballs tore into the slope, raising long streaks of dust as brush shredded and flew in the air. Some landed on the ground among the running Maoris, and scattered them. The palisade wall vibrated and buckled in spots as cannonballs crashed into it.

The salvo stopped, and the echoes died away. Dust rose from the village wall, and there were gaps in it where palisades had been shattered or knocked down. The warriors stopped, spread out on the slope, and looked back at the ship. Seconds dragged by, the silence seeming loud after the roar of the cannon. The side of the ship suddenly disappeared in a cloud of smoke as it fired all cannon in broadside.

The thunderous, awesome noise rang through the

hills. Dust boiled into the air all over the slope, obscuring it. The village wall snapped and jerked from the impact of the cannonballs, heavy timbers falling and splintering. The gates and long sections of the wall collapsed. Perry rose to his feet, drawing his sword and shouting, "Fix bayonets! Advance at double quick time!"

The marines climbed to their feet, and trotted down the hill behind Perry. Garrity drew his cutlass and beckoned his men forward. The other volunteer officers rose and shouted orders. The brush tore at Garrity's clothes as he pounded down the hill in front of his men. Then the brush thinned out and the overland force moved in to take the village.

Smoke rose from fires that had started among the thatched roofs, and the Maoris formed into ranks in front of the ruins of the gate. The marines whooped and shouted, increasing their pace to a run. Garrity led his men around the flank of the marines and struggled to catch up with the front ranks. The Maoris began to chant, advancing slowly to meet the charge.

The marines fired a mass volley at a range of fifty feet, and the Maoris wavered as warriors in their front rank staggered and reeled backwards. Garrity cocked both hammers of his pistols and fired at a warrior who was leveling a spear. The warrior sagged and dropped and Garrity killed another Maori with the second pistol ball. Then he drew his cutlass and chopped at a man's head.

The warrior parried the blow with a large hardwood sword, and slashed back at Garrity. A musket barrel slid across Garrity's shoulder and belched smoke, shooting the warrior in the face. His head snapped back and he died. The marines had broken through the Maoris with the weight of their disciplined, organized charge, climbing over wounded and dead. The Maoris fell back and began a retreat into the village.

The battle turned into a fierce melee of individual fights, a noisy confusion of hoarse voices, weapons clashing, motion on every side. The marines were invincible, a deadly hedge of jabbing bayonets that streamed with blood.

Thick, choking smoke swirled along the street, and flames shot up from roofs. Women and children screamed and darted about through the smoke, and a drove of pigs that had escaped from a pen somewhere in the village raced by and almost knocked Garrity and other men down. He fought his way forward, shouting at the top of his voice for Meghan as he parried blows and chopped with his cutlass.

Then he saw Tench, Porter, and other men fighting Maoris in front of a house up ahead. He shouted to his men, and threw himself at the Maoris. His men charged, wielding their muskets like clubs, and the Maoris fell back from the furious onslaught. They began to break and scatter, and Garrity pressed on with his men. Tench was stabbing at a warrior with a broken spear. A Maori in front of Garrity dropped a cutlass as a bullet dropped him. Garrity snatched up the cutlass and shouted at Tench as he threw it.

Tench plucked the cutlass out of the air and swept it down across a warrior's neck in a single motion. His aquiline features were rigid with determination, his head cocked to one side as he looked around him with his single eye.

The battle swept on past the house, then far along the street. Tench clapped Garrity on the shoudler. "By God, that cannonade was a welcome sound, and you're a welcome sight, my lad. Where's Captain Buell, and what kept him so bloody long?"

"He's dead, and it's a long story. Where is Meghan, and is she all right?"

"She's inside, and she hasn't been physically harmed." He caught Garrity's arm and held him as he started to rush into the house. "I said not physically harmed, Earl, but she's endured grief that would drive a multitude mad. These fiendish sods have been taking a couple of men every day or two for a while now, and they've been cooking and eating them up the street there. Yesterday they took a lad named Dickon Muir, who was very dear to her, so proceed with caution."

Garrity sheathed his cutlass. He pushed his pistol under his belt as he ducked and went into the house. It was dim inside, and a few baskets and a pile of wood were scattered around a fire in the center of the floor. At first it looked like no one was in the house, then he saw the grass mats hanging in the corner. He walked toward the corner, calling to Meghan. A soft, whimpering moan came from behind the mats.

Meghan sat on the floor, looking up in terror. Her hair was disheveled, her face was pale and her eyes were red and swollen from crying, and she wore a dark, shapeless shift. And there was only fear in her eyes, not recognition. He hesitated, calling her name again. Her hands trembled as she lifted them to her

318

lips, looking at him and frowning in concentration.

Her eyes opened wide in astonishment and overwhelming relief. She burst into tears, wailing and sobbing as she said something in a plaintive tone, and she held out her arms. He stepped to her and lifted her, and he held her to him, trying to calm her.

───────── Chapter 17

THE HELMSMAN TURNED AS GARRITY bent over the binnacle, looking at the compass in the dim light of the lantern. "We're rolling right down to Sydney, Mr. Garrity," he said. "A few more days of this easterly, and we'll be in port."

"Aye, we will," Garrity replied, glancing up at the sails. "Steady as she goes."

"Aye, aye, sir."

Garrity crossed the quarterdeck to the taffrail and leaned against it, watching the steps to the main deck. It was almost dawn, well into the morning watch. Meghan always got out early, and she occasionally came on deck to watch the sun rise. He waited hopefully, and she suddenly appeared in the moonlight. She climbed the steps to the quarterdeck, and he lifted his hat.

"Good morning, Meghan."

"Good morning, Earl," she replied, walking to the rail to him, and leaning against it, looking up at the sails. "*Pamir* seems to like this wind she's getting."

"She does indeed," Garrity agreed. "And Captain Johnson and I like the victuals we've been getting since you came aboard. He said last night that you've come closer to beaching him than anyone ever has, because he might have to look for a wife who can cook like you. But I told him his searching would be in vain, of course."

Meghan laughed softly and shook her head. "It's only been pantry victuals, Earl."

"That's true, but the difference is in how you cook them."

She smiled up at him, then looked out at the waves in the moonlight. Outwardly, she had largely recovered from her ordeal during her captivity, but raw wounds remained. The Cargills had wanted her to stay with them for at least a few weeks, but she had chosen the uncertainties that awaited her in Australia over being near Maoris.

Captain Johnson had offered her passage back to Australia, and Garrity had moved out of his cabin so she could use it. During the first days of the voyage he had tried to broach the subject of marriage when he had private moments with her, but she had avoided discussing it. She was more quiet and withdrawn than she had been before, and she seemed reluctant to think of anything more distant than the moment at hand.

Her long days of constant terror were still fresh in her mind. The savage, grotesque death of the men she had known and the cannibal orgies in the village still haunted her. At times when he passed her cabin at night, he heard her weeping. He could understand

322

why she would want to withdraw, and wait for time to heal the wounds. But she was still legally a transported convict.

He glanced down at her and looked away again. "We'll be in Sydney within a few days, Meghan."

She sighed. "Aye, and it'll also be daylight soon. I'd best see to the fire in the galley."

He reached for her hand and took it, holding her. "Stay and talk to me for a moment, Meghan. I beg you, talk to me for a moment."

She hesitated, looking up at him apprehensively, then pulled her hand out of his. "For a moment only, then. And let's talk about happy things, because I don't have to search for cause to be heavy-hearted."

"I'd like nothing better than to make you smile, but I'm worried about what might happen to you when you return to Sydney. Do you know if the commutation of your sentence remains in effect now that Buell is dead?"

She drew in a deep breath and released slowly. "No, I don't, Earl."

"Nor do I. Reason would say that it does, but reason has naught to do with laws, lawyers, and such. However, it would put the matter to rest and fulfill my every dream in life if you'd marry me."

She was silent for a long moment, looking out at the ocean, and she lifted a hand and pushed at her hair as she replied in a soft, sad voice. "Earl, I've been trying to keep you from asking me, because I don't want to refuse you. But I can't marry you."

"Will you tell me why, love?"

Her voice broke with a sob as she started to speak.

323

She swallowed and brushed at her eyes, controlling her tears, and shook her head. "Because I love you, Earl," she whispered. "I love you, and you'd grow to despise me if I married you as I am. I'm only a shell of a human being. Buell degraded me, used me like a . . . The Maoris were worse . . . they degraded me in ways you can't imagine. I feel dirty."

"I could never despise you, Meghan," he replied, putting an arm around her and pulling her to him. "Neither you nor anyone else can make me do that. And there's more of a human being in your small finger than in any other ten people I've met. You've been hurt, but you'll heal. And with my love to help you, you'll heal that much quicker."

She pulled away from him, shaking her head. "Earl, I've plainly told you that I can't be a wife to you. In time, your love would turn to hate through that. I can't help it. I think what men and women do is dirty."

"And I'm telling you that it isn't, Meghan," he replied firmly, taking her hand again. "If you'll stand up with me and take your vows, then that'll be wife enough for me. I know what you've been through and I can understand your feelings, and the rest will come in time. And if it doesn't, then it doesn't. But you'll be mine, and you'll be safe from any conniving to return you to Parramatta. Now that's as plain as I can be."

"It's plain, and more," she sighed, shaking her head. "But I can't ask you to do such a thing, Earl."

"You're asking for nothing, Meghan. I'm begging you to stand up and take your vows with me."

She looked out at the waves again, silent for a long moment, then her shoulders began trembling as she wept quietly. "I'm so afraid that I'll make you despise me, Earl," she sobbed. "I love you, but I've been so grievously wounded that I can't reach beyond the hour or bear to think of more than a week behind me. And my most earnest desire is to be a wife to you, but I can't."

He put his arm around her again, holding her and wiping away her tears. "If you'll do as I asked, you'll make me the happiest man alive, Meghan," he said tenderly. "And I take my oath that my only thoughts of you will be the love I've felt for you since we first met. Please tell me that you'll marry me."

"Is that truly what you want, Earl? Are you sure?"

"I'm sure, Meghan. Truly, it's what I want more than anything else in life."

"All right, then. And I pray God I've not made a decision that will destroy your love for me, because it's more precious to me than life itself."

He lifted her hand and kissed it. "You've made this day a new life for me, that's what you've done, Meghan."

"I hope so, love. I'd best go see to breakfast, because it'll soon be daylight."

"No, not yet. Tell me again that you'll marry me, and tell me you won't change your mind."

She smiled faintly. "Aye, I will, and I won't change my mind. When do you wish to have it seen to?"

"Could we have Captain Johnson do it? He's very fond of you and he's been a good friend as well as my captain, and I know he'd like to."

"If you wish," she replied. "And as soon as you wish."

"Then it'll be as soon as he will, because I want to make sure you don't change your mind or get away from me by some other means."

The first light of dawn was beginning to spread across the sky, and her beautiful face was dimly visible as she looked back at him. Then she went below. Garrity turned back to the rail, glowing with happiness. He watched the sun as it peered over the horizon and inched up into the clear blue sky.

The sun rose higher into the sky, and the helmsman rang the forenoon watch on the ship's bell. The bosun came to the quarterdeck to take the watch, and Garrity went to the galley. Meghan was at the stove in the tiny galley, which also served as a wardroom. Captain Johnson was at the table. Captain Johnson was a portly, jolly man, and he was chuckling over something Meghan had said. He was delighted when Garrity asked him if he would perform the wedding ceremony, and he shook hands heartily with Garrity and kissed Meghan.

Captain Johnson insisted on making the ceremony as much of an event as the circumstances would permit. He wrote out the certificate, brushed his clothes, and was generally merry. He conducted the ceremony on the quarterdeck during the second dog watch, as the sun was setting. The bosun and a leading seaman were witnesses. The crew gathered on the main deck and watched. They cheered when the brief ceremony was concluded and lined up with pannikins for drinks of rum. Captain Johnson and Garrity distributed the rum, then went into the galley for the wedding breakfast that Meghan had prepared.

There was an awkward moment when Garrity and Meghan were alone in the small cabin he had vacated for her to use. He had gone to the forecastle to bring back his sea chest, and she was in bed when he returned. He put his sea chest in the corner and blew out the lantern, then undressed and lay down beside her. They were silent for a long moment, then she whispered softly.

"I'll not deny you your rights, Earl."

He slid an arm under her and pulled her to him, pillowing her head on his shoulder. "We don't have rights between us, Meghan. We have love, and that's all. We also have a lifetime ahead of us, and time for everything. You're my wife, and nothing else matters to me."

She lay against him, sliding an arm across his chest and pulling herself closer. She began to cry quietly. "I didn't think there could be such a kind and loving man in the world, Earl," she said.

He patted her, kissing her forehead. "And I don't see how anyone could be other than kind and loving to you. Good night, Meghan."

"Good night, love."

She burrowed her head against his shoulder, settled herself, and stopped weeping. He lay with his arm around her, with her body soft against his, the scent of her hair filling his nostrils. He burned with desire for her. But his desire was only an element of his love for her, a far more powerful emotion that possessed him completely, and the fact that she was actually his wife still seemed a dream to him. He fell asleep, listening to her breathing.

327

The bosun tapped on the door during the early hours of the morning and woke Garrity for the morning watch. And Meghan rose and dressed in the dark to prepare breakfast for him. When he came off watch, she had taken everything out of his sea chest, rearranged it neatly, and she had washed his shirts and linen. Then she brushed his clothes and shined his boots, and searched for other things to do for him.

She was a tirelessly industrious woman, always working at something, and she was pathetically eager to do things for him. He let her, vaguely understanding her compulsion to compensate for what she was unable to do. Their hours alone were richly enjoyable for him, and they talked about their families and childhood. She was distressed when he told her about the estrangement between him and his mother, because she regarded family ties as vitally important.

Her captivity by the Maoris was a closed subject between them, because she was unable to talk about what had happened. A reference to New Zealand, the voyage of the *Baleen,* or anything that could remind her of the degradation she had suffered was not to be mentioned and he learned to avoid everything connected with the incident. She had frequent nightmares, when she woke screaming until he calmed her.

The ship's log from the *Baleen* was among her belongings, and she had a whale's tooth covered with scrimshaw. He occasionally found her looking at the whale's tooth, a treasure she prized, but it seemed to make her sad as well as give her pleasure. She never talked about it, and he resisted the impulse to ask her.

The ship drew closer to Sydney, and they discussed

what they would do when they arrived. He had already thought about it and decided to leave the ship and take her to the Garrity property on the Georges River, because he had no intention of leaving her by herself in Sydney. Meghan had been reared in the tradition of seafarers' wives and she objected at first, then she relented when she saw he was adamant on the point.

He told Captain Johnson about his decision on the night before they arrived in port. They were on the quarterdeck, with the coast a dark blur to the west, and the ship crept toward it under light sail. Captain Johnson nodded understandingly. "I suspected as much, Mr. Garrity. You'll at least want time to get properly settled into being married, won't you?"

"I will, sir. And I don't want to leave her by herself, considering what she's been through."

"Indeed you shouldn't," Captain Johnson said. "She's borne that better than I'd have thought humanly possible, but she'll be a while getting over it completely. What are you going to do?"

Garrity chuckled wryly and shrugged as he shook his head. "I don't know, Captain Johnson. There's not a lot I can do, and I'll always be grateful to you for taking me on and suffering with me until I finally began finding my way."

"Nonsense!" Johnson snorted. "You earned your way from the first day, Mr. Garrity. And I'm sure there are many things you can do."

"Well, I'll have a look around. I hope that this short notice doesn't make it difficult for you, Sir?"

"No, it doesn't," Captain Johnson replied. "I'm going to try to talk the owners into letting Poage and Venable do some repairs on *Pamir*. She's overdue it. If they agree, and I believe they will, that'll give me ample time to look around for another mate." He glanced up at the stars, and yawned as he walked away. "I believe I'll get some rest. Mr. Garrity. We'll want all hands on deck to take her into port."

Garrity nodded, touching his tricorn. "Aye, aye, sir."

Garrity had a lot to think about. He disliked using the Garrity property on the Georges, because his mother had ordered him off the sheep station and he had no intention of returning until she asked him, but it was a financial necessity. And he had thought about what he could do to earn money, but there were few possibilities. There was an added complication in that his mother was well known in Sydney. No one would hire him if they thought it would displease his mother.

The bosun came on the quarterdeck to take the midwatch, and Garrity went to his cabin. Meghan was still up, sorting through their belongings and packing his sea chest in preparation to leave the ship. He helped her put the things away, and they went to bed. The ship's bell ringing the morning watch awakened him.

Johnson came up to the quarterdeck at sunrise, and the opening between the Jackson Heads came into sight as the ship approached the coast. An onshore breeze was blowing, making it easy to negotiate the opening between the headlands and the long, winding entrance to the harbor. The ship slid smoothly into place at the end of a line of ships. The men finished furling the sails and securing the ship at anchor, and Garrity went to his cabin.

Meghan was wearing one of her pretty dresses, and she tied her bonnet and picked up her bundle as he lifted his heavy sea chest. The bosun ordered men to lower a boat and put a ladder over the side of the ship when Garrity and Meghan went out on deck. Captain Johnson was there to see them off. He put out his hand and said, "Well, it's been a pleasure having you as a mate, Mr. Garrity, and I'd more than welcome the chance to do so again. If you'll go by the offices of Drexler and Suggs tomorrow, they'll pay you for the voyage."

"Thank you, Captain Johnson," Garrity replied as they shook hands. "I'm most grateful for everything."

"I'm grateful for your dedicated service. Mistress Garrity, you've quite spoiled me for eating common fare, but it was well worth it."

"And you've spoiled me with your compliments, Captain Johnson." Meghan laughed. "I'm much obliged to you for all your kindnesses."

"It was my pleasure, you may be assured of that. Here, Mr. Garrity, we'll give you a hand with your chest." They lowered the chest to a small boat waiting below.

The men rowed the boat through the lines of ships, and across the harbor to the end of a pier. Two of the men climbed up to the pier and took the sea chest. Garrity helped Meghan up the boards nailed to the pile and climbed up behind her. He lifted the chest to his shoulder, and they walked along the pier toward

331

the street.

Meghan tucked her bundle under her arm and looked up at Garrity. "I have a very dear friend here, Earl. Her name is Mary Whittacker, and she's in service at Mr. James Wyndham's house. Would it be possible for me to visit her?"

"Of course, Meghan. I know Mr. Wyndham, and I'll be glad to take you there. But it might be better to wait until we're settled in, and you can invite her to visit, if you like."

"Aye, that would probably be better. I'm anxious to see Mary, but I'd like to receive her properly. How far is it to the house?"

"It's much too far to walk," he chuckled. "And particularly while carrying this chest. We'll go up Bridge Street to see some people I know, and I'll ask them for the use of a cart."

The crossed the street, weaving through traffic, and turned into Bridge Street. It curved up the slope, with carriages, horses, and people moving along it. They walked up it to the center of town, and Garrity sighed in relief as he put the chest down in front of the Cummings Brothers office.

The head clerk failed to recognize Garrity at first, and a businesslike frown formed on his face. Then his frown faded as Garrity took off his hat, and he nodded gravely to Garrity and Meghan and climbed down from his stool. He crossed the office to a door, and stepped into the inner office.

Jeremiah Cummings came out, the brother with the large, dark brown birthmark covering half of his face. He was putting on his swallowtail coat. He stared at

Meghan, but recovered from his surprise and smiled politely. Garrity introduced Meghan to him, and he was intensely proud of her. He had difficulty talking to the man because of the birthmark, but Meghan seemed not to notice it. She was composed and self-assured, smiling as Cummings bowed.

"You must forgive me for being taken aback, Mistress Garrity," Cummings said. "In these dry and dusty precincts of commerce, we rarely have the pleasure of receiving one so refreshingly attractive. Mr. Garrity, you have my most sincere congratulations.

"Thank you, Mr. Cummings. I have need of a cart and horse, and I stopped by to see if I could borrow them from you."

"Of course, of course," Cummings replied emphatically. "But wouldn't you rather use a carriage?"

"No, a horse and cart will suffice quite nicely, thank you."

Cummings nodded, glancing at the head clerk. "Send a boy for a horse and cart, please. Mr. Garrity, please bring Mistress Garrity in and sit down while you wait. It will only take a few minutes to have the horse and cart brought here."

Garrity and Meghan went into the inner office with Cummings. They talked for several minutes, and Garrity told Cummings about his plans to live in the house on the Georges River. Cummings expressed discrete approval that the house would finally be put to use. The head clerk looked in and told Cummings that the cart and horse had arrived.

The front door was open, and the apprentices were carrying Garrity's sea chest and Meghan's bundle out

333

to the cart parked on the street. Garrity turned back to Cummings. "I'm much obliged, Mr. Cummings, and I'll bring the cart and horse back tomorrow."

"Please keep them as long as you wish, Mr. Garrity, and please don't hesitate to call upon us if there is any other way we can assist you. Mistress Garrity, it was a pleasure meeting you."

Garrity nodded in thanks to the apprentices as he and Meghan went out. He helped her into the cart, then walked around it and climbed in. Meghan glanced back as the cart began moving along the street. "He's a most pleasant man, isn't he?"

"Aye, Cummings Brothers have been the factors for Wayamba Station for many years, and they've always been more helpful than most factors. I find it difficult to talk with Jeremiah, though, because of that birthmark."

"Well, he can't help that, Earl."

Garrity smiled, recalling that his mother had said the same thing. "That's true enough. Perhaps we'd best get some provisions before we leave town. You'll want things that Mayhew won't have, and I'd like to get the things you need to make some beer."

"Very well, but I thought you had to wait until tomorrow to get paid."

"Did you think you married a man with an empty purse? I'll have you know that I'm not one to squander money on riotous living, and I still have much of my wages from other voyages."

Garrity smiled at her as he snapped the traces. The horse lifted its head, increasing its pace to a fast walk, and Garrity guided it through the traffic. He turned onto a street leading to the market near Fort Macquarie, and there was less traffic here.

Garrity and Meghan walked through the lines of vendors' wagons and carts. Meghan smelled, tasted, and examined peas, beans, rice, flour, and other things. Garrity paid for the purchases and carried them to the cart. Then they drove on, and the street became a track leading away from the town.

The last of the houses disappeared, and Meghan looked around at the trees and open fields. "This has a very agreeable aspect, Earl. I know I'm going to like it here."

"As much as being on a ship?"

She hesitated, then smiled. "Almost as much, perhaps."

"I hope you'll like me as much when I'm wearing a stockman's hat instead of a tricorn."

She laughed. "I love you, and I'll like you in any sort of hat. The kind of hat you wear isn't important." Her smile faded, and she looked musingly into the distance. "And I don't have to live on a ship to be happy, either. But I would like to have the principal shares in one or own one outright some day."

"I'd be thick if I didn't know that by now," he said. "You've told me that a score of times if you've said it once. And I promise you that I'll do my utmost to see that you get your wish."

Chapter 18

THE HEAT OF THE LATE summer afternoon had settled
by the time they reached the selection on the Georges,
but it was cool under the trees near the house and
along the river. Mayhew was awed by Meghan, and
Meghan was delighted with the house. She walked
through it, gazing around in wonder, and Mayhew
stumped after her on his wooden leg and pointed
things out.

A breeze stirred. Garrity and Mayhew unloaded the
cart and took the horse to a paddock. The aborigines
were still living along the river. The two men returned
to the house, and they sat on the front veranda and
smoked their pipes while Meghan prepared dinner.
The house seemed to have come to life, now that
Meghan was there. Garrity listened to her humming
in the kitchen, and felt a deep sense of contentment.

Meghan was up early the next morning, writing a
note to Mary Whittacker in Sydney. Mayhew hitched
a horse to a cart and followed Garrity when he took
the borrowed horse and cart back to Sydney. Garrity

returned the horse and cart to the Cummings Brothers office, then went to the offices of Drexler and Suggs to collect his wages for the last voyage to New Zealand.

Ezra Drexler came through the outer office while Garrity was transacting his business with the head clerk. Drexler was a pompous but a friendly man, and he nodded pleasantly to Garrity as he passed and commented on the large load of lumber that the *Pamir* had brought back from New Zealand on the last trip.

Garrity finished there, and went to Government House to give James Wyndham the note for Meghan's friend. Wyndham told Garrity that Mary Whittacker had married a man named Joshua Venable, a partner in Poage and Venable, shop brokers and refitters. Garrity walked back through the town to the Poage and Venable offices. Joshua Venable was a small, thin man with stooped shoulders and ink-stained fingers. His sharp, tight-lipped features were those of a reserved, calculating businessman. But he was cordial, telling Garrity that his wife had often spoken of Meghan. He appeared pleased that they would be able to visit each other.

The few remaining convicts and those who had served out their terms filled all of the laborer's jobs in the town, and Garrity visited a few businesses to see if he could get a job as a foreman or supervisor. He knew many of the owners of the businesses, and they greeted him heartily. But they became vague and uncertain when he asked them about work. Few wished to hire someone with no experience in their business. None wanted to risk incurring Elizabeth

Garrity's displeasure.

Meghan had passed over the salt pork and beef at the market on the previous day, preferring fresh meat that she could preserve herself. Garrity walked to the market at the edge of town and found Mayhew, who was waiting there. After looking over the stock, he bought a young bullock, a sow with piglets, and a large shoat. Mayhew helped him load the swine into the cart. They tethered the bullock to the rear of the cart and started back toward the Georges. It was almost sunset when they got there.

Garrity and Mayhew left the swine in the cart for the night, and began working on a pen the next morning. During the afternoon, a rider arrived with a note for Meghan from Mary Venable. Mary Venable and her husband were coming for a visit the following Sunday and were bringing with them a woman named Alma Beasley, another friend of Meghan's, who worked as the cook in the Wyndham household.

When the pig pen was finished, Garrity and Mayhew began repairing the sheds behind the house. Nails were needed to finish the work on the sheds, and Garrity rode to Sydney to get them. He went to other places to ask about work while he was in the town, with the same results as before. It worried him, but Meghan seemed unconcerned.

She was more concerned about their unauthorized use of the house. So was Garrity, but he knew it would be months before he heard of his mother's reaction. He was reasonably sure that Jeremiah Cummings would inform her, and the news that he was married and living in the house would reach Wayamba Station by word of mouth. But it was near shearing time, which took the full time and attention of everyone on the station, and travel would be difficult during the winter months after the shearing had been completed.

The Venables and Alma Beasley arrived at noon on Sunday in a sporty, four-wheel chaise with a leather calash top. Mary Venable was a tall, slender, attractive woman, several years younger and much more personable than her husband. Alma Beasley was a stout, cheerful, middle-aged woman. Meghan ran out as the women climbed out of the chaise. She kissed them and took them inside. Everyone was laughing. Garrity and Mayhew helped Venable unharness his team, and the three men sat on the veranda while the women talked and finished preparing the meal. Garrity found it difficult to talk to Venable. The man seemed to have nothing to say. He became interested only when Garrity mentioned that he had been on the *Pamir*, and he asked about the lumber and naval stores trade in New Zealand. Captain Johnson had attended to the transactions in New Zealand and Garrity had never been curious about what was involved. After he exhausted the little he knew on the subject, the conversation consisted of polite remarks punctuating long silences.

Venable became more talkative when they went inside and sat at the table. Mary commented that Venable had received a ship the previous week to broker on commission, and he nodded. "A very good commission," he murmured in his dry, grave manner. "And it'll soon be an absolutely topping ship."

Meghan was passing dishes of vegetables around

340

the table, and she looked at Venable skeptically. "Then it'll be the first one I've seen in Port Jackson. What ship is that?"

Venable blinked in surpise. "The *Noel.*"

"The *Noel?*" Meghan laughed. "She's a sweet little barkentine, but you'll never put her in tip-top condition without stripping her to her stringers. We were anchored a few ships from her in Port Jackson for a time, and I didn't need the bell to awaken me. The hammering of her pumps woke me every morning."

Mary cleared her throat nervously, uncertain as to how Venable would take this. "I believe I did mention that Meghan was knowledgeable about ships, dear."

"Yes, you did," Venable said. "We're working on the hull, and the leaks will be stopped very shortly."

"Aye, I know what you're doing," Meghan chuckled. "You've got her careened, and you're caulking her. And she could well use it, because fish were swimming in and out of her bilge. But there are loose frames in that hull, or I'll miss my guess, and you wouldn't caulk a hull and sell it to me as a top quality ship."

Venable smiled. "If the purchasers wish to pump the bilge and inspect it, I might reconsider the price. Otherwise, the ship goes at top quality. And in my experience, few of those who invest in ships care to crawl about in the bilge."

Meghan laughed, nodding. "I'm sure that's true, and I'm also sure that ship will be leaking as bad as before after she weathers a couple of hard storms. But I wouldn't have to pump out the bilge and climb down into it, because one can tell if a ship's been freshly caulked just by opening the bilge hatch. I used to go

341

down to the ways with my father all the time, and he showed me what to look for."

Venable pursed his lips in keen interest. "Indeed?" What's that?"

"Oil from the fresh tar in the caulking," Meghan replied. "If one holds a lantern so the light strikes the bilge water at an angle, one can see the oil gleaming."

Venable frowned. "Yes, that sounds reasonable," he said. "I'll have to remember that."

"Aye, my father knows all there is to know about ships," Meghan said, passing another dish. "And much of it he learned from his father." She laughed again. "Of course, if you see the buyers carrying a lantern down to the bilge hatch, you can always say that the ship has been carrying cargoes of oil."

Venable blinked, then he laughed. "Yes, I suppose one could, couldn't one? My word, we could well do with you in our employ, Mistress Garrity."

"I'm fully employed now," Meghan said with a smile. "I saw a ship at the Bay of Islands that you'd be eager to broker. It was none other than the *Pommern.*"

"The clipper?" Venable replied. "Yes, I've seen her when she's put into port here. That would be a substantial commission indeed. The clipper *Galatea* also calls at Port Jackson frequently, and it wasn't that long ago that she changed owners."

Meghan was interested. "Indeed? When did this happen, and who bought and sold her?"

"Let me think for a moment," Venable said. Then he began to describe the circumstances of the sale.

Garrity recalled seeing the clipper at the Bay of Islands and another at Port Jackson, impressively large ships with massive spreads of sail. He ate, listening to conversation between Meghan and Venable. Mary appeared surprised and pleased by her husband's animated conversation with Meghan. Alma and Mayhew were lost in this talk about ships.

Meghan's and Venable's ship talk dominated the conversation for a while. Then Mayhew commented to Alma that he had known her husband, and they discussed him and mutual acquaintances. Mary had heard of Wayamba Station and asked Garrity about it. Meghan and Venable continued to talk about ships.

Venable had been bored while on the veranda, and he had obviously made the trip to please his wife. Now his attitude underwent a complete reversal and he was fascinated by Meghan's encyclopedic knowledge of ships. He took the initiative in making plans for a visit the following Sunday, and he delayed in leaving until Mary and Alma began hinting that they would still be on the track at nightfall unless they left immediately.

Garrity returned to Syndey the next day and investigated other possibilities for employment, again without success. He met Tench while walking along a street, and they talked for a few minutes. Tench had returned to Australia on a ship that had arrived the day before, and he was also searching for employment. He had seen Captain Johnson and had heard about Garrity's marriage with Meghan, and he was keenly pleased by it. Garrity told him where he and Meghan were living, and he promised to visit.

Tench arrived at the house at midmorning two days

later, perched awkwardly and uncomfortably on a horse that he had borrowed. Meghan had been waiting for him and tears of joy filled her eyes as she ran out of the house to greet him. He spent the day, and tactfully avoided mention of subjects that would distress Meghan as he reminisced with her about the voyage of the *Baleen.* The owners of a small schooner had hired him as captain, and he would be sailing the coastal waters of Australia and Van Diemen's Land.

Garrity and Meghan finished working on the sheds behind the house, and made bins for the potatoes, carrots, pumpkins, and other produce from the garden. The fence around the selection and some of the fences in the paddocks needed repair, and they began working on them. The Venables came to the house on the following Sunday. On the Sunday after that, the Garrity's visited the Venables.

The Venables lived in a large stone house on several acres at the edge of Sydney, and they had a cook, maids, and a gardner. Most of the day was spent at the Poage and Venable shipyard, in a cove on one side of the wide entrance to Port Jackson harbor. It was a maze of sheds, piles of lumber, skeletal frames of ships, muddy slopes with ships careened on them, and Meghan and Venable spent hours in conversation as they walked around the shipyard.

The visits became a Sunday routine, and most of the day was always spent at the shipyard when Garrity took Meghan to Sydney. He found the shipyard uninteresting, but he was deeply gratified that Meghan had found something of such intense interest to her. Mary Venable's interest in ships was even less that Garrity's but she was pleased by the relationship that developed between her husband and Meghan. Venable had found a friend and confidant in Meghan, one who was knowledgeable about his business, and who represented no threat to his business interests.

The small, stooped man and the slender, attractive woman were incongruous friends, and in many ways they were amusing as they discussed pieces of equipment, looked at hulls, and probed at heavy timbers for rot. They disagreed and argued heatedly at times, their voices carrying across the deserted shipyard, and they laughed over jokes that were obscure to Garrity and Mary.

Venable had a warehouse he used for storing salvaged cargoes, which he bought by bidding on entire shiploads and disposed of in piecemeal lots through dealers. Most of it had been soaked by seawater and condemned by underwriters, but it included valuable items and he had furnished his house out of it. He sent wagonloads to Meghan, bolts of cloth to make curtains, carpets, pieces of furniture, and other things. Meghan soaked the fabric and carpets in the river, removed stains from the furniture and made curtains. The house was transformed.

Meghan was happy in her surroundings and looked forward to the visits on Sundays, and she gradually began overcoming her experiences as a captive of the Maoris. Her nightmares were less frequent and less terrifying for her, and she talked about some of the men who had been killed by the Maoris. It was painful for her, often making her burst into tears, but she seemed driven by an inner compulsion to exorcise her grief. The process was slow and erratic, and Garrity let her set her own pace.

The weather turned cool and autumn rains threatened, and Garrity and Mayhew harvested the vegetables in the garden. When it turned colder, they slaughtered the shoat and bullock, and built a smokehouse for Meghan to preserve the pork. Garrity harnessed the horse to an old plow he found in a shed, and expanded the garden to plant more vegetables the following spring. They were virtually self-sufficient on the selection, but buying staples and other expenses had taken most of his money, and he was still unable to find work in the town.

The wool on the few sheep Mayhew had in the paddocks was worth very little, and he had let them turn into woolies, overgrown masses of thick, deep wool. The aborigines living along the river asked for a sheep for its wool and for winter food, and Garrity and Mayhew went to the paddocks on a cold, gusty winter morning and looked at the sheep. They picked one out and the aborigines drove it toward the river. A carriage came through the gate as Garrity and Mayhew walked back toward the house.

The carriage was large and heavy, and muddy from its trips along the rutted track. Mayhew and Garrity reached the house and waited for it, and the driver reined up in front of the house." "Is this where Mr. Earl Garrity lives?" he asked.

"Aye, it is," Garrity replied. "I'm Garrity."

The driver climbed down from his seat, and opened the carriage door and looked inside. "We're here, sir."

Ezra Drexler heaved himself off the seat and looked out, pale and flustered from the jolting along the track, and he smiled wanly. "Good day, Mr. Garrity."

"Good day, and welcome, Mr. Drexler. Please step down and come in."

Drexler nodded, wheezing as he pulled his fat body through the door. The carriage shifted as he climbed down the steps. "My word, you do live at a distance from Sydney, don't you? I've heard of the rigors of traveling in the outback, and now I've experienced them."

"Well, the track is rough enough," Garrity laughed. "But I don't believe you've yet reached what most people call the outback."

"Indeed?" Drexler sighed. "Then I do admire the courage of those who venture there. I was certain we'd end up in the ditch on the way here, and my heart was in my throat a thousand times." He smiled as Meghan came out the front door, and he lifted his hat and bowed. "Well, well, here's the lovely lady herself. And it's Mistress Garrity now, I understand. My most sincere congratulations and best wishes, dear lady."

"Why, Mr. Drexler!" Meghan exclaimed. "It's such a delight to see you!"

"And you, my dear," Drexler said. "Suggs and I often discuss how utterly charming you were when we met you, and we remember the treat you prepared for us with special fondness."

"Then you've come on the right day." Meghan

347

laughed. "I've only just finished taking some pastries out of the oven."

"Pastries! Mistress Garrity, someone should devise another word for the delicious morsels you bake."

Meghan took his arm, smiling up at him and pulling him toward the steps. "Whatever you wish to call them, you shall have some while they're still warm from the oven. Come along, Mr. Drexler."

"Indeed I will," Drexler agreed, walking toward the steps with her. "I can stay only a moment, because the thought of being caught by darkness whilst in the wilderness unmans me, but I'll stay long enough for that." He glanced back at the driver. "Turn the carriage around, Tom, and I'll be back out directly."

Garrity followed Meghan and Drexler into the house. Meghan took Drexler's coat and hat, and led him into the kitchen and seated him at the table.

Meghan made tea, and filled a plate with apple pastries and put it in front of Drexler. Drexler devoured the pastries, sighing and murmuring to himself, and washing down huge mouthfuls with gulps of tea. He took the last one from the plate and Meghan reached for the plate to refill it, but he lifted a hand and shook his head regretfully.

"No, I'm afraid that's all I can eat, dear lady," he said. "Ordinarily I could eat a dozen or more, but the bouncing on the road has upset my stomach. However, these have been a feast I'll long remember."

"I'll put you some in a napkin to take with you, then," Meghan said. "I have some jam tarts here as well, and I'll also put in a few of those for you."

Drexler nodded eagerly, pushing the rest of the last pastry into his mouth and chewing it. "That's very kind of you, and I'll have them when I get home. And perhaps I'll even let Suggs have one or two. He had an opportunity to come with me, but he won't venture out of the town for fear that he'll meet up with a bushranger."

Drexler took a handkerchief from his sleeve and wiped his mouth. "And now to business, dear lady. The underwriters have settled with us on the *Baleen*, and we're in the process of tidying up the accounts. It came to our attention that we owe you certain monies. I inquired as to your whereabouts, and here I am."

"Would that be the master's share of the cargo of oil that was sold at the Bay of Islands?"

"Indeed it would," Drexler replied, smothering a belch. "And I must say that I'm pleased to be dealing with someone so alert and intelligent, because I can dispense with hours of explanations. As you know, the master of the vessel was due part of the profits from that cargo. In our records, which is what we'd normally consult in a situation of this nature, he listed no relatives. But we know that you were his wife, so the monies are due you."

"My word," Meghan murmured. "Then I'm due some fifty-two guineas, aren't I?"

Drexler blinked, taken aback. He pursed his lips reflectively. "Actually, we computed it at forty-one guineas and odd shillings."

"Indeed?" Meghan replied in mild surprise. "Then I must have cast the numbers wrong, but it'll be easy enough for you to point out where I went wrong. I have the log from the *Baleen,* and we can compute the master's share from the entries in it."

"No, no, there's no need for that." Drexler chuckled. "I can put my finger on the exact place where you went amiss. You failed to take into account the repairs and stores charged to the *Baleen* at the Bay of Islands, and I can tell that from the amount you derived."

Meghan folded her hands and smiled blandly, nodding. "I did, because they're expenses to be charged to the second voyage. The *Baleen* put into port and unloaded her cargo, which qualified as a voyage for a whaler under maritime law, and only the expenses she incurred at Port Jackson are to be charged against the cargo sold at the Bay of Islands. The expenses incurred at the Bay of Islands are between you and the underwriters, I believe, but I doubt that the full value was underwritten, was it? That would have been terribly expensive."

Drexler's smile faded for an instant, and he looked at Meghan as though seeing her for the first time. Then he smiled again and nodded. "Yes, it would have been beyond reason. We did take some loss, but we received cash in hand on the settlement, which gives us the opportunity of immediately investing again. And I do believe you're absolutely correct, dear lady, in that we charged expenses against that cargo which weren't due. In that event, you're owed the larger amount instead of forty-one guineas and odd shillings."

"I could have miscalculated the amount," Meghan said politely. "I'm often between wind and tide when casting accounts."

"No, no, I'm sure you're correct in the amount," Drexler insisted. "I'll not see you take a penny less than fifty-two guineas, and the money will be waiting for whenever you or your good husband here can come by our offices and collect it."

Meghan hesitated. "Very well, but it must be with full good will."

"My dear, you could never have anything but my full good will," Drexler laughed in expansive good humor. "My affection for you wouldn't waver over a thousand times that amount of money."

"Then I'm content," Meghan replied. She took his arm and walked to the door with him.

They went out on the veranda, still discussing the settlement on the *Baleen.*

"It's fortunate that you received cash in hand on the settlement," Meghan said. "I'v heard of some who lost cargoes and ships, and who waited years for the underwriters to settle with them. Will you buy shares in another whaler with the proceeds of the settlment?"

Drexler said he wasn't sure. "It depends upon how a certain matter transpires. We heard about a ship being sold in Bombay, and we went together with a few people and made a bid on it. If our bid loses, then we might buy shares in another whaler."

"May I ask what ship you've bid on?"

Drexler winked. "The *Orion,*" he said.

"The clipper *Orion?*" Meghan gasped in delight. "She's the sister ship to *Galatea*, isn't she? Oh, I do so hope that you're successful in your bid, Mr. Drexler."

"So do we." Drexler sighed, and shook his head doubtfully. "But clippers are very expensive and others are bidding, and we could bid only so much. We'll know the outcome in a few weeks, though."

"I'll pray every night that you get her," Meghan said. "I'd like you to have the good fortune of owning her, and I'd like her home port to be Port Jackson so I could see her now and again."

"If we get her, I'll see that you have a chance to come aboard her and look to your heart's content, my dear. You have my word on it. And for now, I'd best be on my way lest I be caught on the road by darkness. Goodbye for now, dear lady, and goodbye to you, Mr. Garrity."

Garrity watched the carriage moving away, and thought about the conversation between Drexler and Meghan, and about his mother. His mother would have been beligerent in her demands for the amount she considered correct, but no one could have been more firm than Meghan. Meghan had been amiable and courteous as she demonstrated to Drexler that he was dealing with acumen equal to his own. And under the pleasant exterior, she had been absolutely unyielding.

He also thought about the times he had talked worriedly with Meghan about being unable to find work, and she had been unconcerned. She had known that she would be due money from the settlement on the

Baleen, and she had quietly waited for the settlement to be made. When he had married her, he had thought he knew her well. Since then, he had found unsuspected depths to her personality. And he was still finding them.

"I like Mr. Drexler," Meghan said.

Chapter 19

THE MONEY FROM THE SETTLEMENT on the *Baleen* was more than Garrity had possessed when he had brought Meghan to the selection, and it would maintain them for a year or more as long as they remained there. It was also enough to invest in cargo shares, which could result in anything from outright loss of the money to a manyfold profit.

Garrity knew nothing about investing in cargo shares and considered the money Meghan's, and he left the decision to her. She thought about it for a day, and decided against risking the money. Garrity went to Sydney to collect the money and to bring it home.

The weather turned colder in June. This was full winter and it rained for days. The track to Sydney became a quagmire, and the Venables were unable to visit. Venable also had a weak constitution and was frequently ill during the winter months, and he was often bedridden and unable to go to the shipyard when Garrity took Meghan to Sydney in the cart. But both he and Meghan enjoyed her visits and Meghan worried about him. Garrity took her to visit him each Sunday except those when the track was too dangerous for the cart.

Leaks had developed in the roofs on the sheds during past years, and because of his wooden leg, Mayhew had been unable to climb up to make repairs. Garrity found the leaks during a rainstorm and fixed them.

The roof on the house began to leak one day during a heavy downpour of rain. Water was dripping in the kitchen and the front room.

Mayhew helped Garrity carry the ladder around to the side of the house while Meghan heated the tar pot in the kitchen. The rain beat against Garrity's oilskins and hat as he walked along the roof over the front room, stepping carefully to avoid starting more leaks. He daubed tar on likely-looking spots, and Meghan called out to Mayhew that the leak had stopped.

The leak in the roof over the kitchen was more difficult to find, and the tar became cold while Garrity was daubing it on places that looked like leaks. Mayhew took it inside to reheat it while Garrity waited on the roof, then he brought it back out and handed it up to Garrity. Meghan called out that the leak had stopped after Garrity daubed tar on a few more places. In winter, there was a lot of work like that.

A rider approaching the house became visible through the rain as Garrity climbed down the ladder. Tench had visited twice, but the rider sat his horse with accustomed ease instead of Tench's awkward wariness. The hat was a stockman's instead of a tricorn, and the man's outline looked very familiar. Then

Garrity recognized his younger brother Colin, and he whopped and ran toward him.

"Colin! What the bloody hell are you doing here during winter?"

Colin laughed as he leaped down from the horse and threw his arms around Garrity, pounding his back. "By God, it's good to see you again, Earl! And it doesn't look as though you're any the worse for being a sailor for a while, does it?"

"No, it didn't shrink me or anything." Garrity laughed. "But what are you doing here in the middle of winter? You must have had a hell of a trip!"

"Aye, it was a trip and then some," Colin chuckled ruefully, and he turned as Mayhew came around the house. "By God, here's old Alf! Are you all right, Alf?"

"Well, look who's here!" Mayhew hooted, hobbling toward the brothers. "Aye, I'm all right so long as I can keep my peg from getting stuck in the mud. What are you doing here in the winter?"

"Thus far I've been fighting mud and floods," Colin laughed. "Every creek between here and Wayamba is running a banker, and never mind what the bloody rivers are doing."

"Come on, and let's get you in out of the rain," Garrity said, taking his brother's arm. "There's someone in here I want you to meet."

"Aye, I've heard about her, and I've been looking forward to seeing her. How did you come to meet her?"

Garrity briefly told Colin about Meghan as they walked toward the house through the rain, and he shook his head in warning as he finished. "But don't mention the cannibals to her, because it can put her in a bad frame of mind. She's getting over it, but she still has a way to go."

"I'm not bloody surprised," Colin replied soberly.

"She has a strong will, and she can deal with things better than most. I expect everyone at Wayamba has heard about her, haven't they? And I expect that's the reason you're here."

"I expect it is," Colin agreed, smiling again. "Ma said there were some things she wanted from Sydney come hell or high water, but she did tell me direct out to stop by the Georges."

Garrity laughed and nodded, and Colin chuckled as he stopped at the corner of the veranda to tie his horse. They walked up the steps to the veranda, Mayhew stumping behind them, and Meghan opened the front door. Colin blinked, and his eyes opened wide. Garrity introduced them, and Meghan smiled.

"Aye, I knew immediately who you are, because the blood runs true," she said. "I'm pleased to meet you, Colin."

Colin still gazed at Meghan, then he smiled. "By God, she's lovely, Earl!" he exclaimed, and his smile turned into a wide grin. "And I'm most pleased to meet you, Meghan. I'm your brother, so there's no harm in a kiss, is there?"

Meghan laughed, shaking her head. "No harm at all, Colin. But I'm also your sister, and I'll make free to belay sauciness with my hand across your chops."

Colin roared with laughter, stepping toward her, and Meghan laughed as she reached up to him. Garrity was glad that they liked each other immediately.

"Come on in, Colin," Meghan said. "You look as
though you haven't eaten in a week. You can talk to
Earl while I prepare dinner."

Colin nodded. "I can stay for a bit, but I must get on
to Sydney and see to my wagons and men. I'd have
brought them with me, but I didn't want to take those
wagons a foot off the track. But I'll be back tomorrow."

The men took off their oilskins and hats, and hung
them up and sat down at the table as Meghan built up
the fire and began preparing dinner. Garrity told Colin
about his trip to New Zealand on the *Pamir.* Colin
talked about what had been happening at Wayamba
Station.

An aged stockman had died, dingos had savaged
and scattered the flocks in one of the paddocks, and
there had been floods, grassfires, and accidents. The
litany of events sounded wearily familiar to Garrity. It
was the monotonous routine and hardships he had
longed to escape. At the same time, he felt a poignant,
longing nostalgia as he listened. He remained a part of
Wayamba Station, and the sheep station remained a
part of him.

Meghan prepared dinner, and she carried the food to
the table. A long platter was filled with smoked sausages, plump and juicy, with crisp, crackling skins.
There was a tray of bread still hot from the over, bowls
of pickled cabbage and potatoes fried with onions.

They ate in silence for several minutes, then Garrity
looked across the table at his brother. "When I saw
you, I fancied you might have a message from Ma for

me to get myself and mine off Wayamba property."

Colin took a drink of tea, shaking his head. "We first heard you were here from old Ian Higgins, who picked it up somewhere along the track. Then Ma got some mail from Cummings Brothers, and there was a note about it among the other things. She didn't appear at all upset, and the only comment she made was that isn't Wayamba Station."

"That surprises me," Garrity said musingly. "She's always seemed to have a special feeling for this place."

"Aye, she has," Colin agreed. "But that's all she had to say about it. I'm sure she'd be so taken with Meghan, though, that you could return to the station and commence where you left off."

"No, Meghan and I have plans of our own."

"That's true," Meghan said. "But this bad blood between you and your mother isn't right, Earl. It isn't the way people in a family should be, particularly a mother and her children. Perhaps we could go for a visit so I could meet your mother, and you could heal this rift."

"No, we're not going to Wayamba Station. Ma sent me away, and she'll have to ask me back before I'll go. And she'll never do that."

Colin looked at Meghan. "There you have it, Meghan, clear and plain. If you haven't found out already, a hard head goes with the Garrity name. I'm not calling Earl and Ma on it, because from time to time I also get like an old ox with a yoke gall. Well, it's near dark, so I'd best be going."

Garrity got up. "You'll be around for a few days, won't you?"

360

"You may be assured of that," Colin laughed, rising from the table. "I don't intend to get back on that track any sooner than I have to. Meghan, I don't know how Earl managed to do it, but he did us all a good turn when he talked you into marrying him."

"I'm most proud to be a member of the family, Colin," Meghan replied. "I knew it to be a good family from the kind of man Earl is, and meeting you has confirmed it."

Colin took his hat and oilskins off a peg. "I'm not sure everyone would say that, but I do know we're better off for having you in the family, Meghan. I'll see you again tomorrow, then."

"Aye, goodbye for now, Colin."

Garrity and his brother went out to the veranda, and Colin put on his oilskins and hat. He tugged his hat down, looking out at the rain.

"You're a lucky man, Earl," he said.

"Aye, I am," Garrity agreed. "She's a most wonderful woman in every way that makes a difference, as well as in those that don't."

Colin nodded. "I trust you won't take it wrong, but it's strange how much she puts one in mind of Ma. It's strange, because she doesn't look or act like Ma in the least. But at the same time, they seem similar in some way or other."

"I've noticed it myself," Garrity replied. "Meghan doesn't have Ma's sharp edges, but she's as quick in her own way to achieve her ends. She knows what she wants and goes after it, and they're alike in other ways."

"Well, if I could find one like her myself, I'd start

thinking about getting married," Colin chuckled, walking down the steps. "I'll see you tomorrow, Earl."

"Aye, that you will."

Colin untied his horse and mounted it, and waved as he reined it away from the house. Garrity waved, and stood on the edge of the veranda and watched his brother ride away. The gray, dim light was fading rapidly into an early dusk, and Colin disappeared into the heavy downpour of rain.

Garrity went back into the house. Mayhew had gone to his room, and Meghan was washing the dishes. She smiled as he took out his pipe. He filled it and lit it, and sat down at the table and watched Meghan as she moved back and forth.

"Would you like some more tea, love?" Meghan asked.

"No, I've had my fill, thanks all the same. Colin was mightily taken with you."

"And I was with him," she replied, smiling as she put the pannikins on the shelf. "He's a very congenial man, and very entertaining. The women hereabout appear to be dreadfully slow for him to still be running loose. You ran loose long enough yourself." She looked at Garrity, touching his face. "Colin's a very fetching man, but I have the more handsome one."

Garrity took her hand and kissed it. But her smile faded as she looked down at him, her large blue eyes moving over his face. She suddenly bent over him, her fingers combing into his hair and gripping it, and she kissed him with fierce intensity. Her lips were damp and hot against his, moving over his lips. He reached

362

to put his arms around her, but she twisted out of his arms and walked rapidly away.

Her features were flushed, almost crimson. She cleared her throat as she paced nervously and aimlessly across the kitchen, wiping her hands on her apron again. Then she stopped and glanced around, her eyes avoiding his. She stepped to the fireplace and picked up the shovel, and she scooped up hot coals in the shovel and carried it out of the kitchen. Garrity watched her as she walked out of the kitchen with the shovel.

Months before, when they had arrived at the house, she had laid wood for a fire in their bedroom fireplace. There had been no need for a fire during the summer months, and the wood had remained in the fireplace without being burned during the autumn and winter months. Meghan's footsteps came back through the house, and she walked into the kitchen and replaced the shovel by the fireplace. Then she turned and walked out again without looking at him, her face still flushed.

He knocked the ashes out of his pipe and blew out the lamp on the kitchen table, and walked through the house to their bedroom. The dry wood in the fireplace was blazing hotly, filling the room with a flickering, ruddy light. Meghan's alluring, feminine fragrance filled the room and she was in bed, the bedclothes outlining the contours of her slender body. He undressed and slid into bed.

His leg brushed her warm, smooth leg as he lay down by her. She pushed the covers down, turning to him. The front of her chemisette was open, and the firelight played over the swelling mounds of her firm, resilient breasts and shone in her eyes. He moved toward her, and she melted into his arms. She lifted her lips to his, and fiery, throbbing desire exploded to life within him as he kissed her passionately. He pulled at her chemisette, and she lifted it and wriggled out of it.

She was frightened, trembling in his arms even as she pulled him over her and surged toward him. He struggled to control the raging desire that possessed him, moving slowly and gently. She gasped softly, and a shuddering tremor raced through her as the damp warmth of her body opened and enfolded him. He hesitated, and she arched up to meet him as she murmured demandingly. Her fingers dug into his back, her lips searching for his, and she pulled him into her as she bit at his lips.

They clutched each other and throbbed together in a heated rhythm, seized by a driving compulsion to release the torrents of demands that had been suppressed. She smothered a soft, wailing cry against his lips, lifting herself higher, and numbing pangs of ecstasy seized him. He collapsed on her and she was motionless under him, and the feel of her slender body under his immediately stimulated his desire for her again.

He moved slowly and leisurely, kissing her. She remained motionless, her eyes wide in the moonlight as she looked up at him, then she began moving again. Her fingers combed through his hair and caressed his face as she looked up at him, lifting herself more strongly and meeting him. Then her features tensed and she dug her fingers into his shoulders, surging under him.

Time collapsed, each second seeming an eternity as her lithe body moved in a quickening pace, urging him to greater exertion. The contact between them seemed to acquire a force and life of its own, and the swift plunge into ecstasy rushed over him. Her breath came in panting gasps as she strained, then she moaned softly and surged in a frenzy of movement as wrenching spasms raced through him.

They clung together, damp, panting breathlessly, their hearts pounding. Meghan drew in a deep breath and released it in a sigh, lifting a hand and pushing his hair back. "I wish I had been a virgin for you, love," she whispered. "And I wish I had been a proper wife for you from the beginning."

"You were a woman for me," he murmured. "And our love has made you a proper wife from the beginning."

She smiled, moving higher in the bed and wrapping her arms around him, and she pulled his head down to her. He pillowed his head on her breasts, and she made a sound of satisfaction in her throat as she settled herself comfortably and caressed his face with her fingertips.

Chapter 20

MEGHAN WINCED AS THE CART jolted through a deep rut, and looked ahead impatiently. "Can't we go a bit faster, Earl?"

"We're going fast enough, love," Garrity replied. "You must remember your condition."

"My condition," she sighed in exasperation. "Earl, I'm with child, but that doesn't mean I'm made of glass."

"No, but it does mean that you're with child," he chuckled. "We're going as fast as you need to go and as fast as the horse needs to go, and that ship will be there when we get there."

"But everyone else will already be there."

"And they'll also be there when we get there."

Meghan sighed again, craning her neck and looking around. The cart was rumbling along the road between Sydney and the Jackson Heads, at the entrance to the sound leading into the harbor. The glint of the sunshine on the sound shone through the trees on the left, and the masts of ships at anchor in the harbor were visible through openings in the trees. A narrow road branched off to the left, and Garrity turned the horse onto it.

The road went downhill, to the cove at the side of the harbor entrance where the Poage and Venable shipyard was located. The trees ahead thinned out, and the mast heads and upper spars of the clipper anchored in front of the shipyard came into sight. Drexler and the Venables were at the yard, standing near their carriage and chaise. Captain Spencer and Thomas Mabry were standing with them, talking as they looked at the clipper.

The clipper dwarfed two other ships at anchor in the cove, its long, slender hull seeming to fill the cove and its masts towering into the sky. Some of its spars were missing, and the main rigging on the port side was in process of being replaced. Its boats, windlasses, and other items of equipment had been taken off, but it was still impressive. And its long, raked prow made it appear to be racing through the water even when it was at anchor.

People waved and called out to Garrity and he waved back. Meghan waved absently, and turned back to the clipper. Garrity reined up and lifted Meghan down as people came over. Meghan had never met Spencer and Mabry, and Garrity introduced her to them. The two men lifted their tricorns and bowed as Meghan bobbed in a curtsey.

"Mr. Venable has been telling us about you, Mistress Garrity," Spencer said. "We're given to understand that there's very little about any sort of ship that you don't know."

"Mr. Venable makes too much of my small knowledge," Meghan laughed. "I know only bits and pieces I learned from my father."

Venable coughed hoarsely into a handkerchief and shook his head. "I should also add that Mistress Garrity is too modest," he said, clearing his throat. "Are you feeling well, Meghan?"

"Better than you sound, Joshua," she replied. "Have you been using that eucalyptus oil and poultice?"

He nodded and shrugged, clearing his throat again. "Yes, but this warm weather we're having will do me more good than anything else. Are you ready for a closer look at the clipper?"

"Aye, but let me give Mr. Drexler his basket first. I brought you some pastries and tarts, Mr. Drexler, as well as some smoked sausages you might like. Would you hand out the basket, Earl?"

"Pastries?" Drexler exclaimed in delight, rubbing his stomach. "And tarts? I was waiting with bated breath, dear lady, hoping you might have thought to bring something of the sort along. And smoked sausages? I'll certainly look forward to having them for my dinner. I'll take the basket and put it in my carriage, Mr. Garrity."

He beamed with pleasure, taking the basket as Garrity lifted it out of the cart, and he trotted to his carriage with it. The others walked toward a longboat at the edge of the water, and Drexler put the basket in his carriage and caught up with them. Venable, Drexler, and Spencer climbed into the boat as Garrity lifted Meghan and Mary Venable into it, then he and Mabry pushed it out into the water. They jumped into it, and picked up the oars and rowed out to the clipper.

A ladder hung over the side of the ship, but Garrity refused to allow Meghan to climb it. She sat in the boat with Mary and fumed as Garrity and the rest of the men climbed up the rope ladder. On board, they rigged out a bosun's chair on a boom that had been set up to hoist repair materials onto the ship. They lifted Meghan up to the deck, then lowered the canvas sling to bring Mary on board.

Meghan walked across the deck to Venable, looking at coils of rope that were being used to make the new main rigging. "I see you're using the hemp rope again, Joshua."

He coughed, nodding in disgust. "Yes, I'm doing as you suggested even though the flax rope is far stronger and not nearly as expensive. I still fail to understand why sailors don't like it."

"They say it doesn't take tar as well as hemp," Spencer said. "And they say it doesn't hold up to chafing as well as hemp does."

"Nonsense, Captain!" Venable snorted. "I've had lengths of flax and hemp rope chafed across a board at the same time, and the flax holds up better. And my men have no difficulty in tarring it."

"The sailors don't trust it, Joshua," Meghan said. "And when they don't trust something, they'll think of all manner of reasons not to use it regardless of its excellence. For my part, I'm inclined to put faith in the feelings that seamen have about things. When an old salt starts rubbing a shoulder or a knee, I'll look for a storm whether the mercury barometer says so or no."

"And I will as well, Mistress Garrity," Spencer said. "Come, let's have a look at the cabins. I glanced at them yesterday, and they're most commodious indeed."

Garrity followed the others as they walked back along the main deck and entered the passageway under the quarterdeck. The cabins were enormous compared to those on the *Pamir* and other ships Garrity had seen, and they were luxurious. The walls and floors were varnished, highly-polished oak, with trim and accents in mahogany. The captain's cabin was large and comfortable, and there were cabins for a first and second mate, as well as passengers. The galley and wardroom were spacious, with polished oak furniture fixed to the deck and walls.

Drexler glowed with pride of ownership, and Spencer and Mabry radiated satisfaction over their new command. Garrity had been offered the position of second mate and had declined it, refusing to leave Meghan while she was pregnant. Venable had hinted about the possibilities of employment for Garrity in the shipyard, and Garrity had ignored the hints. He knew they were motivated by Venable's friendship with Meghan, rather than by a need for him. But the money Meghan had received from Drexler and Suggs was steadily trickling away on necessities.

The people straggled back out on deck, and Garrity went up to the quarterdeck. The helm was a large double wheel, more convenient than a single wheel for two helmsmen to grip and hold the rudder steady when the massive spread of sail was exerting pressure against it in a tack. The binnacle was large and well-sheltered from wind and rain, with small lanterns mounted around it out of the field of the compass. Garrity looked at the helm and binnacle, and walked back across to the edge quarterdeck overlooking the main deck.

Meghan talked with the men as she picked her way around tools and materials scattered on the deck. Garrity smiled fondly as he watched her. When he had been offered the berth of second mate on the ship, she had left the decision to him. There had been no question in his mind on what to do, even though the thought of sailing with the clipper had been appealing, and Meghan was pleased at his decision.

Mabry opened a hatch cover and the men climbed down into a hold, helping Meghan as she came. Mary came up to the quarterdeck and chatted with Garrity while they waited. Meghan and the men prowled around in the hold, then came back up on deck and looked at the masts and rigging. Then they went into the forecastle and looked around, and climbed down into a forward hold.

The summer day was warm and bright, and the sun was at its zenith when Meghan and the men finished looking at the ship. Meghan was fascinated by the clipper, and she left it reluctantly. Mabry and Garrity rowed the boat back to the shipyard, and Mabry and Spencer went with Drexler in his carriage. Garrity helped Meghan into the cart, and she continued talking about the ship as they followed the Venables' chaise to their house on the outskirts of the town.

The scullery maid at the Venable house was an aged

widow named Martha Fisher, who was known throughout the town as an expert midwife. Meghan and Mary Venable went upstairs with the woman so she could examine Meghan and talk to her. They returned, and Meghan went on discussing the ship with Venable during and after lunch.

It was late afternoon when Garrity and Meghan left, and it was nearly dark when they left the last houses of Sydney behind. Bushrangers occasionally lurked along isolated roads and tracks at night, and Garrity checked his pistol and put it back under his coat. Darkness closed in and the moon rose, dimly lighting the track as the cart trundled along it, with Meghan still talking excitedly about the clipper.

Garrity listened absently and murmured responses, thinking of his promise to her the first time they had traveled along the track. He had promised to try to satisfy her yearning to own shares in a ship, but the possibility of fulfilling her wishes had never seemed more distant. Her excitement over the clipper had nothing to do with his promise, but at the same time it was a reminder of his inability to give her what she wanted. More importantly, he remained unemployed and was making no progress toward what she wanted or any other goal.

They reached the selection, and Garrity opened the gate and led the horse through it. He closed the gate and climbed back up to the seat, and the cart bumped along the rutted track leading through the paddock to the house. The kitchen window in the house glowed with yellow light, and fires flickered around the aborigine huts by the river. Meghan had fallen silent at the gate, and she looked up at Garrity.

"Have I bored you with my nattering about the *Orion,* love?" she asked. "You've been very quiet."

"No, no," he said, putting an arm around her and squeezing her affectionately. "No, nothing gives me more pleasure than to see you enjoying yourself. I was only thinking that I'd once promised you a ship, and I might have to ask you to content yourself with a rowboat."

Meghan's smile faded a little. "Are you reproaching yourself, love? My word, if every woman had as much as I have to be happy about, there'd be few tears from women in this world. You're the best of husbands, Earl, and I won't have you reproaching yourself."

"But I know how you feel about ships, and I did say that I'd try to see that you'd have shares in one some day."

"So you did, and perhaps you will. If you don't, I'll certainly never think twice about it, because you've made me the happiest woman alive. In any event, Earl, we're young and we have years ahead of us."

Garrity nodded as he reined up in front of the house, still feeling the same in spite of what she had said. He lifted her down from the cart, and she went in as he led the horse around to the side of the house. Mayhew came out with a lantern to help unharness the horse. Garrity shrugged off his guilty mood as Meghan prepared a late dinner and they ate, but it returned after they went to bed. He stared into the darkness, thinking of the promise he hadn't even begun to keep.

Roosters crowing awakened Garrity at dawn, and life seemed more promising as the sun rose and another summer day began. The chicken pen was crowded with chickens from broods hatched during early spring, and two sows with litters of pigs rooted in the pig pen. The ground that Garrity had plowed the previous autumn was planted, along with the rest of the garden, and the vegetables were flourishing.

A large flock a drover had taken to Sydney the previous spring had left strays scattered for miles along the Georges. Garrity and Mayhew had rounded up more than a hundred of them, and Colin and Dennis had left two more horses at the selection when they had visited while on a trip to Sydney during late spring. The paddocks were less overgrown with the additional stock in them, but the fences needed constant attention. When Garrity and Mayhew finished the new pig pen, they walked around the fences and looked for holes and weak spots.

A swagman came along the track as Garrity and Mayhew were returning to the house for tools to repair a hole in the fence, and they stopped and waited to see if he would turn in at the selection. He came through the gate, carefully closing it behind him, and walked through the paddock toward them. Mayhew looked at the man more closely, chuckling. "That's old John Pringle," he said, and shouted, "Are you all right, John?"

"Aye, I'll do, Alf," the man called back. "Are you?"

"I'm still moving around enough to keep my peg from sprouting roots," Mayhew answered. "It's been donkey's years since I've seen you."

"It's been donkey's years since I've been this close in," Pringle replied. "And I intend getting back to

375

where a body can breathe just as fast as I can." He approached, a tall man in dusty, ragged clothes and hat, with a bedroll slung across his back. His features were baked dark brown by the sun, and he walked with a long, swinging stride. "Are you and your ma still on the outs with each other?" he asked Garrity.

Garrity had never seen the man before, but the questions and attitude were typical of the swagman. "It's been a while since we've seen each other," he replied.

Pringle stopped by Garrity and Mayhew, taking out a rag to wipe the dust and sweat off his face. "Aye, I saw your brother Dennis on the track to Menindee a few months ago, and he said as much. And a body could opine as much without asking, because Garritys have always been quicker to take offense than they have been to get over it. Do you have any work that wants doing?"

"No, we have everything in hand. Do you have a tucker bag there?"

Pringle nodded, taking the bedroll off his back, and he knelt to untie the rope from the ends of the bedroll. He took a canvas bag out of the bedroll and handed it to Garrity, who took it around the house and handed it to Meghan at the kitchen door.

The bag contained smaller cloth bags for tea, salt, sugar, and flour, and Meghan filled them. Pringle and Mayhew came around the house and stood by the door talking. Meghan added potatoes and a piece of smoked pork to the other things and handed the bag back out. Pringle weighed it in his hand, and lifted his hat to Meghan.

"That's a most generous ration, Mistress Garrity, and I'm much obliged to you."

"You're more than welcome. Will you be spending the night?"

"No, I feel closed in hereabout, so I'll be on my way."

"Godspeed and good fortune, then."

"Thank you, Mistress Garrity, and I pray the little one will be hale and hearty."

She smiled and nodded, walking back into the kitchen, and Pringle knelt to put the bag of food in his bedroll. He unrolled his dusty blue blanket, looked up at Mayhew. "So I've passed no fewer than forty who were heading there, and it was probably more like sixty. People are heading there from all over, so it must be true."

"Aye, it must be," Mayhew agreed, and looked at Garrity. "There's been a big gold strike down by Adelaide."

"There has? When did this happen, John?"

"Just a few days ago," Pringle replied. "And from what I've heard, it's one of the biggest yet. One fossicker found a nugget twice the size of your fist, and others have found enough to put them right for the rest of their lives." He wrapped the blanket around the bag of food, retied the rope on the ends of the bedroll, and pulled the rope over his shoulder as he rose. "So it's a big one."

"Are you going down that way, John?" Mayhew asked.

"No, I'm not a fossicker, and that's not for me," Pringle chuckled. "I don't know what I'd do with money if I had it, and there'll be too many people down there to suit me." He nodded to Garrity and Mayhew, turning away. "I'll be on my way. Good luck to both of you."

Garrity and Mayhew replied, waving. Pringle waved, and disappeared around the corner of the house. Garrity and Mayhew collected the tools they needed out of a shed, and walked back out through the paddock to repair the hole they had found in the fence. Pringle was far down the track when they reached the fence, walking along with his long, swinging stride. Garrity and Mayhew began working on the fence, and Garrity pondered over what the swagman had said about the gold strike.

There had been several gold strikes in Australia, and people had flooded into the colony from as far away as Europe following the news of the first ones. His mother had always regarded prospectors and their hopeful optimism with scorn, as had many others he had known, and for good reason. Most of those who had come to Australia to find gold had left when ships brought stories of gold strikes in other places, and most of them had left as penniless as they had been when they arrived.

But a few had found vast riches. Some who had arrived in the sordid misery of crowded accommodations on small, leaky ships had left on clippers, wearing expensive clothes and taking along cases of costly wines and supplies of delicacies to last them on the trip. A few who had come to Australia as convicts had returned to England as wealthy men. Some of the businesses in Sydney had been established with capital that had come from deposits of gold and precious stones.

Many of those who had been unsuccessful had been defeated by Australia. And some had found death instead of riches. Australia could be inhospitable to those unfamiliar with the land and its moods. Flash floods, poisonous snakes, the vast deserts, grassfires, the devastating heat of the interior, and other perils had taken their toll. Some had left bones bleaching in the sun and others filled lonely graves, and still others had become discouraged by the grueling hardships and left.

Australia could be a perilous land. But from childhood, Garrity had dealt with the perils and hardships daily, and the land was a part of him. He had longed to go to sea, and while at sea he had felt the tug of the land pulling him back to it. The lonely monotony of a sheep station still repelled him, but the land was his birthright. He was Australian, and he could deal with the land. And it was a land of precious minerals and stones.

Prospecting offered a possibility of fulfilling what he wanted to do for Meghan. It was a remote possibility, because the chances strongly favored failure, but it was the only possibility that had presented itself. He thought about it without mentioning it to Meghan, considering various ways to proceed. The next time he went to Sydney, talk about the new gold strike was widespread in the town. Some laborers had left their jobs to go to Adelaide, and the latest edition of the newspaper was filled with stories about the gold find.

Garrity bought a copy of the newspaper, and took it home with him to show Meghan. She read the newspaper, and Garrity told her what he had been considering. She objected strongly.

"You turned down the second mate's berth on the *Orion* because you didn't want to leave me," she said. "But you'd leave me to go off in search of gold. Now where's the sense in that, Earl?"

"Because I wouldn't be going as far or for as long," he replied. "I could come home at any time, and I'd be here when the baby's born. You couldn't possibly go, because the gold fields are no place for a woman. And particularly a woman in your condition."

"Considering where I've been in the past, I doubt that the gold fields would represent any great terror to me. However, I do agree about my condition. We could wait until the baby is a few weeks old, or do you think all the gold would be gone by then?"

Garrity shook his head. "No, gold is always spread over a large area whenever it's found, and one find usually leads to many more. I daresay we could wait until this time next year and still have as much chance of finding gold. But I don't favor the idea of taking you and a baby to the gold fields, Meghan."

"And I don't favor the idea of sitting here and twiddling my thumbs, Earl. We're married, and it's right and proper that we should do things together insofar as possible. And as long as the baby has proper food and shelter, it won't know the difference between here and the gold fields. We could have some sort of shelter, couldn't we?"

Garrity thought about it for a moment, then slowly nodded. "Aye, we could. I wouldn't feel right about taking a horse and cart from here, but we have enough to buy a horse and a small wagon. And we could buy sail cloth to make a tent. We could load the wagon with food from the garden and things you've preserved, and that should last a long time. In event of bad weather, you and the baby could shelter in the wagon. That should suffice, shouldn't it?"

Meghan nodded happily, and she became more excited over the idea as they continued discussing it. Garrity told her about prospectors he had known, and the methods they used. He knew how to identify the terrain formations where gold was most frequently found, and how to extract placer gold. Several years before, he had even spent a few days in prospecting on a low mountain on the southern border of Wayamba Station.

The mountain was called Broken Hill, and with his limited resources and time he had been unable to find worthwhile deposits of precious metals. But the area had seemed rich in metals, and later developments had proven him to be right. A consortium of investors had prospected the area, and found silver and other metals. Extensive mining operations had begun on the southern border of Wayamba Station, enraging Garrity's mother.

Garrity's doubts about taking Meghan with him faded as they discussed it, and Mayhew had mixed feelings when Garrity told him what he and Meghan planned to do. He was disturbed over the prospect of their leaving, but enthusiastic about their joining the search for gold. When Garrity and Meghan visited with the Venables the following Sunday, they had reservations about the undertaking. They considered it too dangerous for Meghan to go along and take a small baby.

Their objections failed to dim Meghan's enthusiasm, and it continued growing. She had positive feeling about the venture, viewing it as a promising opportunity. Each issue of the newspaper had more stories about the gold find, and she read them with avid interest. Tench visited while his ship was being loaded in Port Jackson, and he brought news that thrilled Meghan. On his last trip around the coast from Adelaide, he had brought several thousand ounces of gold to the bank in Sydney.

Garrity priced horses at the market in Sydney, and looked for a wagon small enough for a single horse to pull but large enough to provide the space they needed. The price of horses had risen sharply because of the number of people buying horses to go to Adelaide, and he decided to wait until the initial excitement faded and the price went back down. He saw no wagons that would fit his needs, and he placed an order with a wainwright in the town to build one.

Meghan had exchanged several letters with Mary Cargill in New Zealand, and Garrity routinely stopped at the postal office each time he was in town. He went to the postal office after he left the wainwright's shop, and the clerk dug through a large box of letters and gave him one for Meghan. It was addressed to her as

Meghan Buell, and it was a large, thick letter from England. She had told Garrity about having written to an uncle in England well over a year before, when she had been in New Zealand, and the letter was apparently a reply to her letter.

Garrity hurried back to the selection, riding at a fast trot through the heat of the afternoon. He rode around the house to the kitchen door, and took out the letter as he dismounted and went in. Meghan squealed in excitement when she saw the letter, and she tore the thick packet open as she sat down at the table. She unfolded the pages, reading rapidly, and her smile faded. Her eyes filled with tears, and she put down the letter and slumped in her chair.

"My father's dead, Earl," she said quietly.

He stepped to her and put his hand on her shoulder. "I'm very sorry to hear that, love. I'm very sorry indeed."

Meghan glanced up at him and nodded, and she brushed at her eyes as she picked up the letter and began reading again. Garrity took out his pipe and filled it, and he lit it at the fireplace and sat down on the other side of the table. Meghan shuffled the pages of the letter, reading it through. A smaller sheet of paper fell out of the pages, and she looked at it and put it aside. She folded the pages to put them back into the packet.

"Well, he was released from confinement a few weeks before he died," she said in a resigned tone. "And he saw my letter."

"That much is good, in any event."

"Aye, but his sentence was only commuted and not revoked," she replied bitterly. "Queen Victoria is ill-served by some of that foul lot who call themselves her ministers. I pray God that pack of scurvy dogs will someday be made to pay the price of their perfidy against one who truly and bravely served God, queen, and country." She sighed again, picking up the piece of paper she had put aside. "Here's my inheritance from my father, and it's a goodly sum. It's almost sixty guineas."

Garrity took the bank draft and looked at it. "There's money we could well do without."

"We could indeed," she agreed sadly. "But at least we'll not want for anything when we set out for the gold fields, will we?" She pushed the letter back into the packet, smiling faintly. "My uncle was on beam's ends as to how to tell me about my father's death. He always looked after me when my father was at sea, and we've always been most fond of each other."

"I can tell that by the way you speak of him."

Meghan nodded musingly, looking at the letter. "If our baby is a son, would you mind greatly if we named him after my uncle? His name's Patrick, the same as your grandfather's, so there's reason on both sides of the family to use the name. I know it's your right to name him after yourself, but we'll have others."

"I've told you before, there are no rights between us," he replied, smiling at her as he reached across the table to pat her hand. "And you're having the baby, not me. If you wish to call him Patrick, then I don't mind in the least, love."

"That's good of you, Earl," she said gratefully. "If it's a boy, then, we'll name him Patrick. It will please my uncle to no end."

He patted her hand again, and pushed his chair back and rose. "I'll go unsaddle my horse. You should write back to your uncle as soon as you can, and I'll take the letter to town and post it."

"Aye, I've a lot to tell him, and I'll begin on it tonight."

Meghan put the writing materials on the kitchen table after dinner, took out her uncle's letter, and began writing a reply. She finished the letter the next morning, and Garrity saddled a horse and took the letter and the bank draft to Sydney. After he mailed the letter and cashed the bank draft, he went to the wainwright's shop where he had ordered the wagon. Work on the wagon had already begun, and it would be ready well before he needed it. He went to a chandler's shop and bought sail cloth to make a tent, and rode back to the selection.

Joshua Venable had recovered from his illness when the weather turned hot, and Garrity and Meghan were again exchanging visits with the Venables on alternate Sundays. The jolting of the cart along the road caused Meghan to have abdominal pains when Garrity took her to Sydney on a Sunday in late summer, alarming him and the Venables. The Venables began coming to the selection each Sunday after that, and Meghan fretted over being unable to visit the shipyard.

Garrity finished making the tent, and he soaked it

with whale oil to waterproof it. He let it dry in the sun for several days, then folded it and put it away. The wagon was completed, and Garrity paid for it and brought it to the selection. He soaked the canvas top with whale oil to waterproof it, and built shelves and bins along the sideboards in the wagon to hold food, utensils, and his and Meghan's belongings.

Martha Fisher came with the Venables more often on Sunday as the weeks of the summer passed. When the old woman estimated that the baby would be born within two weeks or less, she and Mary Venable brought clothes with them and moved into an empty bedroom. The two women helped Meghan with her work, and sat and chatted with her in the shade at the side of the house on hot afternoons while the three of them sewed on small clothes. They were nonchalant about the situation, but Garrity was constantly distraught and unable to sleep, awakening every time Meghan moved during the night.

Garrity and Mayhew were transferring the sheep from one paddock to another on a hot afternoon when the women had been at the house just over a week. It looked like Meghan was close to her time. The fire in the kitchen had been built up, even though it was sweltering, and smoke poured from the chimney. Mary Venable was hastily gathering linen cloths from the clothesline by the house, and neither Meghan nor the old woman were outside. Garrity ran toward the house, leaving Mayhew far behind as he hobbled along on his wooden leg.

Mary came to the front door with the cloths folded

over her arm when Garrity called to her from the veranda, and she nodded. "Yes, it started just a little while ago, Earl."

"Is she all right? What can I do?"

"You can do naught!" the old woman said peevishly inside the house. "Your doing was done some months ago. Mistress Venable, I do need those cloths in here now!"

"She's all right, Earl," Mary said, turning away from the door. "And it's only just started, so it'll be some hours yet."

He nodded. Mayhew puffed breathlessly as he approached, calling out. "Was that it? Is it a boy or a girl?"

"That's it, but it'll be a while yet," Garrity replied, walking toward him. "It takes a woman longer than it does a ewe. We might as well finish moving the sheep over to the fresh grass."

Mayhew stopped, looking deflated, and turned and stumped along by Garrity as they went back out into the paddocks. The sheep were scattered between two paddocks. Garrity and Mayhew got them together. They finished driving them into the paddock with deeper grass, and walked back to the house. The doors and windows were open so the house would cool when the late afternoon breeze began, and Meghan's soft cries of pain carried outside as Garrity and Mayhew sat on the steps in front of the house.

Sunset approached and a breeze stirred, breaking the torrid heat. Each cry of pain from Meghan grated on Garrity's nerves, and he writhed inwardly in an agony of frustration. Some vital factor also seemed to be missing, something crucially important that someone should be doing and was overlooking. Then he saw the aborigines filing through the paddocks from the river to the house. The missing element fell into place in his mind, a sense that the situation was complete.

Aborigines had always been a part of his life. An aborigine village was on the creek at the home paddock of Wayamba Station, and tiny family groups were scattered widely across the vast distances of the paddocks. He had often passed them—a man standing on one leg with his other foot tucked behind his knee as he leaned on a spear and gazed inscrutably into the distance, with a woman and a child or two in the shade nearby. They were as unnoticed as the trees and grass, and at the same time they were as much a part of the land and of life as the trees and grass.

Stockmen were under firm orders from his mother to give them what they wanted, but they rarely wanted anything from Wayamba Station. The sheep station seemed irrelevant to them, its boundaries a meaningless convention, their concerns and activities on a different plane. Individuals among them were distinct personalities, but as a group they were as impersonal as the weather and the seasons.

Aborigines frequently offered assistance in some of the more fundamental aspects of life. Their help took obscure and nebulous forms, but he thought he understood it. They stopped a hundred yards from the house—three men, five women, and eight children of various ages at the end of the line. Garrity beckoned, and they continued walking toward the house.

The adults wore rags and loincloths made of bark, and the children were naked. The children's hair was yellow, varying from bright yellow among some of the smaller ones to brown fading into black among the older ones. A wisp of smoke rose from smoldering tinder a woman carried on a stick, and others carried their digereedoos and rhythm sticks. The men nodded to Garrity as they passed, and they filed around to the side of the house.

The sun set in a blaze of color, and the breeze freshened. Smoke eddied around to the veranda from the fire the aborigines built at the side of the house. Digereedoos whispered, rhythm sticks tapped, and voices chanted softly in a low throbbing that was almost lost under the rustle of the breeze through the grass and the chattering of birds. Meghan moaned again, her voice rising to a wail. Then she was silent, and Mary and the old woman moved around in the house and lit lamps.

Garrity looked up at the two woman as they came out on the veranda. "How is Meghan?"

"She's resting now, and her strength is holding up well," Mary replied, and she pushed at her hair and glanced around. "It's cooling off nicely, and that will help. But that noise those aborigines are making could drive one mad."

"It's not bothering Mistress Garrity," the old woman said firmly. "I've had their lot about before during lying-ins, carrying on with that noise, and I opine they do more good than harm."

"Perhaps you're right," Mary sighed. Meghan cried out inside the house, and she turned back to the door. "We'll put out something for supper directly, Earl. It'll be in the kitchen."

Garrity nodded indifferently, and the two women went back inside. Meghan's cry rose to a shrill scream, and Garrity got up and paced back and forth in front of the house. The sound of the digereedoos, rhythm sticks, and chanting was louder. Meghan was silent again for several minutes, and the women moved around in the house. Mayhew rose and walked around the corner to go to the kitchen and eat.

Darkness fell and the moon rose, and Mayhew came back around the house with a lantern and the bottle of rum from the kitchen. Garrity took a drink of rum, and continued pacing back and forth. Meghan's screams came at more frequent intervals, shrieks that rang through the house. The groaning of digereedoos, clatter of rhythm sticks, and chanting voices at the side of the house became a pounding crescendo that blended with Meghan's screams.

Then there was quiet, the digereedoos sobbing softly and the rhythm sticks tapping. A baby cried in the house. Garrity was walking in a wide circle in front of the house, and he ran to the house and up the steps. He stopped on the veranda, listening. The women bustled about inside, their voices cheerful. Minutes dragged by, then Mary came to the door with a lamp, smiling and beckoning. Garrity rushed inside.

Meghan's face was pale and wan in the lamplight, and lined with fatigue. The aborigines had put green branches on their fire, and the room smelled of smoke. Garrity stepped to the bed and bent over it, and leaned down and kissed Meghan. She smiled wearily and plucked at the bundle nestled in the bed by her.

"Here's our son, Earl," she whispered weakly. "Shall we name him Patrick, then?"

Garrity chuckled and nodded, looking down at the small, wrinkled face. "Aye, we'll name him Patrick, love. He's a fine boy, and we'll make a proper little fossicker out of him when we get to the gold fields."

PART FIVE

Chapter 21

THE BILLY BEGAN BOILING BRISKLY, and Meghan glanced at Garrity as she lifted it off the fire with a stick. "Would you like some tea now, Earl?"

He was playing with Patrick, laughing as he held the baby's hands and helped him to walk. Then shook his head. "No, I'll wait until supper. Look, Meghan, young Patrick is almost walking by himself."

Meghan smiled and nodded, stirring dough to bake bread. Over a year had passed since they had left the Georges, and the baby had become large and chubby, seeming to thrive on the wandering about. They had found only a few ounces of gold, enough to keep the money from disappearing too rapidly on necessities, but Meghan had enjoyed it. It had been a complete release from cares and worries, with the wagon always ready to move and leave everything behind. But it had also been a lazy time, the days slipping past without fruitful results, and she felt guilty about it.

The tent was pitched by the wagon under a copse of trees at the side of a rutted track, and a rivulet·

gurgled through a ravine a few yards away. It was autumn, and the late afternoon air was cool. During the past months, they had drifted north from Adelaide and traveled along tracks by the Murray River, and they had followed the news of other gold strikes and gradually worked their way south toward Melbourne. The forested foothills of the Australian Alps surrounded them, and the setting sun gleamed on the tips of higher peaks to the east.

Meghan finished mixing the dough to bake bread for the next day, and divided it into small pans. The oven was a cast iron box, and Garrity rose and came around the fire to move it for her. He placed it in the fire, and laughed as he stepped back to the baby and snatched him up, tossing the baby in his arms. Meghan put the pans of dough in the oven, closed the lid, and piled hot coals around and on top of the oven with the shovel.

The baby squealed and gurgled in delight as Garrity laughed, tossing him and catching him. Meghan smiled and watched them as she prepared dinner. The pots and pans were blackened by hundreds of camp-fires, and Meghan had adapted to the necessities imposed by living out of the wagon. But she had refused to adapt as other prospectors did, by living on damper, tea, and mutton or salt pork or beef. The pots and pans contained beans, peas, and rice that had soaked through the day, and she cut pieces of pork to fry and sliced a loaf of bread.

A family of aborigines appeared in the fading light, walking around a curve in the track a short distance aways. Meghan pushed hot coals around the pans with the shovel, looking at Garrity and pointing to the aborigines. "It's unusual to see them on the track, isn't it?"

Garrity turned and looked, holding the squirming baby in his arms, and he nodded. "Aye, they're not usually inclined to travel the tracks. But it appears those live in closer than most you'll see."

Meghan nodded, turning the pork in the pan. The aborigines had lived near a town or on a station at one time, because the man wore ragged trousers and a shirt, and the woman had on a tattered, faded skirt and blouse. The two children were naked, and the woman and children carried baskets and bundles as the man walked ahead and carried his weapons. Garrity nodded and spoke to the man as he approached.

"Are you all right, then?"

The man stopped and leaned on his spear as he shook his head. "White pellow digger him say bloody bugger off," he muttered.

"Some fossickers ran you off?" Garrity replied. "Well, that's no good, is it?"

The man shook his head, his thick, primitive features reflecting no emotion. "No bloody good," he agreed, and his dark, aloof eyes moved to Meghan. "Coppatea, please."

The woman and children had sat down on the track behind the man, and Meghan glanced at them and put the billy back on the fire. "Would you like something to eat?"

The man grunted disdainfully, shaking his head again. "White pellow tucker no bloody good for abo."

"Perhaps so, but those children look hungry,"

Meghan replied. "If you want some tea, tell them they can eat what I give them."

The man's lips twitched in remote amusement, and he glanced back at the woman and children and murmured. The woman and children looked at him, then at Meghan. She poured treacle on three slices of bread, and beckoned. They stepped closer to the fire and took the bread, and the children devoured theirs as the woman held hers and watched them. She divided hers and gave it to them, and Meghan poured treacle on another slice of bread and handed it to her. The woman ate part of it and gave the rest to the children as they moved away and sat down behind the man again.

Meghan made tea, and filled a pannikin and handed it to the man. He held the hot pannikin on the flat of a palm and sipped the tea, conversing with Garrity in grunts, monosyllabic, broken English, and occasional words of aborigine. The man was from the moutains west of Melbourne, and he had worked on a cattle station. He had left there and had been living in the hills several miles away, and prospectors had driven him and his family out of a valley where they had been camped.

"You're on a walkabout, then," Garrity commented.

The man sipped his tea, nodding. "Bloody walkabout," he replied.

Meghan stirred the food in the pots and pans, listening to the men. Garrity had told her about a few aborigines who had worked at Wayamba and other stations. They were excellent stockmen, looking after their flocks as carefully as any white man, and they were unaffected by the loneliness that made life difficult for most stockmen. But they were prone to unexpectedly disappear on a "walkabout" and be gone for a year or more, wandering through the wilderness. And when they returned, they were midly surprised and offended by the indignance of their employer.

The man finished the tea and put the pannikin down by the fire, sucking his teeth and belching. "Bloody good coppatea," he said. "I'm bloody oblige." He straightened back up and looked down at the baby in Garrity's arms. "Bloody good *birrahlee,* big like you."

"Aye, he's a fine boy," Garrity chuckled proudly, tossing the baby and making him squeal. "His name's Patrick."

"Patrick," the man repeated in a murmur, his eyes moving from the baby to Garrity's face. "You gotta piece of abo?"

"Aye, I have," Garrity replied. "Mother of my father was an abo. Have you got a piece of white fellow?"

The man stiffened in surprise, then snorted and made a rude sound with his lips. Garrity laughed merrily, and a smile slowly spread over the aborigine's face. He chuckled in acknowledgment of the joke, looking back at the woman and children and beckoning, and he nodded to Garrity and Meghan as he walked away. The woman and children rose and followed him, and they disappeared around a curve in the track.

Meghan broke up sticks and tossed them on the fire, smiling at Garrity. "He wasn't expecting that, was he?"

"No, he wasn't," Garrity laughed. "If you want to

get an abo's wind up, just ask him if he's part white. Mix up Patrick's frumenty, and I'll feed him while you're finishing there."

Meghan picked up a pan of cold rice that had been boiled to a soft pulp, and put it on the fire to warm. She spooned part of it onto a plate, mixed treacle and a pinch of cinnamon into it, and handed the plate to Garrity. He propped the baby up on his lap and fed him, smiling as the baby hungrily devoured the sweet, soft mixture.

Darkness fell and the breeze became a cold, gusty wind. The baby dozed off as soon as he had eaten, and Garrity wrapped him in his blanket and put him down by the fire. Meghan filled plates with food and moved the pans off the fire to cool, and she and Garrity discussed the gold strike near Melbourne as they ate. Large nuggets and deposits of flake gold had been found in creeks north of Melbourne several weeks before. The news had been like a magnet, drawing crowds of people along the tracks toward Melbourne.

Meghan washed the dishes after they finished eating, and took the baby's dirty clothes to the rivulet and washed them. She hung them on sticks by the fire to dry during the night, then spread out the bedroom in the tent. Garrity got his long, double-barrel pistol from under the seat in the wagon, and checked the priming in the pans by the light of the fire. Lawlessness in the gold fields consisted mostly of penniless, half-starved men stealing food, but bushrangers preyed on those who were known to have found gold, and some men had been killed for it.

He put the pistol on his side of the bedroll, and un-

dressed. Meghan put a bowl of cold frumenty within
reach in event the baby woke during the night, then
undressed and lay down with the baby nestled by her.
Garrity was large and warm, and she wriggled closer
to him as he put an arm around her. He kissed her and
settled himself to go to sleep, and Meghan lay and
looked up at the flickering light of the fire on the tent
as she waited for sleep. She thought about the aborigine man on his walkabout, and about her enjoyment of
the prospecting trip, her walkabout.

The birds stirring in the trees in the gray light of
early dawn woke Meghan, and she shivered in the cold
and dressed as Garrity built up the fire. The morning
routine was completely familiar, and Meghan heated
the leftovers as Garrity rolled up the bedroll, took
down the tent, and put things into the wagon. They
ate, and she changed the baby's clothes and washed
while Garrity harnessed the horse to the wagon. Then
they put the last things into the wagon and climbed
into it.

Others were moving along the track by sunrise.
Riders passed leading pack horses or with bundles of
belongings behind their saddles. A few men on foot
and with bundles on their backs overtook the wagon,
struggling and panting as they hurried along the
track. The wagon passed some who were pushing
carts. Everyone was on the move.

An occasional cart or wagon, broken beyond repair,
was in the trees and weeds at the side of the track.
Sometimes they saw a dead horse or donkey. Clothing,
books, tools, and other belongings were scattered
along the track, discarded by those who had over-

loaded themselves and become weary. The wagon passed some who were working on disabled carts and wagons, and some who had become exhausted and were resting by the track.

Every occupation and class of society and age was represented. Smooth-cheeked boys strode along with the enthusiasm of youth, while wrinkled, grey-haired old men leaned on staffs and labored along the track with the determination of age. Some wore canvas trousers and shirts, some wore good woolens and cravats, some wore seafaring clothes. All of them were men, and women were rarely seen in the gold fields. They looked at Meghan in surprise, then touched caps or lifted hats and they bowed.

At noon, Garrity guided the horse off the track and onto a level, grassy spot. Meghan built a fire to heat the leftovers as he unhooked the horse so it could rest and gaze, then he sat by the fire and played with the baby. An old man came walking along the track in the opposite direction from everyone else, and he looked at the pots and pans hungrily as he lifted his cap to Meghan. Garrity invited him to share their food, and he thanked him and Meghan effusively as he took off his pack and sat by the fire.

The old man wolfed the food down. He talked about the gold strike. It was rumored that several men had found substantial amounts of gold, but he had worked several claims during the past month without success. He had run out of money and food, and he was going to a relative's cattle station several days' travel away to try to replenish his supplies.

"Of course, I'll eat up most of it getting back," he

said ruefully. "But perhaps I can get the loan of a horse or a few shillings, that would put me right." He wiped his plate with a piece of bread and ate it. "That was most tasty, Mistress Garrity, and I'm obliged."

"You're more than welcome. Are we near the main diggings?"

"It's not far. This track runs into the track between Bendigo and Melbourne just a few miles from here, and you turn south toward Melbourne. Then your horse and wagon should get you to the main diggings in about another day. It's almost within sight of Melbourne."

"Where's the land office?" Garrity asked.

"You can take your pick between Bendigo and Melbourne, because there's a land office at both of them. There's a place called Cypress Ridge to the east of the track as it goes into Melbourne, and you'll want to stay clear of it. The ones who've filed on claims around there are rowdies more than they're fossickers, and some say bushrangers loiter around there, too. In any event, it's no place a man would want to take his wife."

"I'll bear that in mind," Garrity said. "And you say bushrangers loiter around Cypress Ridge?"

"That's what I've been told," the old man replied. "No one I know has been robbed or killed, but no one I know has any gold. And I've been told that anyone who ventures around Cypress Ridge should either be armed or in the company of sturdy and trusted friends." He sighed heavily, rose to his feet and lifted his pack. "Well, I'd best be on my way while that good tucker is sustaining me. Thank you again, and good luck to you."

The junction with the track between Bendigo and Melbourne came into sight an hour later, and it was a wide, well-traveled track. Dealers in stock and foodstuffs were taking advantage of the heavy traffic along the track, and had brought wagons of produce, preserved foodstuffs, and stock to the junction. A large sheep fold was on one side of the junction, and butchered sheep hung from a tree. The dealer was haggling with men who had stopped, and was selling them portions of the sheep.

Others had horses, cattle, and wagons and carts filled with baskets of vegetables, barrels of salt pork and beef, ship's biscuit, and other foodstuffs. Men milled around the wagons and carts, looking and arguing with the dealers, and some men were trying to trade horses and other belongings for supplies of tea, salt, flour, and salt meat. Meghan had cooked the last of their potatoes a few days before, and Garrity stopped the wagon by a vegetable dealer's wagon and helped her down.

Men moved aside for her, bowing and lifting their hats, and she nodded to them and looked at the baskets of potatoes. The dealer was a large, beefy man with a thick, black beard, and he touched his cap as he moved closer. "The potatoes are five shillings the bushel, Mistress," he said. "And a bargain at the price."

"My word," Meghan said amiably. "It's good you have such a fine beard hiding your face, because you must blush when you say such a thing. These potatoes are worth a shilling a bushel, and not a farthing more."

The man frowned and started to reply impatiently. Then he glanced at Garrity and moved closer to Meghan, speaking softly. "My price is five shillings the bushel, and I'd be mobbed by others who've bought from me if they knew I'd sold them to someone else for less. I'll let you have a bushel for two and sixpence, but don't broadcast it, Mistress."

"That's very good of you," Meghan replied quietly. "And it'll be worth the money if a peck of those onions over there goes with a bushel of potatoes at two and sixpence."

The man hesitated, then sighed in resignation and beckoned a boy. "Aye, I'll do it, then. A bushel of potatoes and a peck of onions for two and sixpence, but I wouldn't do it for anyone else."

Meghan smiled and nodded. "I'm most grateful for your consideration. I'll have two bushels of potatoes and two pecks of onions. That'll be five shillings, won't it?"

The man blinked, his mouth dropping open in surprise. His mouth snapped shut and he tugged at his beard. Then he snapped his fingers at the boy. The boy began dragging out baskets of potatoes and onions. Garrity took out his purse and paid the dealer, who shook his head morosely as he pocketed the money.

"It wouldn't be fair for you to find gold," he grumbled. "You made your fortune when you got married," the dealer said.

"Aye, and I wouldn't trade her for all the gold in Australia," Garrity said. "Are we near the main diggings, then?"

"You should get there late tomorrow," the dealer replied, then he smiled wryly. "But if you loiter and let your wife spend as much as a guinea, she might load your wagon down so heavy that you won't get there for another week or more."

Garrity laughed, lifting a basket of potatoes and carrying it to the rear of the wagon. Meghan went back to the wagon and climbed up to the seat, and picked up the baby. Garrity and the boy loaded the potatoes and onions into the rear of the wagon, and Garrity climbed up to the seat and shook the traces as he clucked to the horses.

The track was a wide swath through the forest as it wound among the hills, following the contours of the land. It was deeply rutted by large drays and wagons that had transported goods from the port at Melbourne to the hinterland. Creeks crossed it in valleys. Trails made by woodcutters from Melbourne and smaller tracks leading to isolated houses and selections turned off to each side at long intervals. The wagon bumped and rattled along the track, and the sun sank lower into the west.

There was a movement in thick brush at the side of a narrow track that turned off ahead of the wagon, then the aborigine they had met the night before stepped out of the brush. He acted cautious and secretive as he peered along the track in both directions, craning his neck to see behind the wagon. Then he pointed to the narrow track and shouted something, and he darted along the narrow track and disappeared.

"What's he doing here?" Meghan asked. "And

what does he want?"

"I've no idea what he's doing here," Garrity replied. "He was going the other way. And he wants us to follow him. I suppose it'll do no harm."

The wagon jolted heavily across the earthen berm at the side of the main track, turning onto the narrow track, and brush and tree limbs scraped along both sides. The track was an old one, overgrown with weeds and sapplings that scraped along the bottom of the wagon. It curved, and the aborigine came into sight again. He beckoned, and ran on along the track and disappeared around another curve.

The track went to an old, deserted selection a mile off the main track. A small house and fences were weathered and falling to pieces. A vast, grassy valley stretched out beyond the house and sloped up to a tree-lined ridge several miles away. The aborigine was awaiting by the ruins of the house, and he beckoned again and ran out into the valley. Garrity started to rein up, looking at the aborigine with a perplexed frown, then he sighed and he snapped the traces.

Part of the valley had been plowed at one time, and the wagon slammed over old furrows hidden under the deep grass. Then it became smoother, and the grass whispered around the wheels and under the bed of the wagon as it trundled along behind the horse. The aborigine became small in the distance, a tiny, dark figure racing through the grass with a long, effortless stride. He ran up the other side of the valley, leaving a faint trail behind him in the grass, and disappeared among the trees on the ridge.

The wagon was halfway across the valley, the track

far behind, the sun low in the west. Then the ground underneath was suddenly boggy, the wagon wheels sinking into it, and Garrity urged the horse into a trot to keep the wagon from miring down in the mud. The ground was beginning to slope up toward the ridge when the wagon was completely out of the mud.

The horse trudged slowly up the long, gradual rise. It reached the top, and the aborigine was standing under the trees, almost lost in the shadows. Then he beckoned and ran through the trees. The trees were closely-spaced, with dense brush growing under them, and Garrity looked ahead for a path wide enough for the wagon as he slowly guided the horse through the forest. A bare limb snagged the top of the wagon and ripped the canvas, and Garrity glanced up at it and winced.

The trees opened out, and a small, grassy valley dotted with copses of trees lay on the other side of the ridge. A creek ran through the valley, and the aborigine was standing by the creek at the head of the valley. The slope was steep, and Garrity seized the rope on the brake lever and threw his weight back against it as the wagon went downhill. The brakes squealed, and the wagon slid down the slope.

The head of the valley was a precipitous wall, almost a cliff, and a network of streams and rivulets ran down it and joined together to form the creek. Smoke rose from a copse of trees father down the creek, and the aborigine leaned on his spear and looked at the smoke in disapproval as he waited for the wagon. The wagon bumped across rocks and uneven spots under the deep grass as it reached the bottom of the slope and crossed the valley to the creek. Garrity reined up.

The aborigine looked up at Garrity and pointed to the creek with his spear. "Here."

Garrity lifted his hat and scratched his head quizically. "What's there? Gold?"

"Bloody gold," the aborigine grunted, nodding, and turned to walk away. "I go."

"Wait a moment," Garrity called, jumping down from the wagon. "Would you like a cup of tea or something?"

"I go!' the aborigine barked over his shoulder, shaking his head brusquely. "I bloody go!"

Garrity shrugged and turned back to the wagon, and reached up for the baby. He took the baby and helped Meghan down, and she stepped away from the wagon and looked around it at the aborigine. His family had come out of a copse of trees, and they were following him back toward the ridge. Meghan turned and looked at the creek, then looked up at Garrity.

"Do you think there might be gold here, Earl?"

"I've never heard of aborigines doing any fossicking," he replied doubtfully, tossing the baby in his arms. "But it looks like a good place to try. And it appears someone else is trying down there."

Meghan nodded, glancing around. "It also looks like a good place to camp. There's water and plenty of wood."

"And we're much too far from the track to get back to it by dark," Garrity said, shrugging. "So we might as well stay and try it. Here, take the baby, and I'll get the tent and other things out of the wagon."

Meghan nodded, taking the baby from him. She

409

walked toward the creek as he began taking the things out of the wagon to set up camp. The wide creek rushed across and around large stones, sparkling clear in the warm light of sunset. And it looked promising to her, but other places that had yielded only isolated flakes of gold had appeared promising.

Anyway, it would have to wait until morning.

——————— Chapter 22

MEGHAN HEARD GARRITY AND ANOTHER man talking while she was washing the breakfast dishes. Garrity had walked along the creek, and he was returning to the fire with the man who was camped down the creek. The man was about forty, smaller than Garrity but sturdily-built. His closely-trimmed beard and mustache was streaked with gray, and his clothing was conspicuously neat and clean for the gold fields.

The baby was crawling around on the ground.

"Meghan, this is Mr. Ned Cooper," Garrity said. "Ned, this is my wife Meghan and my son Patrick."

"I'm most pleased indeed to meet you, Mistress Garrity," Cooper said, doffing his hat. "It isn't often we have the pleasure and benefit of a woman's company whilst in the gold fields."

"I'm pleased to meet you, Mr. Cooper," Meghan replied. "There's tea in the billy if you'd care for some."

Cooper smiled and shook his head. "I'm obliged, but I had my fill at breakfast. This is a fine-looking boy, Earl."

411

"Aye, he's the youngest fossicker in the gold fields," Garrity laughed, kneeling by the fire and reaching for the baby. "You feature John Cooper, so you must be kin."

Cooper nodded, sitting down by the fire. "John's my brother, but it's been five years or more since I've seen him. He was born to be a swagman, because he was restless even when he was a boy. How long has it been since you were at Wayamba?"

"About four years now," Garrity replied, tossing the baby in his arms. "I was on a ship for a time, then Meghan and I settled not far from Sydney for a while after we were married. Then we thought we'd try our hand at fossicking."

"Well, you might have some luck here," Cooper said, looking at the creek. "Like I said, I got here yesterday and I haven't had time to do any more than dip a pan a time or two. But I did find some color right away."

Garrity looked around, nodding. "And at least we aren't crowded. This creek is out of the way, and most of the people are south of here."

"Aye, that's true," Cooper agreed. "The only other ones I've seen were some aborigines who were up here yesterday, but they appear to be gone now. It's a caution the way you got that wagon in here, and I'd have said it couldn't be done. The reason I chose a pack horse over a wagon was so I'd be able to get off the track, but you appear to go where you wish."

"It's a good wagon, but I don't fancy hauling it back out of here just to file on a claim. At the same time, I don't fancy leaving Meghan here by herself while I go and do it, but I feel more easy in my mind knowing you're here."

"You could stay here if you wish," Cooper said. "We can pace off our claims and stake them, and I'll take your paper in and file it for you if you'll keep your eye on my claim. My horse can move right along, and I'll be back by this afternoon."

Garrity nodded, putting the baby down and rising. "Let's do that, then. I'll get an axe to cut the stakes."

Cooper rose as Garrity stepped to the wagon and got the axe out of it, and the two men walked to a copse of trees a few yards away. They cut down a slender tree and chopped it into lengths, and carried the stakes to the creek and began pacing off Garrity's claim. Meghan climbed into the wagon to get the writing materials.

The men finished pacing off Garrity's claim, driving in stakes to mark the boundaries. Then they walked along the creek to pace off Cooper's claim and mark it with stakes. They returned to the wagon and wrote out the claims to be filed in the land office, and Garrity gave Cooper the ten shilling filing fee for his claim. Cooper took the money and the papers, and walked back along the creek to saddle his horse.

Garrity took a gold pan out of the wagon and went to the creek, and Cooper rode out of the valley and disappeared over the ridge. Meghan looked through all the clothes in the wagon, then gathered them up and piled them on the tailgate. They were dingy from hurried washing in creeks and ponds during the past weeks, and needed boiling to whiten them. And during the past weeks, the meals had also been hurried.

She put dried apples and peaches to soak so she could make pastries, then peeled potatoes and cut slices of pork to cook for lunch.

She finished preparing lunch and called Garrity, and he waded out of the creek and came to the fire. The creek appeared promising, because he had seen color in each pan of gravel and had found a nugget almost as large as a pea. The nugget was heavy in Meghan's palm as she looked at it, and she went to the wagon for a small vial to put it in. Garrity hurriedly ate lunch, then returned to the creek.

When the dishes were finished, Meghan put slices of salt beef in water to soak out part of the salt, and dragged the large kettle out of the wagon. She carried water from the creek and started some of the clothes boiling in the kettle, and mixed dough to bake bread and pastries. She hummed cheerfully as she worked, pleased at being in one place for at least a few days, and the valley was a pleasant place.

The wind was cold and the blue of the sky was touched with gray that warned of the approach of winter. Still, autumn was very pleasant. Other places had been crowded and noisy, with each foot of ground claimed by someone, and boisterous, argumentive men all around. The valley was quiet and private, and it was beautiful. The wind stirred the deep grass and rustled the trees, and the birds chattered as they flew back and forth in flashes of bright color.

Meghan tied a rope between two trees, and hung the clothes over it to dry. When the washing was finished and the pastries and bread were baking, she unfastened the canvas top on the wagon and dragged it off.

She sewed the tear that had been made in the top the day before when they crossed the ridge, then moved things around in the wagon and cleaned out the weeks' accumulation of dust and dirt.

Cooper rode down the slope from the ridge as she was cleaning the wagon, and his horse was weary and sweaty from being ridden at a hard, fast pace. He smiled and touched his hat as he reined up by the wagon. "Are you doing your housecleaning, Mistress Garrity?"

"Such as it is," she laughed. "When one has a house that travels along the roads, it does get dirtier than most."

"No doubt, but it's far better than my house at present," Cooper said. Garrity came up from the creek, and Cooper took the mining licenses from his pocket and separated one of them. "It looks like we're still here by ourselves, Earl."

"Aye, there's been no one about," Garrity replied as he took the license. "I'm much obliged, Ned."

"You're more than welcome. Have you found any color?"

"Aye, it's like you said. I might get out my sluice box tomorrow and see what I can do with it."

Meghan looked at Garrity. His manner and tone were casual, too casual. She knew him well, and she could tell that he was seething with excitement under his outward calm. He had found something he wanted no one else to know about, not even a trusted and friendly man like Cooper.

"You're going to try a sluice box?"' Cooper asked, reining his horse away from the wagon. "By God, I like the sound of that, and I think I'll get on down to my claim and get busy myself. I'll talk with you again tonight."

Garrity nodded and waved as Cooper rode away. He stood watching Cooper until he disappeared behind a copse of trees, then he looked up at Meghan. A wide smile slowly spread over his face, his eyes sparkled, and he winked. Meghan stepped to the side of the wagon, and he silently helped her down and walked toward the creek. The baby was waking and stirring by the fire, and Meghan picked him up and followed her husband to the creek.

The gold pan was by the edge of the water, and Garrity picked it up and rocked it. The pan contained water and a thick layer of concentrates, black sand and flecks of pyrites, stream tin, platinum, and other metals. The tiny bits of metal sparkled as the sand and water swirled. Then a large spot of yellow surfaced. Then another. The rich gleam of gold winked through the black sand and sank out of sight again, all over the pan. The pan contained dozens of large flakes and nuggets.

"This is all from one panful," Garrity said quietly.

"One panful?" Meghan gasped. "Where did you get it?"

"Over there in that pool," Garrity said, nodding toward a quiet pool in the creek. "I kept finding more and more color as I worked my way across the creek, then I found this. It looks like a lode has washed down from the hill there and settled in that pool." He glanced sidewards down the creek, then looked back at Meghan. "Ned's a good man, but this is something

416

one shouldn't talk to anyone about. Fetch me a bucket, then keep on with what you were doing."

Meghan rose and walked back to the wagon, and held the baby in one arm as she reached up and lifted a bucket out of the wagon. She carried it to the creek, and put it at the edge of the water. Garrity poured the concentrates into the bucket to separate the gold later, then he waded out into the creek to the pool. He scooped up a panful of sand and pebbles from the bottom of the pool, and swirled the pan and spilled out the pebbles and other lighter material.

Cooper was out in the creek with a gold pan, the water boiling around his boots as he swirled the pan and examined the contents closely. Meghan looked down the creek at him as she walked back toward the wagon, and he was carefully avoiding curiosity about what was happening up the creek from him. She returned to the fire and brushed the ashes off the top of the oven, and opened the lid with a stick. The pastries and bread were baked, and the clothes on the rope were dry. She took the pastries and bread out of the oven, and began gathering the clothes off the rope.

Garrity brought the bucket to the wagon shortly before sunset, and he sat between the wagon and tent and separated the gold from the concentrates. Meghan sat where she could watch along the creek for Cooper. Garrity finished by dark, and he had filled a small vial with three ounces or more of flakes and tiny nuggets of gold.

Cooper waited until dinner was over before coming up the creek, and he sat by the fire and talked for a few minutes. He was considerate, and brought along his own billy of tea to keep from imposing. He was also polite, calling out loudly before he approached, and Garrity put the vial of gold away. And he was also finding gold, because he was vague on the subject during the conversation.

When Cooper left, Meghan and Garrity went to bed. Meghan lay and waited for sleep, thinking about the gold and how it had changed things. The valley was now a place of wealth, its beauty and comfort irrelevant. Garrity had lost his carefree, nonchalant attitude and had become intent on finding gold. Meghan also felt a change in herself, brought about by the increasing possiblity that she would be able to fulfill her ambitions. Her walkabout had come to an end.

The sluice box was disassembled and tied along one sideboard of the wagon, and Garrity took it out after breakfast the next morning. An old prospector who had run out of money and supplies had sold it to them several months before for a few shillings, and it had almost become a joke between Garrity and Meghan during the months of hauling it about without using it. Meghan took the lighter pieces and helped Garrity carry it to the creek and assemble it.

It was a long, wide trough without ends, with a series of wooden baffles across one end to catch and hold concentrates as the flow of water carried pebbles and other lighter material on through it. Garrity dragged it out into the creek when it was assembled, and arranged large rocks to make an inclined foundation for it just under the surface of the water. Meghan went to the wagon and brought back a shovel, and Garrity began shoveling up sand and pebbles and tossing it into the box.

The sky was clouding over, threatening rain, and the wind was cold and gusty. Meghan finished cleaning the wagon, and dragged the canvas top back into place and roped it down. She prepared lunch and fed the baby, and when he went to sleep she took a plate of food and pannikin of tea to the creek for Garrity. He put the shovel down, and waded through the creek to the bank.

His trousers were soaked up to his knees and he was shivering with cold, and Meghan looked at him worriedly as he sat down on the creek bank. "You'd best come to the fire and warm yourself while you eat, Earl."

"I'll be all right," he replied, taking the plate and pannikin from her. He put them down and groped in a pocket, then held out a hand to her, his fist clenched. "Here's something for you."

Meghan put out a hand, and he dropped an elongated, irregularly-shaped nugget almost as large as her forefinger into her palm. It weighed several ounces, and she gasped as she darted a quick glance down the creek and looked at the nugget closely. "It's huge, Earl!"

He nodded, picking up his plate, eating rapidly. "I saw it as it went into the sluice box, and I stopped and dug it out. And I saw any number of other nuggets as I was shoveling sand into the box, some of them as large as walnuts."

Meghan sighed and shook her head, turning the

419

nugget over in her hands. "We finally found the right place, didn't we? Or rather, that aborigine pointed it out to us. I wonder why he did this for us?"

"He apparently took a fancy to us," Garrity replied. "So many people treat them like dogs that a bit of kindness wins them over entirely. The good will you showed in giving his family food was probably what did it."

Meghan nodded, examining the nugget and flicking grains of sand off it. Garrity finished gulping down his food and took a drink of tea as he rose. "Your food hardly touched the sides of your mouth, Earl," Meghan protested. "You shouldn't eat so fast, and you should rest for a bit after you've eaten."

"I'll rest when I'm old," he said, taking another drink of tea. He put down the plate and pannikin and waded back into the creek. "Or when we have the money to buy shares in a ship." Meghan climbed into the wagon and put the nugget with the vial of gold.

Shortly after Meghan and Garrity had left the Georges, they had met a sundries dealer on the track, and the man had been selling leather bags he said were favored above all others by prospectors for storing their gold. Garrity had bought two bags, and he and Meghan had never seen any others like them during the time they had been in the gold fields. Like the sluice box, they had become something of a joke. And like the sluice box, they turned out to be useful. When Garrity emptied the concentrates out of the sluice box and separated the gold that night, the gold made a large, heavy lump in the bottom of one of the bags.

420

There was drizzle that stopped short of being rain that night. The clouds lifted again and the drizzle stopped after daybreak. The wind whipped the fire and made it roar, the flames licking out from it, and Meghan wrapped the baby warmly and kept him on the upwind side of the fire. At the end of the day Garrity cleaned out the sluice box and separated the gold, collecting even more gold from the concentrates than he had the day before.

The cold, cloudy weather continued, heavy rain threatening but remaining only a threat. Garrity began hitting large rocks and bedrock in the pool and spent a day scraping up pockets of pebbles and sand and shoveling it into the sluice box. Then an anxious day passed while he panned in other pools around the head of the creek. He found another pool that was rich in gold, and he moved the sluice box and began shoveling pebbles and sand again.

Two men rode over the ridge late one afternoon, and camped down the creek from Cooper. Meghan watched down the creek the next day, dreading the time when word would get out and the inevitable flood of people would pour into the valley. She occasionally glimpsed the men as they moved among the trees and waded out into the creek with gold pans. One of them rode a horse across the creek and out of the valley in the opposite direction from the track. The other one remained in camp.

The two men approached the wagon the following morning while Meghan and Garrity were eating breakfast. They stopped at a fair distance and waited for an invitation to come closer. They were old men, with long, gray beards, mustaches, and hair, and they had on sturdy, well-worn clothes and heavy coats. Garrity called them over to the fire and introduced himself and Meghan, and one of men introduced them as they lifted their hats to Meghan.

They were the Carline brothers, and Meghan had heard many stories about them. The two men had been prospecting in Australia from the time of the first gold strikes, and they had also prospected in California, South America, and South Africa. Strangely, they were said to care little for wealth, which was borne out by their appearance, but they were compulsively dedicated to searching for gold. And they were reputed to be supremely skilled and lucky in finding gold.

"Aye, I've heard of you," Garrity said. "Like everyone else who's ever been in the gold fields, because fossicker and Carline amounts to the same word to most people. It's Simon and Seton, isn't it?"

"Aye, I'm Simon, the one who does the talking for both of us," the one who had introduced them replied. "People in the gold fields do give us and what we do some attention, and that's why we came here to talk to you. From the looks of that sluice box out there, you probably don't want a lot of people gathering in here just because we're here."

"That's true," Garrity agreed. "And regardless of the sluice box, I don't enjoy having a lot of people underfoot."

Carline nodded emphatically. "Neither do we. I rode

to Melbourne yesterday and filed our claims, and I rode in and out in such a direction that no one could tell where we are. But I was noticed, and I didn't want to buy supplies and chance being followed. We have most everything we need to last for a while, but we need some flour to make damper. Cooper doesn't have any to spare, and we thought you might."

Meghan nodded as Garrity looked at her. "Aye, we can spare about ten pounds or so of flour."

"That'll be plenty to last us for a while," Carline said. "We'd be most obliged if you'd sell it to us, and I'll pay an ounce of gold for it."

"No, I couldn't possibly take that much, Mr. Carline," Meghan protested. "That's a hundred times what it's worth."

"Then I couldn't take the flour, Mistress Garrity," Carline replied firmly. "We're in the diggings and not in a store, and I expect to pay diggings prices. If I can't do what I think is fair, then I'll have to go for supplies and none of us wants that."

Garrity nodded and motioned to the wagon as Meghan hesitated and glanced at him, and she shrugged as she turned and walked to the wagon. The men continued talking as she climbed into the wagon, and found a cloth bag and filled it out of the flour barrel. She climbed back out of the wagon with it, and Carline thanked her and gave her a large nugget in exchange for the bag of flour.

The two men left, and Meghan and Garrity sat down by the fire and resumed eating breakfast. Meghan smiled and shrugged as she took a bite of food from her plate. "If we could engage in trade with such profit, there'd be no need for you to get your feet wet. And with the gold those two men are said to have found at one time or another, it seems odd indeed for them to be living out here on a creek bank and eating salt meat and damper. Or do you think it might be only talk?"

"It could be true," Garrity chuckled. "Human nature is sometimes impossible to fathom. I knew of a swagman who inherited a fortune, and he wouldn't touch a farthing of it." He took a drink of tea, and sobered as he put his plate and pannikin down. "But the important thing to us here and now is that people believe what's said about the Carlines. And as soon as word gets out that they're here, we'll be overrun with people."

"He said that he rode in and out of Melbourne in such a direction that no one could tell where he is."

Garrity nodded somberly. "But he's known to be hereabouts, so it's only a matter of time until we're mobbed with people. I'd best get to shoveling while I still have elbow room to do so."

He walked toward the creek, and Meghan gathered up the dishes to wash them. She picked up a bucket, and carried it to the creek for water. Garrity was shoveling sand and pebbles into the sluice box, and she thought about what he had said. An unspoken comment behind his words was that it would be dangerous to keep a large amount of gold in the wagon if numerous men were around. At the same time, it would be unwise to leave the claim for even as long as it would take to get to a bank with the gold, if numerous men were around. Mcghan dipped up water and carried it back to the fire, looking worriedly up at the ridge line.

Chapter 23

THE DAY PASSED UNEVENTFULLY, AND no one else appeared on the ridge above the valley. The Carline brothers had brought a disassembled sluice box, and they put it together and carried it out into the creek. Cooper continued working around his rocker box, completely intent on what he was doing. Garrity cleaned out the sluice box near dark and carried the concentrates to the tent in a bucket to separate the gold, and one of the bags was almost full of gold when he finished.

Meghan's concern about others finding the creek began fading when another day passed without incident. Drizzle fell intermittently on the following day and the cold air was laden with moisture, making it difficult to dry the clothes she had washed. She was hanging some of the baby's clothes on sticks by the fire to dry them when a movement on the edge of her sight made her turn her head. Two men had ridden down into the valley from the ridge. They were yards away from the wagon.

The two men were not prospectors. More than anyone else she had ever met, they reminded her of the guards at Parramatta Prison. Their faces reflected the same craven personality as the guards, servile toward authority, overbearingly arrogant to those in their power. They were slovenly and unkempt, even though they wore good clothes, and their horses were thin and scarred from merciless beatings. The two men looked at Meghan in bold, brazen insolence, their eyes moving up and down her.

One of them murmured a sneering comment about Meghan to the other one as they rode past the camp. The other one laughed. They were violating a rigid rule of the gold fields, entering a claim without express invitation, and Garrity frowned darkly as he waded toward the bank. "Who the hell are you, and what are you doing on my claim?" he barked.

The two men reined up, some of their arrogant self-assurance evaporating. They were big men, one with a bright red beard and florid features, and the other one dark and swarthy. But Garrity was even bigger. Now his fists were knotted, and the tension in the bulging muscles in his shoulders made his coat tight over his shoulders as he waded out of the creek.

"I'm Harv Lawson, and this is my mate Ed Slocum," the swarthy man growled. "And I didn't see any door to knock on."

"You saw those stakes!" Garrity snapped, pointing. "And if you've ever been in the gold fields before, you know what they mean!"

"Lawson and Slocum you say?" Cooper called from the other side of the wagon. "Those might be names a body would hear over at Cypress Ridge. You two look and act like that lot of rabble."

Meghan turned and looked at him. He was breathing deeply from running up the creek, and he glowered at the men as he walked toward them. Meghan picked up the baby and held him in one arm as she climbed up to the seat of the wagon. She put the baby down under the seat and picked up Garrity's long, heavy double-barrel pistol. Cooper passed the wagon, looking at Lawson and Slocum with a steely glare, and they glanced between him and Garrity as they backed their horses away from the creek.

"There's no more rabble over there than there is anywhere else," Lawson growled defensively. "You'd be well advised to have a mind as to who you're calling names."

"And you'd be well advised to ask before you ride onto someone else's claim," Garrity said in a quiet, ominous tone. "Get those horses back on the other side of those stakes."

"Aye, it looks like you might have something to hide and all," Lawson chuckled sourly. He and Slocum slowly backed their horses toward the line of stakes. "I see you have a sluice box there."

"What I have on my claim and what I'm doing on my claim is none of your affair!" Garrity barked. "If you've come prowling around here to see if you can find trouble, then you've found it!"

Lawson replied in a blustering tone as he and Slocum continued backing their horses toward the stakes, and Meghan lifted the pan lids on the pistol to check the priming. Days of damp weather had passed since the pistol had been checked, but the gunpowder in the pans was still soft and dry, without a crust that would warn of a potential misfire. She snapped the pan lids closed and pulled the large, heavy flintlock hammers back to cocked position, and rested the pistol across her lap.

The baby writhed and howled indignantly over being snatched up from his nap and shoved under the wagon seat. Lawson and Slocum sat on their horses on the outside of the line of stakes, exchanging heated retorts with Garrity and Cooper. The Carline brothers passed the wagon, their aged faces rigid and stern, and both of them were carrying muskets. They joined Garrity and Cooper, and Lawson and Slocum reined their horses around to ride away.

"Well, this lot don't know how to be hospitable, Ed," Lawson said sarcastically. "We might as well ride on, and see if we can find a place where people have less to hide and where they're more matey." He pulled back on his reins and stopped his horse, looking at Meghan, and he whooped with derisive laughter. "And what are you going to do with that pistol? Your man would do well to take you in hand before you shoot yourself or someone else." He took off his hat and held it out at arm's length. "Here you are," he jeered. "See if you can hit that."

Meghan quickly snapped the pistol up, resting the heavy barrels across her left forearm and aiming down the right barrel. She tugged the front trigger, the right hammer slapped forward, and the pan flashed. Her movement with the pistol had been sudden, and Lawson's sneering smile was starting to fade as the pistol cracked and belched smoke. A large hole appeared in the top of the hat.

Lawson looked at the hat, stupified. His bewilderment overcame Cooper's anger and he exploded into uproarious laughter, stamping his feet and howling with glee. The Carline brothers looked between Meghan and the hat in startled surprise. Garrity glanced at Meghan and nodded approval, and continued glaring at the men. Lawson's face flushed with rage, and he slapped the hat back on his head and kicked the horse viciously. It sprang into a gallop, and Slocum kicked and whipped his horse, following Lawson.

Cooper continued whooping with laughter, and he lifted his hat to Meghan. "Good on you, Mistress Garrity!" he laughed. "By God, that did my heart good! Did you see the look on that blackguard's face, Simon? He'll learn to still his wagging tongue, won't he?"

"Aye, he will and all," Carline agreed with a dry chuckle. "But that took me by surprise as much as it did him. Mistress Garrity can shoot a pistol, and it doesn't take her all day to get ready to shoot."

Garrity relaxed, smiling at Meghan and looking at the other men. "Aye, it doesn't do to provoke her when she has a pistol in her hand, and that wasn't a lucky shot. He could have been another twenty paces away, and she'd have hit that hat with the same ease. Do you think those two are some of the Cypress Ridge lot, Ned?"

Cooper sobered, nodding. "Aye, I'd stake my life on it. What do you think, Simon?"

Carline shrugged and shook his head musingly. "I don't know where they keep their bedroll, but I'd opine they're bushrangers. At the same time, I don't think we'll have any more trouble out of them. They saw too many guns and too many ready to fight them."

"I think you're right," Cooper agreed. "They certainly weren't fossickers, and they had the look of bushrangers. And I don't think we'll see them again. They'll stab a man in the back, but they won't look a man in the eye." He shrugged, turning to walk back toward his claim. "In any event, they've been sent on their way, like the curs they are."

"They have indeed," Garrity said. "I certainly appreciate your coming up to help so promptly."

The men nodded and replied, walking away. They passed the wagon, chuckling and commenting again about Meghan's accuracy with the pistol as they looked up at her. Meghan was reloading the pistol, and she smiled at them. They walked on along the creek, and Garrity waded back out into the creek to the sluice box. Meghan finished reloading the pistol and put it under the wagon seat. She glanced up at the ridge, thinking of the two men. They were gone, because the sound of hoofbeats had continued all the way up the ridge, but they had approached to a distance of yards from her before she had seen or heard them. And even if the men never returned, they had seen too much. They had seen the sluice box, and probably the rocker box and the sluice box that Cooper and the Carline brothers were using. They would talk, and a flood of men would pour into the valley.

Garrity commented on the same thing while they were eating dinner. He was uncertain about the precise amount of gold they had, because they had no way of weighing it, but he was sure it was worth hundreds of guineas. It was possibly enough to buy a ship outright, or shares in two or three ships. And it was far too much to keep in the wagon if others were around. He got the pistol from under the wagon seat when they went to bed, the first time he had taken the pistol out of the wagon since they had arrived in the valley. Meghan slept uneasily.

The subject came up again while Meghan and Garrity were eating breakfast the next morning. Garrity fell silent for a moment. "Of course, I could take the gold to the bank in Melbourne today, and we wouldn't have to worry about it. I'd be back by this afternoon, and this place won't be overrun with people before then. But today might be the last day I'll have to do that, because I won't be able to leave the claim once a lot of people get here."

Meghan thought about his suggestion. Fog hung low to the ground and encircled the fire in a misty, clammy curtain, but the pallid light of early dawn made nearby objects visible as it crept through the darkness, overcast, and fog. His suggestion was logical, but for some reason she felt reluctant to be parted from him for even a moment. She reached over and tucked the oilskin cover closer around the baby, then shook her head.

"Do whatever you think best, Earl. Those scurvy swine who came here yesterday put me in such a

433

gloomy frame of mind that I can scarcely think."

"We've seen the last of them," Garrity said, patting her shoulder. "Don't worry about them, love. I do think I should put our gold where it'll be safe while I have a chance, and today might be the last chance I'll have."

"Very well, Earl, if you think that's best."

"I do," he replied, and he took a drink from his pannikin and put it down as he rose. "I'll go get the horse and saddle him. I'll miss a day of sluicing, but at least I'll have dry feet today, won't I?"

Meghan looked up at him and forced a smile, nodding. He leaned down and kissed her, then turned and walked away. Meghan picked up the baby and held him on one arm, and picked up a bucket and walked to the creek to fill it with water. A slight breeze stirred, swirling the fog as she walked through it to the creek. She dipped the bucket into the creek and walked back to the fire, and Garrity emerged from the fog with the horse.

Garrity saddled the horse and put the gold in his coat pockets. He held out the large, elongated nugget he had found on the first day of sluicing. "Let's keep this one, love. It's worth a lot of money, but to me it's worth more just to keep it. And we can always go ahead and turn it in for the money if we need it, can't we?"

Meghan nodded, taking the nugget and putting it in her pocket. "Aye, very well, Earl."

"I'll leave the pistol here for you, and I'll tell Ned Cooper that I'll be gone for a few hours. He'll make certain that you'll be all right, and I'll be back by this

434

afternoon, love."

"Very well, Earl. Be careful."

"No fear about that," he said, patting his coat pockets. "I'll not lose our gold."

"Blast and damn that gold. You be careful about yourself."

He smiled and nodded, kissing her again, then stepped to the horse and mounted it. The horse plodded away, walking slowly toward Cooper's claim. The fog started breaking up as the breeze swirled it around the fire. The copses of trees and then parts of the slope above the valley became visible. There was a movement on the slope through a thin haze of fog, and she suddenly realized that it was Earl and he was waving to her. She waved, but he had disappeared behind a thicker cloud of fog. It appeared that he had failed to see her wave, and she felt a keen, poignant stab of regret.

The fog left a damp chill in the air that the fire failed to dispel. A deeper, more penetrating chill suddenly gripped Meghan, a premonition of impending disaster. She thought about the pistol that Earl had left behind. What he had said about it had scarcely registered on her, and suddenly it seemed crucially important for him to be armed. She leaped into the tent and snatched up the pistol, then she stopped and looked at the baby as she started to run toward the ridge.

She put the pistol down by the fire and picked up the baby, and ran toward Cooper's claim. The trees blocked the view, but she could hear the wooden thumping of his rocker box over the rushing sound of

435

the creek. She burst through the trees. His crude tent was hung over a rope between two trees, a smoldering fire by it, and his horses were hobbled in the grass a few yards away. Cooper looked at her in concern, wading out of the creek.

"What is it, Mistress Garrity? What's wrong?"

Meghan swallowed to make her voice steady, trying to control herself. "I'm very sorry to bother you, Mr. Cooper, but I forgot to tell Earl to get something for me. Could you watch my baby for a moment while I run and catch Earl?"

"Of course, of course," he said. "I'll be more than glad to look after him. Here, let me have him."

"I could just put him down here, and you could watch him while you continue with your work."

"No, no, it's no trouble. Just let me have him, and you go ahead and catch Earl before he's gone. Run, now."

He took the baby, motioning her away. Meghan lifted the hem of her dress, and ran back through the trees to camp. She picked up the pistol and clutched it to her as she raced toward the slope. The bottom of her dress became sodden with moisture from the grass, and it tangled around her ankles. The grass pulled at her dress, holding her back, and she struggled through it.

The ground sloped upward, and trees and brush closed in around her. The pistol was a solid, heavy weight, and she became short of breath. Vines caught at her feet, and brush and low limbs of trees slashed at her. Her thighs and calves began cramping, and the pain became a fiery torment. The imperative need to reach the top of the ridge and stop Earl clamored in her mind, and she ran on. Her steps became labored, and she summoned reserves of strength, but she ran on.

The pain in her legs passed beyond pain, and she breathed in hoarse gasps. The slope leveled off near the top of the ridge, and she threw herself forward. Spots of light danced in front of her eyes and she felt lightheaded, the trees swimming around her. After an eternity, the trees opened out ahead and the wide valley lay below. She struggled the last few steps, staggering and weaving on her feet, and slumped against a tree as she looked across the valley.

He was gone. The trail his horse had made in the deep, wet grass was clearly visible through the thin wisps of fog drifting across the valley.

She returned to the fire and put the pistol down by it, and she straightened her clothes and composed herself and she walked along the creek to Cooper's claim. The baby was crying angrily, waving his arms and kicking, and Cooper was talking to him and awkwardly trying to pacify him. Cooper smiled in relief, handing the baby to Meghan. The baby immediately stopped crying as she rocked him in her arms. Cooper chuckled.

"He knows who his mother is, doesn't he? Did you catch Earl, Mistress Garrity?"

"No, he was already gone, Mr. Cooper. He did intend to hurry there and back, and I was too long getting to the top of the hill."

Cooper smiled reassuringly. "Well, I've been intending to go to Melbourne, and I might as well go today. I daresay I can catch up with him easily enough unless he goes every yard of the way at a dead run, and I doubt he'll do that."

Relief flowed over Meghan. "No, I couldn't ask you to do that, Mr. Cooper. I've already been far too much trouble to you."

"No, you're not putting me to any trouble," he replied. "It's something I've been putting off, because I need to get some things from town. I'll just get my horse saddled and be on my way before Earl gets too far ahead of me."

"Very well, Mr. Cooper, and I'm most grateful to you. I'm most grateful indeed."

"It's a pleasure to be able to help you, Mistress Garrity. What was it that you wanted Earl to bring from Melbourne?"

Meghan was momentarily puzzled. The urgent need to help her husband had been so paramount in her mind that she had forgotten her ostensible reason for stopping him. Then she remembered. And it was a transparent fiction between her and Cooper. His eyes were wise and shrewd, and he knew why she was worried. "Some tea, Mr. Cooper," she said. "I'd like Earl to fetch me back some tea."

"I'll be on my way, then," Cooper said, walking rapidly toward his tent. "And I'll speak to Simon Carline before I leave and let him know that you're here by yourself."

He picked up a saddle by the tent and hurried toward the glade where his horses were hobbled. Meghan walked back up the creek to the tent and wagon. The fire had burned down, and she knelt by it and piled wood on it. Hoofbeats drummed against the ground, and she turned and looked. Cooper waved, riding up the slope at a run, and Meghan waved. He rode into the trees, the hoofbeats fading, then she saw a movement through the trees as he crossed the ridge.

The thick, dark clouds sank lower, and drizzle began falling. Meghan built up the fire and wrapped the baby in his oilskin cover after she fed him, and he went to sleep by the fire. Her relief was short-lived, and her feeling of impending disaster returned as she thought about how long it would take Cooper to catch up with Earl. A nervous, frantically driving need for activity gripped her. At the same time she felt lethargic and listless, the tasks she usually did seeming futile and pointless.

The drizzle stopped, and fog began settling along the creek again. Wisps became more dense, and the clammy chill was penetrating as fog thickened into a dense mass around the fire. Nearby trees were dark, full of lurking shadows. The day turned into gloomy twilight. The fog absorbed sound, turning the rushing noise of the creek into a distant whisper, and the chirping of birds and other normal sounds were stilled. It gave Meghan a feeling of isolation, of being completely alone in the world.

Her sense of time was confused. Each moment seemed like hours, and the gray dusk around her gave no hint of the time of day. When it seemed like a long time had passed, she thought about dishes that Earl particularly enjoyed, and she began preparing a meal for him with meticulous care. She chose a lean piece of pork and looked through the potatoes for the best ones, and she examined handfuls of peas and beans and carefully sifted flour to bake fresh bread.

Nothing seemed to go right. The peas and beans kept boiling instead of simmering, then the coals became too cold and the pans hardly steamed. The baby cried, and the piece of pork had gristle in it. She burned her hand and spilled part of the peas into the fire. The dough for the bread was too dry, then it was too soggy. She almost burst into tears, because she wanted it to be a particularly good meal.

A sound carried through the fog. The baby was crying, and his wails almost smothered the sound. Meghan moved away from the fire, listening. Brush and grass rustled, and hoofs thumped against the ground. Men's voices murmured. The slow, walking hoofbeats of several horses approached, and the voices were those of several men. Dark forms moved through the fog, gradually becoming more distinct.

Cooper emerged from the fog, holding Earl in his saddle in front of him. Earl slumped loosely in the saddle. Three strangers followed, one leading the horse. They dismounted, and lifted Earl down to the ground. Cooper dismounted, and the men took off their hats and silently looked at Meghan. She wanted to run to Earl, but she was unable to move. Cooper's voice seemed to come from a long distance away as he spoke.

"I'm dreadfully sorry, Mistress Garrity. These men here saw Earl's horse running loose, and they were looking for him when I got there. We found him a way off the track, and it was too late when we did find him."

Meghan took a step, then another. Then she rushed to Earl. He almost looked asleep, his strong, bold features in repose, but his brown skin had a deadly pallor. His hair was scattered over his face, and his face was cold and waxen as she pushed his hair back. She took his hand and collapsed on the ground by him, sobbing bitterly.

—————————— Chapter 24

THE COLD WIND SWEPT ALONG the track and keened around the wagon, rippling the canvas top. Meghan huddled on the seat with the baby bundled under her coat. Deep grass and trees on the rolling hills whipped and swayed in the wind, and the narrow track stretched through the hills ahead of the wagon. A wheel rolled over a large rock in the track with a heavy jolt, jarring the coffin in the wagon, and Meghan glanced back at it and looked ahead again.

The track was dim and overgrown with grass in places, and marked with furrows and ruts where only a few wagons had traveled along it. It had been wider and more heavily-traveled during past days, with log corduroy laid down in boggy places and wooden bridges across streams. But it all faded together in Meghan's memory, blending into a dreary succession of freezing winter days that were much the same, beginning with harnessing the horse and ending by a cheerless, lonely fire at night.

When her grief had turned into dull, numb misery

and despair, her memories of Earl had provided a purpose, something she had to do. Each time he had spoken of Wayamba Station, his voice had revealed his depth of feeling for where he had been born. It had been an inexhaustible topic of conversation for him, his point of reference in life, his standard of measure. In his heart, he had never left Wayamba Station. And in death, he had been returned to Wayamba Station.

The dangers that Cooper had warned her about had failed to materialize. The pistol had always been near at hand, but few had been traveling the tracks in the winter cold once she was north of the gold fields. She had avoided people, finding isolated spots to camp and always continuing to the north. The track had led along the Darling River after she crossed the Murray, with junctions and other tracks turning off, and she had found her way along it. And the previous day she had passed the last town, a small settlement called Menindee.

The wagon crossed a saddle between two hills, and a junction came into sight. The track divided into two tracks that angled away from each other. Meghan looked at the junction as the wagon approached it, trying to decide which track to take. At times the track divided and the two branches converged again miles farther along. But she had once turned onto a track that had eventually disappeared, leading nowhere, and she had turned onto one that had led only to a deserted hut and sheep folds.

Meghan reined up at the junction, still undecided. She knew she was nearing her destination, because Earl had often spoken of Menindee. She looked at the tracks, then at the sky. The sky was overcast and she was uncertain about directions, but the track on the right seemed to lead more directly north. She clucked to the horse and shook the reins, tugging on the right one. The horse turned onto the track and plodded along it.

Several miles passed, then a fence came into sight. The track went through a wide gate in the fence, and Meghan reined up at it and climbed down from the wagon. She opened the gate and led the horse through it, then closed the gate and continued along the track. A distant hill seethed with movement. She watched it for a moment, then realized it was thousands of sheep.

Wide swaths were trampled in the grass on both sides of the track where flocks of sheep had grazed. The track crossed a creek in a shallow valley, and the creek banks had been churned into mud by sheep. A few miles beyond the creek there was another fence and another gate to open and close. Then the track went up a gradual incline and crossed a low hill, and Meghan saw buildings in the distance. There was a sprawling house with smoke rising from the chimney, outbuildings, acres of pens for sheep, and pens for horses and cattle.

The track passed within yards of a low shed with pens around it. A man came out of the shed and looked at the wagon, then he was joined by two more. As the wagon drew closer to the three, Meghan saw they were a bearded man and two youths. They looked at the wagon and at Meghan curiously, and walked closer to the track as the wagon approached. They touched their hats and nodded in greeting, and Meghan

445

stopped the horse, She was obviously on the man's property, and she felt obliged to speak.

"Could you tell me if this is the way to Wayamba Station, please?"

"Aye, you can get there on this track, Mistress," the man replied, and the youths followed him as he stepped closer to the wagon. "It's hard to find a track within miles that won't lead you to Wayamba Station so long as you go north. May I ask who you are?"

"I'm Meghan Garrity."

The man blinked, startled. Then he took off his hat, and the youths took off theirs. "You must be Earl's wife, Mistress Garrity," he said, eagerly courteous. "Colin told us that Earl got married."

"I'm his widow. Earl was killed near Melbourne, and I'm taking him home to be buried."

"Then it's true!" one of the youths cried. "What that swagman said he heard is——"

"You shut your mouth!" the man warned him furiously, wheeling on him. "If you don't learn to keep your tongue in check, I'll pull it out of your head and throttle you with it! Now get to the house and tell your ma who's out here, and then you get back here! Move! Move!" He turned back to the wagon as the youth raced toward the house, and looked up at Meghan solicitously. "I'm Luther Newton, Mistress Garrity, and this is my boy Tom. That one going there is Rob. Hand me your baby, and I'll help you down."

"No, thank you very much, Mr. Newton," Meghan replied. "I'm much obliged, but I only wanted to be sure I was going the right way."

"No, no, you must let us help you!" Newton insisted

urgently, alarmed by her refusal. "You're amongst friends, Mistress Garrity, and we'll see to everything and see that it's done properly. Now hand me your baby, and we'll get you inside with my wife while we're getting organized."

Meghan hesitated, looking down at the man as he reached up for the baby. The name Garrity had been well known and respected in Sydney and in the gold fields, but it commanded even more respect in the outback. Newton had become deferential when she introduced herself, and he was demanding to help her. And his name was one Earl had mentioned; she was on Newton Station. She handed the baby down to Newton, and he nodded in relief and satisfaction. He took the baby and held it carefully on one arm, and reached up to help her down.

"Let me say how sorry we are to hear what happened, Mistress Garrity," Newton said. "A swagman came through the other day and said something of the sort, and it took me so ill that I couldn't credit it as truth." He touched her arm, nodding toward the house. "Let's go to the house, and I'll bring your wagon over directly so you can get anything out of it you want."

They walked toward the house, and Tom looked up at his father as he walked by him. "What do you want me to do, Pa?"

"I want you to saddle a horse and ride to the west paddock," Newton replied. "Tell all of the stockmen there except Aberly to get back here as quick as they can. Pick out a good horse amongst theirs, and ride on to Wayamba Station. When you see stockmen on

Wayamba, tell them the errand you're on and change your horse for theirs. You're to ride straight on through to the home paddock, and if you kill a horse then you run on foot. Tell Mistress Garrity that we're bringing in her son Earl and his widow, and you mind your manners when you're talking to her. If you shame me in front of her, I'll sew you up in a green sheepskin. Now do you understand all of that?"

"Aye, I understand, Pa."

"Then what are you waiting for?"

Tom raced toward the stock pens. The front door of the house opened, and a tall, angular woman came out, pushing at her hair and straightening her dress. Rob followed her out, and ran back toward his father. Newton beckoned him impatiently.

"Get a move on, Rob!" he barked. "Go saddle a horse, and ride into Menindee and tell the vicar what's happened. Tell him we should be at the home paddock on Wayamba Station by Friday afternoon. When you've told him, go over to Jasper's place for a fresh horse and ride to Powell Station. Tell them what's happened and ask them to send word to Mission Station, then you head for Wayamba Station and meet us there."

Rob nodded and ran toward the stock pens, straining to catch up with his brother. The woman stood in front of the porch, glancing between Newton and Meghan as they crossed the bare, trampled ground in front of the house. "Mistress Garrity, this is my wife Marcie," Newton said as they approached the porch. "Marcie, this is Earl's widow, and what we heard from that swagman is true."

"We're dreadfully sorry to hear that it is, Mistress Garrity," Marcie said sympathetcially. "I'm pleased to meet you, and I wish we could have met under happier circumstances."

"Thank you, Mistress Newton, and I'm pleased to meet you," Meghan replied. "And I'm grateful for your hospitality."

The woman smiled warmly, shaking her head. "It's no more than you're due. And you came all the way from Melbourne by yourself? There's a journey few woman would undertake, winter or no."

"She's a Garrity," Newton said. "I've never known one of that name who didn't live up to it, and it's clear to see that Earl did his family proud. That's a fine-looking boy, Mistress Garrity. What's his name?"

"Patrick."

"By God, there's a good name!" Newton exclaimed. "It'll be good to have a Patrick Garrity on Wayamba Station again, and everyone will be glad to hear about it. I'll park your wagon by the house and take care of your horse, and we'll get set to leave tomorrow morning. I have a little wagon we use for visiting, and I think it would be best to carry the coffin on that. Then we'll have my big wagon, and Marcie and you can ride in it to keep each other company. I'll have a fresh horse hitched to your wagon, and one of my men can bring it along behind our big one. Does that sound all right to you?"

"Aye, and I'm most grateful to you for your trouble."

"I'm proud to be able to help," he replied. "You just go on in the house with Marcie, and we'll see to

449

everything."

Marcie took Meghan's arm, leading her up onto the porch as Newton walked away. Two horses appeared, the youths leaning over the saddles, burst past the house at a pounding run, and rocks and dust flew up as they thundered toward the track. They swerved, one turning onto the track in one direction, and the other horse raced along the track in the opposite. Marcie opened the door, and Meghan followed her into the house.

It was a warm and comfortable haven after weeks of the cold and lonely hardhsips of the track. But it ws the first house Meghan had been in since leaving the Georges, and it brought back haunting memories and a renewed sense of loss. Marcie had been in the process of preparing dinner, and she had baked a rich, juicy beef roast and vegetables. The baby devoured a bowl of finely-cut beef minced with chopped vegetables, greedily hungry for food after weeks of living on frumenty. Meghan had no appetite, but she forced herself to eat.

Newton was in and out of the house, eating and speaking about things that had to be done, and Marcie talked constantly as she helped Meghan bathe the baby and wash clothes. They were eager to help Meghan because she was a Garrity, and for other reasons that were revealed in what they said. The Newtons were warm, friendly people, genuinely shocked and sorrowful over Earl's death, since they had known and liked him well. The Garrity family was also regarded as an institution in the region, and what affected them affected the area at large.

The giant sheep station to the north represented authority and sovereignty far more concrete then the tenuous ties to distant Sydney. Elizabeth Garrity's wishes were law. Wayamba Station was a kingdom surrounded by allied states in the isolation of the outback, and it was also an umbrella of protection and assistance. Marcie talked about a devastating grassfire during a dry summer several years before that had virtually destroyed Newton Station. Elizabeth Garrity had sent stockmen to help rebuild and then sent flocks of tens of thousands of sheep. She had refused to discuss payment.

Meghan's arrival at Newton Station also broke the deadly monotony of winter in the outback. The cirumstances of her arrival made it a momentous event. Newton Station had become the focus of an episode that would be discussed for years to come, and Luther Newton intended to make the most of it. Stockmen arrived from an outlying paddock in a drumming tattoo of hoofbeats. Newton bustled about, coming in to confer with Marcie, sending men on errands, and ordering others about outside the house.

The Newtons insisted that Meghan sleep in their bed, the best in the house, and they used one of their sons' rooms. Meghan was weary with grinding fatigue that approached exhaustion. Though the bed was luxuriously warm and soft, she slept fitfully. In the dream-like state between sleep and full wakefulness, the events of the past weeks seemed like a nightmare from which she would awake. The dismal reality and grief returned when she eagerly shrugged off sleep and reached out for Earl.

451

The activity around the house also kept her awake. Riders arrived and left until the early hours of the morning. Hammers rang on iron in the blacksmith shop among the outbuildings. The barracks cook had a fire outside one of the buildings and made tea and food for men arriving and leaving, and the glow of the flames shone through the window by Meghan's bed. Wagons rumbled around the house, harness jangled, horses stamped, and men talked quietly. Newton, supervising preparations most of the night, hardly slept.

Meghan heard Marcie coughing and moving about well before dawn. Though the sky had cleared, it had turned colder, and she shivered as she put on the gray wool dress with matching bonnet she had picked out the night before. The kitchen was warm and filled with ruddy light from the roaring fire in the fireplace. Marcie rushed about as she prepared breakfast and picked out utensils and supplies to take along. Newton, his hair and beard freshly combed, and wearing a baggy wool suit with a neckcloth, came in for breakfast.

The moon was still up when they went out, and it was frigidly cold. Men hurried about with lanterns, as horses snorted and pranced in the dark. The wagons were in a line by the house—the small one in front, a huge one behind it, and Meghan's wagon at the rear. Newton helped his wife and Meghan up to the seat of the large wagon, and put thick, warm sheepskins around them. Riders mounted horses as Newton gathered up the reins and shouted, and the wagons moved briskly away from the house.

Light touched the sky in the east, and the stars dimmed as it spread across the sky. The sun rose into the gray, wintry sky, pallid and without warmth. An icy wind swept across the brown, rolling hills. It stirred the grass and the trees, and the black crepes on the coffin and small wagon in front. Newton talked to Meghan as they moved rapidly along the track, reminiscing about past years.

Newton Station had been established by his grandfather and he had inherited it from his father, so his relationship with the Garrity family was anchored in past generations. He talked about Patrick Garrity and his aborigine wife, their children Sheila and Colin, and others Earl had mentioned to Meghan. He repeatedly referred to the baby's name, keenly pleased that there was another Patrick Garrity.

The wagons stopped at midday, and the men ate the cold rations they had brought along. Marcie uncovering kettles in the wagon, passed out cold food to her husband and Meghan, and helped Meghan feed the baby. The men brought spare horses that were being led behind the wagons and harnessed them, then the wagons moved along the track again.

A fence came into sight which stretched across the hills to the horizon in both directions. What Earl and others had told Meghan about Wayamba Station made the fence appear different from others she had seen, more than a barrier to hold sheep, more than a structure to mark a property boundary. The rolling terrain beyond the fence was identical to that which they had been traveling, and at the same time it was subtly different.

Stockmen had gathered, waiting through the night to pay their last respects to a Garrity who had returned to Wayamba Station in a coffin. Their flocks covered nearby hills with carpets of gray, and wisps of smoke rose from their fires. They were waiting along the track, weathered, ragged men with long, unkempt hair and beards, wearing sheepskin coats that trailed to the ground. They stood by their shaggy dogs and horses, taking off their hats as the wagons passed.

The sheer size of the sheep station had been difficult for Meghan to grasp, and she gradually began to comprehend it. The wagons stopped at a spring in a valley at nightfall, and started along the track before dawn the next morning. They traveled rapidly along the track and went through another gate during late afternoon, finally finishing crossing the southernmost section of Tanami Paddock.

Stockmen were scattered along the track, their flocks on the hills behind them. They stood with their horses and dogs and took off their hats. Swagmen were converging on the home paddock of Wayamba Station. They too stood by the track and took off their hats as the wagons hurried past. Aborigines were also along the track, almost hidden among the trees and grass as they stood in small family groups and watched the wagons pass. The vicar from Menindee caught up with the wagon, riding one horse and leading a spare. He camped for a night with the wagons, held a prayer service, spoke with Meghan, then rode on to the home paddock.

Bores that had been drilled deep into the earth to tap subterranean springs supplemented rainfall in some places, and there were vast savannahs of deep grass and thickets of trees. More stockmen were along the track where the grass was more abundant, and their flocks were larger. There were craggy, rocky hills and dry, flinty ground in other places, with few except aborigines along the track. The wagons crossed a wide stretch of miles of grassland in its natural state, then went through a gate in another fence and into the southernmost section of Tambo Paddock.

Tom Newton joined the wagons in a northern section of Tambo Paddock, riding along the track from the north as the men were building fires and making camp for the night. He had found Elizabeth Garrity at the home paddock and delivered his father's message, and his father questioned him closely on what he had said to her and how he had conducted himself. Satisfied, his father nodded in dismissal.

"Well, it appears you didn't make a fool of yourself and shame me, then," Newton grunted grudgingly. "Your ma has your good clothes in the wagon, so see to them and grease your boots."

"That's not all, Pa," Tom said. "There's been a hell of a set-to at the home paddock. Dennis and Colin started rolling their swag to go to Melbourne and decorate some trees with those who did it, and Mistress Garrity told them she'd sew them in green sheepskins if they so much as——"

"Will you learn to check your tongue?" Newton interrupted him in a furious bellow. "What passes between Mistress Garrity and her sons is none of your affair, and you've no call to go wagging your tongue about it! It's also none of my affair, and I don't want to hear about it! Now do as you're told and keep your mouth closed!''

Tom nodded, glancing at Meghan contritely, and scurried away. Newton sighed and shook his head apologetically as he looked at Meghan. He then walked over to where the men were hobbling the horses to check the hobbles.

Meghan expected it, because the affairs of the Garrity family and their battles with others as well as each other were a staple among stories told by swagmen and residents of the outback. She had also expected the reaction from Dennis and Colin that Tom had related. They were like Earl had been, friendly and generous, but with fierce family pride and hot tempers. And Elizabeth Garrity's ability to restrain her sons was a testimony to the authority she exercised.

The wagons started along the track before dawn the next morning. That evening was the last time they would camp before reaching the home paddock. The men carried buckets of water and washed the wagons, greased the harness, and dusted off the crepes on the coffin and small wagon. They were up early the following morning, dusting their clothes, greasing their boots, and combing their hair and beards before starting along the track again.

Smoke from a fire where three men were camped by the track came into sight shortly before midday. The men extinguished the fire, mounted horses, and rode away to the north at a pounding run. The wagons passed the ashes of the fire, crossed the creek where the men had camped, and continued along the track.

Miles passed before the wagons went up a slow incline and the home paddock came into view from the top of the rise.

The row of houses and cluster of outbuildings looked larger than the town of Menindee. The buildings were along a thickly-wooded creek, shaded by tall trees, and a vegetable garden; an aborigine village was up the creek from them. Sheds, runs, and acres of pens were north of a wide track that led away to the west, and warehouses, barracks, repair shops, and other buildings were south of it.

Lines of wagons were parked by the sheds, and dozens of people milled about in the wide, trampled area that separated the houses from the outbuildings. The crowd was much too large for a house, and rows of benches had been set up for the wake on the grass verge in front of the large house. Whole beef and pork carcasses turned on spits over roaring fires in front of the barracks, huge pans of other food were on gratings over smaller fires, and trestle tables and benches were in lines between the outbuildings and houses.

The crowd of people moved to one side and became silent and still as the wagons approached. The men took off their hats. Two remained standing near the tables, apart from the others, Dennis and Colin. They were bareheaded, holding their hats and looking at the first wagon. To Meghan, their features were painfully reminiscent of Earl, though their faces were taut and pale with grief and smoldering anger.

People in the crowd shifted and craned their necks to look at Meghan as the wagons stopped. Dennis and Colin nodded to the man driving the first wagon, and looked at the coffin as they walked toward the large wagon. Newton climbed down from the wagon, shook hands with Colin and Dennis and murmured his condolences. They nodded, replying, and Dennis took the baby from Meghan and helped her down from the wagon.

He handed the baby back to her, then embraced her. "We're thankful you brought him home, Meghan. It was no small thing to do."

"Aye, there's God's truth," Colin said, stepping forward, and he embraced Meghan. "It must have been a sore trial for you, Meghan, but you're among your own now."

"Mr. Newton and his good wife were a godsend," Meghan replied. "I was almost at the end of my strength and my wits when I met them, and their help and sympathy have known no ends."

"Aye, we won't forget that soon," Dennis said, turning to Newton. "We're most grateful for everything you've done."

Newton helped Marcie down from the wagon, shrugging and shaking his head. 'I did no more than anyone would have, and I wish I could have been of help for a happier occasion. This is a sorry business indeed."

"It is and all," Dennis agreed grimly, looking back at Meghan. "We've heard this and that, and I'm not sure we have the straight of it, Meghan. How did it happen?"

The other people were moving closer, looking and listening, and Meghan sighed heavily as she replied. "He was carrying gold from our claim to Melbourne, and was waylaid along the track. No witnesses came forward, and the constable from Melbourne could find no evidence that would point to the one who did it."

"Aye, well, a bit of the gold could have seen to that," Colin growled angrily. "He might even have had a hand in it, knowing some of these scurvy dogs who call themselvs constables."

He was the youngest and the most hot-tempered of the brothers, and his attitude aggravated Meghan. "No, the constable at Melbourne is a good and honest man, Colin," she replied sharply. "I've known no constable I'd refer to in such abusive terms, but that may be because I've never had occasion to be athwart of any. Regardless, I'll not have him maligned and I'll not listen to reproaches on how I saw to this matter."

Colin frowned, shaking his head stubbornly. "I'm not reproaching you, Meghan, because I know you did all you could. But my brother is dead, and his murderer hasn't been made to pay. I won't know any peace on this until justice is done."

"Peace?" Meghan exclaimed. "Colin, I won't know any peace on this until the last breath passes between these lips. And I would feel no whit the better if every bushranger in Australia were drawn and quartered. I did all I could to see justice done, and I did all anyone could except perhaps a witch or a wizard. Looking into people's hearts isn't among my talents, and nothing less would do to find the murderer."

"I'd find the swining, blackhearted bastard," Colin muttered furiously, looking away. "I'd track down bushrangers and hang them until I found the right one, and then it would be settled."

Meghan's aggravation and sorrow made tears well up in her eyes, and she blinked and swallowed. "And you'd make yourself no better than the one who did it, Colin. If there were a way to find out who the murderer is, I'd not rest until I made him pay blood for blood. But there is no way, and you're simply seeking an outlet for your grief. You'd do yourself more credit to seek strength within yourself to deal with it. Moreover, it would do us both credit to let this rest here and now. My husband and your brother lies there, and this is most unseemly."

"By God, it is and all," Dennis growled, frowning darkly at Colin. "I want to see justice done as much as you, but Meghan has suffered enough without having to face this from us."

Colin's anger faded, and he nodded contritely as he stepped to Meghan and put his arms around her. "I'm sorry, Meghan. You've lost more than anyone. Will you forgive me?"

Meghan forced a quick smile and nodded as she shifted the baby in her arms and brushed at the tears in her eyes. "Of course, Colin. I need to see to my baby."

"Aye, and no doubt you need to sit for a moment and collect yourself as well, love," Colin said sympathetically, patting her shoulder. "You've endured too much, and I've been no bloody help at all. But I'll make it up to you, Meghan." He glanced around, and beckoned a woman. "Here's Martha Appleby, the housekeeper. You could go over to her house and see to young Patrick, and we'll get you settled at home later. Martha, would you take her over to your house so she can see to the baby?"

"I'd be most pleased to," the woman replied. "I thought she might want to feed him and such, so I have things prepared. Just bring his things, Mistress Garrity, and we'll see to him."

"I'll bring his things," Marcie said. "Tom, hop up there in the wagon and hand me down that bundle from behind the seat."

The youth scrambled up into the wagon and handed his mother the bundle of baby clothes. Martha Appleby took Meghan's arm, her round, amiable face warm and sympathetic, and Marcie walked toward the houses with them. The people had been still and quiet while listening to the exchanges between Meghan and Colin, but now they began gathering around the wagons and conversing.

The houses looked peaceful and inviting with the massive trees along the creek towering over them. A mound of earth was by a freshly-dug grave in the graveyard between the large house and the first one in the line of smaller houses. Meghan averted her eyes from it as she and the women crossed the grass verge and walked up the steps to Martha's house.

The small, neat house was furnished with heavy, homemade furniture and decorated with things that Martha had made. The kitchen was warm and cheerful, a fire blazing in the fireplace and pans of food keeping warm on the hob. Martha seated Meghan at the table and took the baby from her. She smiled as she unwrapped his blanket and looked at him.

"Would you look at the size of him?" she chuckled. "Here's a sturdy boy if I ever saw one, and he's

461

pure Garrity."

"He's not the only one," Marcie said in satisfaction, glancing at Meghan. "I just saw Colin dealt with as ably as anyone could."

"Aye, he was and all," Martha replied in approval. "We've had such a row here that you wouldn't believe, Colin and Dennis in a rage and Mistress Garrity not budging an inch. Here, you take the baby, Marcie, and I'll make tea and see to his food and bath ."

Marcie held the baby, as Martha moved around the kitchen. The two women had been born and reared on sheep stations in the area, and they discussed mutual acquaintances among those who had come for the wake and funeral as Martha put on water for tea and prepared food for the baby. She had boiled vegetables and mutton to a soft consistency, and she spooned it out into a bowl and gave it to Marcie. Marcie fed the baby, and Martha made tea and put a basin of water on the hearth to warm for the baby's bath.

With pannikins of tea on the table, the atmosphere in the kitchen was soothing and comforting. Marcie finished feeding the baby, and she and Martha undressed him to begin his bath. There was a knock at the front door and a boy called to Martha.

"Is that you, Tod?" she replied. "What do you want?"

The boy opened the front door and looked in. "Aye, it's me, mo'm. Will you be through there directly?"

"We'll be through when we get through," Martha snapped impatiently. "If anyone's getting anxious, they can wait their hurry."

"Nobody's getting anxious, mo'm," the boy replied. "But Mistress Garrity is coming out of the big house."

"Aye, well, we'll be there just now," Martha said, her tone changing. She turned and stepped back to the hearth as the boy closed the front door. "We'll need to wrap him good against the chill, because there's too many here to have the wake inside, and he'll be on the veranda at the big house. Here's a pretty blanket we can put around him for Mistress Garrity to see him."

Marcie lifted the baby out of the basin and dried him, and the two women dressed him and put the thick blanket around him. Meghan rose, put her coat back on, and took the baby. Marcie and Martha retrieved their coats and with Meghan, they went back out.

The coffin was on trestles at one end of the veranda in front of the large house. A tall woman in a severe black coat and dress was talking to Newton, as Colin, Dennis, and the vicar stood by her.

Meghan looked at the woman as she walked toward the crowd. Elizabeth Garrity was old, but ageless. Her hair was gray at her temples and her features were lined and wrinkled, but there was an enduring, eternal vitality about her. Her bearing was regal, her back straight and her head held high. A long, straight nose and a short upper lip gave her features a proud, haughty cast. She had never been beautiful, but she had been and remained a handsome woman.

The conversation died away as Meghan approached. Elizabeth Garrity turned. Her piercing blue eyes probed, searched, and anaylzed Meghan's features. There was a momentary silence as Meghan stopped, then Dennis introduced her to his mother. Meghan murmured a polite greeting. A silence again stretched out for long seconds as the people watched the old woman study Meghan's face. She finally nodded and spoke quietly.

"Welcome to your home, Meghan."

She was a stern, undemonstrative woman, whose manner was one of reserved judgment rather than affection or friendship. But her tone gave the words a literal emphasis, as if stating a fact. Suddenly Meghan had a feeling of a conclusive end to turmoil and upheaval, of having arrived where she belonged. In a way it seemed that her entire life had been a series of events leading up to her becoming part of this proud family. She was a Garrity, and Wayamba Station was her home.

"Thank you, Mistress Garrity. I'm most grateful."

"I'm grateful to you for bringing my son home," the old woman replied. Reaching for the baby, she pulled the blanket away from his face, and a bare shadow of a smile touched her firm, thin lips as she looked at her grandson and glanced around. "Now here's a Garrity, and one with a good name and all."

People moved closer and commented admiringly over the baby. The old woman gave the baby back to Meghan, and started to introduce the people to her. Most of them were men, but several station owners had brought their families with them. She introduced them by name and station, and the stations were

464

those that Earl had mentioned frequently—Powell, Mission, Blair, Stanthorpe, Tibboburran, and others. Many of the men were swagmen, their ragged clothes dusted and their worn boots greased for the occasion, still the old woman knew each of them by name.

The people murmured greetings and condolences, men lifting their hats and women bobbing in curtsies. The old woman finished introducing the last of the people, and glanced up at the sky. "Well, it's almost sunset, so we may as well begin. Dennis, go tell the storekeeper to put out a dozen port and a keg of rum with the food. Colin, drag your long face up the creek and tell the abos to get on down here and commence their heathenish racket if they're going to."

The vicar cleared his throat and plucked his collar. "Do you think that's entirely appropriate, Mistress Garrity?" he asked diffidently.

"I deem it most appropriate, Vicar," the old woman replied crisply. "They deafened me with their clatter when he was brought into the world, and I consider it right and proper for them to help send him on his way."

The vicar nodded uncomfortably, clearing his throat and tugging at this collar again. Dennis and Colin walked away, and Meghan walked toward the large house with the old woman. The other people followed in a quiet murmur of voices and footsteps. They climbed the steps and walked around the settles and chairs to the settle at the front, facing the coffin. Boots thumped against the steps as others filed in front of the benches on the grass verge in front of the house and stood, waiting.

Dennis and Colin came up the steps and stood in front of chairs behind Meghan and the old woman, and the vicar took his place by the coffin. Silence fell as the people bowed their heads. The vicar prayed in a ringing voice that carried out across the benches. Meghan looked at the coffin, tears starting to fill her eyes as an agony of despair gripped her again. The old woman whispered softly, and Meghan glanced up at her. She had shown no indication of sorrow, conducting herself as though the gathering was a social occasion, but she was praying.

The vicar finished. Boots scraped on the floor and chairs and settles creaked, and the people talked quietly as they sat down. Meghan sat down by the old woman, and tucked the blanket around the baby. The vicar tiptoed past and went down the steps speaking quietly with some of the men on the benches. A long line of thirty or more aborigines filed past the veranda and disappeared around the side of the house, men followed by women and several children with bright yellow hair.

Then there was a whispering groan of digereedos, quiet tapping of rhythm sticks, and soft chanting of voices. A hushed silence hung over the people on the veranda except for an occasional cough or scrape of a boot on the floor. The men on the benches in front of the house moved quietly about and gathered in groups to talk in low voices. A few of them went to the fires to eat, and some of the men on the veranda rose and tiptoed down the steps.

Darkness fell, and the fire at the side of the house made a halo of light at the end of the veranda behind the coffin. Women went into the house and brought out lamps and lanterns. Martha was weeping as she put a lamp at each end of the coffin, choking back sobs and wiping her eyes. She returned to her chair and whispered tearfully with another woman. The old woman sat and looked at the coffin, a lamp shining on her face and her features expressionless.

The pulsing dirge of the aborigine music was mournful, awakening depths of grief, and at the same time it was soothing and seemed to exorcise grief. Meghan listened to it, her eyes filled with tears but the tears not spilling over. The baby began crying and wriggling, and Meghan rocked him in her arms to pacify him. He continued crying, and Martha tiptoed to the settle and took him to her house, his wailing carrying back to the veranda as she walked toward it.

Martha was gone with the baby for a time, feeding him and changing his clothes, then she returned to the veranda and gave him back to Meghan. He was asleep, and Meghan held him and looked at the coffin again as she listened to the aborigine music. More people tiptoed down the steps from the veranda and went to eat, sitting on the benches around the trestle tables, then quietly returned. Colin leaned foward and murmured to Meghan, suggesting that she go and eat, and she silently shook her head.

"You must eat," the old woman said, turning to Meghan.

Meghan hesitated, then shrugged. "I'll go when you

467

do, then."

"I'm not hungry."

"Neither am I."

The old woman's lips thinned with impatience as she looked down at Meghan in silence. It was a contest of wills, and Meghan continued looking up at the old woman, her eyes on the icy blue eyes. Then the old woman sighed and nodded, rising. Meghan rose and walked along the veranda with her. Martha reached up and took the baby, and Meghan and the old woman walked down the steps.

A lantern was in the center of each trestle table, and a few people sat around the tables and talked quietly as they ate. The barracks cook sliced thick, juicy pieces of steak and put them on plates, and spooned beans, peas, and potatoes onto the plates. Meghan and the old woman filled pannikins with tea, and took the pannikins and plates to a table.

They talked as they ate, and the old woman asked Meghan about her family and the places she had been. What she asked revealed that she had questioned Colin and Dennis closely after their visits to the house on the Georges, because she was thoroughly familiar with Meghan's background, the places she had been, and what had happened to her. They finished eating and sat in silence for a moment, then the old woman nodded musingly.

"You've had your share of misfortune, haven't you?"

"No more than many others, I'm sure," Meghan replied. "I don't dwell on it, because there's the road to

468

self-pity. And I learned at an early age that much of life consists of tacking up contrary winds."

The old woman shrugged impatiently over the nautical figure of speech. "You're probably right, whatever that might mean. Why didn't you make Earl come home? I know you could have."

"Aye, I could have. And I would have paid a price in resentment, which is the penalty for using love to prevail upon someone against their will. That's why I decided against it."

"So you let him waste his time in the gold fields instead."

"I was his wife, not his ruler, and it was a decision we made together. And it was hardly a waste of time. He had a fortune in gold on him when he was killed."

"Aye, and what do you have to show for it now?"

"The same that you have to show for a flock of sheep when they're caught in a grassfire. Human endeavor will always come to naught when it goes athwart fate or the will of God. I might also say that a single word from you would have brought him running, because he loved this place."

"So you think I should have summoned him home?"

Meghan sighed sadly, shrugging. "It isn't for me to say what you should have done, Mistress Garrity. You laid your course as the winds and tides you encountered permitted, and to fault that now would be as futile as Colin and Dennis wearing out their teeth by gnashing them together. Further, gazing behind only gives one a sore neck and a view of where they sit."

Her eyes filled with tears, and she blinked as she looked away. "He's gone, and there's the bloody end of it."

"Aye, there's the bloody end of it," the old woman echoed, rising from the table. "I could have summoned him home. But if I had, I wouldn't have been able to keep rein on any of the three. The only thing restraining Dennis and Colin is their fear that they won't be able to return if they leave. Come on, and let's finish seeing my son on his way."

Meghan rose and walked back to the house with the old woman. The men on the benches were quieter, and some were slumping on the benches and dozing. A few people on the veranda were dozing, their arms wrapped around themselves to keep warm. Meghan took the baby back from Martha, and returned to the settle in front of the coffin with the old woman.

The murmur of digereedoos, rhythm sticks, and chanting voices continued at the side of the house. The cold of the winter night had settled, and Meghan tucked the blanket around the baby and held him close. Time dragged past as Meghan looked at the coffin in the flickering light of the lamps. Her eyelids began drooping with leaden weariness from the journey and the many nights with too little sleep, then she dozed.

She woke, leaning against the old woman. The old woman's arm was around her shoulders, warm and comforting. Meghan sat up, and the old woman looked down at her as she took her arm from around her shoulders. She straightened Meghan's bonnet, her eyes and features neutral. It seemed to be motivated by a desire for order rather than affection, but it was something she would do for few. Meghan tucked the blanket around the baby and smothered a yawn.

"I'm sorry I went to sleep and leaned against you."

"There's no cause to be sorry, and I didn't mind keeping you warm. It's no more than what one human being should do for another."

"Why do you say that?"

"It's something I learned from someone a long time ago."

"Who?"

The old woman silently shook her head, ending the conversation, and Meghan glanced around. The thick darkness was that of early morning, and the flames in the lamps and lanterns were guttering. The fire by the house silhouetted the coffin as the aborigine music continued. The cooking fires had burned down, and the cook was moving around them and building them up. Men were dozing on the benches and several people on the veranda snored and breathed deeply as they slept.

A few of the men on the benches stirred, and they rose and went to the fires to eat breakfast. People on the veranda began moving about, quietly going down the steps and to the fires. The baby began crying, and Martha stepped to the settle, took him from Meghan, and carried him to her house. The old woman touched Meghan's arm and nodded toward the fires, and Meghan rose and followed her off the veranda.

They drank pannikins of tea, and went back to the

veranda. Martha returned from her house with the baby, and gave him to Meghan. Meghan wrapped his blanket around him tightly and held him close, looking at the coffin and waiting for the time to pass. Light touched the horizon in the east. The droning of the digereedoos, rattle of rhythm sticks, and chanting voices at the side of the house became perceptibly louder.

Dawn came, frigidly cold and gray. People on the veranda shivered, coughed, and smothered yawns. Those around the fires returned to their seats on the benches and the veranda. The vicar moved quietly about on tiptoe, pointing and motioning. Colin, Dennis, Newton, and another man stepped to the coffin. Meghan and the old woman rose. The four men lifted the coffin.

They carried the coffin on their shoulders and walked slowly along the veranda. Meghan and the old woman followed them, and people fell into line behind Meghan and the old woman as they went down the steps. The men at the benches milled about, joining the line. The four men carried the coffin around the side of the house to the graveyard, and they put it down on the boards across the open grave.

The vicar began reading the service. Smoke billowed up from the fire on the other side of the house, and the groaning of the digereedoos rose to a wild, frenzied sobbing. The rhythms sticks clattered, and the chant was a pulsing beat. Meghan swayed on her feet and she began to cry. The old woman put her arm around Meghan. Her arm trembled. Elizabeth Garrity's features were in stern, neutral lines, but she was crying, too.

Chapter 25

TAKING THE THINGS OUT OF the wagon was difficult, because everything in it was evocative of Earl. He had built the shelves and bins along the sideboards while they had been in the house on the Georges, and at each step of constructing them he had discussed the arrangement with her to make certain they would be convenient for her. Each shelf and bin was the focus of the memory of a conversation with him.

At times she had been impatient. Pregnant, weary of the subject, and irritated over being repeatedly called out of the house to look at how a shelf was being placed or how the lid would go on a bin, she had snapped irately at him. He had always been smiling and cheerful, understanding about her mood. And while she was taking the things out of the wagon, she paid heavily in remorse for her moments of impatience.

The wagon contained his clothes, the shirts and linens she had washed for him, and the good wool trousers with a smudge of axle grease on a knee that she had scolded him about. It contained the set of small, light cookware he had found at a chandler's store in Sydney and had rushed home to show her. It contained the tent that had sheltered them, and it contained the bedding that had enfolded them when they made love.

Handling the things and making decisions on how to dispose of them was painful. It evoked rapturously happy moments she wished she had savored more fully, and it brought back moments she wished she could reach back and change, doing or saying something differently. It was also painful because it seemed to be a process of exorcising him from her life, bringing to a conclusive end a time she wished to continue.

Her tears had seemed to be exhausted numerous times while on the long trek from Melbourne, but further depths of grief had brought fresh tears. Her tears had also seemed to be exhausted during the funeral, but she wept while she was taking the things out of the wagon. It was a long, slow process, and she had to force herself to go to the wagon each morning. On some days hours passed while she looked at a single item and wept, and she had to find new courage to return the next morning.

She had the room in the house that Earl had used, and her bed was the one he had slept in as a boy and as a man. One of the bedposts had knife marks on it, and she wondered if he had whittled on the post in a moment of boyish idleness or had been trying out a new knife. Other marks on the floor, the thick wooden walls, and the windowsill provided a source for hours of speculation when she was in the room.

476

The room seemed to retain something of him, some vague shadow of his personality that remained from the years he had spent in it, but it was bare and sparcely furnished. While putting away some of the things from the wagon in the storerooms among the outbuildings, she found a small, exquisitely beautiful cabinet. It had been ordered from England years before, along with other furniture for the large house, and it had been considered too dainty and ornate to be useful in the house.

The storekeeper got two stockmen to help him clean the cabinet and move it to Meghan's room, and Meghan found two large, decorative wall sconces for oil lamps in another storeroom. She polished them and put them on the walls in her room, and she found a small table that was made to fit into a corner and moved it to her room. The crib that Earl and his brothers had slept in as small children was in a storeroom, dark and smooth with age, and she cleaned it and moved it to her room for the baby.

One of the shelves in the cabinet was just wide enough for the whale tooth that Gibbs had painstakingly covered with scrimshaw, and she found places for the log from the *Baleen,* the first large nugget that Earl had found, and her other treasures. In her mind, the double-barrel pistol had become hers on the day she had shot a hole through the top of Lawson's hat with it, and she hung it on a wall. And when she finished, the room was also hers and all traces of Earl had been lost.

Taking the last things out of the wagon was a symbolic ending of a phase in her life, and it produced a conclusive change in her attitude. She delayed and approached it reluctantly, with a feeling of leaving something precious behind, but it was finally done. The empty wagon was parked with others behind the outbuildings, and her marriage to Earl and the time they had spent together was completely in the past.

The results of her marriage remained, and they were a source of joy. The baby was beginning to walk by himself, and Elizabeth Garrity and her sons accepted Meghan as though she had been born into the family. It was easy to derive keen pride and satisfaction from being a member of the Garrity family, and Meghan gradually found her place among them.

Martha Appleby was unfailingly friendly and helpful, but she was also jealous of her position as the cook and housekeeper in the Garrity household. Her ability as a cook was limited, but Elizabeth Garrity also expressed displeasure when Meghan showed any inclination to do any domestic work. The blacksmith found a sidesaddle in the harness room and Meghan went for rides, and she spent the long winter afternoons with books from the shelves in the room that Elizabeth Garrity used for an office.

The family had a reputation for obstinacy, and Meghan had seen it demonstrated in Earl's refusal to return to Wayamba Station. She saw it demonstrated again, because the dispute between Elizabeth Garrity and her sons over their wish to avenge Earl's death showed no signs of abating. The old woman and her sons were coldly formal, and talked only when they had to. Meals were enervating for Meghan, but the old woman and her sons appeared impervious to the atmosphere of raw discord.

Work at the station was at its winter ebb and all three of them were at the home paddock most of the time, and Meghan carefully maintained a neutral position in the conflict. Dennis and Colin were friendly and affectionate toward her, and cautious, tentative mutual respect developed between her and the old woman. Meghan occasionally found herself in the position of carrying on two conversations at meals, talking with both the old woman and her sons as they ignored each other.

The old woman was even more unyielding in her attitude than her sons. A mining firm had discovered rich veins of silver and other ores at a place called Broken Hill, on the southwestern border of Wayamba Station. Earl had told Meghan about it, and the subject came up at dinner one evening. The firm had taken some twenty or thirty yards inside the border of Wayamba Station, and Elizabeth Garrity had marched south with an army of armed stockmen, and constables had come up from Adelaide to prevent bloodshed.

James Wyndham, in his position as an official of the Land Board, had arbitrated the dispute and made a binding settlement. He had ordered the mining firm to pay a substantial royalty for the mineral rights on the land, and the firm had been periodically depositing large amounts of money into a bank account in Sydney. Elizabeth Garrity had refused to touch the money, and she had sent men to build a huge fence along the boundary of the mining operation.

The old woman related the story to Meghan, grumbling about the encroachment on Wayamba Station, and Meghan nodded when she finished. "It does seem unfair, and circumstances can often put one on beam's ends. However, I have a passing acquaintance with Mr. Wydham, and I'm sure he did his utmost to preserve the rights of all parties involved."

"You know that swining pommie sod?" the old woman growled, looking up from her plate. "I'd not own to it if I were you, and there was only one right involved. It was Wayamba Station property, and there's the bloody end of it. And he rode roughshod over the rights of Wayamba Station."

"Not by his lights," Meghan replied placidly. "I agree with you that boundaries are boundaries. But he saw land that would graze a handful of sheep versus precious metals worth a fortune. And it appears to me that he made a most handsome settlement for a few yards of land."

"A few yards of land?" the old woman shouted, exploding in fury. "That was Wayamba Station land, and I'd not trade one bloody inch of it for all the gold and silver in Australia! And I'm just waiting for those buggers to try to take one more inch! When they do, Broken Hill will be bathed in blood! And no scurvy pommie dog from Sydney will stop me the next time, nor will that whining lot of constables from Adelaide! I'll chase those buggers as well, by God!"

She became speechless with rage as she tried to continue, and she threw down her spoon, shoved her chair out of the way, and stormed out of the room. Her footsteps stamped along the hall to her room, and her door slammed with a crash that echoed through the house.

Dennis and Colin continued eating, radiating satisfaction, and Colin nodded toward the hall as he looked at Meghan.

"You see what you're dealing with there, don't you?" he said. "A mere difference of opinion brings the walls tumbling down."

"It would depend on the specific opinion at hand, I should think," Meghan replied, and smiled brightly. "As it would with you. Let's take up the matter of your futile, foolish wish to journey to Melbourne in search of bushrangers, and see how far we get on it."

Colin's smile faded, and they finished the meal in silence. The silence at the table continued at breakfast the next morning, the old woman still resentful over Meghan's attitude toward the incident involving Wyndham and the mining firm. Meghan tried to talk to her, but she replied in monosyllables and remained moody at lunch. Then she began talking again at dinner, relating the history of Wayamba Station.

It was a long monologue, and Meghan saw that the old woman's purpose was to explain the heroic efforts that had been made in the past to maintain the integrity of the boundaries of the sheep station. Meghan had heard most of it in somewhat different versions from Earl, but the history of the sheep station fascinated her and she listened avidly. Each paddock had its story and some had several, and the old woman talked all during the meal and continued the next day.

When the old woman talked about the paddock that bordered on Broken Hill, another reason for her rage toward the mining firm surfaced. Patrick Garrity had grazed sheep in that area when he had been a stockman, working for the owner of what became the nucleus of Wayamba Station. Two of his children, Sheila and Colin, had been born there and their aborigine mother had built a cairn of stones that had some significance to aborigines. When the old woman had heard about the mining activities, she had sent men to dismantle the cairn and bring it to the home paddock, but it had been destroyed during the initial prospecting.

Earl had told Meghan about his father and his aunt, but most of what he had related had been hearsay. They had died during his childhood, and his memories of them had been vague. Dennis remembered them somewhat better, but his memories were obviously colored by what he had heard about them as a boy. Meghan wanted to know more about them, but she hesitated to ask the old woman. The old woman's stern, reserved personality discouraged questions, and she rarely mentioned Sheila and her dead husband.

The weather turned mild, and Colin and Dennis went to a paddock to help exterminate several large dens of dingos. Meghan and the old woman were alone at the house for several days, and the old woman enjoyed spending the mild afternoons in the graveyard by the house. The fresh grave among the others made Meghan melancholy, stirring an agonizing sense of loss each time she saw it, but she enjoyed being with the old woman.

The old woman abruptly began talking about Sheila

Garrity while they sat on one of the wooden benches at the edge of the graveyard one afternoon. She seemed to be almost talking to herself as she reminisced, looking into the distance. Meghan had heard contradictory stories about Sheila Garrity, and she understood why as she listened. Sheila Garrity had been a woman of contrasts. The old woman still loved her deeply, and for the first time Meghan saw an unrestrained smile on her face.

"She had a heart the size of New South Wales," the old woman sighed wistfully. "And she knew no ends when it came to helping one of her own. But the one who crossed her had best be off for China. She was as black as the soot from a smoky lamp, and she was also so lovely that it made my heart ache to look at her."

The old woman's voice faded as she looked into the distance, smiling. Meghan waited a moment, then prompted her. "She must have been a very good friend to you."

"Aye, she was my only friend when I needed one most sorely," the old woman murmured. "No one had a friend more true, and she never tired of helping me to my feet however many times I fell. She was made of steel, but she dealt with me most gently when I needed it." The old woman blinked, her smile fading, then she glanced at Meghan and shrugged as she looked away again. "But just when I needed the huge, black, bloody slut of a cow the most, she up and died on me."

"Her death must have been a grievous blow to you."

The old woman nodded with the abrupt motion of her head that indicated a subject was closed. They were silent for a moment, then the old woman spoke quietly again. "You could make a good life here for yourself, you know. Neither Dennis nor Colin will ever be able to manage this station, but I daresay you might if you put your mind to it."

"No, I love Wayamba Station and I've already come to regard it as my home, but blue water is my life."

"The sea!" the old woman hissed. "I'm sure it would be vastly entertaining for the men on deck to have you climb up to put out sails, with your skirt and petticoats flying about your ears. But considering the fact that you won't even sit astride a horse, you'd best give it lengthy thought before you commit yourself."

"I wouldn't commit myself to that," Meghan laughed. "No, I mean I'd like to eventually engage in the shipping trade. That was the object that Earl and I had in mind."

The old woman grunted sourly and nodded. "Aye, I knew what you meant. Dennis and Colin told me as much, and they said that many in Sydney opine that your knowledge of ships is extensive. But a lot of swagmen who'll never own a sheep know all there is to know about them."

"I believe I could find employment in Sydney, and put what I know to some use. I could invest in cargo shares and such in small amounts at first, and with good fortune I should do well in time. And once I have a start, I should make progress rapidly. Some of the waste I've seen in profitable shipping firms astounds me, and I'd eliminate all of that."

"You know more than others who've engaged in shipping for years?" the old woman asked skeptically. "That's hard to believe."

"Some of the waste I've seen is hard to believe. For example, all ships out of England carry stones as ballast to balance their cargo. Bricks can be had in England for pence and the bricks here are very poor, so why not carry a few ton of bricks instead of stones?"

"Why not indeed? Why hasn't someone else thought of this?"

Meghan shrugged and shook her head. "People seem content to get by with the least effort, and they're satisfied with the profits from that effort. But there are many such things that could be done."

"Aye, well, I know naught about ships," the old woman sighed disinterestedly. "Cummings Brothers see to all that for me, and all I care is how long they let my wool gather dust in the warehouse and how much I have to pay for shippage. And if my wool waits too long or I have to pay too much, I soon let them know my feelings."

"And you make a mistake when you do," Meghan chuckled. "You've almost assured that your wool won't be worth having."

The old woman frowned darkly, looking down at Meghan. "Wayamba Station wool is of the finest quality, and I'll not hear anyone say different. You might know ships, but I know wool."

"It can be of the finest quality when it leaves here, and be something again when it reaches the docks in

London. If you've told your factor to ship quickly at low cost, you've told him to put your wool on the first old leaky scow outbound for England. And if he does, your wool is half mold and seawater by the time it gets there.''

The old woman looked away, thinking, then looked back at Meghan. "I want it to get there ahead of the bulk from other stations, don't I? The price always falls when the market gets flooded with wool.

"Aye, it does. I remember reading the quotations on wool in the newspapers in England, and I'd see it fall from a shilling to tuppence the pound over the course of a few weeks. But the first ship out of Port Jackson won't be the first ship into the roads of the Thames by any means. A well-found ship with a clean hull will be to London and halfway back before an old scow ever sees the Straits of Magellan.''

The old woman nodded thoughtfully, looking away again. They sat for a few minutes longer in silence, the light beginning to fade into early winter dusk and the breeze becoming colder, then they rose and went back into the house. Martha was preparing dinner, and the baby was in the kitchen with her and playing with sticks of wood on the hearth. Meghan took him to the washroom and bathed him, then dressed him in clean clothes for dinner.

While they were eating, the old woman asked Meghan in a tone of idle interest about her plans. Meghan had seen and heard about shippers who had been financially ruined by a loss of a single ship, and she wanted to avoid such a situation. Drexler and

Suggs were too diversified, with shares in too many ships of too many types. If she was successful, she eventually planned a compromise between the two, with principal shares in three or four ships that sailed between Australia and New Zealand, and in one or two deep water ships.

She told the old woman about it, explaining her reasons. "Of course, that would be years in the future," she said as she finished. "When I begin, I'll be more than content with a good return on cargo shares so I can build up some capital."

"Why didn't you think of this before?" the old woman asked. "If you can do it now, you could have been doing it instead of wandering about the gold fields."

"No, I couldn't have. What would Earl have said if I'd announced an intention to seek employment and invest my wages in cargo shares? It would have sorely wounded his pride. And worse, he was searching for employment at the time and was unable to find it."

The old woman nodded. "Aye, dealing with that would have been a problem indeed. It's been so long since I've had a husband to worry about that I've forgotten how burdensome they can be in some ways." The baby had gone to sleep on Meghan's lap after she fed him, and the old woman looked at him. "So you wish to take young Patrick away from his grandmother, do you?"

"Not at all," Meghan protested. "I want him to know you and love you, and I want him to spend time here with you. If I can manage it, I'd like to send him to England, to school. But before I do that, I want him to have his feet solidly on the ground here so he'll return."

"I'd have thought you'd want him to be a seaman."

"I do. When he's finished school, I'd like him to do his duty on a quarterdeck in the Royal Navy, but I don't intend him to spend his life at it. I'd like for him to return to Australia, and I'd like to have something to give him when he does."

"Such as a shipping firm?"

"Aye, if I can manage it. It's only wishful thinking now, but the time might come when there's a Garrity line."

The old woman took a drink of tea and put her pannikin down, and she sighed as she pushed her chair back and rose to leave. "Starting a shipping firm is a possibility, Meghan, because that's up to you. But what your son does is up to him, and there's your wishful thinking. Children without a mind of their own are useless, and those with a mind of their own are prone to seek their own paths."

Her tone was sad, and her shoulders were uncharacteristically slumped as she went out. Meghan watched her leave, thinking about what she had said. She had obviously been referring to her sons and her experience with them. As a mother she loved them, but she also had the stewardship of Wayamba Station as a responsibility to pass on to others. In that they had failed her. Earl had left, and Dennis and Colin had yet to fulfill her expectations. And it also appeared that the continuing conflict with Dennis and Colin was taking its toll on her.

Dennis and Colin returned the next morning, and the conflict was renewed. Meghan had become accustomed to the relative serenity in the house with only her and the old woman there, and the atmosphere at the table during meals seemed even more jarring than before. And she found herself choosing sides. Dennis and Colin had each other, but their mother had no one. The old woman gave the impression of needing no one, but she was also capable of concealing virtually all of her emotions except anger.

Meghan spent most of her time with the old woman, sitting with her on a bench by the graveyard. What Meghan had said about shipping wool to England had made a deep impression on her, and she brought up the subject repeatedly. She looked through stacks of musty papers in her office, and found messages from the Cummings Brothers on the shipment of wool during past years. Meghan read them and discussed them with her, and explained the characteristics of various types of ships used to transport wool.

The subject of clippers came up while they were sitting and talking one afternoon, and the old woman dismissed them as too expensive. "It wouldn't be worth my while to even ship the wool," she said. "By the time I paid the shippage, I wouldn't have any profit left."

Meghan thought about it, then shook her head. "I'm not sure about the precise cost, but it might be to your advantage. Your wool would be on the docks months ahead of the yearly flood of wool, and it would be in prime condition. You'd get a premium price for your wool, and I believe that would offset the higher cost of shippage."

The old woman had a stack of the papers on her lap, and she straightened them and shook her head doubtfully. "Aye, but is a clipper so fast that I could depend on being months ahead of the rest of the wool?"

"There's no question about that," Meghan replied. "They're faster simply because they're so fast. Most ships have to put in at least once between Port Jackson and London to water and victual, and they're often in port for weeks doing that. A clipper can water and victual in Port Jackson, and not drop anchor again until she reaches the roads of the Thames. The problem would be getting the wool on a clipper."

"What do you mean?"

"They don't often call at Port Jackson, and the only one whose home port is here is the *Orion*. The ship would have to be in port just at the right time, and your wool would have to be there and ready to be loaded. Cummings Brothers would also have to be very alert to get space on the ship before it's all let out to others. Messers Drexler and Suggs own the *Orion*, and they don't let the ship loiter around in port."

"Did they have it built at Port Jackson?"

"No, no," Meghan said. "Only a few builders can put a clipper together, and certainly none in Australia. They bought her out of Bombay, and probably got a better ship than a new one. My father always said that a hull is better for seasoning in salt water, so long as it's kept clean and carefully maintained."

The old woman looked down at the papers again, thumbing through them. "What was its name before they bought it?"

"They kept the same name, as people usually do with a clipper or any other well-known ship. I've heard of people changing the name on other types of ships when they buy them, but never a clipper."

The old woman nodded, gathering up the papers on her lap and rising. "Well, as you say, the chances of getting the wool on a clipper are small, so it's pointless to discuss it. It's getting late, so let's go inside. I have some more papers I want to show you."

Meghan rose and went back into the house with the old woman, and she brought another stack of papers out of her office. She had identified shipments of wool that had arrived in London at approximately the same time of year, but the wool had sold for unit amounts that differed widely. Meghan read through the papers, trying to guess the types of ships from the names, and they discussed the probabilities of whether the low prices for the wool had been because of its condition, market fluctuations, or other reasons.

They were still discussing it at dinner, but it failed to interest Dennis or Colin, as it would have failed to interest Earl. As a previously unexplored subject and one she had just realized was important to her, the old woman continued pursuing it and plying Meghan with questions. Meghan also perceived other reasons for Elizabeth's interest. It was something to occupy her during the inactivity of winter, and the old woman enjoyed Meghan's companionship. And Meghan suspected that the old woman still entertained hopes that she would remain at the sheep station.

Meghan had deep respect for the old woman, and affection for her that was close to love. Subjects had arisen in conversation between them that had caused a clash of opinions, but the disagreements had resulted only in a more complete understanding of each other. The old woman had a quick temper, but under her reserve she was also warm and loving. And Meghan discovered within herself a reluctance to think about leaving Wayamba Station. She was happy, and in many ways the sheep station was the first home she had known since leaving England.

The mild weather continued, and there was a feel of spring in the air during the warm afternoons. The activity on the sheep station increased as stockmen began preliminary preparations for the long days and nights of drudgery that would begin when spring arrived and lambing began. Meghan knew that the old women would want to send a man or two to accompany her when she left, and she knew it would be more considerate of her to leave well before lambing began. But she remained reluctant to commit herself to leaving on a given date and beginning her preparations to leave.

A rider arrived late one afternoon leading a spare horse, a courier who had been sent by the Cummings Brothers with important messages and documents for the old woman. A letter from Meghan's uncle in London had arrived in Sydney months before, and someone from Cummings Brothers had collected it from the postal office and sent it along with the rest of the mail. The rider remained for a day while the old woman signed papers and wrote messages back to the Cummings Brothers, and Meghan wrote a reply to her uncle.

The rider left during early morning, and the old woman spent most of the day in her office, still looking over the messages she had received. She was also quiet and thoughtful at the table, and one particular message seemed to be of special interest to her. Meghan saw her reading it several times, standing at the window in the front room, gazing absently into the distance as she thought about it. During the afternoon, Meghan saw the old woman go out to sit on a bench in the graveyard. Meghan followed her there.

The old woman was pouring over the message again, and she looked up as Meghan came around the corner of the house. She folded the message and patted the bench beside her. "Come and sit down, Meghan. It's very pleasant this afternoon, isn't it?"

"Aye, it is, Mistress Garrity," Meghan agreed. She sat down, hesitating for a second, then broached the subject she had been reluctant to even think about. "It'll soon be spring, so I should leave before very long."

The old woman pursed her lips, "Aye. I suppose you must, if you're to do what you plan. I'll have some men drive your wagon and escort you to Sydney when you go."

"No, no need for that," Meghan replied. "I can go to Adelaide and get transportation around to Sydney on a coaster. That sort of travel will suit me better than a wagon, and it'll keep your men away for a far shorter time. And I can go to Adelaide on a horse, which will take even less time."

The old woman shook her head. "No, you can go to Adelaide and take a ship to Sydney if you wish, but you must go in a wagon and take that little cabinet and the other things you like with you. We have plenty of men, and we can spare a couple for that long."

Meghan smiled up at the old woman. "That's very kind of you, Mistress Garrity, and I am fond of that little cabinet and the other things. They'll also serve to remind me of the happy days I spent here." Her smile faded, and she sighed. "I came here on an errand of sorrow, but I've become very attached to this place and to you. I'll miss this place, and I'll miss you very much indeed."

"It won't be the same without you, Meghan," the old woman replied, patting Meghan's hand. "It's easy to find affection for you, and I've become fond of you as I have of few before." She looked down at the folded message in her hand. "I have here a note from a girl named Alice Willoughby, a distant relative of mine who recently arrived in Sydney. She finds herself at loose ends and wishes to come here, and she seems to be a smart girl of some ability. It could be that she'll be of use to me here, so I've made arrangements to have her brought here. But she won't take your place with me, Meghan."

"I trust I'll keep my place with you, Mistress Garrity."

494

"Indeed you will, Meghan. And when opportunity presents itself, I trust you'll come to visit me. You've a keen mind, and you're a very entertaining companion." She looked away, and stared into the distance. "You've also pointed out where I've gone amiss. I've thought of naught but sheep and Wayamba Station these past years, because this place is sufficient for one mind. But there is a larger view to be had, and it's time the Garrity family reached farther. To that end, I've sent a message to Cummings Brothers to make arrangements to deal with you and the bank and advance you the monies to buy three of those ships that trade between here and New Zealand."

Meghan was speechless. "Buy them outright? Mistress Garrity, that would cost an enormous sum of money. To buy three barques or such could amount to as much as two thousand guineas. That's why people deal in shares rather than buy ships outright."

"Aye, and they take shares of the profits," the old woman replied. "It's best to get started right, and the full profits from three should very quickly put you in position that the loss of a ship would be no great risk. And you can go on from there as you will."

Meghan nodded numbly, overwhelmed by the offer. "And I will indeed. With the full profits of three ships I'll go on very rapidly, but I don't know what to say, Mistress Garrity."

"There's another matter in this same connection. You say that the name of a ship can be changed when it's sold from one person to another?"

Meghan cleared her throat and pushed at her hair,

collecting herself, and nodded. "Aye, it's only a matter of changing the registry, and that has to be done in any event when a ship is sold. We can name the ships whatever you like."

"I had in mind another ship altogether. I'd like you to cast about and buy the first one of those clipper ships that's offered for sale. And I want the naming of it myself."

"A clipper?" Meghan gasped. "But Mistress Garrity, that's thousands more! A clipper is the most costly of deep water ships!"

"Wayamba Station has done well these past years," the old woman replied. "We have a lot of money in the bank that the bankers pay us a pittance on so they can loan it out at great interest, and this would be a far better use for it. So the money's there, not a farthing to waste but thousands to use for good purpose. And I see this as a good purpose." She looked down at Meghan, tapping her arm. "But mind you, I want the naming of that clipper ship myself."

Meghan was bewildered, full realization of the enormity of the offer slowly dawning on her. Long years of struggle, risks, and bitter setbacks had been swept away in an instant. She would begin where many ended after years of successful effort. Her eyes suddenly filled with tears of happiness. "You've given me more than I ever dared dream of having, Mistress Garrity. You've given me the world."

"It's hardly the world, Meghan," the old woman said, taking her hand and patting it. "But you'll have your ships."

Meghan squeezed the old woman's hand. "No, I'll have far more than that," she replied. "Far more indeed. When I begin, I'll already have the Garrity Line."

PART SIX

Chapter 26

THICK WINTER FOG HAD RISEN from the long sound leading into Port Jackson harbor, and it surrounded the carriage in the early morning darkness. The coach lamps on the front of the carriage made misty halos of yellow light, and the carriage moved along the road at a slow pace. The driver had dismounted when the fog had become too thick to see ahead, and he was carrying a lantern and leading the horses.

The carriage stopped, then it turned off the road. It swayed and bobbed on its springs, crossing the earth berm at the side of the road. It crossed a wide, level field. The carriage stopped again, the branches on a tree dimly visible through one window, in the light of the coach lamps. The driver walked back and lifted his lantern as he opened the door for Meghan.

"We're here, Mistress Garrity. I'll look around for some wood, and I'll build a fire to cut the chill."

"Aye, very well, Frank."

He closed the door and walked away from the carriage, and the glow of his lantern through the fog dimmed and brightened as he walked through trees at the side of the field. Meghan opened the door and felt for the step with her foot, and climbed down. The fog had the salty smell of the sea, and the sound of drops falling from damp leaves was loud in the early morning stillness.

The enamel and bright metalwork on the carriage gleamed in the light of the coach lamps. The horses stamped and snorted, nervous in the fog and darkness. They were a matched pair of young horses, energetic and excitable. The driver returned with an armload of wood, and he kindled a fire.

Flames licked up through splinters, highlighting the driver's bearded face, and he carefully piled sticks over the splinters. The damp wood smoldered for a moment, then it ignited and began to blaze up. A pool of ruddy, flickering light spread through the dense fog around the fire. The driver piled more wood on the fire, and dusted off his coat, and stood up.

"I asked the cook for a billy, pannikins, and the makings for tea, Mistress Garrity. They're in the boot, if you'd care for some tea."

"Aye, I would, and it was thoughtful of you to bring them, Frank. I'll make the tea, and you take the lantern back to the road and light the way for the others when they get here."

"Very well, mo'm. Are you sure you can manage?"

"I can manage a billy, Frank." Meghan laughed. "If I had tuppence for every time I've boiled a billy to make tea, I'd have the wherewithal to put another clipper to sea."

The driver laughed, picking up the lantern, and he went to the carriage and rummaged in the boot. He returned with a billy, pannikins, and containers of water and tea, and put them by the fire. Meghan pulled her coat and skirt aside and knelt to pour water into the billy. The driver walked toward the road with the lantern.

Meghan had made tea with a billy many times, but she had been wearing clothing other than a camelhair coat with sable trim, a heavy brocade dress with four petticoats, a wide hat piled high with folds of tulle, and silk gloves. The heavy demijohn of water was slippery in her gloves, and smoke from the fire gathered under her hat brim.

She took off a glove and fished pieces of bark out of the water. Then she put the billy on the fire. A slow clopping of hoofs and the rumble of wheels came from the road, muffled by the fog, and she stood up and looked toward the road. The driver called out, and Joshua Venable replied, coughing. The chaise turned off the road, coach lamps glowing on it, and it crossed the field.

Venable reined up by the carriage and climbed out, coughing. "Good morning Meghan," he said, walking toward the fire. "I see Drexler isn't here yet. Do you think he will be?"

"Good morning, Joshua. Aye, he said he'd be here."

Venable coughed hoarsely. "It'll be something to see him up at this hour of the day, if he does."

"Aye, this is a bit early for him, I should imagine. That cough sounds worse, Joshua."

503

He cleared his throat and sighed in resignation as he shrugged. "It's winter, and when it's winter I have congestion. It'll be dawn directly, but we won't be able to see anything unless this fog lifts. Do you think it will?"

"It's been lifting every morning this past week," Meghan replied, glancing around. "And there's been a good offshore breeze with the morning ebb of the tide. If seaman's luck will hold just one more morning, that'll please me to no end. Is Mary still having morning sickness?"

Venable smiled wryly as he took off his gloves and warmed his hands at the fire. "Worse than ever. Mistress Fisher said it's normal and it should end before long, but that doesn't make Mary feel any the better when she's having it."

"No, it won't, poor Mary," Meghan sighed. "I remember well how dreadful that was, but they do say that a more severe morning sickness makes an easier delivery when the baby is born."

Venable nodded. The water in the billy began boiling, and he took it off the fire. Meghan knelt and opened the can of tea, and poured a measured amount into the water. She let it brew for a moment, then filled two pannikins and handed one to Venable.

The impenetrable darkness was starting to dissolve, dawn light creeping down through the fog, and there was a slight movement in the air. Meghan and Venable drank their tea and talked, and the light gradually brightened. The dense fog swirled, the thick clouds rolling across the open field and drifting sea-

504

ward as the movement of air slowly developed into an offshore breeze.

A carriage rumbled along the road, the horses walking. The carriage turned off the road, the driver walking ahead of it, his lantern and the coach lights were dim in the brightening light. The carriage stopped by the chaise, and Meghan's driver opened the door. Drexler climbed out clumsily, bundled in his heavy greatcoat and scarf.

"My word, this fog is thick," he said, walking toward the fire. "We could hardly see to get here."

Venable laughed. "We've had fog like this every morning most of the winter, and you'd know that if you rose before midday."

"This is a bit earlier than I usually rise," Drexler said amiably. "Will we be able to see anything, Meghan?"

"Aye, it appears to be clearing, Ezra," Meghan said, kneeling and pouring tea into a pannikin for him. "It's cleared every morning this past week, and a breeze seems to be rising and pushing it out now. Here's some tea for you."

Drexler's fleshy face was bleary and lined from too little sleep, and he smiled gratefully as he took the pannikin. He sipped the tea noisily. "That tastes good, very good indeed. I hardly had my head settled on my pillow before I rose again, but I'm a man of my word, Meghan."

"You are indeed," Meghan agreed. "But I promise you a sight to behold. Seeing my clipper put out to sea will be worth the trouble I've put you to, and more."

Drexler took another drink of tea. "I'm sure it will, but a few pastries would make it even more worth my while. It's been months since you sent that last batch."

"It's been months since I've had time for pause or pastries," Meghan said. "This business with the clipper combined with all else has kept me at it hammer and tongs these past months, but now I'll have some respite to retire to the house on the Georges for a while and do other things I've been wanting to do. I'll also bake some pastries, Ezra. I promise you some from the first batch I bake."

Drexler smiled and nodded in satisfaction. "I'll certainly look forward to that, Meghan."

"You may depend upon it. On another subject, I believe I remember that we had a small debate on whether or not *Orion* or my clipper might be the faster. And I believe there was passing mention of the possibility of a wager on it."

"I believe I remember the same thing," Drexler replied cautiously. "Yes, I believe I do. But if we're to take the time *Orion* made on her last passage to England and back, you must remember that my captain didn't know he'd be in a contest with another ship. And considering the fact that you've brought the matter up, your captain must know that's he's most likely in a contest against *Orion*."

"The captain of a clipper who doesn't make his best time all the time doesn't deserve his berth. Nevertheless, I'll give you an advantage of two weeks. I say that my clipper will return and have her hooks down in Port Jackson in two weeks less than *Orion* did on her last passage, the time to be measured from dawn this morning to the hour and minute my ship anchors."

Drexler's lips twitched in a sly smile, and he nodded. "That seems fair enough to me. What amount should you like to wager?"

"One hundred guineas."

Drexler was taking a drink of tea, and he almost chocked. Meghan looked up at him with a bland smile, waiting. Venable glanced up and suppressed a smile.

"That's a large sum of money," Drexler said doubtfully. "I'm sure you can afford it, because you've almost taken over all the naval stores and lumber trade out of New Zealand. But a hundred quineas is an enormous amount to a man like me."

"A man like you!" Meghan scoffed. "You own shares in half the ships that put out from Port Jackson, and you have gold that hasn't seen the light of day for twenty years or more. You can afford it as well as I can. Besides, I made mention of the matter in correspondence with my mother-in-law, and she insisted that the wager be for no less than the sum of a hundred guineas."

"She insisted?" Drexler asked curiously. "I thought you were independent of control from Wayamba Station."

"I am, but when she asks me to do something I'm more than pleased to do it. She's my benefactress and

507

the head of my family. Beyond that, my affection for her knows no end and I enjoy pleasing her. But we stray from the subject, Ezra. What do you say?"

Drexler finally nodded. "I'll do it on one condition. If I win, I get a dozen apple pastries. And if I lose, I get two dozen. That way I win even if I lose."

"Done." Meghan laughed and put out her hand. "Here's my hand on it."

Drexler shook hands with her. "You might regret this, Meghan," he said in friendly warning. *"Orion* made good time on her last passage to England and back."

"I know what she did, and that hundred guineas is as good as in my pocket," Meghan replied, smiling happily. "My ship's hull is as clean as new linen and as tight as a new bucket, and she carried more sail than *Orion.*"

"Well, we'll see." Drexler chuckled, glancing around. "It does appear that the fog's clearing nicely doesn't it?"

Meghan looked around. The fog was lifting, breaking up rapidly. The gray, wintry sky was visible through misty veils of fog passing overhead, and the light had brightened into full daylight. Meghan called to her driver.

"Can you see the sound up there, Frank?"

He turned toward the edge of the field, craning his neck and looking, he nodded. "Yes, I can see it in places, Mistress Garrity. The fog down there is almost gone."

Meghan put her pannikin down, and the men put theirs down and followed her as she walked to the edge of the field. It sloped down into a steep, forested hillside, overlooking the sound a quarter of a mile away. Thick clouds of fog were scudding ahead of the breeze along the surface of the long, wide body of gray-green water. Meghan pulled her coat tighter, shivering in the chill, and the men stood by her and looked down at the sound.

Fog floated through the trees and along black, shiny faces of rock on the distant opposite shore of the sound. Tendrils of fog still rose from the water, the breeze whipping them away, and the masses of fog continued to roll along the sound. Then the fog cleared away from Jackson Heads, the headlands on each side of the wide opening to the sea.

"I see masts, Mistress Garrity!" Meghan's driver shouted. "A ship is clearing the roads and coming down the sound!"

Meghan looked up the sound. It curved, and forested hills and points of land jutted out and blocked the line of view up the sound. Misty veils of fog eddied and swirled along the shoreline, concealing parts of it. Meghan saw a movement, the tips of masts momentarily coming into sight as a ship turned and followed the channel in the sound. A moment later, the clipper glided around the curve.

The men in the rigging were tiny dots in the distance. The jibs were billowed in the breeze above the long bowsprit, the sails up to the topsails were spread, and the topgallants were falling into place and opening. The ship changed course slightly, staying in the center of the deep channel. The breeze was coming directly over the stern, and the ship moved rapidly down the sound.

"She's already taking a bone in her teeth," Venable said quietly. "And this breeze is no more than a puff of wind."

"By God, she is," Drexler murmured in wonder. "That ship has a clean hull indeed."

Meghan looked at the white water boiling under the long, raked bow of the clipper, evidence of the ship's speed in the light breeze. The slender, graceful hull glided through the water, leaving a long wake behind. The masts towered high above the deck, the topgallants billowing and the royals tumbling down into place on the spars. The ship continued to pick up speed along the sound as the royals opened and filled with wind, and the skysails opened.

"That's a good crew," Drexler remarked. "They've filled the mast with canvas in little more time than it takes to tell about it."

"That's a good crew, but that's not all the canvas on those masts," Venable chuckled. "That ship carries moonrakers above her skysails."

Drexler grunted in surprise, looking at the ship more closely. The skysails opened, then the moonrakers at the lofty heights of the masts began opening. The sails were a mountain of canvas above the long deck, and the ship rocked gently as it met the swell rolling in from the sea. It raced along the sound, alive with movement as men scrambled about in the rigging and ran back and forth on the deck.

The ship closed the distance rapidly, and passed abreast of Meghan and the men. White water boiled all along the slender hull as it sped through the water, the sails billowed above it. Pennants fluttered from the mast heads, and the flag of the Garrity Line flapped lazily at the stern. Meghan looked at the ship, thrilled. It had been a thing of beauty in the yards, while being refitted, and now it had come alive.

She could almost hear the breeze singing in the rigging, and feel the trembling vibrations of the deck under her feet as the ship sliced through the waves. Captain Tench was on the quarterdeck, and he lifted his tricorn and waved it as he saw Meghan and the men. The men lifted their hats and waved, and Meghan waved. The ship passed, bursting through the higher swell and speeding toward the Jackson Heads.

"By God, you promised me a sight to behold, and you showed me it," Drexler said emphatically. "Whether I win the wager or lose, there's a sight to see, Meghan."

Meghan tried to reply, but a tight feeling in the back of her throat kept her from speaking. Her eyes were stinging and blurred with tears, her heart swelling with exultant pride at the magnificent sight of her clipper putting out to sea under full sail. She silently nodded, and looked at the ship and waved. Then the two men were also silent, watching as the clipper *Sheila Garrity* passed the Jackson Heads and stood out to sea.